THE
GOLDENACRE

THE
GOLDENACRE

PHILIP MILLER

Published by
Soho Press, Inc.
227 W 17th Street
New York, NY 10011

Library of Congress Cataloging-in-Publication Data

Names: Miller, Philip, author.
Title: The Goldenacre / Philip Miller.
Description: New York, NY : Soho Crime, [2022]
Identifiers: LCCN 2021060854

ISBN 978-1-64129-427-0
eISBN 978-1-64129-428-7

Subjects: LCSH: Art—Provenance—Fiction. | Journalists—Fiction. |
Murder—Investigation—Scotland—Edinburgh—Fiction.
LCGFT: Detective and mystery fiction | Novels.
Classification: LCC PR6113.I567 G65 2022
DDC 823'.92—dc23/eng/20211215
LC record available at https://lccn.loc.gov/2021060854

Interior design by Janine Agro

Printed in the United States of America

10 9 8 7 6 5 4 3 2 1

For Frank and Theodore

THE
GOLDENACRE

1

Ned Silver was being banged out.
Across the *Edinburgh Post* newsroom, journalists
were slapping their hands hard on the tabletops. It was a
rhythmic racket—some were banging their feet on the floor,
others tapping the sides of their grey, flickering monitors.
One or two rang peals from their chipped coffee cups, using
stained old spoons. The sound rebounded from the worn
brown carpet to the stained white ceiling tiles, and out of the
open windows to the chilly street outside.

Years ago, typewriters would have been banged, and
maybe even print presses clanged, and then, after the tumult
of industrial percussion, there would have been a long session of
hard drinking in the pub. These days it was only tired hands
sounding on dust-smeared laptops, with little time to party,
commiserate and celebrate afterwards.

Shona Sandison, senior reporter, watched it all. She had
seen many journalists leave in recent months. Unlike most,
Ned had been a friend, once. Now he was just a speech and
a night in a sodden pub away from being another memory.
She watched, unsmiling, as Silver looked out over the newsroom and took a piece of paper from his rumpled corduroys.
Colm, the news editor, had already handed Ned a bottle
of whisky in a pale cardboard case, an envelope of money

gathered from the office, and a fake front page, announcing his departure.

"Speech!" someone yelled.

"Don't encourage him," Shona said. She was working, holding a telephone receiver close to her ear, cupping her hand over it to muffle the noise of the newsroom. The phone was ringing and ringing. She was waiting for a police contact to answer his mobile.

Opposite her, swivelling on his seat, the crime reporter, Hector Stricken, grinned. "He'll love this," he said. "He's been waiting years. It's his grand exit. It might be funny. It probably rhymes or something. Give him a listen, Shona."

"I'd rather set myself on fire," she said, lolling back in her chair. Her walking stick, which she had hooked on her armrest, fell to the floor with a clunk. She had a new story to investigate. It was probably a murder, and she was gathering information—an old man in Stockbridge had been found dead in his ground-floor flat.

Shona nodded over to the office of the *Post*'s new editor, Ron Ingleton, who appeared to be hiding. "Where's that wee prick, Ingleton?" she whispered loudly to Stricken. "Squatting in his Führer bunker?"

"Shona," Stricken said, shaking his head.

"The man's a fuckwit," she said.

Colm was saying some words about Ned's long tenure as arts correspondent at the *Post* . . . broken many stories over the years . . . how he had been an important asset.

"Ass-et," Shona snorted. Some people looked around. "Near enough," she muttered. The phone was still ringing, somewhere.

Shona looked over at Silver, his hair thinning, his nose redder that it used to be. When they had been friends, he had not worn his glasses, and now he wore better clothes. Back in those days, he had been floppy-haired, and thin, and funny. This was before she had been stabbed. Then, sometime after that, he had married and didn't seem to want her company anymore, with no more drinks after work, or coffees at lunchtime. Now he was going to London for some communications job, and that was that. She doubted they would speak again.

She tilted her head and turned away from the hubbub in the room, as the phone was finally picked up with a click.

Detective Reculver answered. "Ah, Shona Sandison," he said. "The impossible pencil."

"Ya what?"

"Both blunt and sharp. Go on."

"I hear a man's dead," she said.

"What's that racket?"

"An old timer is leaving," she said. "Doing a speech. Anyway, I heard it's a murder."

"You might have heard right," he rumbled. "But I can't say more at the moment. You'll get the news release like everyone else. No exclusives, this time."

"Whatever. Was it a robbery? Who was he?"

"Yes, maybe, and a suspicious death. The name was Love. An artist." Reculver lowered his voice. "Nasty business—a bloody mess. Look, meet me tomorrow, eleven A.M., normal place."

"Give me an address for this fella?"

"How about a 'please'?"

"You can have my 'thank you' tomorrow."

"No. But look near the bookshop on the main road—there's polis everywhere. Shouldn't be too hard to spot."

"A Mr. Love?"

"Aye. Do one of your internet searches—you'll find him right enough."

"Okay, see you tomorrow."

Shona put the phone down and checked her email, but there was nothing from the police communications department yet.

Silver was speaking. "I saw us all at this wee newspaper not as friends or rivals or colleagues, but more a kind of a gestalt . . ."

"Jesus H. Christ," Shona said. She picked up her walking stick and got out of her seat. Limping on her left-hand side, stick tapping on the thin carpet, she moved through the rows of standing newspaper staff who were nodding, murmuring and chuckling at Silver's speech. Shona needed some fresh air: to see the silken clouds weaving over the city, casting pale rivers of shadow over the stones and statues. Another good journalist was leaving the *Post*. Every one that left the paper was like the gasp of a dying man. There were only so many breaths left that it could take before it breathed its last.

She stood in the office block landing, waiting for the lift. Someone outside on Rose Street was playing a saxophone. Then her phone buzzed—a text from Reculver: *Statement with you now*, it shouted.

"Fucking hell," she said, turning around and heading back to her desk. The staff had dispersed again, and the noise had fallen. Silver was in the editor's glass-walled office, and Shona wondered what they were saying to each other.

Colm ghosted over to her desk.

"What do you want?" she said, as her computer screen blinked back to life.

"Six hundred words on the Stockbridge death, Shona," he said, beginning to roll a short cigarette in his stumpy fingers.

"Fine. Has Silver found his balls in there?"

"What do you mean?"

"Is he lamping Ingleton with the whisky bottle?"

Colm smirked. "Exchanging platitudes, Shona," he said. "The time for melodrama is over."

"Don't I just know it."

Colm nodded, looked as if he was going to say something, didn't, and then stumped off again.

Stricken looked over his monitor and raised his eyebrows. "Another corpse for you, is it, Shona? You must be delighted."

"Fuck off, Stricken."

"You used to be nice, you know," he said, rattling his fingers on his keyboard. "Charming, even."

"Remember when you were quiet, before you decided to grow a character?" she said. "I preferred it that way. What are you working on?"

"Wouldn't you like to know?" He tapped his nose. "It could be the big one."

"The big one?"

"The big one," he repeated.

Shona shook her head. "Cock," she said.

Stricken leaned back in his chair. "Have you ever thought, Shona, of living more in the moment, of being less annoyed by the past, and less worried about the future?"

"Like what . . . a whelk?"

He laughed and carried on typing.

Shona checked her email. The police press statement had come through. There it all was, in black-and-white, from the city police: a suspected murder. An ongoing investigation and an appeal for witnesses. She read the news release through again and then began, with a familiar and comforting sense of relief, to write.

Half an hour later, it was done.

The death of Scottish painter Robert Love, who was found in his Edinburgh home this morning, is being treated as suspicious by city cops, the Post *understands. The body of acclaimed artist Love, 67, was discovered in his home studio in Stockbridge. Love, a graduate of Glasgow School of Art whose lauded work hangs in the Public Gallery and institutions across the UK, was well known in the arts world. He leaves a daughter.*

The story, completed with police quotes and more background about Love's life and career, was barely edited before being laid out on the page. Colm was reading it over again as Shona prepared to leave the office.

She was about to ring her father. Shona lived with him, and she usually rang at this time to check he was back from the allotment, and what he wanted for dinner. Or whether he was cooking—which he usually was. Silver and some other colleagues had gone to a pub on the corner of the street, and she wondered whether she should join them. Through the open window, she thought she could hear their voices.

Colm walked over from the newsdesk, his shirt half out, a rolled cigarette behind one ear. He was squinting at a large piece of paper: a printout of page three, which he put down on her desk. Her story was the lead. There was no headline, just "headeryheaderyheadery" typed in its place. There was also a large picture of Robert Love, taken in his pomp in the early 1980s: he had a drooping moustache, a wild frizz of dark hair and a velvet suit. Dark eyes and a smile.

"He has a daughter, then?" Colm said.

"That's what it says," Shona said.

"Have you spoken to her?"

"Not yet."

"Have you tried?"

She hadn't. "Of course, I have. Number rang out," she said. She didn't have a number. Shona was already planning to track her down for a second story, but she wanted to get home. She had no desire to knock on the door of a grieving woman and ask her how she felt. She had done enough death knocks for one lifetime.

Colm snorted. "Try her again tomorrow, and knock on her door," he grunted. "And you got an idea for the headline?"

"Colm," she said, standing up, grabbing her stick, "that's your job. The most important three words are already there."

"*By Shona Sandison?*" he said, his mouth twitching. They had exchanged these lines before.

"Exactly," she said. "How about 'Cops Probe Shock Artist Death'? Something like that."

"Fine," he said, tucking his shirt in. "Straightforward."

"Why's it not the splash?" she asked. She peered at him, and he sighed and rubbed his eye.

"There's a drug story. A load of cocaine has been found in a boat from Whitby that shipped up in Pittenweem. Worth ten million, apparently. Stricken's done it."

Shona looked to Stricken's seat, but he was gone—he had filed and fled. "Ten million? That's a lot of coke. And my plans for the weekend ruined."

Colm smiled. "I can't imagine you ever doing that sort of thing, Shona, for some reason."

"I've had my moments. Since when is a drugs haul more important than a murder?"

Colm's eye twitched again. "Since the editor decided that was the case," he said, his voice low. He rolled up the page into a baton and gently beat the desk with it. The new editor was another angry white man from Glasgow, short and shaven-headed.

"Rightio," she said, and slammed her notebook in her bag.

Colm's voice changed to something softer. "The man is settling in. Give him time. Here—you going to Ned's bash? I won't be done here until late. Maybe see you there?"

"Not a chance."

"Fine," he said. "Why were you shouting at poor Hector about whelks earlier?"

"Mind your own business, Colm."

There was a shout from the other end of the office. Colm's deputy was standing up at the newsdesk, looking for him. He called to Colm and held up a telephone receiver in the air as if it was on fire.

"Westminster!" the deputy shouted.

"Great. Another clusterfuck to sort," Colm said. He sighed and walked slowly back to the newsdesk, and Shona pulled on her coat. It was late now, and only editors and a few writers were left in the office. In the glass office in the corner of the newsroom, the editor was watching a football match. Green and blue flashed on the flickering walls.

Shona made her way to the street outside. The air was cool and the sky was still a cloudless blue over the Scott Monument and the rise of the Old Town to the Castle. The old city glittered under a vast sky. She passed the pub that Ned and half the newspaper were now inside. Another wake, she thought. The newspaper was dying, and Ned leaving was another blow to its life. She could not wish him well, or celebrate his exit: the paper needed journalists like him to stay. And she needed the newspaper for her life to stay as it was.

She felt a sink of sorrow as she walked, her stick clipping on the stone streets. Ned had loved her once, probably. A long time ago. She pushed the thought away from her mind. Back into the shadows.

Shona took her bus, and the city moved past in a blur of light and shadow, its hills and peaks, its ruins and boulevards, ready to be lost into the night. To be sunk into a darkness, as if it were underwater.

Her keys battered against the old scratched lock of her flat, but she entered quietly enough. Her father was asleep on the couch, in front of the football. Hugh Sandison, snoring into his chest, and she was glad he was asleep.

She took a blanket and laid it over him, pressing it under his shoulders to keep it in place. He smelled of mud and sweat—he had been gardening all day. There was dirt under his nails, and a smear of green across his stubbled cheek. She took the half-drunk cup of tea from his lap, turned the noise of the TV down and left him to his sleep.

Shona walked slowly to her dark room and sat on the edge of her bed, her side aching again. She pulled off her black trainers and placed them by her wardrobe before lying down on her bed. She thought of the past: her memories, and whether they were the same as other people's memories. She saw green mountains, ruins on the high ground, and the endless dark sea: a long weekend in Ireland with Ned. Before things had got complicated. Before he felt he had to leave.

Shona turned onto her good side and, before long, she fell into a pit of sleep.

Suddenly, her eyes were flashing with a cold blue light. A flickering and a persistent dull buzz.

"Dad?" she said, still half-asleep. She sat up. The splinters of a dream slithered from her mind—there had been a city in ruins, great fires, a strange boy with eyes like spun galaxies, a floating dog. She shook it from her mind, and it drifted into nothingness. Forgotten forever.

The light strobed again. It was her mobile phone, which was on the floor. She was still dressed. It was dark outside.

"Jesus fuck," she said.

Her phone continued to ring, buzzing and shaking on the bare floorboards. She grabbed it and put it to her ear. She looked under her bedroom door, but the hall light was off. Her father must still be asleep.

"Shona Sandison. Who is this?" she whispered as loudly as she could.

"Hey, Shona, it's me," a voice said.

3 A.M.

You never answer this bloody phone number. It is me again. Yes, another message to delete. To ignore and erase.

And do you even get these messages? The

words leave my mouth and disappear somewhere. I assume this is being recorded. Are you even listening?

Maybe you order transcripts, so this is all set down, justified and printed in italics.

You know, the last time I saw you, you turned your back. You did not even wave.

Tomorrow, I take another step on this new path. But if they find out, I am finished. And this time, for good.

Anyone can lose their balance.

I know—I suspect—you helped cover it all up. Got me this post here. That would be just like you: just cleaning things up, making things nice and tidy, and empty, and then leaving—but leaving no traces.

I hope you did. Because I could not.

Sons disappoint their fathers, and fathers disappoint their sons. And the world keeps turning.

And so to bed, in this strange new place. I cannot sleep, of course.

Every life ends with death, I once read. And every day with sleep.

Enough.

2

Through the phone Shona could hear the sound of the street: cars and people shouting, the echoes of lanes and doorways; piped music leaking from pubs, and car engines revving up hills, tyres battering over cobbles. A shrieking noise that rose and fell.

"Who the fuck is 'me,' at three in the morning?" But she knew who it was. She recognised his mild northern English voice. Ned Silver. "Ned," she said, before he could answer.

"Oh Shona, it's good to hear your voice," he said drunkenly. There was a whooshing noise all around him. It tunnelled and boomed. "I thought I might see you tonight. But no luck."

"Do you know what time it is?"

"Who knows where the time goes, Shona?"

"Enough, Ned," she said quietly, rubbing her eyes. Her vision was all speckle and fuzz. Then the edges of her furniture emerged from the static, gilded by the gentle touch of the soft golden light from the streetlights outside.

The phone whooshed again. "Where are you anyway, Ned? In a freakin' wind tunnel?"

"Just down by the river, you know."

"Don't fall in," she said. She flicked on her bedside lamp.

Her bedroom came into order again. Everything was where it should be. The surfaces were hard and real.

"Where were you?"

"I was busy," she said. "Shouldn't you be at home?"

"On my way. It was a long night. Listen, I have something for you."

She paused. "I dread to think," she said eventually.

"It's actually something you would want—it's a story. I might have a news story for you."

"Can you not tell me in the morning?"

"I am very drunk now and feeling nostalgic. And I won't feel that in the morning."

"Okay, carry on."

"I haven't got all the information you will need. But it's an interesting thing," he said. "I was going to tell you earlier, before I was drunk. But it's not all there."

The whooshing continued.

"So, it's a story, but not a story—sounds just like you, Ned. If it's so interesting, why don't you write it?"

He said nothing. There was just the sound of cars, and the wet darkness, and unsteady steps along an invisible street.

"Oh, go on: tell me more," she said, reaching for the pen and pad beside her bed.

"Even if I could, I can't do it. There's . . . sensitivities. Who I got it from. The people who know these things—it's a small circle. It would be traced to me pretty easily," he said.

"Och, who cares?"

"It's . . . a personal thing. I don't want to let someone down."

The wind tunnel intensified. There was a clattering. The dull roar of engines.

"Are you at the bus station, Ned?"

"Yes. On me way home."

"So, not by the river?"

"I'm never by the river. I don't like watery expanses. I don't trust tidal currents. I nearly drowned as a child, you know."

Shona smiled. "I remember you mentioning it. Tell me more about this story. Come on, I need to get to sleep."

"Wait," he said. "I'll call you back, then."

The line went dead.

"Fucking hell, Ned."

The flat was silent again. She rolled onto her back and stared at her phone. Then it rang again, and Shona, with a jolt, immediately took the call.

"Sorry," Ned said. The background noise had gone—a numb drone had replaced it.

"You on a bus?"

"Yeah. I'm the only one on it."

"I hope there's a driver."

"Like I say, I have a story for you," Ned said. "It's about this guy. He's coming to Edinburgh. To work at the Public Gallery."

"Right," Shona said. She knew nothing about the art gallery world. That had been Ned's remit. The Public Gallery was the city's large gallery, set in parkland in the West End. She had never been there. "So? 'Man gets job in Edinburgh'— world exclusive."

"Fucking hell, Shona," Ned said softly.

"Carry on," she said.

"So, this fella . . . He's seconded, or visiting. Or something. But he used to work in London, at the Civic Gallery. I met him once at a press launch. Nervous. Didn't do well in front of the press. Anyway, he left the Civic under a cloud. More than a cloud. And now he's making big art decisions for the government."

"More than a cloud?" Shona said.

"A whole weather system. Of his own."

"High pressure?"

Ned chuckled, or seemed to. Shona had not heard his gulping laugh for a while. It sounded like he was crying.

"Anyway. Whatever happened there, I know for a fact he signed a Non-Disclosure Agreement—you know, an NDA. His superior left at the same time. There's been nothing on it so far. In the papers. It's all been—"

"Hushed up," Shona said. She looked at her bedside radio. It was 3:12 A.M.

"Aye, well—exactly. I've been on to the Civic this week and poked around but no one is saying anything. And on the face of it, what is there to see? Two staff members have left—so what? People move around in the art world all the time. But it's fishy. An NDA was definitely signed. The Civic gave him a glowing reference anyway, for the government. The lawyer who arranged the paperwork told me."

"What's his name?"

"The lawyer? It's a she. And I'd really rather not say."

Shona sighed. Ned's wife was a lawyer. It might have been her. "No, not the lawyer—this guy? Who has come to Edinburgh?"

"Tallis. Thomas Tallis."

"Sounds familiar to me," she said.

"Yeah well, he shares a name with some old composer or other. His real first name is Raymond. And this is where it gets even more interesting."

"All right," Shona said, scribbling in shorthand. She was fully awake now. She reached to the other side of her bed, where there was a slim silver laptop. She opened it. The glow lit her face.

"His old man was, unbelievably, Sir Raymond T. Tallis."

There was a silence.

"So?" Shona said. "Am I meant to know who that is? Is he an artist?"

"Shona," Ned said, in mock exasperation, "for God's sake."

"Come the fuck on, just tell me," she said. She had now wedged the phone under her chin and was searching for Raymond T. Tallis on the laptop's internet.

"Deputy director of MI6," they both said at once.

"Former," Ned said. "Former deputy director of the national spy agency."

"He's dead?"

"Nope," Ned said. "Retired and disappeared from public life."

"So he could be dead. Hang on, while I have a swatch."

Shona searched for notice of his death, but there was none. Just a few articles on his retirement, all using roughly the same language: the words of a press release that had been copied and pasted by several newspapers. A glowing quote from the prime minister.

"I hear he's abroad somewhere or other," Ned said. "That's the goss. Not my kind of thing. But I know his son evidently fucked up royally at the Civic. His boss took a bullet, too. Not a literal one. But she's away at some private gallery in Berlin now. Apparently."

"A pretty lawyer lassie told you," Shona said. "So I'm guessing, anyway."

"Fuck off," Ned said abruptly.

"Blimey," Shona said. "So, what happened—any clue at all?"

Ned sucked on his teeth.

"Where are you, anyway?" Shona asked.

"On the way to Falkirk."

"Fucking hell. Poor you," she said. "That'll sober you up."

He smiled and chuckled. "True enough."

"Did they have an affair?"

"Nah. Don't think so. He's devoted to his wife, it's said. She's a musician. And his boss was married with kids."

"Nicked money? Together?"

"There'd be proceedings, then. The Civic wouldn't mess about with fraud or something like that. Public money. We'd know about it. Nah. It's something else."

Shona quickly searched for "Thomas Tallis Curator" on

her laptop. A picture came up: a young-looking man in a corduroy suit at an art show. Large eyes and shaggy hair. He looked like a kicked dog.

"What's the worst an art curator could do?" she asked.

"Well, he didn't set fire to the building," Ned said. "I've no idea. But he did *something*, and now he's got a plum job in the culture department at the government. Inspector of provenance. He's in Edinburgh now. I don't know any more, but it's interesting, right?"

"Interesting, for sure. I guess I should meet him, front him up. I don't really know the arts world. Have you ever spoken to him?"

"Yes, just a couple of times," Ned said. "Just Civic stuff when I've been down in London: an exhibition he worked on, some fundraiser or other. He's a bit funny."

"Funny peculiar?"

"Funny ha-ha," Ned said. "But in that kind of public school, dead-eyed way. Defence mechanism humour: evasive. You know people like that. Humour as force field."

There was silence on the line.

"I'm on an arts story now, as it happens," Shona said. "Some painter's been murdered."

"Yeah, I heard. Poor old Robert Love. How?"

"Head smashed in, apparently. Pretty brutal."

"So definitely murder, then?"

"Unless it was a particularly enthusiastic suicide."

"Fuck sake, Shona," Ned said. He sighed deeply. The bus hummed. The night enveloped them both. "Anyway, I'd better go. I'm fucked. But there you have it, a last present from me."

"I don't remember many presents from you."

She could hear the bus more clearly now, its air conditioning, its growling engine, taking Ned through the darkness.

"If you're ever down in London, Shona, we could—" Ned began, in a soft voice.

"I'll never be down in London, Ned. You know that," she said.

"Right, fine, well."

"But I do owe you one," she said quietly.

"A joint byline, perhaps?"

"Just fucking invoice me."

"Maybe just buy me a drink sometime. I wish you had come tonight."

"Go to sleep, Ned," she said, and ended the call with a sudden thumb.

The flat was silent. Silent as stone walls.

She closed her laptop, stood up and walked through the dark flat. Her father was no longer on the sofa and, outside, the streetlights flickered and hummed.

A cat ran across the empty road in a shiver of movement, and there was pale light in the east. Another day was coming, whether she wanted it to or not.

3

Thomas Tallis, agent of the government, hoped that he was in the right place. He fished out his mobile phone. The image of his young son, Ray, glimmered on the screen. He touched it gently then put the phone back in his pocket.

Tallis was standing to the rear of a large stone building in the West End of Edinburgh. He had tried the front door, set large in neo-classical columns, but it had been closed. Now he was at the staff entrance, and an intercom. He pushed the button. There was a brief electronic whine, and a squeak, before a voice answered.

"Yeah?"

"Hello, I am sorry but I think I am a bit lost—I was looking for the Public Gallery."

Tallis rubbed his face. He had barely slept in his lodgings, his aunt's house on the outskirts of the city. He had lain awake for hours in the cold single bed in an attic space cluttered with posters, books and signs. Waiting for the voice to speak again, he looked around at the columns and pediments, and the early light resting weakly on a nearby graveyard, glinting on mausoleums, broken obelisks and the tilting rows of gravestones. Beyond the filed dead, he could see the rising roofs of the New Town, and Edinburgh Castle sitting on its rock. Thin clouds, like pulled wool, hung over the Pentlands.

The squatting bulk of the city's mountain, Arthur's Seat, glowered. He was a long way from London and its noise and chaos. Here, the wild lived amid the silent order.

There was a sigh, broken by static. "You're in the wrong place, pal."

"I was beginning to suspect as much," Tallis said. "Do you know where it is? Could you give me directions? I was told it was on this road."

"It is, aye."

Tallis stood for a moment with his finger on the intercom button. He heard footsteps behind him. He looked around and saw a tall woman in a black raincoat, holding a large black briefcase. She had spectacles and a hat, and she nodded a brief greeting. She had a pale, long face. Her glasses were tinted and her eyes were hidden.

"Hello," she said, in a flat voice. "Are you looking for the Public Gallery?"

"I thought I'd found it," Tallis said and smiled. Still with one finger on the intercom button, he extended his other arm for a handshake. He realised he was now stretched like a ballet dancer at the bar. "Thomas Tallis," he said.

"Ah," the woman said, smiling now, "the man from the government. I am Peters, from Lord Melrose's office. We have a meeting this morning—but not here."

Tallis felt a sudden sharp wire of pain in his temple. "Do we? I'm sure you're right but . . ." He winced, and the pain passed. He dropped his hand.

"About *The Goldenacre*," the woman said.

The mechanical voice in the intercom coughed. "Youse both need to be over the road. This is the Edinburgh City Museum. Looks the same, but it's different. You and the lady can continue your interesting wee chat there."

There was a click and a buzz and the voice signed off.

"Marvellous," Tallis said. He noticed something glinting

around the woman's hand: she was attached to the thick briefcase by a slender metal chain. "Important cargo?" he said, as cheerfully as he could, moving away from the door and onto the path.

"Paperwork, Mr. Trellis," she said firmly.

"Ah, I see," Tallis said, as if he knew. "And it is Tallis. Like the composer."

"I know," she said. "Shall we?"

They walked in silence to the main road, made their way over a zebra crossing, and through black gates into another large green space—the grounds of the Public Gallery. Bronze gleamed wetly in the new sunlight. There was a glimmering pond and, looming before them, another neo-classical building. It had illuminated writing in fluorescent script on its pediment: *What You See Is Unreal.*

A tall, thin man in a dark grey suit was waiting on its front steps, looking at his watch.

Tallis recognised him from the government briefing. He was Sir Dennis Carver, director of the Public Gallery. He was as sharp and severe as a snapped bone. Carver walked down the steps to meet them. He turned to the woman first and smiled, his face pale and oyster-grey around the eyes.

"Ms. Peters, good morning. Would you like to go straight to my office? My man will attend."

"I know the way," she said.

A short, red-haired man in a dark suit appeared and took Ms. Peters away, walking on a shingle path around the building and out of sight.

Carver watched them walk and slightly shook his head. "Marvellous," he said.

Tallis prepared to apologise for being late, but only opened his mouth.

Carver's face was impassive. He seemed to be focusing on a distant object, his eyes calibrating space, time, shadow and gravity.

"I apologise for the time. I got rather lost," Tallis said.

"Anyone can lose their sense of balance," Carver said evenly. "Did you go to our neighbours, the City Museum, instead?"

"I believe so."

"A common mistake. They are like twins, aren't they, these beautiful buildings, and often mixed up. Never mind. So, welcome to Dunedin, Thomas Tallis. How satisfying that you are finally here. A quick visit, I hope. I'm sure that is your plan."

"Indeed," Tallis nodded. His superior, Melcombe, wanted him back in London within days.

Carver nodded and beckoned with a hand. They walked together up the steps and into the gallery. Tallis followed Carver through pale corridors with high ceilings. He peered through to the gallery spaces as they passed: there were large white rooms, hung with paintings. In another room, an art film played: a man shaving his hands with a razor. Fresh, bald, pink hands emerged from the tidal foam and the wracking blade.

"How have you found Edinburgh?" Carver said. He had a brittle, educated accent.

"Well, I took a train north and, after three hours, suddenly I was here," Tallis said, with a deliberate smile.

Carver turned and laughed a slim grey laugh. "Very good. Did your people find you a satisfactory place to stay?"

"I am staying with my aunt Zelda. She lives in Portobello."

"Ah, how wonderful. Better than some dreary old hotel. By the esplanade?"

"Just there, a little place by the sea."

Carver flourished a swipe card to open a large grey door and, after they passed through it, the building changed. They were into the backstage: dark corridors with little light, small offices and a cramped staircase. The stairs rose to the third floor, where Carver and Tallis entered more corridors, past a desk where the red-haired youth was tapping at a computer terminal, a large white door and, finally, into a room with windows on two sides.

They stood together in silence for a while.

"Your temporary office," Carver said. "I hope you find it comfortable."

"Thank you," Tallis said. "It's rather grand."

"It belonged to our former curator of Dutch art," Carver said. "Poor man."

Tallis nodded, not knowing why.

"Ended up in a canal in Venice, you know," Carver added lightly.

"Gosh," Tallis found himself saying.

"So, for your time here, this is yours," Carver said, sweeping a hand around the space before him.

"This is very kind of you."

"My pleasure. It feels suitable for the historic journey on which we are about to embark."

There was a large glass-topped desk, a computer with a rhomboid screensaver slowly bouncing around its frame, empty bookshelves, another door to a walk-in cupboard and a long table with chairs.

"It is your domain, Thomas," Carver said, before adding, "within mine."

Tallis walked to the tall window. The view was wide and deep: he could see the green grounds of the gallery, and the city rising and falling in dales of buildings to the rise of the Old Town. In the parkland outside, the trees gently swayed, their leaves glinting with wet light.

Carver was talking and Tallis realised he hadn't been listening. He turned around, and the red-haired youth was also in the room.

"This is our great friend, Mungo," Carver said. "He can assist you in your work."

"Hello, Mr. Chalice," Mungo said quickly and nervously, and extended a slightly shaky hand.

"Hello, Mungo," Tallis said, as warmly as he could.

"Mungo Munro," the youth said. "Like the mountains. Not like Marilyn."

Carver shook his head and looked at the carpet. Mungo opened his mouth to say something and then thought better of it. He nodded and smiled.

"Mungo, perhaps Mr. Tallis would like a refreshment?" Carver intoned.

"Thank you, that would be lovely, if it's not too much bother," Tallis said.

"Not a bother, in any way at all. Of course. How does one take it?" the youth said. His red hair was thick and perched on top of his long head. Tallis observed its waves and curls, a kind of stacking arrangement.

"In a mug, if you have one. Two sugars," Tallis said.

"Good, good, excellent," Mungo said, and departed in a fankle.

Carver and Tallis sat. Carver was thin and sleek, with closely cropped hair and dry eyes. No light in them. He had small, close, white teeth, like a fox. "I should have realised this Acceptance Instead of Tax process would involve much close work with the government," he said evenly. "Perhaps I underestimated the process. But here you are."

Tallis felt sweat somewhere on the base of his spine. "As we discussed on the conference call, in these cases—"

"Due diligence is required," Carver said. "I absolutely agree. Of course." He tapped out his words on the tabletop. "Absolute propriety."

"Indeed," Tallis said.

With a slap, Carver lifted a pale folder onto the table. It had MACKINTOSH written in red on a white sticker.

The Public Gallery was about to receive a gift: a rare gift—the last precious work of Charles Rennie Mackintosh, the artist and architect. It was *The Goldenacre*, a painting as beautiful as its name. The task for Tallis was to prove the painting had a sound provenance. That it was what they said it was; to establish that its history was certain. He looked at the folder: inside, he could see documents and papers, maps and images.

"It is good to meet you in the flesh rather than down a line," Carver said. "You do look a lot like your father."

Tallis stared at the table. His heartbeat rushed and his skin cooled. He suddenly wanted to be anywhere but here. Perhaps hanging from a branch in a lonely forest. "My father?"

"Yes, we were at Cambridge together. A remarkable man. Of course, his life went in a very different direction to mine. I went to the Courtauld, and he went into . . . his business."

Tallis nodded.

"I'm sure he was surprised by your own career choices. But here we are," Carver said smoothly. "How is your father? Well, I hope?"

Tallis nodded again and made a short murmuring noise as Carver folded over a corner of paper in the file.

"And how long have you been an inspector of provenance?" Carver asked, and smiled.

"Three months."

"This is a sizeable first job for you, then."

"Not my first," Tallis found himself saying.

"Of course. An arbiter of the past. What a philosophical occupation."

"Not of the past, of the present. We just check that objects are real," Tallis said. "That their histories are stable."

Carver smiled and nodded and seemed to say, "Sure, sure."

"In every case of Acceptance Instead of Tax, these matters are investigated," Tallis said. "We explain our work this way: we have to make sure the past of a work of art is secure, so that an acquisition's future can also be secure."

Carver blinked, unmoving for a moment, and then leaned forward. "*The Goldenacre*, for us, for this grand old institution, is no mere new acquisition. This is not a print picked up on a curator's whim from an auction house in the provinces. This is a matter of great and urgent importance. Historic. A watershed. The handling of the painting has been agreed by the minister; and its provenance is indisputable, of course—it is well documented. But we need your good graces for the painting to be transferred to us. Your check is the last full stop in a wonderful sentence, Thomas: 'The Goldenacre, the last masterpiece of a Scottish icon, is the property of the Public Gallery of Edinburgh.'"

Mungo arrived with a tray of hot, sweet tea.

"Everything and everyone has a past," Carver said. "And yet in this case . . ." Carver carried on speaking, in his clipped, efficient way.

Outside the trees shook gently, as if shaking off the rain. The sky seemed wide and deep. Out beyond stood the dark, and the stars. Tallis thought of Astrella, somewhere in the world, moving her long white fingers over black keys and white keys. Her fingertips on ivory and wood, and the strings responding, echoing in velvet and wood. She would practise for hours in her tracksuit at the grand piano in the spare room. Her eyes closed, recalling runs and lines, crescendos and diminuendos, largos, codas.

"So tell me . . ." Carver stood up, having completed his unheard monologue. "Your family has no actual relation to the composer?"

"You should have asked my father," Tallis replied.

"There was no small talk with Raymond," Carver said.

Tallis laboured under the same name as the sixteenth-century composer. But there was no relation. "He would have told you that we are not," Tallis said, as brightly as he could. "In fact, my first name is also Raymond, but no one calls me that."

"Perhaps I could?"

"I would rather not," Tallis said.

Carver raised his eyebrows and seemed to shrug. A shiver skittered across his shoulders. "It's a remarkable name to have, certainly," he said, finishing his tea.

"At least people remember it. If not me." Tallis drew a circle on the desk with his finger.

"Oh, they remember," Carver said, his eyes unblinking, and he suddenly shot out a hand. He peered at his watch. "Enough of this cosiness. Time to meet Ms. Peters!" he said loudly. "I have the little matter of *The Goldenacre*'s transfer to discuss. She is here to fine-tune the handover."

Tallis cradled the warm mug of tea in his hands. Carver turned to leave the room and then stopped.

"Perhaps it would be useful for you to come and meet Ms. Peters, the envoy of the late, lamented lord, at this juncture?"

"Lord Melrose passed eighteen months ago," Tallis said. He was remembering the details of his brief. They floated to the surface of his mind. He grasped them before they sunk again.

"Indeed," Carver said solemnly. "He was a friend of mine, for many years. As you know, his departure left a great deal of inheritance tax to be paid, and the house with many repairs required, including the Sunken Garden, of course."

Tallis nodded, although Carver was speaking of things he did not know.

Mungo, who had been standing in the corner silently, said Mrs. Peaches was still waiting in Carver's office.

"Thank you, Mungo," Carver said.

"My pleasure," he replied.

"And it's 'Ms. Peters.' I would make sure that is correct."

"Sorry, sorry, yes, of course. I just have fruit on my mind today."

"I see," Carver said, and walked towards the door.

Tallis nodded and waited for Carver to leave the room. "I'll be along shortly, Mr. Carver," he said.

Carver and Mungo left, and Tallis moved to the desk.

He dialled a number in London, and it rang and rang. Tallis picked up his mobile phone in his other hand and looked at the BBC website. He moved to "Scotland News" with a dab of his thumb. Four headlines down, he saw the word "artist."

The London number clicked to voicemail—his own voice: "Hello, this is the Tallis household. I am afraid neither Thomas Tallis nor Astrella Nemours are here just now. Leave a message after the beep." He put the phone down and looked at the headline: SCOTS PAINTER ROBERT LOVE FOUND DEAD.

Mungo reappeared. "Are you ready for the meeting?" he said gently. "I can show you where to go?"

"Thanks, Mungo," Tallis said. "I don't think I am ready, really."

"Oh."

"But let's do it anyway."

Tallis read the news story on his phone as he was led through the pale corridors:

> *Love, 67, was found dead at his Edinburgh home yesterday. Police entered after being alerted by neighbours. Love, RSA, has paintings in galleries across the UK and internationally. He was known for his large landscapes and for his membership of the "New Glasgow Boys" group in the 1980s.*

They came to a large door, and Mungo showed Tallis through into a boardroom, where he sat down in the nearest chair.

Robert Love: the name was both familiar and unfamiliar.

He was distracted as Ms. Peters walked past him, with Sir Dennis Carver close behind.

4

Shona Sandison was early. She leant her stick beside the wooden table and waited for her coffee. The stick's grey rubber nub dunted against the tiled floor. She always met Detective Reculver here: a small café on Broughton Street, a steeply descending road on the edges of the New Town. It was miles from her flat, but it was central, quiet and easy to get to by bus. She rubbed her side. In the wet and cold, it ached.

Her bus from Lochend had been driven by a maniac, the journey done in half the usual time. So she had walked into the Scottish National Portrait Gallery, around the corner from the café, for a while. In the central court, there was a frieze of historical figures that stretched from Scotland's deep past through to armoured and crowned medieval times, and on to the suits, soldiers and inventors of the most recent century. A parade of pale, pale faces: some bearded, some with blond moustaches, crowns of glittering gold leaf, and, in the few women pictured, white cheeks like masks. They trod their silent way around the walls, facing forward, blue eyes unblinking. At the end were figures from the twentieth century, which then touched figures from the beginning of human time: a man and woman in rags and furs amid rocks and a stunted tree. The end became the start and the procession went on.

By the large pale statue of Robert Burns, Shona had checked her phone: emails from press officers about this announcement or that. She was a news reporter, so her email was full of press releases, from people or organisations that wanted her to write about them. She did not want to write about any of them. She wanted to find and write her own stories. Copying and pasting somebody else's words did not interest her. That was not journalism.

There was a terse email from Colm reminding her to look further into the Love death. As if she hadn't thought of that already.

There was a note from the editorial secretary saying that Ingleton—the arsehole from Glasgow—would be holding a meeting to "roll out a new digital content strategy." Attendance at the meeting about the scheme was mandatory. She would not be going. It was to be called a "digital transformation."

"Fuck all that shit," she had said out loud. She had looked up at Burns's pale carved face. He would have agreed.

She yawned. The coffee she was drinking now was sweet and milky. Outside, cars moved slowly down the hill and businesspeople strode quickly by. There was the steady tread of feet. The sky was blue, slashed with white cloud. Shona texted her father. He would be up now, and at the allotment. She would see him later.

She looked at the internet on her phone. The dead painter, Love, had lived in Stockbridge—a ten-minute walk from the café—but it would be pointless going there. There would be a police officer outside now. But Reculver would help. She texted the detective again: *You coming?* Her phone made a swoosh as the message hurtled through the ether.

"I'm here," he said, closing the door behind him. Large and well dressed, Reculver slumped down on a seat. He took off his hat and slapped his lit phone on the table. He was wearing makeup again. One of his eyes was closed, red and swollen. Reculver's broad face was thick with foundation, and mascara lined his one working eye.

"Jeezus. You look fucking terrible," she said.

He shook his head. "Ah, wee Shona Sandison—easy, as always, to distinguish from a ray of sunshine."

She tried not to smile.

"Yes, I had a little altercation," he rumbled, gently touching his eye. "What is the matter with you? You look ill."

"Thanks—didn't get much sleep."

"You're too thin these days," he said. "There's more meat on a dirty fork." He looked to the woman behind the counter and asked for a large black coffee and a slice of cake.

Shona had known Reculver for a few years. Her late mentor in journalism, John Fallon, had introduced her to this man, his best contact in the Scottish police. Reculver had, it was rumoured, once been in the intelligence services. Now he was a detective. He was a large man, handsome in a brutal way, had hands as big as spades, and often wore dabs of makeup. Fallon had told her, firmly, not to mention it, and she never had. She did know his first name—Benedict—but he did not seem to need it, and she had no idea about his life. He sometimes looked bruised. He wore cologne. His information was always correct, if sometimes given obscurely.

"Your eye?" Shona said, nodding to his face.

"You should see the other guy," he said, and smiled.

"Domestic?"

Reculver winced and waved a hand. "No comment, officer."

They drank coffee.

"How's your old man?" he said.

She shrugged. "Hugh Sandison is all fine. On his allotment. And no one comments on his appearance, thin or fat or otherwise. So he's happy. What about this Robert Love?"

"Put your pad and pen away," he said, putting his face in his hands.

Shona had not seen him in the flesh for a while: he seemed bigger, bulkier. He always wore a lot of clothes: vest, shirt, waistcoat, suit, large overcoat, a hat, a scarf. He was bundled up against the world.

He opened his hands and peeked with his one good eye through his fingers.

"I don't have my pad and pen," she said, pointing to the empty table.

"Well, whatever, this is off the record, and not even 'sources' or 'insiders,' okay?"

"Right." She nodded.

"Well"—he blew out his cheeks—"as you reported, or suggested in your customary vague way, it looks like a murder case. But it is a strange one. Nothing stolen, we think. Our team are all over it right now, but there's no sign of that kind of disturbance. Nothing rifled, or gone through. It was not a forced entry. But there he lies with his head open. It's a sad thing. I believe his daughter or maybe a son-in-law identified him last night. Which cannot have been pleasant for her. Or him."

"Sad?"

"I sort-of knew Bob," Reculver said, and took a swig of black coffee and winced. He put a finger in his mouth and then looked at it.

"He was a friend?"

"Friend of a friend. He was a brilliant man, was Love. Could capture anything—a horse, a sunset, that shadow, the moon. Could draw a perfect circle, it was said, freehand. He was quite the thing in the early eighties. Eighty-two, eighty-three. When we were young. He used to wear a cape about the place. Sauntering down Rose Street with his big hat on. He had his issues. We all do, of course."

"Drink?"

Reculver shook his head. He wiped his finger on a napkin. It stained pink. "Gambling. Horses. Greyhounds. The lottery.

Football, cricket, rugby results. Anything. He would gamble on raindrops sliding down the pane if you took him up on it."

"Right," Shona said. "So, is this a debt collected?"

"It is rather pointless killing someone who owes you money, is it not?" Reculver rumbled.

"And not stealing anything." Shona nodded.

"Well, exactly," the detective said. He picked up the slice of cake. Silvery icing glinted before it disappeared into his tender mouth. He gulped it down. "His wallet was all there, on the side. No cards stolen. His passport in a drawer beside his bed."

"A love thing?"

"Bob was killed by a man, and he wasn't gay."

"Still can't rule it out."

"Yes, you probably can. It's very unlikely, Ms. Sandison," Reculver whispered, going for his coffee again.

Shona noticed the size of his legs, his thighs like hams, jammed under the table. Red socks, well-polished brogues. "Killed by a man?"

"Yes. Not a pretty end for Bob," Reculver said. "Some kind of metal implement: maybe a screwdriver, a chisel, or something like one of those heavy tent pegs. We're not sure. It was a mess of a scene for the team: he collapsed into his painting table. There was paint everywhere and he or the murderer had knocked over a large painting. It was a work in progress. There's more I could tell you, but I won't. It was complicated."

"Right," Shona said. She was making notes in her head, to remember it all.

"He had been struck with great force," Reculver said, shaking his head. "He was only a little guy. He might not have known much about it."

"A murder," she said.

"Murder. Not an accident. No manslaughter here. Someone got into the house—maybe he knew them—and killed him deliberately. Efficiently. And didn't leave many traces. A little blood goes a long way."

"You have something, then?"

He shook his head. "Something and nothing. A size twelve walking boot. Could be anyone's."

"Size twelve?"

"A big fella," he said.

"How big?"

"Fearless and adept, too, going by the butchery."

"Butchery?"

He flushed. "I'll stop myself there, I think. Fucking hell. Don't ask—you won't find out." He sucked his coffee.

"What do you mean, 'butchery'?"

Reculver held up a large pink hand. He shook his head. "Forget it."

Shona drank her coffee. The sugar sizzled on her tongue. "Okay. Debt collection aside, do you think this was to do with his gambling, with money?"

Reculver brushed yellow cake crumbs from his hands. He shrugged. "Come on, Shona. Who the fuck knows at this stage?" He stood up suddenly, to leave. He gently wiped his bad eye.

"Going already?" Shona said.

"Yes. I can tell you are a trained observer. How are you, anyway?"

"Fine."

"You always say that." He put some money on the table. "You'd say that if you were hanging out the window." He paused and put his hat on. He placed a large hand on her shoulder. "Off the record," he said.

"Of course," she said.

His hand gripped her shoulder briefly. "Be safe, Shona. There are bad people doing bad things out there."

"Don't I just know it."

"To know is one thing, to see is another," he said.

"Thank you."

He paused and looked at her. "There is something else about this."

"What?"

"I can't tell you. You will find out, though. Don't read too much into it. And don't call me again," he said, smiling. He winked with his one good eye and left the café. He stomped off down the street.

Something else? Shona shook her head. She took her pad from her bag and scribbled some notes. She looked at her phone: time soon to get to the newspaper office. At least to show her face, show willing. Sometimes all it took was for her to be present and colleagues thought she was working. Even if you spent most of the day aimlessly online, avoiding the smear of grey despair with sudden, twitchy changes of screen—video, music or a newsfeed. With little shallow lights, twinkling in her eyes. A sinking in her stomach, and pain in her old wounds.

She picked out her phone. There were three missed calls, all from the office. She shook her head and called back.

"Shona Sandison," the thick voice said, in mock surprise.

"Yeah, fuck off," she said.

"What you got?" the voice said. It was Colm. News editor, and sick and tired of it. Rumour was, he had tendered his resignation three times and been rebuffed each time. Now he lived and worked in a state of suspended release. And furious with it.

"Well, it's murder," she said.

"I know, tell me about it. But that's just the business we are in." He sighed. She could imagine him rolling a cigarillo.

"No, Colm, the Love death—it's definitely murder."

"No shit. You've already written that. We all have memories. Well, some of us. What's new?"

"No, this is different, it's confirmation—"

"That our last story was all good? We don't need to write

another saying the same thing. You know that. We need a
new line. So, what's new?"

"Well . . ."

"We need a new line. Isn't there a wife?"

"A daughter."

"Get the daughter, then. She'll be at the house today,
won't she? Try your luck. And don't forget this fucking
meeting this afternoon. It's a three-line whip. 'Digital transformation.' Ingleton has a hard-on."

"Gross. But I'm afraid, Colm, that I can't go."

There was a large sigh. "Come on now, Shona. If I have
to attend, you do. Why the fuck not?"

"'Cos I don't want to," she said, and hung up.

Shona ordered another coffee. She searched on her phone
for articles about Love. There were several profiles, but
from ten or more years ago. Some had mentions about other
Scottish artists from the same period in Glasgow: Campbell,
Howson, Wiszniewski. They had long and varied careers.
Love had had some big shows, at the Gallery of Modern Art
in Glasgow, another in a private gallery in London. He'd had
an exhibition of his watercolours in New York.

Shona read on, looking for a profile, for a biography:
some mention of family, his wives or daughters. If she had
been doing this search ten years ago, she knew, it would
have been easier: she would have called the library at the
newspaper and a trained librarian would have looked up
back copies, or spun through the microfiche. But the newspaper's library had been dumped on a local authority years
ago and the microfiche sent to the landfill. The digital record
only went back to 1996 or so. Older than that, the stories
began to tail off, and disappeared into memoryless darkness.

There was one story: a gallery opening in Edinburgh,
1999. It had nothing to do with Love, but there was a picture
of a row of luminaries at the opening of a seasonal exhibition: an autumn show of paintings and drawings. She peered

into her phone. There was a caption under the photo, in tiny italics. She expanded it with her fingers. She read the names of the people in the photo from left to right. There was a young woman with long hair, smiling, "Trinity Arts Club President Mhairi Brown"; a very old man in a wheelchair, "Lord Melrose"; and there, Robert Love, "with his daughter Morag." A child with blond hair.

She looked again at the picture. Robert Love, long-haired, with a colourful shirt, smiling. His right hand was on the shoulder of Lord Melrose. Maybe they were friends.

The event was at the Arts Club in Trinity, a suburb to the north of the city, with large stone houses and elegant parks. She looked up the club: it still existed. The president was now a Mr. Crawford Dudley. She found the address.

From the website, she saw it was closed on a Friday. She would go there, but not now. Robert Love would still be dead on Monday. He had moved outside time. Any secrets he held would still be as true then, as now.

There were other stories to be written. She turned her mind to them, and the day's work consumed her.

5

It was nearing the end of a long day. Edinburgh was becoming a weave of shadows hung in a net of light. And, as the bus crested a hill and then moved down a long road to the shore of the Firth, glimmers on the sea came into view: ships moving slowly from the sea inland. Over on the far shore, Fife lay in hills and fields, huddled in dimming light and silence.

Tallis was alone on the bus, as it ground its way down Leith Walk, turned right at a large tatty roundabout and edged down the old London road towards the city's small seaside community, Portobello. He did not quite know where he was going. He was warm and tired on the bus. Its engine lulled him. Something began to move in his coat pocket, as if a small animal was writhing there. It was his phone. He fished it out: the number was not registered. "Unknown," his phone said.

"Hello?"

"Melcombe," a solid voice said. It was his superior at the Department. Melcombe was a small man, with a face constructed from a series of stolid horizontals.

"Hello," Tallis said, his stomach turning over. "How are you?"

"When has that ever mattered?"

Tallis did not know what to say.

"How is Edinburgh, and when can you come back?" His voice was as solid as a blocked drain.

"I've only just arrived."

"You need to check it out, get it cleared and come back," Melcombe intoned.

"I need to do it properly," Tallis said softly.

"No one is saying you shouldn't, least of all me, Tallis. But time is pressing. You have an interim review assessment coming up. That's not a foregone conclusion."

"I know," Tallis said. But he had forgotten. A human resources interview: he had fallen asleep at his desk six weeks ago. There would be questions. Beasts and shadows around his shoulders.

"Anyway, that is not why I call," Melcombe said. The receiver seemed to move closer to his mollusc mouth. Tallis could hear his tongue slide over his teeth. "Are you on a secure phone? Have you your laptop? We could use the message system."

"No," Tallis said, as the bus ground its way to the long esplanade by the sea where his aunt lived. A two-storey house in a lane. "I don't have them with me."

"Why not? You are meant to be working. Here's the question: Have you been trying to contact your father?"

"No," Tallis lied. "I have not spoken to him since he left."

"Because you know calls to his number are tracked," Melcombe said. "Logged and noted, categorised and filed. Colour-coded."

"I am sure they are," Tallis said. "But I haven't. No. Why do you ask?"

"What about your mother? Has she tried to call him?"

"I doubt it. She died when I was seven."

"I suppose not, then." Melcombe sighed. His point of superiority made, he was now bored. "Just checking. Someone has mentioned it—that there have been erroneous signals. I thought I had better go straight to the source. I need a report on the Mackintosh by Tuesday at the latest. Okay?"

Melcombe said this firmly, as if it was a new plan. But it had long been agreed that Tallis would confirm the provenance of *The Goldenacre* within the week, sign the requisite documents and return to London.

Tallis felt an irritation rising in him. It crawled across the nerves of his shoulders. A thin, wispy sense, like the legs of a fly dragged across his flesh. "Fine," he said. "That is fine."

"How is Carver? Has he been helpful?"

"He just wants this deal done, so he can hang the painting for a summer exhibition. It's all straightforward. The family lawyer was there today. Carver is chilly. He doesn't give much away."

"He doesn't need to; he's in charge."

"So I gather."

The called ended. Tallis threw his phone into his bag. "Dick," he said.

An electronic bell tringed and the bus came to a stop. Tallis slumped down the stairs and entered the outside world. He walked slowly to the house of Aunt Zed.

Aunt Zed was his mother's sister. She looked like his mother, and sometimes sounded like her too. His mother was long gone. Zed was a living echo of her. She had her eyes, the curl of her nose. A facsimile.

The sea silently ate the shore.

It had been a long day. He was weary. As the bus lurched away around a corner, he wondered if loss could run in families. A strain of mortal pain. His father, widowed; his grandfather, widowed too. And now he was losing Astrella. Now he had lost her. His chest tightened as he thought of Ray and the life the boy had to come. What loss would scar it, what shadows? He would be there for him, though. Holding his hand, until it slipped away.

As he walked, his mind turned over the meeting that

morning, with Carver and Ms. Peters. It had been abrupt. By the time he arrived in Carver's large office, Peters was almost on her way out. She had left papers on the table. She had shaken his hand with a firm grip, her dark glasses still on, her hat on. Then she had left, her hands in her pockets. Carver and Tallis had sat in silence for a time before discussing the documents.

He had been relieved to work. To consider the matter at hand: *The Goldenacre*. It was a large, strange work, regarded as one of Mackintosh's most beautiful creations. It had been in the hands of the Lords of Melrose and Roxburgh since the family had bought it from Mackintosh in 1927.

It was the product of a departure. Mackintosh is now, in these times, renowned for his architecture, for the elegance of his designs. There is a famous picture of the young Scot: resplendent in silk, with a sturdy moustache and intense gaze. But for most of his life, Mackintosh was not that man. Not that adored visionary. In his own time, his architectural practice, based in Glasgow, had foundered, driven deep into a sand of indifference. He mysteriously left his job. He and his wife, Margaret Macdonald, a childless couple, moved to Suffolk. And then, in 1923, to another stage: Port Vendres, in southern France.

There, Mackintosh regained something. Or discovered it. A new and gentler vision of his life. He painted many lovely watercolours under cloudless Mediterranean skies. Little villages in white hills. Striated rock above turquoise seas. Winding paths in chalk. But, then, another departure: a savage illness, cancer in his mouth, which brought him and Margaret back to London. After a brief improvement in his condition there, he seems to have returned to Scotland. But not to Glasgow, where his School of Art building stood. He instead apparently visited Edinburgh, and, working at some height above the Ferry Road in the north of the city—within sight of the sea—painted the fields and buildings in the area known in the city as Goldenacre. He died in 1928.

Tallis had read the Public Gallery's submission on the painting:

> The Goldenacre *(1927, watercolour on paper, board) has been in the family of the Lords of Melrose and Roxburgh since 1927, when the thirteenth Lord Melrose—John Felix Farquharson—bought it directly from the artist. He presented the painting to his wife, Lady Anne, and thus it was formally owned by Lady Melrose.*
>
> *It has been in the family seat, Denholm House ('The House'), ever since. Traditionally it hung in the bedchamber of the Ladies Melrose ('The Green Room') overlooking the eastern Sunken Garden (disused water features in a contrived landscape of architectural follies) of the Denholm Estate.*
>
> *A fire in 1961 damaged a part of the property, since renovated, and the painting suffered smoke damage. It was saved and reframed. The frame, according to the fourteenth Lord Melrose—William John Felix Farquharson—had been destroyed after it fell from the wall. The work itself (120cm x 120cm) was unaffected. The painting was, however, removed from its board and "rolled" for a short time. It suffered little damage.*

And, at its conclusion, the heart of the matter:

> *. . . as agreed by the Minister for Culture, and the relevant committee of the Department of*

Culture and Heritage, the Acceptance Instead of Tax Panel, The Goldenacre is to be transferred to the collections of the Public Gallery instead of inheritance tax. The acceptance of this artwork will generate a tax deduction of more than £12 million.

After an inspection of provenance (IP) by Department officers, it will be moved from Denholm House to the Public Gallery, in Edinburgh, once particulars have been agreed.

Carver had laid his hands on the papers and explained, in his clipped voice, with his eyes closed as if in prayer, that Lord Melrose had been succeeded by his twin children, Olivia and Felix Farquharson, both thirty-three. Ms. Peters worked for them. The painting was still at Denholm House. Tallis, as inspector of provenance, would have to go there to assess the painting.

Tallis walked on through Portobello. People were shrugging their way down the street against the spitting rain, ducking into doorways, trying to put up umbrellas. He turned down a side street, to the sea. There were several of these streets in Portobello, at right angles to the coast, avenues of small, cramped houses, old bungalows and windswept terraces. There were small gardens, fairy lights in upper windows, children's scooters attached to railings. Plastic windmills turned.

Out past the cobbled lane where his aunt lived, he walked past a small park and then on to the esplanade. There, a long path ran beside the wide beach. Tallis stood looking at the sea, the great mouth of the Firth of Forth, its teeth of ships, and the gathering darkness. The setting sun, obscured behind the rushing clouds. Salt adrift in the air.

The great trench, filled with fathoms of cold, with silt and rock and detritus. The dark depth of it and the slow, healing weight of it, if he could dive in and submit to it. He shivered and shook his head: he could not think of these things. If he were alone: perhaps. But Ray was the tiny white hand holding back the tidal wave.

Tallis was suddenly cold and needed to move. He tried to concentrate on his surroundings. A large white car, with its lights on, was parked nearby, a driver behind the wheel, its engine purring. Tallis turned and walked to his aunt's house. There was warm amber light from its windows and, as he took the short path to the large front door, he could see inside. In the kitchen living room, Zed was kneeling before a stove, feeding a log into the flames. A pan was boiling on a hob. On the long wooden kitchen table, a newspaper was spread out.

He let himself into the house with her spare keys.

"Hello?" she called, and he called back. He hung up his coat and bag. In the hall was a large blue poster that stated, "Still Yes." Hanging from a hook were several lanyards. Aunt Zed was a campaigner. She was for many things: Scottish independence; land reform; socialism; a more sustainable world. And against many others: nuclear weapons; pollution; animal testing; the patriarchy; the Orange Order; the free market; Conservatives.

Tallis moved to the warmth of the kitchen. Aunt Zed, wiping her hands on her overalls, came to him smiling and gave him a hug. She smelled of sweet lavender and the tang of firelighters. Her hands gripped him.

"So, how was the first day?" she said and smiled. She turned and went to put the kettle on. "I'm doing pasta. Jack will be joining us."

Jack was her boyfriend. He was a framer and had a workshop in Newhaven, a former fishing village, farther east along the Firth of Forth coast, which was now part of Edinburgh. He was in his sixties and thrawn.

Tallis talked in vague and general terms about his day, and she made him tea. He moved to the fireplace and sat on a wooden chair, the flames coiling pale and high inside the stove. He looked through the kitchen window, out to the street, and could see the white car sitting, still.

"I am not sure I am very welcome there," he said. "But that is fine: I am a footnote in this deal."

"Of course not," she said. "They don't want anyone prying into their cosy transactions. But you get to define it yourself. Don't worry: you can grind this corn slowly."

"I cannot grind slowly—I need to do this quickly. My boss is already moaning."

"That's your damn government for you. Let him moan," she said. "The longer I can see you, the better. It's so lovely having you to stay." She looked at him and added, "You're in Free Scotland now, beyond his jurisdiction. Don't let him put a finger on your soul."

"It's fine, Zed, it really is. And I've taken to reminding myself the same thing when things are . . . sticky."

"What is that, my love?"

"Every time something happens—it happens for the last time."

Zed peered at him. "How bleak and philosophical of you," she said. "You sound like your father."

"Oh Lord, don't say that," he said.

She shook her head and returned to the stove. "Your father—he wasn't all bad."

"'Not all bad'?" Tallis repeated, raising his eyebrows.

"Tom—"

"In the same sense that Fascists make the trains run on time, that kind of 'not all bad'?" he said.

Zed chuckled suddenly and shook her head.

Tallis saw a light outside flash and strobe. He moved over to the window, stepping around Zed, who was stirring a rich red sauce into long slippery strips of pasta. It smelled delicious. She had poured red wine, and there was a large bowl of green salad on the table.

"Anyway, how did you sleep last night, Tommy?" she said, sipping wine, leaning against her wooden dresser.

"It was blessed relief after that train journey. It was like I had fallen into the grave," he lied. He had barely slept. He peered out to the street at the white car. It was a four-by-four, with metallic rims. The driver was still at the wheel, and the engine was ticking over. "Is that a neighbour of yours?" he asked.

She looked. "No, not seen that car before. But it might be one of those private taxis, the ones you can order from your phone. Something like that," she said lightly, and turned back to the food. "Where has Mr. Jack got to?"

"How was your day, Zed?" Tallis said, looking at the white car. It was waiting for something.

Aunt Zed talked about her day: her yoga group, her meeting with Extinction Rebellion, a chat with the local MSP. She was organising a petition. Then emails and bills, and a walk on the beach with some friends. Her voice thrummed with life, with interest. In the glowing light, her eyes glimmered, the frayed ends of her hair seemed to be alight. Fragile wires of copper and brass.

They both sat down at the table.

A newspaper had slipped to the floor and was now a small tent around the leg of the table. He lifted it up. There was a short story about the death of Robert Love, and a photo of him from many years ago, wearing a colourful shirt and with long hair. He stood beside a large canvas, one of his colourist works. Tallis looked at the painting: all daubs and splashes of colour. Paint squeezed straight from the tube onto a harsh canvas.

Zed, keeping the pasta warm on the stove, noticed Tallis reading the article. "Now that's a really terrible business," she said. "Lovely man. In his way. Well, I say lovely. He was interesting. Haven't really liked his work for a while, but he was always around and about. Jack knew him too."

"You knew him? How awful," Tallis said. "Of course, you knew him. You know everyone."

"Many moons ago we stood together at Faslane. But I don't think his heart was in it. I met him many times, of course, for work. He had his demons."

"How long did you work at the Arts Council?"

"Thirty-two years, Tommy."

He smiled at her. The firelight illuminated her face and she was momentarily transfigured. A warm light in her eyes and glowing on her skin like a fine dust. "So, you might know this Carver, then?"

"Oh yes, Sir Dennis," she said, shaking her head. She looked at Tallis and squinted. It was her sign. She did not want to talk any further. She had worked in external affairs—marketing and public relations—for the arts funding council for most of her life. Her husband, Hamilton, had died young in the 1980s. She had taken on causes ever since. Impossible ones, mainly, so that they did not run out. Could not die.

"So, was it suicide?" she said softly.

"They usually say 'no suspicious circumstances' if that is the case. It's a bit curious."

"A robbery gone wrong," she said, nodding. "These things do happen."

"Who burgles an artist? There's never much money lying around."

"It is called 'theft by housebreaking' in Scotland: Scots law," she said, waving a finger. "Have you heard anything about Ray today?"

Tallis glanced at his phone, a silent black slab on the table. "No, nothing."

"I hope that woman is not playing silly buggers!"

"Astrella doesn't play those games," Tallis said, and took a large swig of tea. Zed raised her eyebrows.

The front door to the house opened. Jack appeared, his head wet, his beard fluffed and wiry. He looked at Tallis and seemed momentarily unsure what to say. But he reached forward with wet hands, and they shook. Jack was a big man. His trousers, thick cords, were filthy.

"Dreich," Jack said, and disappeared into the hall, kicking off boots, shrugging off his jacket.

"Okay, Mr. Tallis, shall we eat?" his aunt said, settling down at the table.

"Let's," Tallis said, and they began the hearty meal.

Later, with the fire low, and Jack and Zed gone to bed, Tallis washed up, his hands glad of the warm water and soap, the swish of the full basin and the dutiful clink of plates and bowls.

He sat by the fire, the logs free of flame, but throbbing with heat, scaled with white ash, the glass smeared with black. He had been poured a large whisky by Jack. It swilled cambric in the glass.

At some point in the evening, the white car outside had driven slowly away.

Tallis sipped the spirit, smarting at its strength and seaweed tang. He drank some more, and felt his head become heavy.

He looked into the fire, the alcohol unspooling a giddy gyre in his blood. A new world was being burned from the old. The red ash and the silver ash. The black ash and the red flame.

He rubbed his eyes. He thought of Carver's question: What does "Tallis" mean? It was from the French: *taillis*, for "copse." Or "thicket." He was in a thicket now.

The weekend opened up before him, empty. He could not think what it would contain.

He lay back on the carpet and watched the fire slowly die.

6

Edinburgh City Councillor John Cullen stepped out from the tall, grey council buildings, through an arch and onto the cobbles of the Royal Mile. He checked his watch. In seventeen minutes he needed to be at Edinburgh Castle. There was an event there, some kind of late morning tourism shindig. A brunch reception, his private secretary had said. And, as head of the Planning and Finance Committee, he had been invited.

The rotund man churned his legs up the hill. He moved with a rolling stomp. He quickly checked his watch and smiled. He had time. He would nip into a pub on the way. It had been raining that morning, and the old street was wet, the cobbles gleaming like the sheen on his happily bald head. Tourists were about, ambling under plastic ponchos and umbrellas. They milled around shops that sold ginger-hair hats and kilts, the whisky and cigar shops, the pubs, restaurants and cafés. The brooding bulk of St. Giles' cathedral was dread and dark in the morning sun.

Councillor Cullen's tired mind ran over the events of the previous few hours. There had been a full council meeting, with every councillor in the city running over the decisions made by committees. They had discussed the tramline extension; new housing in the north of the city; the proposal to extend, by artificial means, the beach at Portobello. And, most pleasingly, one of his decisions had been ratified: to reject the building of a proposed "international film studio" on a site at South Queensferry, near the Firth of Forth. A large acreage of drowsy wasteland overlooking the three bridges across the estuary. The full council had agreed with his committee's dismissal.

Cullen was especially content, as the main developer behind the opaque and shambolic proposal was a particularly arrogant and annoying one. An entitled dick. One day, they would go the way of their forebears. One day.

The developers, Oldmeg Reach, led by this prick. were furious, he knew. But they would be back with another plan, another shell-game, in a few weeks or months. People like that, all they literally want is money, he thought, as he tramped up the hill. As prosaic as that. Stark, simple. And people with money, such as Oldmeg Reach, always want more money. It was the way of this, the fallen world. No other way to dress it up. It was down to good men, as Cullen knew he was, to stop them. Greed is, after all, a sin. Every other sin flows from it. All the savage sorrow of the world.

Men of good intention, he thought. We need more men of good intention. He huffed up the steps into the Ensign, a pub near the last rise of cobbles to the castle. It was cosy and small, with low ceilings and exposed beams. As he rolled to the bar, Cullen nodded at a face he recognised by the empty fire, and the barman also nodded to him. It was warm, and there was a low murmur of conversation. Diffuse light glinted from brass and optics. He exhaled and leaned against the bar. He ordered a whisky. A single malt. He pondered the day and gently rolled the whisky glass in his fingers. The liquid slowly moved as one, a caramel eye caught in the thin glass.

A large, lithe man sat by the door, reading an old paper. Cullen could just make out the headline of a story about an artist that had been found dead. There was a photograph of a bearded man, smiling, but Cullen did not recognise him. The man peered over his paper. He had short grey hair and grey eyes.

Cullen needed a piss. He nodded to the barman, who took his whisky and held it for him, for his return. As he made his way to the toilet, the councillor smiled as he thought of his dog: she was pregnant. He thought of puppies and yowling, of tiny scrunched balls of fluff and their tinny squeaks. He would call home from the castle and check how she was doing.

He pushed at a wooden door and entered the small toilet. There were two urinals, a cubicle for a lavatory and a sink. It was windowless and tiled, and smelled like drains. Cullen looked at his watch. He would have to hurry. He stood in front of the urinal, unzipped his bulging trousers and began to pee. Behind him, someone entered the toilet and put something under the door. The councillor did not want to turn.

The man grabbed Cullen around the throat. He was suddenly stiff with fright, as hard leather fingers closed on his soft neck. There was a sudden stab of pain. A knee struck the back of his knee. Another gloved hand forced a plastic bag onto the councillor's head, and it was pulled over his hair, his forehead, his face. He began to choke. Cullen tried to turn around, his zip down, his wet dick flapping, but the man had him tight. The grey-haired man was strong and tall, his body like a tree trunk, and Cullen could not move. He was clamped in his vice.

The bag was yanked from the back, and the plastic closed over Cullen's face like a second skin. He tried to kick back, away from the urinal, into the man. But he could not find any strength. The grey-haired man brought down a sharp, short spike of metal into the side of the councillor's head. With a hard puncture, his head was broken. The bag filled with a gout of black blood, his muffled cry and his last breath. He crumpled, slowly, his heavy fall broken by the man's large hands, to the piss-pooled floor. He lay slumped and punctured.

The large man washed his hands under a twist of warm water and removed the wedge from the door. He left the toilet, and the dead councillor. Dark arterial blood pooled from the bag and spread, following the lines between the neat white tiles like a red net of released life.

The grey-haired man made his way to the front door of the pub and walked outside to the Royal Mile. An aeroplane glimmered over the Pentlands.

A white car pulled up beside the path, a door opened, and he stepped inside.

8 A.M.

Astrella and I are all over. Finished. Not quite divorced. Not together. So . . . I'm not sure how she is, but she's always busy, and when she's not busy with work she's too busy to talk. She's doing really well still: recordings and concerts all over the place. Living that life. She has this big new deal with Deutsche Grammophon, so if you look her up online . . . I don't know whether you have online. The internet. I'm sure you do.

I'm in Scotland now. In Edinburgh, as part of my new job. I don't know how long I'll be here. Who knows how it will work out. Better than the last one . . . Edinburgh is beautiful. I don't know if it's more than that. Do you remember we came to visit Zed and we watched the New Year fireworks from the top of that hill? The whole city lit up. And I saw that unusual Vermeer in the gallery, and those Titians. That Rembrandt self-portrait, that hugely sad one? It's still here. It reminds me of you.

I'm staying with Zed. You'll have her address and phone number. If you want to get in touch. Which you won't, but anyway. Ray is doing fine, he's in his third year now and is a good little student. He has friends, collects football cards and loves maths—that must come from your side of the family.

Right now I'm in Zed's spare room. It has a window and I can see the sea from here, and the ships on the Firth of Forth. I think she is still on her antidepressants.

Today I am being introduced to more people. I must just try and find my feet. The Public Gallery is smaller than the Civic Gallery. It's a little held together with string and Sellotape, I think. But that's fine, so am I.

Not feeling my best. I'm having dreams of death.

7

The Trinity Arts Club was down a cobbled lane, off a quiet, wide street lined with large houses and old trees. There were drifts of blossom at the kerbs, pink and white. Shona paid the driver and the taxi grinded its way along the street. She did not know Trinity. A northern enclave, it had silent houses, separate and gardened, some with high walls, some with towers. It had straight streets and narrow, interlaced lanes. There was the smell of the sea, from half a mile away to the north, and a deep silence. It also smelled of wealth and long holidays, elderly quiet and old money. It felt like an empty market town. Around the green parks were elegant railings, and the trees were old, their roots breaking through the tarmac, bubbling the paths.

Shona walked down the lane. It had been a quiet and watchful weekend. Films and books, and getting her father to the allotment and back. A drink with her friend Viv in the Roseleaf, talking over the same old journalism tales. Feeling empty as she watched the news scroll over the screen of her laptop late into the night. Both days, she had been uneasy. Time seemed to drag. It had a clenched gravity of its own— like the curling wave, pulling itself back before delivering its blow upon the land.

Her feet and stick thumped on the stones of the street, cut

in better times. Everything in this place seemed clean, and ordered. There was a green sign, lettered in gold, hanging from two little chains: *Trinity Arts Club. Private Parking.* Shona stopped, leaning on her stick. There was no noise, just the distant burr of cars, somewhere south, somewhere on a major road, far from here.

Her mobile phone juddered and buzzed. She answered it. It was Colm.

"See the fucking *Journal?*"

He was annoyed and impatient. The *Journal* was a rival paper: a weekly, but still staffed with a small team of competent news reporters.

"Nope. Don't read it."

"You should."

"What do you mean?"

"The Love murder. Says nothing was nicked, no money stolen, no paintings nabbed. Makes it a bit more interesting, doesn't it?"

"I see," she said, annoyed.

"We need more on this. Can you speak to your spooks and get more? Need a line on it by afternoon news conference—confirmed, denied or otherwise."

The phone went click.

"Fuck you," Shona said.

She had an urge to throw her phone into the ground. She almost called Reculver. But she didn't. She put her phone back in her pocket and walked slowly to the Arts Club sign.

Her side hurt. An old wound, from an old story. And now a new story, with pain inscribed.

Past the sign was a gate in a stone wall. There was a buzzer and post box, inlaid into the stone. The gate opened with a push, and she was in a garden, with cut grass and various chairs and small round tables. Ahead was a large stone townhouse, separate from its neighbours. There was a green front door, and blinds over the ground-floor windows.

The door was slightly ajar.

She stepped up to it and looked inside: beyond another windowed door, there was a tiled hallway, a wooden staircase. There were dark busts of bearded men on plinths.

Shona pushed open the second door. Her feet clopped on the tiles. There was a deep and plush silence. There were paintings all over the walls, hung one above the other. Portraits and rural landscapes. Scenes cut from another time. Shona looked to the right: there was a large room, with a bar. Shutters were pulled down over whisky and optics. There was a man on a tall stool at the bar, drinking from a small white cup of coffee.

"Hello?" He had a large moustache, wore a shirt with the top couple of buttons undone, and his face was the colour of smoked salmon. "Can I help you?"

Shona moved towards him. The bar was in some kind of restaurant or café. For members only, probably, she thought. "I am looking for Crawford Dudley," she said, as brightly as she could. "I am Shona Sandison, a reporter for the *Post*."

"I am he," he said.

Shona was aware of the space between them. It could have been a mile. "I am doing a piece on Robert Love," she said. She summoned up her usual reporters' tone, a special kind of learned, and curated, energy: to seem reasonable and open-minded, to try and sound like a human. Just engaging, at a light level, in talk, in a roundabout chat. In reality, the conversation was a certain scenario, a discussion in theory only. There were two key questions that needed answering, and that, for the reporter, was the point of the exchange, whatever the surrounding conversation sounded like. And she was always hunting for those two answers. The thickets and woods of words around those two facts were just cover—a distraction. They would be forgotten. She had had enough conversations, chats, interviews like this, and she knew that at some point she would stop living in the present and already be thinking about the eventual story being printed on the page. Even as she spoke, and heard a response, the lede was being typed.

"What kind of piece? The poor old man has barely left us," he said. He spoke in a neutral tone. He did not seem annoyed. He took another sip of coffee. "He was a member here, but latterly we had not seen him much." He opened a hand to the stool beside him.

Shona smiled and moved towards him. He noticed her limp and stick.

"War wound?" he said, pointing, still, with a face unsmiling.

"Car crash," she lied, still smiling.

He offered her coffee. She nodded and he poured thick, hot, black liquid into another cup from a silvery pot.

There were steps from the hall, and a woman carrying flowers came into the room. The blooms shook around her face. Perfume drifted.

"Hello, Liz," he said brightly.

"Crawford," she said. "My, my. What you here for, this early?"

"Ah, picking up some paperwork, you know how it is."

"I see. Well, I'm just going to do lilies in here, for the do," she said.

"Fine by me, Liz, all good," he said, looking at Shona, who had removed her pad and pen from her bag. She had put her phone on the bar top and turned on the Dictaphone app.

The flower woman was wearing a light blue coat, which the water from the flowers had stained. She had silvery eye shadow. She looked to Shona and smiled. "Are you going to be in the papers, Crawford?"

"Ms. Sandison here is talking to me about Bob Love," he said gently.

The woman stood still and nodded. The flowers swung around her ears and hair. Green stems glimmered. "Well,

well. It's a frightful business," she said. "We all loved Robert here. I hope you are writing nice things about him?"

"Of course," Shona said.

"Well, I'll leave you be, Crawford," Liz said, and rustled out of the room. Her heels clipped on the tiled floor, and disappeared.

The man turned to Shona. He patted his moustache. His eyes were watery. "Well, I will give you a formal quote on Bob in a minute. But what have you heard about this whole terrible business?"

"Just what you know, Mr. Dudley. He was found dead in his home. He had been painting, and someone killed him. Nothing seems to have been stolen. I can understand how shocking it must be."

"Shocking, yes," he said, with no obvious emotion. He picked up the metal pot of coffee and poured more black liquid into his cup. He seemed to be thinking something over. Taking his time. "Turn that off," he said, pointing to her phone.

Shona nodded and pressed the Dictaphone closed.

"I don't want you contacting his daughter," he said.

"I might have to."

"That's what newspapers do, eh?"

"Yes."

He sighed. "You know, someone once said art is a lie that happens to be true. What do you do for a living?"

"I don't lie, Crawford."

"I don't want you bothering Morag."

"Why don't you tell me why?"

He looked around the room, as if searching for someone to talk to. There were large framed pictures: landscapes of sea and city. Somewhere in the building, glass clinked. "I fear for what happened," he said quietly.

"What do you think happened?"

"Bob had been having a tough time lately," he said. "It

has been tough for him, and for his daughter especially—
she had been looking after him, really. He had some issues
that never seemed to go away. Never seemed to alleviate."
He stirred his coffee, even though he had not put sugar in
it. "Robert had always loved the horses, back in the day. Of
course, he had painted Ayr races, and Musselburgh. He ven-
tured down to Liverpool once, painting the Grand National.
We have one of his race-day paintings upstairs. He always
painted: he always gambled. I think he even started in Art
School, when none of us had any money. Not two brass far-
things. You won't know, of course, but in the eighties it was
harder to gamble than now—betting shops were closed on
Sundays. All that business. He still lost a lot of money. But
there was none of this internet stuff. Now you can throw
away three hundred quid on your phone. And he did."

He suddenly peered at her, as if the entire rotten super-
structure of worldwide organised gambling was all her fault.
But the fierce look passed.

"It's an addiction, as bad as any other. Don't let anyone
tell you otherwise. So, he had a lot of debts, and a lot of
problems with money. And with that, frankly, came darkness.
But"—he grinned a tight line and shook his head—"he was
still a damn fine artist."

He rubbed an eye and took another swig of coffee. A tear
gathered and rolled. "I'm sorry. Bob and I . . . We didn't
always see eye to eye. He hadn't paid his subs in years. And
the last time we met, it wasn't a happy experience. But I'm
crushed. That he went like this."

Dudley rubbed his eyes again and drank his coffee. Somewhere in the building Liz was cutting something with a sharp,
swishing noise.

"Do you think his death had something to do with his
gambling?" Shona asked.

His eyes narrowed. "No, I do not. If anyone did know
him, they knew he had no money. So why try and rob him?

I wish he'd had a happier life. He deserved more than this. Much, much more."

She waited again.

"Have you seen the papers?" she said.

"No. I heard a wee report on Radio Scotland. I don't need to know any more."

She did not want to mention how Love had died. "Show me some of his work—do you have some here?"

He nodded and smiled, before leading the way. There were deep red carpets, a hall with closed doors and, at one end, a long room: the gallery. They walked in, and there was clear light through large windows. The roofs and towers of Trinity were solid and silent in the sun. In the distance, the castle rested on its rock. The walls were hung with heavy, large paintings, and there were sculptures on plinths and in cases. There were fresh flowers by the window. The room smelled of their scent, polished wood and carpet cleaner.

"Here, this is one of his best, that we have. Of course, his best-known ones are in Kelvingrove, and I've always liked his portraits too." Crawford gestured to a painting near to a corner. It was a seascape, a whirl of colour, bordering on abstraction. "There's a wee bit of MacTaggart in there, of course, and he was awfully good at watercolours. This is a watercolour, from 1983. He was in his pomp then. He really could control the watercolour so well. He was very exact. Look—this looks wild, but it's actually not."

Shona looked closer. In the foreground of the painting— *Camber Sands, 1983*—there stood people on a beach. They were painted clearly, but they were not real. They looked like ghosts, or spirits, gazing out to the sea, waiting for something to arrive, or waiting to depart on the final journey. "It's beautiful," she said.

"So, you see—this is what we will remember of him. Not all the noise of his life, the ugliness, the unpleasantness. This is why humans create art, so that something beautiful remains of us after we are gone. The individual life is a mote of dust in the fire. A dot of light, and then darkness. But nothing else on earth can create something like this. Until the sun swallows the world, Bob's art will be here."

They stood for a while.

"Why do you not want me to speak to Morag?" Shona asked quietly. She felt, suddenly, as if she needed his permission. Not that it was his to give.

"She's about to get married, she's pregnant, and her father has just been murdered. Is there any way you could avoid talking to her? For a time?" He had raised his voice. He held up a hand, put the other to his eyes, and winced. "Sorry."

Shona nodded. "It's okay."

They walked downstairs. Crawford and Shona exchanged email addresses, and he said he would email her a formal statement about Love later that day. She thanked him, and he responded with a warm handshake. He rubbed his eyes again and turned to go back to the bar. She left the Arts Club.

Her phone, which she had ignored, had several missed calls from work, and a text from Hector Stricken, the crime reporter: *Shona. Councillor Cullen. Found dead in pub. I'm on it, don't worry. Get back ASAP, Colm going batshit.*

She shook her head and walked down the lane to the main road. The large houses, windows like open dead eyes, were silent. The trees rustled in the light breeze. Shona called a taxi.

8

It was a misty morning in Portobello. Outside, the world had been erased by the haar. The houses across the narrow, cobbled street were gauzy and vague, only their dark square windows firm in the thick mist. Tallis was eating porridge and looking through a downloaded book on his tablet. After some flicking backwards and forwards, he found what he was searching for: *The Goldenacre*.

He was looking for a clearer image. On the table, next to his cold tea, was an opened manila folder: Ms. Peters had left a series of legal documents and a poor photograph of the work. Badly lit. At an angle.

Tallis sat back and expanded the image on the screen with his fingers. *The Goldenacre* glowed. It was a landscape: a rural scene in a city. It showed a broad urban field, green and yellow, dappled with dots of sun-yellow, the hedges brindled and shadowed. And around the expanse of grass, and its splashes of wildflowers, there were high stone houses with flashing windows. There was a watery sky, with the distant hills sulking in purple and mauve and, black and straight, a spire on the plain of the road. Looking closer, he could see the images within the image: pale figures around the edges of the field. Sexless, drifting in shifts and robes. There was a bird, in clear view. A single robin, tiny, but exactly painted, on the lumpen twig of a tree, close to the artist's eye.

Tallis moved his fingers gently over the screen. The image scrolled. There were silvery things, maybe alive, on the pitched roofs of the tenements. Mackintosh had painted a blaze of white sky, and, within that blaze, something living and diaphanous. In the distance sat the black of the Pentlands. They had been rendered as if they were not bare hills stripped of their native trees but two giant legs and a mammoth body: a distant giant cut from the landscape. The perspective of *The Goldenacre* was unnerving: the field was both flat and three-dimensional, and the height down to the foreground was precipitous. Throughout, the colours were bold and watery, as rich as a passing reality, as sorrowful as a dream departing upon waking.

Tallis put the tablet down on the table. He rubbed his face and shook his head: it was heavy from wine, he had been drinking all weekend, and he needed air. He closed his eyes, to listen. A piano was playing, its chords drifting from the sea.

Aunt Zed was still asleep with Jack. He left the half-eaten porridge in the sink and moved upstairs, to dress quickly. Through the small loft window he could see nothing but the sea mist. A colourless screen. After a time, a difference gathered, and there was now only a faint distinction between the beach, the sea, the sky. The world hung striated in three melting bars of light.

Tallis stepped carefully down the stairs and, taking a key from a hook near the door, left the house. The air was cold and wet, and he gasped briefly. He moved through the thick air, his feet clumping. He turned from the little street to the path to the long beach. His phone buzzed. He looked at it—a message from Astrella: *Hi. Ray will spend half term at home with Gretchen. He is doing a lot of drawing! A.*

For a moment he felt like throwing his phone into a bin,

into the beach, into the sea. But there was music. A piano playing, slow and deep. Then a series of rolling notes. A turning tide. A deep and melancholy tumble of chords. He recognised the music. It was the opening to Rachmaninov's second concerto. It emerged from the thickness of the fog.

Along the esplanade, cafés had put out their boards, and dark figures walked with dogs. The people were all faceless, the animals slow.

A man stood against the sea wall, tall and grey.

The music was coming from somewhere near the broken wooden groyne that led down to the tide. Tallis peered into the haar. There was a dark presence there, a shadow. The music changed. A second movement. A slowly breaking wave of tender loss.

Tallis walked down pocked concrete steps to the beach. There was a murky smell, a sudden drift in his nose of brine and salt. The sand was wide, stretching to the east and west as far as the mist would let him see. He walked across the damp sand. The music continued. He could hear it clearly now: it came from an upright piano, with some notes out of tune—flat, sharp—but someone was a skilled pianist. Astrella may have even been impressed.

Slowly it came into view.

The piano was on the beach, and, on a stool before it, a figure was playing. There was no sheet music. An ivory was missing from a low B, and the exposed key was brown, like a bad tooth in a clean smile. The figure was dressed in some kind of overall, was pale, and had a shaved head. The pianist sat still, fingers moving quickly and accurately over the keys. Tallis stood for a time and watched and listened. His arms crossed over his chest, his skin cold and wet from the sea-fret.

He found himself looking briefly to the sea wall. The man stood there still. Looking at the pianist, or looking out to the hidden sea. Or at Tallis. He was smoking.

The notes sunk into the cold white air. The melody was beautiful. The old piano resounded.

Then it ended. The pianist turned around. Her face was even and pale, the mouth tinged with lipstick, the eyelashes dark with kohl. Some people on the esplanade, gathered outside a café, clapped. The single watcher stared into the mist.

"Did you enjoy?" the pianist said, turning around, facing Tallis.

"I did. You are very good," Tallis said. "That was very beautiful."

"Thank you. It is. I practise. You are lucky. Tomorrow, it's Oasis standards."

The mist was still all around but becoming more liquid. There was a sense of slow and subtle drift. Tallis could see the café more clearly now, and the signs in its windows. Seabirds waited in a hopping white line on its roof. The watcher was gone. He had retreated into nothingness.

"Do you play here every day? And Rachmaninov?"

"Well recognised," she said. "No, I am moving around. Today and tomorrow, the beach. Then somewhere else. Come closer."

It was darker underfoot near the piano. He could smell perfume. The pianist had pearly fingernails, and her skin was as smooth as eggshell.

The pianist pointed to a small, neat glinting hole in the piano, just above where sheet music would be. The hole was glazed with a tiny circular lens.

"A camera?"

"You were my filmed audience today . . . Mr.?"

"Tom, just call me Tom."

"Mr. Tom," the pianist said, smiling. "You will look very striking, emerging from the mist. You will look like you are escaping purgatory. Or entering."

"Is this for a . . ."

"I am an artist," the pianist said, rising and extending a hand to shake.

"Is this for a project, an installation?" Tallis asked. He had the melody of the second movement in his mind, cycling over and over. He reached to shake her hand. It was cool.

"Yes, for something I am working on," she said.

Tallis said he was working for a while at the Public Gallery, and the artist nodded.

"I must go," she said, standing up. The player opened the top of the piano, reaching inside to pull out a small camera. "Recorded forever."

"When can I see your work?" Tallis said, feeling the warmth of the sun nudging through the mist at last.

"I shall let you know. Say hello to Theseus for me," the pianist said.

"Theseus?" Tallis asked.

She nodded. A small bag had been retrieved from somewhere, out of which came a raincoat.

"And what is your name?" Tallis said.

"I am Vorn," the artist said, "and you should know Theseus: Theseus Campbell at the gallery? He commissioned me. I am gathering footage for . . . a gathering. I must call the people to take the piano away. What are you working on there?"

"I'd love to see your finished work," Tallis said.

"One day soon. What did you say you did? Apart from glooming around the beach early in the morning."

"Right now, it seems I am being landed with a Charles Rennie Mackintosh mystery."

"Oh really? Well, his wife was more talented than he," she said. "I am sure you know that. She stayed spooky to the end."

"Really?"

"You should do more research, Thomas. She was on to something." Vorn quietly closed the piano lid, pulling the curved wood veil over the notes. A small key was produced, and the lid was locked. "You should attend the Summoning this week. You can see some of the work we do. Come as the sun sets."

"The Summoning?" Tallis asked.

"An event. Calton Hill, by the ruin." Vorn said goodbye and padded away across the sand, holding a mobile phone to her ear.

Tallis walked slowly up the beach, hands in pockets, to the café. He stopped to look at the piano being hauled up the beach on wooden skis by two large men. He entered the café and, at the take-away counter, bought a coffee. He saw rows of sweets, and thought of his son: he would be waking up right now, somewhere in London. Warm in his pyjamas, moaning about his breakfast. Astrella would not be there. A nanny, Gretchen, would be. Coaxing Ray out of his bed, into his day. Tallis's heart hurt.

He realised his hands were clenched and his eyes closed. The coffee came, and he moved to a table for a moment, to look at the newspaper left by another customer. It was a tabloid, red emblazoned on its front page. The main story was about some footballer having an affair. But a smaller piece pointed to an article inside the paper about the death of the artist Love. He turned the page.

ARTIST MURDER MYSTERY the headline said.

Tallis read the piece.

". . . cops last night refused to confirm or deny whether money had been stolen from murdered Love's house."

Tallis dropped the paper and stepped out into the slowly blooming day.

On the esplanade, a recently extinguished cigarette was caught up by the wind and floated by in a light cloud of ash, drifting in parabolas.

9

As Tallis was finally arriving at work, a solicitor in London called. Astrella wanted a divorce. She wanted custody of Ray and hoped for a quick agreement. They would sell the house and split the money. This was presented as a concession.

"Tough news for a morning," the solicitor said. "Take your time to think it over. But not too long."

"Okay," Tallis said. "Think what over?" He thought of Ray, and thought of recording a video on his phone, and sending it to . . . to whom? There was no way of speaking to him. He would be at school. Who knew who had taken him to the gates, or whether they had kissed him goodbye. "The parental rights: I need to think on that," Tallis said at last.

"If you want this to be quick, I would consider that very carefully. Do you not want to have equal access?"

"No, I want custody, or whatever it is called," he said. "I want to be with him all the time. He can come and live with me."

"Oh? Really?"

"Yes," he said. "Really. He's my son."

"She is claiming unreasonable behaviour."

"She has not been unreasonable until now."

"No, your behaviour: as the reason for the divorce."

"It could have been worse," he said.

They closed the call.

Thomas Tallis walked slowly up the long drive to the gallery and sat on its stone steps. It had been raining, but it was a fine day now and the sun glittered on leaves and grass and water. He sat with his head in his hands, breathing in sobs.

A large Black man walked up the path to the gallery. He was dressed in a finely chequered suit, and held a hat and a briefcase. His hair was finely razored, close to his gleaming skin. He stopped before Tallis.

"Well, hello," he said. His voice was deep. "Can I help you?"

Tallis looked up. "I am . . . sorry, I am just having a moment," he said, wiping his eyes.

The man held out a hefty hand. "I thought as much. Theseus Campbell," he said. "Deputy director."

Tallis stood up. They shook hands and Tallis introduced himself. Theseus's hand was large and warm.

"You look like you need to rest up, Tallis-from-the-government. To have a chat?"

Tallis nodded.

They walked to the café, which was in the basement but opened out onto the gardens at the rear of the gallery. They talked. They sat at a table outside, in the sunshine. The garden was green and neat. Box-cut hedges and tidy flowerbeds.

"I have this Mackintosh painting as my project," Tallis said, looking out over the manicured lawn. The drifting greens, the shimmering sunlight, reminded him of *The Goldenacre*.

"Ah yes, the Melrose designation," Campbell nodded. "A fine thing. Beautiful painting, of course. If anyone asks me, not that they do, I find Mackintosh's watercolours more beautiful than his architecture. Which I can take or leave. Overrated. Have you been to the Mackintosh Building in Glasgow?"

"The School of Art? Yes, a while ago," Tallis said.

"Well, that painting should be a straightforward provenance check for you?" Campbell said. He put another sugar into his coffee.

"Yes," Tallis said, "there is nothing to suggest it will be complicated. I wish I could say the same about everything else."

Campbell turned his head slightly and stroked away a blown seed from his hefty knee. "Look, a tradition of this place . . . Well, it's not a tradition. Let's start the tradition this week. You come round to mine, this Friday? For dinner?"

Tallis smiled. "That would be very nice, if I am still here. I've really only seen Portobello and my aunt's house since I came." He remembered the pianist on the beach. The offer to come to the Summoning.

"If you are still here? Are things that bad?" Theseus rumbled.

"I mean, I might be back to London by then," Tallis said.

"Well, in my view, it's a date," Campbell said, and stood up. "Right, I must go. I have the artists for the 'Vision' show coming in today. And I will try and match their ambition with our budget, which may be a losing proposition."

"Who are they?" Tallis asked.

Campbell put a hand to his forehead. "Hm. Well, we have a portraitist, very interesting; we have a filmmaker and musician, Vorn; and an excellent new sculptor from Glasgow, whose name escapes me."

"Vorn?"

"Vorn, yes. You know the work?"

"I think I met her this morning," Tallis said, "on the beach."

Campbell raised an eyebrow and sunk his hands deep into his pockets. "You may have—Vorn is hard to pin down. She is doing something for a new show we have coming. It might be enlightening. Or darkening. So have you seen this Mackintosh? You will know of the plans for the big show."

Tallis shook his head. "Not in person," he said. "Not in the flesh. No. The big show? Only in brief."

"Carver—has he really not informed you?" Campbell laughed. It boomed around his chest and rattled. He shook his head. "Typical of this place. Typical of him. Sir Dennis. You are not in the golden circle of his trust, yet. Or ever will be. And I will never be."

Tallis raised his eyebrows, and Theseus patted his hand.

"They are planning a big show, a serious exhibition around *The Goldenacre*. Mackintosh loans are coming from all over the place. With your painting at the centre of it."

"Well, it is not my painting," Tallis said quietly.

"Oh, but Thomas, it will come because of you. And the galleries are all very excited about it. Money-making. I believe big marketing plans are already afoot. They are probably manufacturing *The Goldenacre* mouse mats and tea towels and key rings and VIP viewings as we sip our coffee this fine morning." Theseus put a heavy hand on Tallis's shoulder. He put his head close to Tallis's ear. He smelled of a fine cologne. "Don't rush things. Give yourself time. Carver is tricky. Keep your distance from him. He will think of you as a fellow traveller. Just don't get involved, keep yourself on the down-low. Do your job but don't make a scene, or an impression." He gently rapped Tallis on the shoulder. "Don't get involved," he repeated, and put a finger to his nose. Then he got up quickly and left.

Tallis slowly wended his way to his temporary office: he needed to make arrangements. He needed to make an appointment to see *The Goldenacre*, *in situ*, at Denholm House.

Mungo was at his desk, playing a card game on the computer screen. Tallis stopped and smiled, and asked him to make the arrangements. Mungo scribbled it all down on a notepad.

"There is some post for you," Mungo said. "I've put it

on your desk. And you have a ten o'clock meeting with Dr. Roberta Donnelly in Conservation and Archives. I call her Bobby."

Tallis nodded and went into his office. On the table were some letters and a small parcel.

He needed to speak to his son and hear his voice. Feel his head in his hands again. His thin hair like silk. Tallis rang his old home phone number. The phone rang and rang. He closed the call.

Tallis moved over to the table. Two of the letters were for his predecessor, a Dr. G. Newhouse. He opened them anyway: circulars from private contemporary galleries in the city, and an invitation to a "live-art installation" on Calton Hill. It was unnamed, and there was no RSVP. The event Vorn had mentioned.

The parcel was light. A small, brown square box, with a typed name and address. It had no postmark. He looked at his watch—it was time for the meeting in Conservation. He took the parcel with him, and Mungo, hanging by his door, led him down a corridor, into a tiny lift and down to the basement. Here the walls were painted green and there was lino on the floor.

"Welcome to the underworld," Mungo said cheerily as they walked, feet tapping on the hard floors, down a long corridor. "There's no windows down here and no light," Mungo added. "Everyone in Conservation has pale skin and massive eyes. Bobby is the same. Have to take Vitamin D supplements, no doubt. I went potholing once."

"Yes?" Tallis said. He wondered what was in the box. It was light, felt weightless, as if it was empty. The corridor ended in a smoky glass door.

"Yes, at school. We went under this mountain in Yorkshire. Well, I say mountain, nothing compared to the Highlands, of course, but it had all these caves. Outward bound. That's what they say. But it was more inward bound.

Anyway, we were under the ground, maybe a mile under. This was a school thing, don't get me wrong."

"I'm not," Tallis said.

"No. Anyway, we entered this huge, dark cavern. And the teacher, Mr. Dodds, he told us all to turn off the torches, the headlamps, the handhelds, and we did. It was the blackest, pitchest dark I have ever known. Pitch black. Like space. This is Conservation."

Mungo opened the glass door and they entered a large, well-lit room. There were two large easels leaning on a far wall. There were three long tables and several metal shelves. A wall of books and documents faced the window. There was the scent of cleanliness. There was the trace of ionized perfume and fresh paint.

"Bobby is always late," Mungo said. "Anyway, so we did."

"Did what?"

"Turn off the lamps. On our helmets. And we were in the darkest dark, darker than space, really, where at least there are stars. The cosmos. But under that mountain, we were in the darkest place you could be. Then the teacher shone his torch. It was like the sun exploding. My friend Freya just started crying. And he shone it into this underground pool. It might have been a lake. It could have been a sea."

"Perhaps not, but still."

"It was still. There was no moving air down there—I mean, not a breath. And in the water there were these shrimps. Little crustaceans. Shrimps. I could not believe it. Moving around in the underground lake. A swarm of them." Mungo was leaning on one of the long benches now, his eyes closed, his hands moving in the air. "I couldn't believe there were wee animals in the water. So far under the ground, under a mile of rock and earth. In the water. I tried to hold one in my hands, but they were, like, they were projections. Not real, like clear shadows."

Tallis nodded. There was no sign of any conservation

staff. He noticed a canvas lying, face up, on a table at the far end of the room. He moved to it. Mungo followed him.

"But I learned a lesson," Mungo said.

"What was that?"

The painting was a modern work. Its frame had been removed. It was a patterned work, all oblongs and triangles. Not representative, not Cubist. But an arrangement of shapes and colours. A hint of a spiral in a serrated column of edges. It was maybe from the 1950s. The ochre and brown were unpleasant to his eye.

"That, I don't know," Mungo said.

Tallis looked around the room, wondering if *The Goldenacre* was there. Somewhere in the room, under a cover. Hidden under plastic. He thought about answering Mungo, to keep the conversation going. He felt alone without noise. "Well, that life finds a way? Something like that?" he said eventually.

"That, maybe," Mungo said lightly. "Something more than that. I think it was that if we—and this might sound morbid and depressing, but hear me out—if we, I mean, the whole school party, had just then died, the shrimps, these see-through things, wouldn't have noticed or cared. If the bomb had been dropped while we were underground, and the world above had been incinerated and everyone killed, the shrimps wouldn't care, or notice. They might hear a bang. Maybe there would be radioactivity in the water, eventually. I guess. But they would carry on, gliding in that freezing lake, blind and oblivious. The underground shrimps. Victorious."

"Nature doesn't care about us," Tallis said. He was leaning on a desk.

"No, it doesn't," Mungo said. "And the Earth will be fine. Humanity maybe won't be. The way things are going. But the Earth will be fine."

"And the tiny subterranean prawns," Tallis said, smiling at his red-haired colleague, "they shall endure!"

"The victorious shrimps. I feel we should have a toast," Mungo said brightly. "But, sadly, no drink. What's in your box?"

Tallis realised he was still holding the package. There was a scalpel on a green rubber mat beside the ugly Cubist painting. He put the box down and slit the taped side open. Suddenly, there was an odd smell. It wasn't plastic or glue. It smelled like mulch, or something sharp, organic. Something meaty. A wet fart of blood.

"Is it chocolate?" Mungo said, peering over. "A welcome present?"

There was a bundle inside the box, bound in a ball of bubble wrap. It had not been professionally packed. It was a rough bundle, a knot of yellowing Sellotape about it.

"I don't think so," Tallis said.

It could have been pottery, or a fragile piece of glass. He used the scalpel to cut the tape. Whatever was inside the bundle was soft and giving, and light. The bubble wrap squeaked and slid in his fingers. It caught the light, strobing. The bobbled plastic came apart, suddenly. Something cold and slippy slid over his fingers. It plopped onto the coverings.

His hand withdrew, as if burnt. There, in the cradle of plastic, was a strip of thick flesh, creased down the middle, ripped and ragged at one end. Thick, like a raw steak. There were orbs of dark red blood, like berries, tangled in the shaggy tears.

It was a tongue.

10

"That Cullen death—it was a mugging gone wrong, they are saying," Hector Stricken murmured.

Shona was at her desk. There was dust in her keyboard. Crumbs. A brown sickle moon of old coffee had been welded to the hard-drive box. There was a low hum of activity in the newsroom. People were murmuring. TVs were on, but no one was watching.

Her desk was a mess: there were old notebooks in a sliding scree, and post she had not opened. There was a brown bottle of cider sent by a new brewery looking for coverage, its flanks frosted with dust. There was a ripped-open packet of large white envelopes, a crumpled packet of paracetamol and half a bottle of nail varnish remover. A faded photograph of her dead mother was tacked to the side of the monitor screen. Her wild hair, glinting, and Gorbals behind her. Brown spots on the paper, where Shona had kissed it sometime in the past.

"Oh really? Is that what they said about Cullen? Well, it's a murder anyhow," she said. She was trying to remember her password to log in to the editorial system. It escaped her.

Her newspaper had once been a substantial one: hundreds of staff, a national audience. Shona remembered that it used to make the news, rather than just recycle it. But it had been reduced to a distressed rump after various management and editorial system changes. The new editor, Ronald Ingleton, thought newspapers were a "legacy industry": as redundant as shipbuilding or gas-lighters.

Stricken went on. "Yeah. That's what the cops say. Brief statement. Council has put out a press release. His party already has a tribute out. There'll be some kind of by-election, I guess?" Stricken was talking and typing. Light filled his spectacles.

"Guess so," Shona said. "Any family?"

"A wife. She's not talking."

On his desk was a large printed-out photo of the councillor. Cullen had been chair of the Planning Committee, a local politician of the old type: representing an area of the city where he had grown up, alert to the subtleties and limitations, the complaints and whims of his council ward. He had been good at pub talk, and remembering names, and which school you had been to. A pensive presence at official functions. Happy to frustrate business interests when their plans endangered the balance of the public realm. He would never have been leader of the council: he had been too disinterested in the national picture, and only in his party because it approximated his personal views, modest and limited as they were. He was not a zealot.

Shona suddenly remembered her password: "Fuck-This2019." She logged in and stared at the screensaver: a nighttime picture of Glasgow. A silhouette of its high towers and rises, its university tower, against a darkening evening sky, the distant hills looming and bruise-blue, the city lights a scatter of soft neon. Glasgow was her hometown. A city in the dusk of its life, a valley of shadows and memories. She could not live there again, and her father lived with her now. But her mind went there at night. A dream of Glasgow—with all its beauty and poison, its flaking glamour and disfigured elegance.

Her desk phone rang.

"Could be the big one," Stricken said.

Shona stared at her phone. It was a surprise: she rarely gave out her number. She preferred to pursue and not be pursued.

"Is that Shona Sandison?" It was a woman's voice, young and nervous.

"Yeah, it is," she said. "What's up?"

"Sorry, my name is . . . Look, I am Robert Love's daughter."

Shona picked up a pen. She grabbed an envelope and turned it over. The nib poised over the bare paper. A group of men at the sports desk burst into laughter. She held the phone closer to her ear.

"I was. I was . . . I was told you were asking about Dad. I was wondering if you wanted to meet and talk. There might be something I could tell you. If that's something . . ."

"Yes, of course," Shona said. She could hear the woman's nervousness, her shaking voice. A handkerchief clutched to the receiver. "I'm sorry for your troubles."

"Thank you."

"Where is good for you? I can come to wherever you think is best. Do you live in Edinburgh?"

"No, no. We live in Fife. I don't want you to come here, though. Can you meet me halfway? Or somewhere else?"

"Of course. Where is best? Sorry, I didn't catch your name."

"Morag," she said, and spelled it out. "Maybe we can meet at my work."

"Oh aye, where's that?"

"I work part-time at Jupiter Artland—do you know where that is? It's a park, an art-park near Edinburgh Airport. I could meet you there. There is a wood there, a walk through the trees. We would have privacy. It's a drive from Edinburgh, but—is that okay?" Her voice was hardening now, gaining confidence.

"I can find it," Shona said. She had never heard of it.

"Thank you. Shall we say the morning. Eleven?"

They made arrangements.

Shona also asked where the funeral would be. Morag hesitated and then mentioned a church in Goldenacre. She did not want to go into detail.

"See you in Jupiter," Shona said.

"Jupiter Artland," Morag said, and hung up.

Shona opened her email. There were hundreds unread. One was from the City of Edinburgh Council hidden amid the scree of communications.

COUNCILLOR JOHN CULLEN

It is with a profound sense of shock and horror that the City of Edinburgh Council note the death of Councillor John Cullen (Ind. South Leith) at the age of fifty-eight. Cllr Cullen represented the people of South Leith with vigour and probity for more than twenty years, and was a respected convenor of the city's Planning Committee.

His death has robbed the city of a dedicated council man and champion for his ward. The City of Edinburgh Council note his important work on the tram extension and . . .

She stopped reading. Hector was covering the story, after all.

If it had been the nineteenth century, Councillor Cullen might have a new library named after him, or a public swimming pool, perhaps. A street in a new suburb. Even, if the fundraising succeeded, a statue or bust somewhere. But not in these sad and shabby days. Just 400 words on page twelve and a swift by-election. And then, the chasm.

There was a bustling next to her. Stricken was gathering

his notebook and pens, stuffing them into his bag. He pulled on a red waterproof raincoat. "Well, that's me away," he said. "I take it you have the Cullen stuff. I've filed on it."

"Aye, 'course," Shona said, irritated. She needed a coffee. She wanted the morning to come, to see this daughter.

"I was meant to be meeting Cullen for a coffee today, weirdly enough," Stricken said. He jammed his mobile in his pocket. His eyes were red behind his frames. He had been on the early shift and looked beaten up.

"Well, that saves you the cost of a latte," she said.

"Murder, though, eh? That's two now."

"It's very much a crime wave, Hector."

He paused. "Well, it's not normal."

"Normal for what?"

"For Edinburgh."

"Neither are you, and you fit in well enough," she said.

"Yup. I guess I'll have to tee up the vice-convenor now," he said. "That sluggish guy."

"Why's that?"

"They knocked back the film studio plan. The one on the brownfield site out by the bridges. I was gonna speak to Cullen about it."

"What film studio plan?"

"It's in the cuts, Sherlock," Stricken said, leaving, spinning his chair around. "Big plan, £100 million thing, fell apart last week. Cullen basically took against it. He marshalled his troops to vote against it, and that was that. It's been a story. Controversial. I did a splash on it. You know, the front page? I know you're not familiar with the concept."

"I don't read the paper," Shona said, now clacking away on her keyboard.

"Why not?"

"It depresses me. And it's full of your shite."

"Nice. Well, you've hardly been setting the heather ablaze yerself recently," he said, and wandered away.

"Knob-end," Shona said.

"I love you too," he yelled, as he left the office.

She looked on the newspaper's internal picture system and clicked on the search function. She typed in, "Robert Love Artist."

The computer made a mild cranking noise. A lot of the newspaper's archive of photography had been given by its new parent company to the city library. To save space, and to save on the cost of conserving it. Which meant no one used it or looked at it. Thousands of images, lost to dust and boxes. Shona suspected there would be no digital shots of Love, with likely none taken since dark rooms and film became obsolete in the late 1990s.

The computer screen went blank for a second, and then five small thumbnails appeared. Four of them were images of pictures hung on walls at exhibitions. Love's work—she recognised it now. Expert and florid. There was one image of the painter, a black-and-white shot. She expanded it with a click. He was leaning on a stair bannister in a dark house, looking over at the photographer. His eyebrows were raised and he had a short, spiked beard. He was smiling and wearing one leather glove.

Shona stared at the picture for a while, then closed the screen. She picked up her phone. It rang for a while, and then her father answered.

"Hello there, darling," he said. His voice deep and feathery.

"How did you know it was me?"

"You always ring around this time."

"Just checking," she said.

"Aye, well, I'm still alive. Been at the allotment."

"I'm shocked. What's for tea the night?"

"I've got my old chilli con carne on."

"Grand," she said. "I'll be home later."

"Don't rush now. The snooker is on."

She smiled and said goodbye.

11

The police had come and gone. Tallis sat, cold, in front of his computer. The day had been a smear of activity since the opening of the box. A hefty detective wearing eyeliner had asked Tallis some questions. They had carefully lifted away the tongue, with pincers, and slipped it into a plastic bag and taken it away. The box had been taken too.

"It is a human tongue, isn't it?" Tallis had said.

"How would you know that?" the detective had said, not ominously, as his colleagues bustled about. There were two white vans on the gravel outside, and the gallery was shut. Visitors were outside, staring at their phones.

"It looks like one," Tallis had said. "It was the right size. It had . . . fronds."

"It may well be a human tongue. But it is, for certain, a tongue."

"Why would anyone do something like that?" Someone had put a soft blanket over his shoulders. His hands, no longer shaking, clutched a warm cup of tea. His mouth, still rank with sick, his nostrils tart and scorched. "Why?"

The detective had shrugged. A forensic officer snapped off his gloves and left Tallis's office. "A prank. A joke. Do you have any funny friends?" the detective, a Mr. Reculver, had asked.

"Not like that."

"Well, think on."

"I will."

The detective had then spoken quietly. "Could it be a warning of some kind?"

"About what?"

"You tell me."

Tallis had sat down, heavily, and shook his head.

"As I say, think about it," the detective had said, rubbing an eye.

Now the police were gone, and Mungo, pale, shivering, had taken the rest of the day off. Tallis had been kindly asked by Theseus to go home. But he said he would rather work.

A yellow Post-it note curled on the edge of the computer screen: *Olivia Farquharson called*. The Melrose family wanted Tallis to see *The Goldenacre*. He would have to drive down to the Borders to visit Denholm House. He opened an internet search on his computer and looked at pictures of the house. It stood in a forest of old trees. There were high hedges and overgrown beds. Something like a sunken swimming pool, choked with weeds and mud. A half-ruined dovecote with a shattered wall like a smashed ribcage. In the picture, there were gusting clouds, heavy with imminent rain. The trees were black against the sky and the disused, abandoned gardens. There was a cold, dark lake.

He sat back. The room now smelled of chemicals, and there was a fine dust, like gunpowder, on the table where the parcel had been. An opened but empty small, clear plastic bag lay open on the floor. The light caught the edges of its mouth.

Reculver had left a business card on the table, and Tallis put it in his pocket.

The tongue flashed in his mind. Its berries of blood. Its softness, and the scraggy neck of thin flesh beneath it. Someone had ripped it from a mouth. Reached into a human and sawed into the scrag and slime of it. Somewhere, a human mouth gaped wet crimson.

The detective was right—it was a warning. Of what, he could not bear to figure.

He shook his head. Tallis wanted to leave now. He wanted to speak to his son.

Outside it was cool but clear. Tallis looked around for watchers. For people in the eaves of the trees. For figures in the shadows of the walls. His shoulders pinched and stiffened. His feet crunched on the driveway of the gallery.

He called "Home" on his mobile and stopped still. The call rang and rang. He found himself panicking. But then, a receiver was lifted.

"Hello?" It was Gretchen. He spoke to her, as cheerfully as he could. He said he was wondering if Ray was about. No, she said, he was on a playdate with Reuben.

"Who is Reuben?" he asked.

"His friend," Gretchen said, distracted.

"How old is he?"

"Who?"

"This Reuben?"

Gretchen sighed. "What do you mean, Thomas? He is seven. He is in Ray's class."

"Great. Well, of course," he said. "How is he doing?"

"Ah, well. Ray is fine. He misses his mummy," she said.

Tallis stood still. Gretchen was making some kind of scraping noise—metal against a pot. A blade being scraped around a ceramic edge. He could hear a radio in the background. There was no noise from the piano. Astrella was away.

He thought of that kitchen. The square of light that fell on the kitchen table from the high window. He saw the range and the old fireplace, now with a pot of flowers in it. He saw the large fridge, with its baby photos and splodgy hand-paintings.

"And his daddy, of course. I'm making biscuits," Gretchen said.

"Tell him I miss him too."

Yes, yes, she said. She said Astrella would be back in a week.

"Tell him his daddy loves him," Tallis said.

"He knows that," she said.

"Tell him again."

"Oh, and Thomas: there was a man from the estate agency today, wanting to look around the house. Yes? He says he will email you and Mrs. Astrella. I hope that's okay."

"Yes, yes. Of course. Everything is A-okay." They said goodbye, and he hung up. The phone dropped into his pocket like a sleeping hand.

He slowly trod the paths into the centre of Edinburgh. Tallis walked over a bridge and smelled the river below, fresh with brown water from the high hills. Thick with vegetation and minerals. It ran white over the rocks, like it was grinning in pain.

Tallis needed a drink, so he decided he would find a pub and have one. He was into the New Town now: all straight roads and high tenements, locked, gated gardens and cobbles. He stopped at a junction and looked about him. No one else on the streets. Black cars hugging the roads. Bin bags slumped from gaping sheds. Silent offices, silent homes.

He screwed up his eyes. There were better places than this. There had been a place he had gone to as a boy. He would go there: the bend in the river. In the town where he had been sent to school, there were woods that followed the river up to its source. A mile outside the town, the river—wide and slow—slowly turned. There was a beach on the slow side of the bend, and a broken viaduct. There, the shadows of the trees plunged into the moving water and oaks grew. There was cool shade in the summer, and in winter the river ran swollen, and covered the shingle beach. He dreamt of it often.

He walked past high tenements, wide and opulent, until he saw a cathedral ahead: St. Mary's, set in parkland of its own, and towering with three black spires. Like the hand of a wounded man, it lay upright on its fields. He walked to its huge doors and entered, and the sounds of the city were suddenly muted, replaced by the murmur of air moving in the high vaults.

He walked to the rows of pews and sat down. In front of every chair there were handmade cushions, bulky and red, decorated with pixelated images of saints. Tallis looked up. The central tower rose into beams and obscured height. The cathedral stood, massive. Hazy light strained by stained-glass windows cast shimmering fractals on the stone floor and illuminated the pulpit. Blue and pink glinted on the brass eagle lectern suspended in flight.

He did not want to pray, just yet. Out there, the city rumbled and groaned. Somewhere out there in the fallen world his son was playing. Little fingers tapping on plastic soldiers in some sunlit bedroom. Astrella, playing too, her hands over the keys, automatic, controlled.

He knew that, now, he was no longer in love with Astrella. The love had slipped away, like light leaving a room. He had lost something faint, beautiful and delicate. Like a once-heard but forgotten music, gradually fading into silence. There was a countermelody: he knew she was not in love with him. Astrella was kind and loved their son. She was better than him, and sensitive to the delicacies and tender moments of their slowly dislocating lives. But she was impatient to move into another world, another plane of her life.

Six months ago, it had all fallen down. Tallis had been curating a show at the Civic Gallery. He had come home to a note and an absent child: Astrella had written she was going to France for a while, to see her parents in the Île-de-France. Ray was with her. They were gone a month, and when they returned, something—mysterious and grave, tender and light—had gone. The air between them was no longer freighted, no longer waiting for movement towards a centre. Just air, and two human bodies with no connection or desire to connect.

Ray was still growing, and thriving at school, and they kept going in their own lives. Tallis was consumed with work, and, in the end, a series of calamities. Astrella was also busy again: with concerts, with recordings. Everything was numb and numbed. The home was clean and provided for, and Ray was happy in his myopic world of toys and TV, food and play. He would still come into their bed at night, a warm bolster between indifferent bodies.

It was no one's fault, Tallis thought. It was like a collapsing cliff. Or a forest fire. A lightning strike on an exposed peak. The turn of the tide on a green beach.

"It's not my fault," he found himself saying.

He looked up again: a crucifix hung from the high rafter. Christ hung in agony. His blood, bright varnished paint, his skin, varnished bright paint. The nail in his pinned feet as long as Tallis's arm.

Hung nearby was an icon of Mary, holding the Christ child. Underneath it was skeletal black ironwork, holding small candles. There was a black iron box with a slit in its lid, for coins. He wanted to light one, and pray now. But he did not know what he would pray for. For himself, or for others. He moved to them anyway. The candlelight shook on the face of the mother of Christ. The divine baby's hands were around her body, clasped over her bending neck. He knew there were messages in the icon, in the way the hands were splayed, in the folds of the clothes, in the eyes, and in the position of the fingers. But he did not know what they were, or how to read them.

Someone was in the higher end of the cathedral. There was a movement and a noise. There was a faint smell of new flowers and released perfume. Like roses. The roses of Mackintosh.

A great sound suddenly rose in the cathedral. Tallis almost jumped. Someone was practising on the organ. A great chord rang out. Major and plangent, like the sea, it suddenly filled the vast spaces. It rose and fell.

He thought of *The Goldenacre*, and its creator. Mackintosh had spent his final days dumb—the cancer had silenced him. A doctor in London had cut his tongue away, and the great artist had spent his last days denied speech, conversation, music. So he had painted *The Goldenacre* as a last message. As a vision of the world to come: an enclosed field, spirits in robes, bird song and distant mountains. A deep silence sunk in the urban grass. The lengthening shadows of what men had built darkening the trees, the flowers, the animals. A warning, then—and a vision, held forever in watercolour.

Tallis looked to the icon and the candles. They burned on, flickering eyes of fire.

10:54 P.M.

Remember the time when I was allowed to visit you in Cyprus? I must have been twelve or something. It was so hot, I had never been so hot. In the back of the car that picked me up from the airport at Larnaca, my legs sticking to the seat. The flamingos standing in the salt flats: I had never seen flamingos before.

Arriving at that empty house, with the swinging metal gate, the silent cleaner who made my dinner and breakfast. Until you showed up.

At that beach club, with you and your espionage friends. Making your awful jokes about

Greeks and Turks and Jews. You pointing out to me a big white hotel on the Larnaca front, which was full of Russians and call girls, you said. You would know. It smelled of bad suntan lotion and cheap beer and bad burgers. Red-faced squad-dies' shoulders. Endless empty days on that penned-off beach. Listening to rock music on my Sony Walkman. Alone.

There was that day, though, in the mountains, in the Troodos Mountains. We walked in the trees and you gave me a paper bag full of figs. They were full of maggots. Walking in the high ranges, pine needle path under cool pines, with your man walking ten steps behind.

Then on the yacht—do you remember?—your drunk, one-eyed friend's boat. The white yacht on the blue sea and in the blue sky. Dropped anchor off those white stucco cliffs.

You took that long rifle and began shooting fish in the bay. You and your hairy friend. You handed me the rifle and told me to kill a fish. I held it wrong and I fired and the rifle recoiled into my eye.

Terrible pain. Blood and bruises. I took the military plane home, with all the knackered sol-diers. My eye was black and swollen for days. Lots of headaches, and a day in the sanatorium. Hairline fracture of the orbital bone.

Dreams, I still have, of you leaning away from me, a gun at your shoulder, killing creatures in the blinding blue sea.

All these memories will die with me. Do you have any of mine?

Good night.

12

Over breakfast, with light filling Zed's kitchen, Tallis read the documents from the Melrose family. *The Goldenacre* had been profiled in various publications, magazines, websites and books. But it had never been shown in an exhibition—the general public had not seen it. Even when Denholm House was open to visitors, *The Goldenacre* had been out of view.

In the Melrose document, printed on thick paper, there was a poor photograph of the work. It seemed to have been taken down from the wall. It was lying on a bed. It was a strange, unprofessional image. It was murky. The clean watercolour paints looked blotchy and mottled. Mackintosh's brilliant eye looked deranged in this instance—gentle tonal contrasts were made savage and clumsy.

"Is that the painting?" Zed said, appearing in the kitchen. She was wearing her large jacket, covered in badges. Somewhere behind her in the hall, Jack was pulling on boots. They were going to a demonstration. A march to Arthur's Seat, followed by speeches.

Zed leaned over Tallis. He could smell her toothpaste.

"A very bad facsimile of it," he murmured. He took a swig of black coffee. He had slept badly. Upon waking, he had been greeted by an email from his solicitor in London, wanting a brief rundown of his financial status: income, outgoings, savings and so on. It made him feel vomitus.

"It really is," Zed said, tearing at a crescent of crumpet. "I can't believe the government lets them get away with it, really."

"A bad photo?"

"No, Tommy, this whole Acceptance Instead of Tax thing," she said. "Swapping due tax for art. A pensioner misses out on a new hip replacement but the country gets a painting. I am not sure about that equation. How many children's cancer treatments is that painting worth? Maybe they can give the millions to the food banks."

Zed munched loudly. Jack was swearing at his walking boots. He seemed to mutter something about mud and shrinking leather.

"Well, it does not work like that," Tallis said. "And the key thing is, the country—the nation—does not lose the art overseas. The Melrose family could be selling this at auction."

Zed stood back and raised an eyebrow. "Thomas, you have been indoctrinated. Battered into submission. They should sell the bloody thing, and then give the money to charity. I can look at the picture online. You should join us today! Jack and I are going to be marching again this morning."

"If I can bloody walk," Jack said in a strangulated voice. He was on the floor, pulling on a boot.

"No, they would sell it at auction—Sotheby's, probably— and it would be bought by some anonymous collector in Japan or China and never seen again," Tallis said.

He had again emailed Mungo as he had waited for the kettle to boil. He wanted to know when he could go to Denholm House and see the painting himself.

"How much is the silly thing worth?" Zed said.

"Worth—well, that is one thing. Price is another," Tallis said. "But about twelve million is the deal."

Zed snorted. Tallis did not know if she thought this was too much or too little.

Jack pulled on his boot successfully. "Halle-fucking-lujah," he said.

"And what will the Melrose family do with twelve million?" Zed said.

Tallis looked at her. Despite the sun, she was wearing a hat and her coat was fastened to the top. "It doesn't work like that. The government offsets twelve million of tax due—in this case, and usually, inheritance tax. The old lord died last year, didn't he? So they obviously have a hefty bill. There's a daughter and a son."

"Aye, twins," Jack said from the hall. He swore as he dropped the house keys.

"Yes, twins," Tallis said. "So they give the painting to the nation, and they don't have to pay the tax."

"Why don't they sell it at auction, and then pay the tax, and make a profit?" Zed said. She was shaking her head.

"Come on, Zelda," Jack said from the hall. "Let's get fucking on wi' it before noon."

"Because they wouldn't be guaranteed to get the price they want at auction," Tallis said. "It's a mighty risk. Paintings don't reach their estimate all the time. And also, the nation—"

"Would lose this work of genius. Okay, okay," Zed said. "So the UK government takes it off their hands."

"It's thought of, in gallery circles, as a win-win," Tallis said.

"I am really not sure about that," Zed said, shaking her head again. "It seems the kind of tax avoidance wheeze only the landed and loaded could get away with. Nationalise all the private collections, that is what I say. After land reform!"

Tallis laughed. "All right, Commissar Zed."

"Zelda," Jack said again.

"Coming," she said. She beamed at Tallis. "The iniquities

of the landed classes aside, I do hope you have a better day than yesterday." She put a hand on Tallis's shoulder and squeezed gently. The sun cast a net of shadows across her face as it filtered through the window lattice.

"No nasty post today, I hope," he said. "No parcels, anyway."

She shivered. "Who would do something like that? It must have been a joke, or some kind of prank, or . . . Do you think it was one of Astrella's friends?"

Tallis shook his head. He briefly imagined the pink bloody tongue sitting silently on her hand. "No, of course not," he said. "Anyway, I am not sure who among Astrella's friends would even think of that. I mean, she has friends, of course. But no one who would do that. Or who works in a mortuary."

"I always felt she thought friends were just another kind of audience for her," Zed said, moving to the door. With Jack, she left the house.

Tallis, alone, sat in silence, and somewhere in the house a sharp electronic noise sounded. An edging, chiming call. His phone, left in his room. He slumped up the stairs. The phone was still glowing blue on his bed, an irradiated black hand. Tallis picked it up and listened to the voicemail: "Melcombe here. Call me back. I've emailed. You need to wrap that up and get back. Call me at nine A.M. A sense of urgency, Thomas."

Tallis turned off the phone and slid it under a pillow.

Later, on the bus to his work, with the city sliding by outside the windows—chimneys and grey roofs, the hills and terraces rising, unfolding like a gently opening pop-up book—Tallis read the notes on *The Goldenacre* from Carver's file. There was a footnote on its creation: it had been painted in 1927. There was, it said, a "prep. sketch (pencil, charcoal, paper) in Glasgow School of Art archives." He wanted to see it.

He arrived at the Public Gallery late. A police car was

outside, its luminous yellow stripes aglare in the cool sun-shine. An officer was talking to Theseus Campbell on the stairs. As Tallis crunched up the drive, Theseus ushered the officer inside. Tallis walked past the security guard and into the white main hall, but Theseus and the officer had gone.

He did not feel ready for his large empty office. He walked left, into a new exhibition. It was a small display of new contemporary art, from Scottish artists, or artists trained in Scotland. There was a dark room. He walked into it and sat on a soft leather seat, opposite a large screen. But the film did not play. It was just a blank screen, and he was sitting in twilight.

There were footsteps in the corridor outside. Tallis began to shift away from the door. Mungo passed, holding a file, rubbing his hair.

"Mungo," Tallis said, from the dark.

Mungo stopped. He looked back, and then looked around.

"Mungo—in here," Tallis said, louder.

Mungo bent slightly and peered into the darkened gallery. "Mr. Tallis?"

"Yes, indeed. Will you join me?"

Mungo sloped in. He looked at the empty screen. "Well, that's not working. What are you doing here?"

"Just having a sit-down. I was wondering, have we heard any more from Denholm House about my visit?"

"Well . . ." Mungo said, perching on the end of the seat. There was a silence. Mungo was chewing his bottom lip and holding the file close to his chest. "That parcel you received was absolutely horrific," he said quietly.

Tallis nodded. "But I am fine. Are you?"

Mungo shuddered. "Who would do that? I mean—"

"I think it is some kind of prank. No one will want to own up to it, though," Tallis said. "Someone has bought a pig's tongue from a butcher and given everyone a fright."

"But why?"

"Some people have a strange sense of humour, Mungo. What's in the file?"

"Ah, yes," Mungo said, his eyes screwed up. "Well, this is from Sir Dennis, for you."

"Another file? Has he heard of email?"

"I think so," Mungo said. "But he doesn't like anything, he says, being permanent. He does not like setting precedents." He turned to face Tallis and added: "I think I may have made an error, a mistake. To be honest."

Tallis peered at the young man. He looked suddenly stricken. "What kind of mistake?" he said softly.

The room was dark, and the corridor outside bright.

"I mentioned, I shouldn't have. I mentioned to Sir Dennis, to Carver, that you wanted to see the Mackintosh yourself."

"*The Goldenacre*? Yes, of course. That is why I am here. Why should that be—"

"I should have just called the Farquharsons myself and arranged it for you. Just like you asked."

Tallis wondered what was going on.

Mungo raised his head. "This is how I lost my job in the press office. That's why I'm stuck being your gofer." He looked up and added, "No offence."

Tallis put a hand on Mungo's side of the bench. "But what is wrong with mentioning it to Carver? He knows why I am here."

Mungo muttered. "It's . . . He doesn't want you to go. He said there—he was quite cutting, actually—he said you didn't need to see it in person, and that it would be a waste of time and you are here to do paperwork only. He nixed it. Basically. So, I was all of a dither but didn't, in the end, cancel the appointment I made for you. He was so rude. Dismissive."

"Mungo, that's fine, it's all fine," Tallis said. "I am sure there is a misunderstanding."

Mungo looked up. "There's no misunderstanding, Thomas.

I am an anxious person but I am not stupid. If you forgive me. He doesn't want you to go. He was quite forceful."

Tallis looked away, to the blank screen. He heard footsteps in the corridor, and a member of the public—looking curiously into the room—walked slowly by. There were other noises, and a black-clad member of the technical staff walked in.

"Oh, hello, Mungo," the woman said, and then turning to Tallis, she nodded and smiled. "The film will be running presently." She opened a panel in the wall and began pressing buttons.

Mungo said he should be going, he had met with the police officer and needed a rest.

"About the parcel?" Tallis asked.

"Yes, of course," Mungo said, rubbing his eyes. "It was brief. She didn't ask many questions."

"Okay," Tallis said. Mungo looked as if his brain was not working. He was slumped now. He was still holding the manila file to his chest. "Let me see it, then," Tallis said. Mungo handed it over and then crossed his arms. Tallis opened it. It was the rough draft of the press release announcing the Mackintosh show, planned for later in the year. THE GOLDENACRE—A GIFT TO THE NATION said the putative headline. There was a good image of the painting, in all its loveliness and strangeness.

Mungo looked at him. Images were flickering on his eyes. The film had been turned on, and stags and deer were moving rapidly over the screen. "I made the appointment anyway," Mungo said. "Maybe I should cancel. Sir Dennis is my boss."

"I have to honour it," Tallis said.

Mungo's eyes widened. "But he doesn't want you to go."

"I need to see it, in the flesh," Tallis said. "I cannot leave until I have witnessed it myself."

"I think we have all seen enough flesh this week," Mungo said, shuddering.

The deer and stags were moving in lines over colour-saturated glens and moors. They loped over Mungo's pale face. His cheeks became snowy hills, his eyes icy ponds. Antlers spread across his forehead.

"When did you arrange it for?" Tallis said softly.

"What?"

"My visit to see *The Goldenacre*, Mungo."

"Ten, at Denholm House. With that strange woman, Ms. Peters. The twins might not be there, she said. But—"

"It's fine, Mungo. There's nothing to worry about." Tallis put a hand on Mungo's tweedy shoulder. "I will talk to Carver . . ."

"I would really rather you didn't."

". . . if he mentions it. But look at it this way: I am the government, am I not? It is my job to check and ascertain and study and investigate and, in the end, come to some kind of conclusions about this painting. Yes?"

"Yes," Mungo said weakly.

"This painting is a major gift to the Public Gallery. Yes, it's well documented, and it's clearly a Charles Rennie Mackintosh masterpiece. But it's joining the collection, it's down the road in the Borders, and it's worth twelve million. Twelve million pounds, Mungo. That is of tax that will not be paid, in whole or in part. So, why cannot I run my eyes over it? Make sure it is, indeed, what we think—and let's face it—know it is? What's the problem?"

"Sir Dennis was resolute. He was rude," Mungo said. "He was definitive."

"Does he scare you?" Tallis asked.

Mungo looked at him. He shook his head gently. "Of course, he does. And if he asks where you are, I shall plead absolute and total ignorance." Mungo turned and looked at the film. The stags were moving across a brown landscape. Rusty heather and a dark sky. "This is a very clever film," he said. "It makes me feel both lonely and afraid and yet hopeful. What if, Thomas, you are driving down to Denholm House, and you crash, and die, or are seriously injured?"

"I'm loving this fantasia of yours, so far."

"Mangled, in some way."

"Mangled . . . okay."

"And then Carver comes cutting into the office and interrogates me, grills me, on why you were in a car going to the Borders," Mungo said, hissing his words in the gloomy room. "What shall I say then?"

"Just say I ignored your—his—request not to go. Which is a weird one, anyway."

Mungo shook his head. "You don't know how this place works," he said. He seemed to have composed himself a little more.

"I don't work here. Carver is not my boss. What he says, does not necessarily go."

Mungo shook his head and rubbed his face, his eyes closed. He stood up.

"Mungo, which room is Theseus Campbell in?"

"E06. He always has excellent coffee."

"Thank you, Mungo," Tallis said, and made a play of waving his hand in the direction of the door. "You are dismissed."

Mungo glared at him. "Don't say that." He walked out.

Tallis watched the film for a while. The island landscape unfurled under stormy skies. The copper sea buckled and bent. The stags proliferated, glitched, changed in size and shape. Colours strobed and shifted in and out of phase. Luminous colours flashed around the antlers. There were tiny lightning flares and forks.

A young bearded father with two flossy-haired boys walked into the room, one in a pushchair, head slumped asleep. The older child stood, his eyes glazed, unblinking, and pointed at the screen. "Boring," he said loudly. The man and children left.

Tallis walked out and along the corridor, past other new installations, to the lift. He thought he remembered the way the rooms were organised: E meant Campbell's room was on the fourth floor. He exited the lift and walked into the dark corridor. No public came here. There were drab, colourless walls and a rough carpet. No art on the walls. The ceilings were lower—staff quarters, these rooms had been, when the gallery was an orphanage, many years ago. He found the room and rapped with his knuckle on the green painted door.

"Yes?" a deep voice said.

Tallis walked in. It was spacious, deep with books. Large abstract paintings on the wall. There was an orange painting leant against the wall between two square windows. Sheer colour, it frazzled his eyes. At a large wooden desk sat Theseus Campbell and, in a soft chair pulled up to the desk, was a woman in jeans and a sweatshirt.

"Thomas, my man. Good to see you," Theseus said, smiling. "Wait, are you lost?"

"No, no," Tallis said. "I just wanted a word."

"This is Dr. Roberta Donnelly, Thomas, our mysterious and wonderful head of conversations," Theseus said, extending a hand to the woman and smiling.

"Conservation," she said, unsmiling. "You can call me Bobby."

Theseus chuckled.

"Welcome to the Underground," he said, offering Tallis a chair. "Bobby and I meet here with fellow conspirators and try to bring down the Carver regime. But you are now sworn to secrecy."

"Oh, really?" Tallis said, who found himself eager to be in on the joke: if it was one. He was still standing in the middle of the room.

Bobby crossed her legs and rolled her eyes. "Actually, we were just talking about your unpleasant postal delivery," she said to Tallis. "I was deeply shocked. I am so sorry. Surely it is a police matter?"

"Her Majesty's finest were with me just now, Roberta," Theseus rumbled. "Asking me all sorts of questions. None of them very perceptive."

Tallis moved to a metal office chair and sat. He looked at his shoes. "So the police came to see you . . . about the tongue?" he said eventually.

"If that indeed is what it was," Theseus said.

"There was blood on my worktop," Bobby said.

"Yes, a human tongue," Tallis said.

"Fuck and yuck," Bobby said.

"Very awful," Theseus said, rising from his seat. "An obscenity." He moved across the room, large and looming. He walked past shelves that covered an entire wall, full with books and papers. There was a framed photograph of him with a woman and two small children. "And inexplicable," he said. He was looking for a book.

Bobby stood up. She had been holding a small cup. "Thank you for the coffee, Theseus," she said, and put the cup on the desk. "And, Thomas, we must talk about this Mackintosh item. Have you been out to see it yet?"

"No. I . . . I will do," he said. He wondered whether he should mention Carver's reluctance on the matter. He did not.

Theseus had found a book. He pulled it from the shelf and handed it to Tallis. *C.R. Mackintosh: The Late Paintings*, written by Dr. P. Thread. Tallis flipped the heavy pages. There were Mackintosh's beautiful French watercolours: sculptural, lovely depictions of the south of France. Fragile cliffs, villages and fields. Dry rock and barren hills, and pitiless skies.

How different the landscapes in these watercolours were from Mackintosh's home, from wet and black Glasgow. No noise in these paintings. No urban racket and buzz. No hint of Glasgow. No echo of the horn that sounded the turn of the shifts in the shipyards, and the insistent throng of work, and bent and riven metal. Amid that clamour, Mackintosh's stone buildings—the School of Art on its steep hill, his church in Maryhill, his school—had risen blackened and used, lovely and lonely amid the ruin and the smoke. Those watercolours from France were so clean in tone, so precise, long-laboured and delicate. They spoke of release and resettlement. Of a keen vision, and hope for something real, beyond design and build, beyond the vagaries of desired or lost commissions and the tenuousness of architectural competitions. Beyond uncertainty, and failure. Instead, here were the sure lines of the sea's edge and the antique hug of low villages huddled against stone and sun.

Tallis sat and looked at the book as Theseus and Bobby chatted. He moved the pages to the end. There was a large plate of *The Goldenacre*. Shadows over the tenements, and ghosts in the grass. In the notes it said:

> The Goldenacre *(1927, private collection).*
> *Believed to be C.R.M.'s last painting, created in*
> *his final months, before succumbing to cancer*
> *in London. How and when he visited Edinburgh*
> *is unknown, but a rough preparatory sketch in*
> *the Glasgow School of Art archives suggests it*
> *may have been painted from memory, and in this*
> *author's view shows the design and philosophical*
> *influence of his wife, Margaret.*

That preparatory sketch. Tallis nodded to himself. He had to see it.

"Interesting?" Theseus said, with a smile. "You are making approving noises, Thomas."

"Am I? It is. Who is the author: Mr. Thread?" he said.

Bobby looked like she was ready to leave.

"Percy. He's passed away now, I believe," Theseus said,

"but he was quite the expert. He wrote an excellent book about Mackintosh's wife and her sister. Very interesting too. Margaret is not given enough credit, of course. For her own art, or indeed for her influence on her husband."

"How immensely surprising that is," Bobby said. She had moved to the windows and looked out over the parkland and the grey city. She seemed to peer at something in the gardens. "I must go," she suddenly said, and moved to the door. She left. The door clicked behind her.

Theseus sat back in his leather swivel chair. "I actually have some more work for you," Theseus said, running a finger along his desktop.

"I work for the government, Mr. Campbell," he said.

"You have not always."

"Actually, I wanted to speak to you," Tallis said. "About Carver, and his . . . strangeness."

"I have something more of interest for you than the machinations of Sir Dennis," Theseus said, holding up a large hand. "This is a matter of delicacy."

Tallis nodded and smiled. He realised, at that moment, that he did not mind more work. He valued the way work filled up the spaces in life. The spaces that could echo with far worse. "Tell me more," he said.

Theseus nodded and seemed to ponder. "It is a delicate matter. Perhaps for the ears only of us, in this room right now," he said.

Tallis leaned forward. "Is this another matter about Mackintosh?"

Theseus smiled. His teeth glittered. "No," he said. He turned to Tallis fully, his body dark against the light of the window. "Many years ago, after the Second World War, we received a great collection of art. Marvellous French paintings—Degas, Cézanne. Two Manets. Some other work from the earlier, large works of the late nineteenth century. Some wonderful prints and sketches. One Picasso. You may have seen some of them; they are in our first room, on the first floor."

Tallis nodded—he had not.

"The Bradley Collection: forty pieces, in all," Theseus said. "They were not actually given to the Public Gallery. They are a long-term loan, but are a foundational part of our collections. The Bradley family have, since Sir Arthur Bradley first loaned us the works in 1946, been solid supporters of our work and our further acquisitions."

Tallis nodded. "Is there another tax issue?"

"No, we have a weightier issue than that. The Bradley family—well, actually the last remaining Bradley, Edie—has indicated she is planning something rather serious."

"What is that?"

"She wants to remove the works. I think she wants to sell them and donate the money elsewhere. To charities. To philanthropy." Theseus stopped and tapped his fingers on his desk. "You may have noticed a change in the climate, Thomas, of late. A sense that museums and galleries such as ours are facing a reckoning. A debt to be paid, to history. You may guess that I am sympathetic to this view. That we stand, here, with our pillars and our colonnades, full of the plunder of Empire. Of slavery. Of exploitation and nullification."

Tallis nodded. "Are these Bradley works connected to Nazi spoliation?"

Theseus shook his head. "No. There were Victorian genocides, too, Thomas. Indeed, they taught many white men in power how it was to kill, to eliminate, en masse. They taught some impressed men in the cool drawing rooms of Europe how inconvenient peoples could be dehumanised, enslaved and exterminated. Especially, of course, people like me: the Black man. The African."

"Of course," Tallis said.

Theseus smiled and held up a hand and smiled. He was signalling something. "Now, a few years ago there was a conference on the decolonisation of museums. It was held in Glasgow. Edie, herself an artist—a fine artist, we have some of her work—attended. She listened and was convinced. I was there too. Edie Bradley said she needed to do something. Something dramatic, historic."

"Why so?"

"Do you know Glasgow at all, Tallis?"

"Not really. I know Mackintosh was from there. I know about the Colourists, the Glasgow Boys, the art school."

"Fine, great city," Theseus said, nodding. "You may not know something else. There is a network of streets in its centre. The Merchant City, they call it. Merchants of what? Tobacco. Sugar. They made a lot of money. Pots of money, in that city, in the eighteenth and nineteenth centuries. The Bradley family was one of them. Mountains of money, they made. People think of Glasgow's former wealth as deriving from shipbuilding. Not so."

"Right."

"You look at the map of the city. There's a Jamaica Street. Virginia Street. Blood runs in the channels of its grid. This Merchant City? Much of it, built on the profits from the plantations, from free labour: slaves. The Bradleys made their money in sugar and tobacco. Edie knows it, of course. She has long wrestled with that. Her family's wealth was based on slave labour. Not hers, but she inherited it. She has never needed to worry about money. Plantations are behind that ease, that comfort."

"She has spoken to you about it?"

"Yes. She sought me out. I am a Black Briton, with Campbell as my surname. There is an historical reason for that. There are whole arteries of pain there. But, right now, I am a curator here. My job is to keep art here, not to let it go. Not see it sold off. So I am caught in a very unusual situation. But also, I could not have been a more appropriate vessel for her concerns."

Tallis nodded. He briefly thought of his father, in his younger life, tramping around the African veld in khaki, gun toted and loaded. Boots in blood. "How can I get involved?" Tallis asked.

"I would like you to see her on the down-low. Offline. In secret," Theseus said.

Tallis nodded.

"Edie is an artist, a lovely woman," Campbell said. "Do not tell Carver. Go to her, ask her if she is interested in a compromise. This is it: in return for the treasures of the Bradley Collection remaining here, in the Public Gallery, we institute a permanent exhibition, a full display, on the slave wealth of Scotland. A full public reckoning. Her family's history and works would be part of that."

Light glimmered on the office furniture, edging it with copper.

"Why are you asking me to do this?" Tallis said. "Surely this would come better from you, from Sir Dennis? I am just a functionary of the government. I am here for a simple task, to approve *The Goldenacre*. Then I will be gone."

Theseus nodded. "Yes, Thomas, you are an ephemeral presence here. You will arrive and be gone. You will be as transient as a ghost. So when Edie Bradley approaches me with this suggestion, it has come from her, not me. Not from the gallery. Her suggestion will have dignity, integrity. And not be anywhere, should we be asked, on email. No letters, no submissions." Theseus put his reading glasses on. "The Bradley Collection, they are such marvellous works. It would be a tragedy, for us, to lose them." He looked to Tallis. "I would be very grateful if you could speak to her. She is a good person. She needs a whisper, a nudge."

"Where does she live?" Tallis asked.

"Milngavie," Theseus said, and smiled.

"Where is that?"

"Where do you think?"

"It sounds like some kind of eye infection," Tallis said.

"Glasgow, of course," Theseus rumbled. "A wee train trip. Milngavie is a suburb. It's not spelt as it sounds."

Tallis nodded. "Okay," he said. "I will need to go to Glasgow anyway, to see something at the Glasgow School of Art."

"Well, perfect, then," Theseus said. "You can see her as well."

"How should I introduce myself?"

"Say you are a friend of Theseus. Someone will let her know you are coming."

Tallis nodded. "An emissary of Theseus," he said.

"Sounds rather ancient, doesn't it? Appropriately so, perhaps. For the assuaging of inherited sins. Now! For something more congenial—are you still coming to our home for dinner on Friday night?"

"I might not be here anymore," Tallis said. "I may be done by then."

"We could all say that, Thomas."

"But, yes, that would be lovely," Tallis said, and Theseus nodded.

Tallis walked back to his office, down grey corridors and granite steps. He would visit Denholm House and go to Glasgow.

Mungo was not at his desk. A window had been opened, and there was rain on his desk. Another Post-it note, curling at its edge like a fallen leaf, was stuck to the sleeping computer screen: *Your aunt wants to meet you after work. Give her a call.*

13

Shona was at her desk. The newspaper office was deserted. There was a meeting, delayed twice already, on the floor above, where Ronald Ingleton was telling staff about his plans. She could hear people moving their anxious feet on the thin floor.

Shona had been a journalist for twenty years: she had seen such plans before. They involved cutbacks, staff losses and "savings." She did not want to hear it anymore.

She rubbed her eyes. The office air shivered in electric light and dusty air conditioning. Papers lay strewn on desks. Computer screens hissed. She was looking at an online map, checking the way to Jupiter Artland, where she would meet Love's daughter. She didn't drive anymore, so it would be an expensive taxi fare.

Staff began to filter into the office. White shirts and white skin. Drifting between desks and computers. Shona didn't want to talk to any of them.

On the rattling bus journey into work, she had remembered her last conversation with Ned Silver and the tip-off about Thomas Tallis. Somewhere in the scree of papers in her bedroom, she had mislaid her notes. But she minded the basic facts: Tallis, a London art curator who had lost his previous job in strange circumstances. And now he was in Edinburgh, helping the Public Gallery with something. She searched for him on the internet, but the search returned thousands of articles and webpages about the composer of the same name. It is a good way to hide, she reckoned—have the same name as someone more famous. You could slide out of sight into the digital quicksand.

She searched again, refining her terms: "Tallis Curator London." There were more useful returns: Civic Gallery press releases from the last ten years, with stock anodyne quotes from a Thomas Tallis, deputy head of modern collections. She shifted the search to images. Several versions of the same photograph flashed up on her screen: a crumpled man, with large eyes, wearing a cord suit. An average man, crushed by something.

Shona flashed through a series of searches on social media: he did not seem to use any of the various platforms. There was nothing there.

She shifted her search terms again, to his father, Raymond T. Tallis, former deputy director general of MI6. There were many articles about his departure from the post—ten years ago. She again switched to images. There was a picture of the elder Tallis at a parliamentary inquiry into extra-judicial killings. He had his son's large, watery eyes—or his son had his—but his face was leaner, and deeply lined. His shoulders were squarer. His body contained a trim, potent power.

Who would know about Tallis and why he was in Edinburgh?

She ran a hand over her face. Her fingers smelled faintly of cleaning fluid: she had cleared up the mess her father had made in the kitchen that morning. She smiled briefly.

She did not have any contacts at the Public Gallery—the art world had been Ned Silver's area of expertise, and she did not want to phone him for any more favours. She did not want to ask him for a number or a name to speak to—no.

The city's council, however, ran museums and galleries of its own. Municipal places, underfunded. They were run by the council's leisure department, headed by a tired Irishman called Martyn McCarthy. She had spoken to him before— stories about problems, usually: strikes, closing facilities, overspends, budget problems. But she had written a story, a year ago, on a new exhibition of protest art he had set up: banners, badges, flags and tracts from the 1920s and '30s. He had been helpful and funny. He was wry and, through a fog of exhaustion, sharp.

She did not have a direct number for him. And she would not bother trying to get him through the council's press office. That would be a waste of time, an inevitable denial of access: council press offices wanted you to speak to councillors, not officials. Even though officials knew what was going on, and councillors often did not. She found a number for his department on the internet and picked up her receiver and put it to her ear. She looked about her. The office was repopulated: staff had drifted back from the meeting above. Everyone looked shocked and pale.

Hector Stricken sat down heavily. He wrote something roughly on a piece of paper and held it up to her.

ALL FUCKED, it said.

"Thought you had a day off," Shona said to Stricken.

"Came back in for the shit-show," Stricken mumbled.

She dialled the switchboard number.

Her colleagues were murmuring in small groups: knots of pale faces whispering and muttering. One reporter on the business desk stood up suddenly and stalked out the office, slamming a notebook into a bin.

Down the line, the phone began to ring. Somewhere in a council office, a plastic phone was bleating. While it rang, Shona said, "What's happening?"

Stricken, now sipping black coffee from his flask, raised his eyes to hers. "We're all fucked. New editor wants to downsize the paper, concentrate on the web, 24/7 digital shifts. Man's an idiot. Looking for redundancies."

"Heard it all before," Shona said.

"Yeah, true. But Ingleton has the eyes of a murderer and the wit of an angry bed stain. I think he means it."

Someone picked up the phone at the other end of Shona's call. A woman's voice said, "Department of Leisure Services?"

Shona was from Glasgow—Pollokshields, she would say, to be exact—but she could alter her voice with little shame or embarrassment when she needed to. She slipped into an accent that she used when she wanted to sound more middle class. Her "G12" accent, she called it.

"Rita Maxwell Davies." Across from her, Stricken looked up from his glum coffee and began to grin. "From Orkney Museums," Shona added.

"From Orkney?"

"Orkney Museums, director of . . . new acquisitions."

"Director of?"

"That's the one," Shona said.

There was a pause, in which nothing stirred. Then the woman spoke again. "Thank you, Ms. Davies, how can I help?"

"I have a call scheduled with Mr. Martyn McCarthy. About joint workings. And synergies."

"Ah, right. Thank you, I will see if he is ready," the secretary said.

Holding music slid into place. An orchestra, manoeuvring through a slow and wrenching melody. Shona wanted to hear more. But it was cut off.

"Hello, Ms. Davies," the woman said. "Mr. McCarthy did not seem to have this call in his diary about joint workings and synergies, I am afraid. But I will put you through."

"Thank you so much, that's terribly kind of you," Shona said. Stricken laughed a short laugh and shook his head.

There was a click and McCarthy answered the phone. "Hello?" he said uncertainly.

"Martyn," Shona said, her normal voice jolting back into action.

"Shona," he said, and laughed. "Shona Sandison. Who I believe has just lied outrageously to Moira there, for some reason?"

"Are you saying you never lie to Moira?" Shona said perkily.

McCarthy snorted. "That's funny. You have sixty seconds, sleuth, before I turf you off this call."

"I need a favour."

"Clearly."

"There's a fella up from London, working at the Public Gallery. Name of Tallis. I was wondering if you knew anything about him?"

She could hear McCarthy sucking his teeth. "Now, how do you know about that?"

"Little bird told me. Is the gallery in trouble or something?"

"No, no, Shona. No. The opposite."

"The opposite of trouble?"

"You know, of course, the Public Gallery is funded by the government and has nothing to do with the council."

"I know, Martyn. But I also know you know everything."

"I wish."

"Who is this Tallis?"

"Experienced curator, worked at the Civic—he handles provenance checks for the government now. He's up helping the Public Gallery with something."

"Why did he leave the Civic?"

"I don't know. I wouldn't know," he said.

Shona thought she could hear a slight edge to his voice. Or she may just have imagined it. "What's he helping the gallery here with?"

"Look now, Shona. I can't say more. I'd give the whole shooting match away. You should really speak to them, you know. But it's a good news story—I think."

"Provenance?"

"The history of a piece of art. It's his job to check it. Now, Shona, your enterprise is to be admired, but I need you off this line, you know. I have real people to speak to."

"I am real, Martyn."

"I'm not so sure you are," he said, and appeared to be laughing. The call ended with a clunk.

She put the phone down.

"Nice," Stricken said, pushing his glasses up his nose. "Was that McCarthy?"

"Might have been," she said, and wrote some notes in shorthand in her notebook.

"What's this tale you are working on, anyway?"

"Could be the big one," she said, shrugging.

"Could be the big one," he said, nodding, staring at his computer screen.

14

Aunt Zed said she wanted to talk. First, Tallis had to sit through a meeting. The heads of department in the gallery were giving Sir Dennis Carver updates on their work.

Carver had briefly introduced Tallis to the team, but not asked him to speak. The room was long and cold, with various men and women sitting straight-backed around the dark table. Some had brought laptops, although they remained unopened. Mungo sat to one side, taking notes. Theseus had spoken well, and with humour. People had smiled. He had not mentioned Edie Bradley.

Tallis did not mention that he planned to visit Denholm House, and no one mentioned the incident with the tongue. It was like it had never happened. Perhaps, he thought, they did not know about it. He had watched Dr. Bobby Donnelly go through her list of projects, twiddling a pen around in the air in a windmilling motion, which seemed to irritate Carver.

Aunt Zed texted him again. Had he got her message? She was in town, and at Calton Hill, she said.

The meeting came to an end, and they all filed out of the cold room. Carver had not looked at Tallis. He barely acknowledged him.

Tallis walked to a bus stop in the mild sun, clouds unravelling in a grey and silver array over the purring city. Edinburgh did not have London's constant noise, or its clamorous youth, or its pressing crowds. It had another sense instead: of resolve and observation. Everything waiting. Prim surveillance, and hidden dark. Decisions, conversations and important moments sliding in and out of view behind sandstone and glass.

On the bus to the end of Princes Street, Tallis pondered Mackintosh in the Scottish capital. He must have visited. As a young man he had been a pupil at Glasgow School of Art. He would have travelled here, to see the Old Town, the shambles on the castle rock. Its layers and tunnels, dark overhangs and daytime shadows. The young Glaswegian artist, moustachioed in those days, would have walked the New Town, its planned boulevards and avenues, its fenced private gardens. He was of Glasgow: sooty closes, and a clanging river birthing giant ships, locomotives and boilers. Glasgow was then an engine of industry, with a swollen populace. Massive wealth squatted in the west and south, in townhouses and shady new housing, beside miserable poverty in the inner-city slums.

Mackintosh, in his first job at Honeyman & Keppie, the architects' firm, had leaned towards the rational, the new. His lines then were restrained, conventional. There was little evidence of the esoteric and the occult, the strangeness of his Art School days. The Spooks, people had called them then: Mackintosh and his girlfriend, Margaret Macdonald, and their friends. They were regarded by their peers as slightly weird. Tending towards the secret and the gnostic. There were symbols and signs and shapes in his and Margaret's work that seemed to swell from somewhere other, somewhere troubling. The voices of the other side. Mumblings from séances. Words picked out by glasses on boards of letters. Theirs was a world of dreams and half-remembered images, glimpsed through daydream and gauzy half-thoughts. Watercolour memories, pale and fading at the edges.

Tallis looked at an image of the artist on his phone. Who was this moustachioed man, Mackintosh? Who was his wife? He was more than just a maker of fine, uncomfortable furniture, and of severe and elegant buildings. There was something other, something elusive and ghostly, in his lines.

There was a whole tourist industry in Glasgow now dedicated to this misapprehended man. Some called it "Mockintosh": fake jewellery and mirrors, trinkets and art deco tat. But he was not just some whiskery dandy, a fragile genius whose uneven career was cut short by failure and the shifting tides of fashion. There was something else there.

Tallis pocketed his phone, alighted from the bus and walked up the steep path to the top of Calton Hill. A short, nubbed hill at the east end of Princes Street, it was topped with monuments in grey and green: blocky memorials and fluted columns. He walked slowly up steep stairs. Tallis reached the top and a sudden open view of the city, the capital laid out from the Pentlands to the sea. The old volcano, Arthur's Seat, glowered behind. Tallis was out of breath. As he recovered from the climb, the sea glinted like shook silver paper, and oil tankers glided on the light. Fife, across the Firth, was hazy, smoke rising from some refinery in the dim distance. Down below, traffic skittered to and fro. Aunt Zed was sitting on a nearby bench, drinking from a takeaway cup. She waved.

Tallis sensed some kind of important conversation was about to take place. Zed's shoulders were tense, her smile thin. He sat down beside her and dropped his leather shoulder bag. She smelled of sweet honeysuckle. "What a view from here," he said.

"Beautiful." Zed sucked on her herbal tea. A waft of something organic and zesty drifted healthily from its lid. "How is work?" she said, in a formal way.

"It's been interesting so far," he said.

She drank tea. She gulped. "Any more from the police?"

"No, nothing."

They sat in silence for a while.

"Have you heard from your father recently, Thomas?" she said eventually.

He felt his face blanche. "Well, no," he said.

"And they haven't told you where he is?"

"No. I have his number. I mean, it is the same number they gave me when he went away."

"Poor Raymond," she said.

"Poor nothing," Tallis found himself saying.

Zed flicked a sharp stare at him. "Have you tried to contact him?"

"No. There are rules, Zed. You know the rules. To only call in the event of life-threatening illness, or death. Or if something occurs that might endanger national security. That's it. None of those things have happened."

Zed turned to him. "Thomas. Raymond Thomas Tallis," she said.

"That is, indeed, my name."

He smiled. She didn't. The sunlight was gleaming on a half-built monument behind her, what looked like a colossal copy of the Parthenon. It was ragged and unfinished and sad.

"You are probably going to be divorced," she said, "and you may or may not shortly be in charge of your son and his only grandson. Named in your father's honour."

"Not in *his* honour. Every male in our family is Raymond Thomas."

"You are being divorced, you may shortly be a single parent."

"There's worse things . . ."

"A single parent, and you are essentially homeless." She emphasised the last word, and carried on. "You've left your job, a job you loved, in the galleries, to work in some hazy role for this dreadful British government. You seem miserable, Thomas. All these things: I just think your father should know, and would want to know. I think you should call that number and see what happens. I know Lydia—your mother—I know Lydia would be so, so worried about you right now. And you have never properly explained what happened at the Civic Gallery. It's all very unlike you, Tom, and it's been building up inside me, all these questions and uncertainties, and then the tongue . . . I feel I have to talk to you about it now, before it becomes something unsaid and awkward between us, and . . ." She turned to Tallis with moist eyes, and one hand held his arm. "I do love you so, Tom. It's so strange, what has happened to you. You were all so settled and accomplished and brilliant, and little Ray is so wonderful and . . ."

She fell into silence.

They both sat and looked into the Firth of Forth's shimmering plane of light and water. Tallis felt a knot in his chest, and a pain slashed across his temple.

"I have never called that number," he lied. "And I don't think—as unusual as the past year or two has been—that anything which has happened to me, or been done by me, or to me, falls into either category, the categories defined, where I can call him. Or, even if it is him—it's probably just the mobile phone number of some grey drone at MI6 who takes down a message and passes it to Control."

"So, it's a mobile phone number?" She took another sip of tea.

He peered at her and smiled. "I am just saying: it's a number. Maybe he is married again with three young children and amnesia. I simply don't know. And I don't think, even if I did find the number, that calling it would lead to . . . would lead to my marriage reassembling, or who sent that tongue—"

"I think you should. Your life has changed, dramatically."

"He went away before I had even married Astrella

Nemours, Zed. As far as he is concerned, I am still a young junior curator at the Serpentine. He did not care for what I did. Remember what he said about me studying History of Art? Anyway. Is this all because you're still miffed about the Acceptance scheme?"

She smiled. "I don't give a stuff about your government's shady tax schemes. Not compared to my concerns for you." Her body relaxed and she leant a head on his shoulder.

Tallis breathed out.

"Was he cruel to you, your father?"

Tallis pondered a reply. "Absence is cruelty."

She looked up at him. "Lydia loved you so. Her beautiful boy. She was proud of you."

He shook his head, for a reason he could not immediately fathom. He looked at the sea.

"Thomas, what happened to you at the Civic?"

Tallis's mind moved away from the answer. There were traps there, black shadows. He didn't want to think about it. He had been unlucky. And mad. "It was just unfortunate. Everyone makes mistakes. You hope not to make them at work, but I did. It was an almighty mess. It just so happened . . . it just was cruelly timed, that I made a mess at work at the same time Astrella announced she was no longer in love with me. So, there we go. It was a thing . . ." He waved his free hand over the landscape. "So here I am."

"Were you sacked?" she said very quietly.

"No. Not sacked. They gave me a nice reference for this job. There was another job in Berlin, but for Ray . . . I didn't take it."

Tallis sat for a while, and Zed held him. Down the slope, towards some trees, Tallis noticed that young people in hoodies and anoraks were setting up some kind of event. A low-bed truck had been driven up the sole access road, and on it were poles and lights, large rigs and boxes of other equipment. A large tent was in the making, being attached to the unbuilt rear of the monument. There were people with clipboards, and some flooring was quickly being laid.

"Someone is planning on having a party," Zed said. "I'm cold, and this tea is cold too."

"I wonder what it is—maybe a wedding," Tallis said, relieved that the conversation had turned.

"I don't think you can do that up here," she said. "I saw a poster for some kind of festival event. A Summoning? Some kind of DJ thing, no doubt. Shall we go?" She stood up, her eyes still watery.

Tallis remembered the event Vorn had invited him to. He saw a young woman, her arms blue with tattoos, carting a large mixing desk. An accomplice carried a box of records.

Zed looked at the columns of the monument. "On our Independence Day, this shall be completed," she said. "You know, Thomas, they called it Edinburgh's Disgrace?"

"I'm sure there has been competition for that title," he said.

She laughed. They walked together, arm-in-arm, down the path to the city, which was slowly moving from day-time to evening. Commuters with grey eyes slumped in buses. Cyclists veered between stationary cars. Lights paced Princes Street like the lanterns of birthed ships in the harbour.

"Let's get a curry in for tea," she said brightly. "Jack is working late again, some commission or other. Let's make sure we leave him some."

Tallis looked down at her. "How are you and Jack, anyway?"

She peered up. "None of your business. Going steady, as they say."

"No one says that anymore," he said, and they arrived at the bus stop.

6:14 A.M.

So, it seems my marriage is over. Did I mention that? I may have. There's been lawyers' letters, and so on and so forth. Missives. Transmissions. Agreements. Sensible, sober, pragmatic, adult conversations. All that tedious fucking shit.

And I can't see Ms. Nemours, anyway. She is away, somewhere, playing. The first time I met her was seventeen years ago, this month, you know. At a friend's leaving do, she was there, a friend of a friend. The most beautiful girl I had ever seen. We kissed on the university steps. One thing led to another, as they say. You don't need to know this.

I guess I will always love her, even though we will never speak to each other in the way we used to. Not again. Not in the way we once did. It is so easy to become intimate, sometimes. And then, once it is gone—it's gone. That's why there are so many love songs. Too much pain. Too much pain in the world, in life, in living. What makes it worth carrying on? I would have once said art. Or music. Now I think it is just desperation. Maybe children—you hang around for them, to give them love. To be with them. Children as the antidote to suicide. It's a theory.

Why did you have children? Are you dead?

It's time to get up. Light is edging the curtains.

I don't really know if you saved me, back then. If you truly intervened. With the mess. If you did: I suppose a thank you is in order. Celia can thank you, but I won't. There's someone else I won't speak to again.

Someone sent me a body part in the post. I

guess those kind of things happened to you all the time. Fingers in envelopes. Eyes in film tubes. Maybe you dismembered bodies yourself. Or got other people to do it. You liked the former SAS types, didn't you? Small tough men with shark eyes.

Oh—I hear movement in the house. I am by the window now. Portobello is awake. The sea is far out, I can see it—the beach is exposed. The ruination of it all.

Good morning, Dad.

15

Meet me by the weeping children, the text said. Shona was in a taxi, and she had left Edinburgh. They passed by the airport, through industrial lots and warehouses, and then, suddenly, they were into fields.

The text was from Morag, Robert Love's daughter. Shona did not know what she meant. They had agreed to meet in a cultural attraction called Jupiter Artland. It lay in parkland around a beautiful old house in the West Lothian fields. The owners had installed works of art in its wood, and built a large terraced artwork with hills and pools in its grounds.

The weeping children may be one of the art things, Shona reasoned. Or there were just a lot of upset kids there.

The taxi driver was whistling quietly. He was happy with a large fare.

She had kissed her father goodbye in the morning. They had lived together since his stroke. He had a room, and his allotment. He was there now, she knew, sitting in his shed. They had managed to get a power point in there, and he had a heater, a radio and a kettle. He liked to listen to classical music and drink coffee.

She looked out of the taxi window. There were large open fields and little woods. But also there were the memories of lost industry: heavy roads for trucks, and towering red-sided bings, the remnants of old mine workings. The Pentland Hills loomed beyond, stark and treeless.

The taxi driver pulled in through ornate gates to a tree-shadowed drive, which curved through to the Artland. Shapes loomed in the trees. There was a large, open, grassy space, with some scattered parked cars. Sleepy sheep dozed in an enclosure. Through branches and leaves, a large country house stood, immaculate. Orange walls and minarets. A tall plastic sculpture—garish and lumpy—loomed nearby. Shona got out of the taxi, her stick rapping against its side. The air was fresh and clean. A breeze took her hair and moved it across her face. There was silence, and the tingling scent of water nearby.

She paid the driver with her card, and the taxi grinded its way back down the track. She took out her phone and replied to the message from Morag, and asked where the weeping children were. As she waited for the reply, she walked slowly, following signs to the ticket office. There was a coffee shop in an old stable yard. The stables were now small galleries. Old people sat at a table, drinking tea. Her phone buzzed.

Follow the path into the woods.

Shona moved into the woods. Her stick was tacky on the earth. There were glimpses of arable fields beyond the trees at first, but then the woods became thick, and the canopy dark, although there was a clear path through the tall trunks. She passed the first large artwork: a hole in the earth. She stopped. A large cage had been built around it, in umber iron. The hole was smooth-edged, a disappearance into the core of the world. You could not see the bottom. It could be straight through the Earth, she thought. A hole in New Zealand was open somewhere, with leaves from Scotland blowing through and up, out into the antipodean sky. She walked on, her stick softly indenting the drying path. More sculptures were revealed: there was a construct of pipes and rods, which looked like a dinosaur, and then a small

neo-classical bridge over a dry stream. The city was long
gone. She smelled mulch and weeds, herbs and wildflowers.
There was a fresh breeze, it touched her skin and hair, and
bent the long grasses and nettles that grew thick around the
roots and trunks.

She kept following the path. It was quiet, apart from her
feet and stick and breath. She passed a cottage, its doors
closed, its open window filled with stones. Shona stopped for
a time. Light rippled on green, and flashed on lolling branches.
The sky was clear, a fragment of blue set between branches.

The path led into an open space in the trees, a clearing
nodding with ferns, and scattered life-sized statues of children. Their faces were gone. Where there should have been
eyes and noses and mouths were holes. They had cavi-
ties instead, framed by long metal tresses. The metal girls
appeared to be weeping, their hands to their heads. One leant
against a tree, disconsolate. Another, in a farther glade, was
a perch for a bird.

On a large fallen tree, a young woman was sitting,
scrolling through her phone. She had a pregnant bump and
was wearing a large black T-shirt and work trousers. The
pattern on her T-shirt showed a red hare pounding a tabor.
"Ms. Sandison?" she said, looking up.

"That's me," Shona said, and walked towards her with
her hand out. They shook. Shona down sat on the smooth
wood. Her stick rapped against the bark.

"Thank you for meeting me," Morag said.

"No problem. This is a lovely place," Shona said. "If a
little spooky."

"Everyone loves the crying girls. Especially children, for
some reason."

"I'm sorry about your father," Shona said.

Morag nodded and looked at Shona sideways. She moved
her hand to put a strand of hair behind an ear. "He was
murdered," she said, her voice catching.

"Yes," Shona said.

The daughter shook her head. "It wasn't a robbery, a burglary. Nothing was taken. The police don't seem to be doing anything. The house is still a mess." She began to cry, but wiped her eyes. "His body, I haven't seen it," she said quietly. Morag looked at Shona directly. "The police, the policewoman who spoke to me, she said Daddy's face had been . . . messed up."

"I'm sorry. I thought you had identified him," Shona said.

Morag shook her head. She wiped her eyes with the back of her hand and breathed out heavily. "It was too much for me. Martyn—my partner—did it for me."

They sat in silence for a while. Shona wondered if she should take out her notepad.

Light moved in fields of dappled shadow across the trees, the still rivers of branches, the tender leaves. A cold, damaged summer was slowly emerging from a long, harsh spring. Somewhere beyond the trees, beyond the fields, a plane took off from the airport.

Morag smiled. "I work here part-time. Dad was pleased—he loved it here, too, even though he was quite old-fashioned in his views. Liked the coffee, and the walk. We were here only six weeks ago, or so. Is your father still alive?"

Shona looked at Morag's face. She had her father's long nose and his watchful eyes. "Yes, he is. He likes gardening."

"What does he do?"

"He was a hack, like me," Shona said. She smiled. An image of her mother, gone for many years, glimmered in her mind. Candles, lit in a black-out—the flicker of light across her face in a Glasgow tenement. Pale faces reflected in a dark window.

"There's other things I need to tell you, Ms. Sandison," Morag said. "Things that have been bothering me. I don't know what you can do with this. It might just be nonsense. I am anxious because of this"—she rubbed her pregnant stomach—"and I am not sleeping. Bad back, swollen ankles."

Shona reached into her bag and took out her notepad. She clicked open a pen.

"Dad had some issues," Morag said, still gently rubbing her stomach. "He had a big issue—he was always brassic. He never seemed to have enough money. He had paid off the house, thankfully, a while back, but . . . the money issue wasn't something he could seem to get on top of. He owed people. He owed me. I dread to think what going through his papers will be like." She ran a hand through her hair.

"Was he busy? Did he have a lot of work on?"

"He hadn't been." Morag stopped, and then nodded. "He hadn't really been busy. I mean, he always worked steadily. He was always working on something. He had some work to do for the Arts Club annual show. So there was that. Then, recently, he had this big commission. He had mentioned it to me, all excited. This is the interesting thing."

Shona nodded in encouragement.

"This is what is bugging me," Morag said. Her voice was clear and firm now. "Because he never showed it to me."

"Was that unusual?"

"Yes," she said. "He always showed me what he was working on, always. Ever since I was little. His studio was not like a cell, or secluded. He liked me being there. He would sit me down and talk to me as he worked. I mean, he always worked hard, but he was not precious about his space, and he didn't like silence. He is always listening to the bloody radio. Usually the sport." She wiped her eyes again. "But this one . . . He said it was a private commission. He was hard at it. It was a big watercolour."

"Is that unusual?"

Morag turned her head. "It was. For him. Unusual. I mean, really unusual. He usually painted in oils. Not always, okay. But, mainly, he painted in oils. He sometimes did watercolour—but ages ago. Ages and ages. Before I arrived and my mum departed. And I knew this one was bothering him. He kind of moaned about getting it done. He moaned about the woman he was painting it for, how demanding she was."

"Who was that?"

"An awful woman. Always on the phone to him. I answered the phone to her once, so rude. Such an aggressive voice. Well, she has the bloody thing now, I know that. He finished it a few weeks ago."

"What was it?"

"That's what I mean: I don't know. I know it was a big picture, because Daddy said it was. Complicated. And in watercolour. One day, when I was in town, he asked me to go to his favourite art supply place, and buy some gold and silver paint too."

They sat for a while, in silence. Shona made notes.

"Do you think this painting might have something to do with his . . . money problems?"

"How could it?" Morag said.

Shona shrugged. "I don't know."

"But it just doesn't feel right. I think he was worried about it, that's for certain. I wonder if he was even paid for it. Bloody woman." She stood up, and so did Shona. They walked slowly back through the trees to the converted stables.

"Do you mind me asking, why do you need the stick?" Morag asked.

Shona said she didn't mind. "I was out on a story. In Glasgow, a while back. Bampot attacked me. He did some damage."

"I'm so sorry." Morag looked dismayed. "How horrible."

Shona nodded and shrugged. "It was. But I got the story," she said, and smiled.

"Is journalism usually so dangerous?"

"Only to your mind."

They walked through the high grass, the bracken and nettles, the stands of trees. The sun recast the plants as numinous. For a short time of silence, the world seemed at peace, in balance. Eventually, they reached the cobbled square of the stables and bought tea and coffee. Holding the small of her back, Morag sat on a metal chair. Shona sat too.

"You know I think I saw that woman once," Morag said. Shona looked at her expectantly. "The rude woman?"

"Yeah. I was outside the house, trying to find his keys in my bag—I have a set—and this woman came out. She was in a suit, and she had a soft briefcase kind of thing—like a leather folder. She had a bleak kind of face, big glasses, hat. Not a nice person to look at."

"Did you ask your father who she was?"

"I did, and he said it was just someone he was talking to about money. I remember because she walked to this big white suburban tractor thing, this big four-by-four. There was a man in the driver's seat. Huge guy."

"Do you remember her name?"

Morag closed her eyes. "Dad didn't tell me her name, but I did find it in his diary. I would often check his diary, because he would forget things like lunches, dinners at the Arts Club. Doctor's appointments. Meetings with the bank. My birthday." She smiled. "Daddy was such a gentle, kind man. That someone would do that to . . ." Her face crumpled, and her shoulders shook. She cried for a time. "I'm sorry."

"Don't apologise," Shona said. "It's an awful thing."

"Catherine," Morag said. "Or Katherine with a *K*. Pieters, that was her name. *I* before *E*. I don't know who she was. I'd love to know."

"Have you looked her up on the internet?" Shona asked.

Morag nodded and shrugged. She blew her nose and rubbed her face. "I guess those are common names. I could find nothing useful. I'm sorry. I must go. I can't . . . I don't know what you can do with all this. But I had to tell someone like you. I think there is more to it all. I do." She moved her foot suddenly and knocked over her tea. Pale liquid ran between the embedded stones. She shook her head and held her swollen stomach.

"I'm sure there is," Shona said. "I'm sure there is."

16

Tallis was on his way to the Public Gallery, where he and Bobby Donnelly, head of conservation, would drive to Denholm House to see *The Goldenacre*.

Edinburgh shrank in the mist and rain, huddling to its hills as the bus steamed through the sodden streets. The rain had painted sudden spattered pictures on the pale flagstones: new galaxies, Dalmatians, the shadows of a canopy of trees. Acne.

He had a missed call from Melcombe. He wondered whether he should check his work email. He turned his phone off.

At the gallery, Bobby was waiting by her car, leaning on it.

"Good morning," Tallis said.

"Is it a good morning, Mr. Government Inspector?"

"I was told you were always late."

"You were told wrong. Get in."

The small car was warm, its back seat a mess of comics, sweet wrappers and small plastic toys. There were two bulky child seats, engrained with crumbs and sand.

"Sorry about the mess," Bobby said. "I must get this car cleaned at some point. Or condemned."

"How old are your children?"

"Eight and six. They're with their father this week,

however. So I am getting some sleep. Or trying to." She looked across at Tallis and smiled. "You have any?"

"A boy. Ray. He's seven."

They drove out of the gallery grounds and into the quiet, wet streets. Raindrops skidded across the windscreen, and they travelled in silence, at first. As they drove, Edinburgh was slowly reduced to fields, the stone tenements falling to bungalows, single streets to suburbs, and then the road cut south, through farmland and old grey towns. They talked. Bobby and Tallis spoke of their past, their educations. She had grown up in Northern Ireland and then Glasgow, and had trained in Glasgow and London. She had been head of conservation for three years. She was divorced, something she mentioned with an eyebrow raise. She wore a band around her left hand, made from strings and beads.

"And you?" she said, as the road led to the Borders. They were heading for Hawick. The land was old and green: woods and farmland, studded with old barns and stonewalls. Hills rose in the distance, bare and blue.

"It's been complicated," Tallis said. He was looking out of the window. "There's been a lot of changes."

"I imagine the government is a lot to get used to," she said.

"You have to forget about yourself."

They came to a roundabout, and Bobby swung the car around it. They headed onto a road with high, thick hedges either side. They were in deep country now, with dead silence over heavily farmed land. Man had taken this land and dug and planted and burned it into submission. It lay, mud-deep and defeated.

"I think we must be close," she said.

"Have you been before?"

"No. I don't think anyone from the gallery has been to Denholm House, apart from Carver. Sir Dennis. He knows the family."

They pulled over in a passing place. She looked at her phone. "No signal," she said, trying to make a map app work.

"I'll look," he said, fishing out his phone. He turned it on. It buzzed. There was a missed call from a number he did not recognise.

"I have an email with the instructions somewhere," Bobby said. "This is so annoying. I should have printed it out." She was sucking her bottom lip.

His phone was lit and seemed to have a signal. He searched for Denholm House on the map. A pulsing blue blob appeared on flat green: that was their car. A red mark appeared, not far from the blue mark. "Just keep going to the junction up ahead."

They drove on.

"What is it with you and not driving?" she asked, as they waited for a tractor spattered with mud and grime to rumble past. Birds scattered overhead. The road groaned.

"I don't have a licence," he said.

She briefly looked at him.

"I had one, but lost it. It's a pattern I follow."

"Me too," she said. There was a burr in her voice. It was deep, with a lustre.

"I've not noticed your accent before," he said.

"Bog Irish."

"Don't be so hard on yourself."

"Oh, I leave that to other people," she said.

He looked at her, to see if she was smiling—she wasn't. "My father is in Ireland. Apparently," he said mildly.

She grinned. Dimples appeared. "I like the 'apparently.' Is he on holiday?"

"No, he lives there."

"Apparently?"

Tallis just nodded. Through a break in the trees he saw flat plain fields, with mist rising from them, rolling to a dim horizon. They came around a tight corner to a long, straight road. It seemed to emerge from another time. It was walled on one side, overcome with ivy and weeds. The land was thick with trees beyond. There was a wide verge and a ditch, heavy with vegetation. They came to large metal gates, with pediments either side topped with smooth statues.

"I think this might be the place," she said.

"How can you tell?"

"I can smell old money."

They waited for a large white car to pass, and then pulled the car across the road to the gates, which were closed. There was a plaque and an intercom on one of the pillars.

"So," Bobby said, "I assume this is us."

"I guess so," Tallis said. He looked at the map on his phone: the red dot was hovering uncertainly over a large green nothingness. He got out of the car, his leather shoes sinking slightly into the mulch of mud and gravel. The plaque said, DENHOLM. He pressed a metal button set beneath an array of holes. He listened. He could hear the car engine, and silence. Bobby was staring at her mobile phone and gently shaking her head.

Suddenly, the gates moved, sliding on rails. Tallis moved back inside the car. Bobby drove forward, and they were into a wood of conifers. The drive was straight, plunging deeper into the trees. Pine needles and verticals. Deep in the distance, the shadow of a large house loomed, and they drove closer.

"Did they say anything on the intercom?" she asked.

"No, nothing."

A large and uneven house, covered in ivy and with a central pile with many glinting windows, came fully into view. Its form was complicated, and it looked like it had grown, rather than been built. There was a craggy, circular tower. Another wing had a square tower, from a later era, and, behind it, there were more buildings and outbuildings. As they pulled into the circular drive, they saw a large lake to one side, with an island in the middle and, on its far banks, a jumble of overgrown ruins. Light sank in the deep water.

Denholm House and its lake were heavy with shadow. They had a sense of enormous weight.

"Well, well," Bobby said. "What a pile. Who is meeting us?"

Tallis opened his small leather folder and pulled out a note from Mungo. "Olivia Farquharson, and maybe her brother, Felix."

"So, the family, then. Olivia is back in Scotland—she usually lives in England."

The central door seemed outsized, as if it had been removed from a medieval cathedral and installed there. There was a smaller door inside the frame, which began to open.

They stepped out of the car, and brushed themselves down.

"Is it Lady Olivia?" Bobby asked quietly.

"I've no idea. Possibly," he said.

"Nice research, Government Inspector," Bobby said, and left the car.

A woman wearing bright blue stepped out of the door. She had blond hair wrapped in intricate braids around her head. She smiled and held out her hand. Bobby shook her hand with a large winning smile.

"How lovely to meet you, Mrs. Tallis," Olivia said, moving to shake Bobby's hand. Pink varnish glittered on her fingers. Her voice was warm and direct. It rolled, Tallis assumed, from a lacquered lifetime of access, assumption and ease. Peach cushions and inherited furniture. Skiing holidays.

"Lovely to meet you, too, but I am Bobby Donnelly—conservation. This is Mr. Thomas Tallis." Bobby held a hand out to Tallis.

They all produced polite chuckles. They stood in the drive and manoeuvred through small talk—about the drive down, weather, finding the house. Tallis watched Bobby, and

Bobby seemed to be watching Tallis. Tallis watched Olivia. She seemed to be in a hurry.

"So, to business," Olivia said, seemingly in high spirits. "I can't wait to show you our wonderful prize."

Tallis made approving noises.

Olivia walked into the entrance hall, a voluminous dark room with many doors and stairs leading to another floor. They followed. There were doors and mirrors, and light glinting on armour. Weapons were pinned and crossed on the walls. Gloomy portraits glowered as Olivia spoke.

"Of course, we were quite reluctant to part with something so precious to our family. But after Daddy's passing: well, we need all kinds of upgrades and redevelopments. We have all kinds of marvellous ideas. This way . . ."

They moved through one corridor to another. The house was drenched in silence. Their footsteps padded on old carpet.

"I don't live here. I'm really just back to sort things out, but my brother, Felix—he is in a meeting right now but will join us, I don't know if you have met him—has all kinds of plans for the place. They're quite exciting. He thinks he is a super businessman. We are trying to diversify, vivify, redefine what Denholm House really is. We are not the kind of people to simply sit in our house and let it fall down about us. So, thank the Lord for the Acceptance Instead of Tax scheme."

They came to a long hall, with mullioned windows along one side. It looked over the lake, and beyond, to the ruins. They stopped for a moment as Olivia pointed out a small work by Constable that had also been under discussion as the "gift to the nation." Tallis nodded and murmured. But his eyes were drawn to the ruins. It looked like another house, a mirror of the one they were in, but broken down, overgrown, swamped in weeds and roots, sinking back into the land. The scale was impressive. Cyclopean.

He pointed. "What are the ruins across the water?"

Olivia beamed. "That is the famous—or should I say infamous—Sunken Garden. Built in 1786. Our family have used and abused it for generations. It is in a parlous state now, as you can see. It was, basically, a water garden. You can probably not see from here, and it's such a dreary day, but there were pools, water channels, a temple of Poseidon, nymph statues, pyramids, watercourses. Now it is . . . rather messy. And dangerous. But we do love it. We are doing a big fundraiser later this year . . . Anyway, on to Mr. Mackintosh."

They walked on. Before leaving the hall, Tallis looked again at the ruins. He could see architectural shapes now. There were walls and structures under the undergrowth, the creepers and the ivy. It looked like a castle melting into the ground. Sucked under. Mist laced between the mounds and ruins, the shattered pillars and tilting statues. And around and about it hung the blackness of the fir tree woods, with sterile darkness between the trunks and arrowing green.

They all walked through a large and damp-smelling drawing room. The walls had pink Venetian wallpaper. Gilt-edged brittle furniture sat nervously around its wide walls. There was a mess of a glass chandelier hanging from the ceiling: its wires crossed, its glass akimbo and yellowed with stains. Like the glass had fallen from a great height into a metal net.

"It is through here," Olivia said, opening her hand to a door in the corner.

"Actually," a loud voice called out suddenly, "it's not, darling. No."

They all turned around. Behind them, a tall man with a shock of white-blond hair had appeared in the room. He was in a business suit, tieless.

"Felix," Olivia said, surprised. She introduced them all.

"Ah, Mr. Dallas," Felix said, smiling, to Tallis. "We have

heard so much about you already. Formerly of the great Civic Gallery! Settling in to your new role, I hope?"

"I am certainly trying."

"I've heard that too," Felix said. "And you must be Roberta Donnelly?"

Bobby nodded.

"Felix, what did you say about *The Goldenacre*?" Olivia said. Her voice had changed. A bass tone in her alto.

"Yes, sorry. Sorry, sorry," he said, holding up his hands. "I must apologise to all. There's been a tiny change of plan. You weren't here, Olive, when it was all discussed and decided. It's just having a little brush and tickle before it goes. Bit of an assessment and a bit of conservation. And it's not ready. Not quite. I should have said. I didn't quite know that today was the day for the big reveal. So, if you go through that door, you would see nothing but a space on the wall."

Olivia seemed momentarily confused. Tallis looked to Bobby—her face a disapproving mask.

Felix sat tentatively on the arm of one of the antique chairs and ran a hand through his hair.

"Where is this conservation work being done?" Bobby said.

Felix crossed his arms. He looked like Olivia, Tallis thought—same straight nose, hooded eyes—but there was something crumpled and defeated about him. He reminded Tallis of himself. An imploded man.

"Ah now," Felix said, smiling and shaking his head. "I knew you might ask—Catherine Peters would tell you. She's the woman to speak to on that. She is handling it all. I believe you've met?"

"I believe so," Tallis said. "But maybe Ms. Donnelly here and I can speak to Ms. Peters now? We are here, after all. Be a shame to waste the trip."

"Again, I must disappoint you," Felix said, looking down at his shoes. "She is not technically here. I know this is all terribly awkward."

Olivia sighed. The loudness of the sigh seemed deliberate. "So the painting is not here?" Bobby asked.

"No," Felix said. He looked up. "There's our Constable, of course—our little policeman—which you may have seen in the East Corridor, and there's a marvellous Raeburn in the lounge. Our prints and drawings are in the library—"

"We are not here to see them," Bobby said.

"Let's have some tea and biscuits," Olivia cut in, "and talk about where we are on this whole matter of *The Goldenacre*. Let's get to a better place." She asked Bobby and Tallis to retrace their steps to the windowed corridor, and then moved to Felix, bowing her head to him, and spoke in low, hard tones.

They rewalked the corridor, the light rising over the silent old building and its wooded landscape.

Bobby looked to Tallis and raised her eyebrows, shaking her head. "Furious," she said evenly.

Olivia caught up with them, smiling, and led them down a tight spiral staircase to a large pantry and kitchen. Sunlight hung around windows, set back in thick stone. There was a vast old stone fireplace and several iron ovens. A young woman was making tea and coffee. On a long wooden table, plates of biscuits and small cakes had been laid out. They sat, and the young woman, whose dark shirt had a crest embroidered on its breast, poured tea.

"Thank you, Sasha. This is the oldest part of the house," Olivia said, taking a biscuit and breaking it with her fingers. "The whole house was built and rebuilt many times. Additions and augmentations and subtractions. Where we have just been—the coloured rooms—is eighteenth century, and that is where we mainly do hosting and parties and, we hope, more corporate hospitality and so on. The picture corridor was added later, once the Sunken Garden had been built, to afford the view. But this takes us back to the original house, which was fortified. Some of the battlements remain—it was all very stormy around the Borders, of course, for a long time. This is my favourite room, the kitchen. My father's, too. He would sit here and read the papers by the big fire in his muddy boots with the dogs. And when I was home, as a child, we would always come here for snacks and naughtiness. And then, as now, I spent a lot of time cleaning up after my brother."

They drank tea, sitting on wooden chairs around the table. Bobby tapped her phone on the wood. "So, *The Goldenacre*," she said.

"Look, I am so horrifically sorry your journey here has been fruitless," Olivia said. "A breakdown in communication, not for the first time. I have been away, and he has been away, and this is how these things happen. He tends to do things out of order: out of our plan. Daddy always says I am good at strategy, and Felix is better at tactics."

Tallis looked around: Felix was absent. They had lost him, somewhere in the house.

Bobby leaned forward. "I can see there's been a foul-up here. But obviously, as head of conservation I am very interested in the state of the painting that we will inherit— is it undergoing a conservation process right now? Your brother mentioned cleaning up? It is watercolour and mixed media. I assume you know this is a very delicate piece of work and . . ."

Olivia crunched her biscuit. "Yes. I can put your mind at rest on that. My brother was talking vaguely and euphemistically—not for the first time, again. I understand there is an issue with the frame, primarily."

"It is not the original frame, is it?" Tallis said. "It was damaged in a fire?"

"The frame is integral," Bobby said. "It is all of a piece."

"Well, it fell from the wall in the fire in 1961," Olivia said, answering Tallis. "The original frame was, as you know, very decorative, designed by Mackintosh's wife, who was as you know also an artist. Margaret. The Glasgow Style."

Tallis nodded. Sasha arrived again, with a thick paper file, and then swished away.

"Thank you," Olivia said. She opened the file, which was full of papers and pictures of *The Goldenacre*. She passed an old black-and-white image of the painting in its original frame to Tallis and Bobby. "Rather exquisite, isn't it?"

The image was old, rendered in light grey and plunging black. The frame was moulded and designed—a bespoke rectangle in the late Glasgow School style. There were stylised roses in three corners, and a lily in the top right-hand corner.

"The lily," Olivia said softly, "is a reference, apparently, to C.R.M.'s health, which was obviously fading at that time. His final weeks, as you may well know, were not spent in Glasgow or France, but in London. Cancer of the tongue and mouth. Terrible."

Bobby nodded, sipping her watery tea. "No smoke damage, at all?"

Olivia turned to her.

"Not really. The fire in 1961 was a close-run thing, but luckily only furniture and decorations were severely damaged. The picture chains you see here and here, they snapped or buckled in some way, and the picture fell about five feet, from the wall to the carpet."

"Was it in glass?"

"No. The frame was delicate but not glazed. The frame just came apart; it was just destroyed. It was beautiful but fragile—it was actually handmade by Margaret."

"What a disaster," Bobby said, and Tallis nodded.

"But the painting survived. Perhaps the frame saved it," Olivia said, smiling. "As for that frame—my father's father just replaced it, with a rather banal, also decorated, frame. That also did not last too well—that is what is the source of our current little rehabilitation. It needs to be touched up."

Bobby sucked on her tea and said, "May I?"

"Be my guest," Olivia said.

Bobby riffled through the papers, and found an ochre-tinged photograph from the early 1980s. An old man in a three-piece suit was pointing to the painting, which was now in a wooden frame, decorated with simple geometric patterns. "And now it is being touched up?" Bobby said.

"Indeed," Olivia said.

"Who by?"

"Felix has the details."

Tallis peered at the photograph. The old man, who he assumed was Olivia and Felix's father, was the fourteenth Lord Melrose—William John Felix Farquharson. The picture had been taken at some kind of party—there were people in fine dress, and a decanter on the table under the painting. Lord Melrose had a glass in his hand, full of coppery liquid.

"Where is your brother? Perhaps I could get those details now?" Bobby asked.

"He has a meeting in Haddington," his sister said evenly. "Of all places."

The small town was an hour's drive away. Outside there was a sudden loud thrumming noise. A rhythmic throb. Tallis stood up and moved to a window, and peered up at the treetops. A small white helicopter skipped over the conifers. It flittered and whirred, and was gone, an engine wittering through the air.

"Is that Felix?" he said.

"Oh, I doubt it," Olivia said.

"It either is or it isn't," Bobby said lightly. She was holding the image in both hands, staring. "It seems to me here, the frame is plain wood—unpainted." She put the picture down on the long table.

"Oh, that's an unusual angle," Olivia said. "I think the light is strange."

Bobby raised her eyebrows.

Tallis walked over to the window. The lake was at the

height of the glass, and was ruffled with wind. Tiny white-caps sloshed on the water.

"Will the tax scheme cover the inheritance tax bill?" he said.

Olivia affected a gasp. "Well, Mr. Tallis, I am sure you know we cannot talk about family matters such as that. But—"

"Well, the painting will soon be public," he said.

"But, as I was about to say, it does mean we can offset a large proportion. There are many accountants at work right now, as you might imagine, trying to disentangle our father's affairs. There is the house, but also the little place in London where I live, our place in south Gloucestershire, and then there are the trusts and companies."

"Companies?"

"Melrose Jam and Honey, of which you must have heard," she said brightly.

Bobby shook her head.

"And Oldmeg Reach, Daddy's investment portfolio. Ms. Peters is mainly in charge of that. He had some successes with that company and, shall we say, challenges also. Felix and Catherine are looking at all that. Our main plans are for this house. Felix has ideas for a music festival, a gourmet boutique event, all kinds of things. But once things are settled, I will return to London. Felix will become lord of the manor."

"And the hidden gardens?"

"The Sunken Garden? Our dream is to revive it, to rebuild it, to allow the waters to run again. That's the dream. It always has been. Come and have a look at this, if you like."

Tallis turned—Olivia was now standing next to an old picture, an engraving, which was framed on the stonewall.

Bobby came closer. "Lovely engraving," she said.

"Yes," Olivia nodded. "This is the original. It shows the Water Gardens as they were intended. The lord at the time had travelled in Europe, seen Versailles and especially

Fontainebleau, and that place in Prussia whose name I can never remember. He wanted to outdo them all. I think he succeeded."

Tallis peered at the faded picture. It showed the house, in slightly different form, overlooking the lake. The perspective was strange and slanted, as if the artist had seen the house and the surrounding forest from a hot-air balloon. Beside the lake, a tiny man in a bicorn hat walked with a lady in a large dress. The Sunken Garden was not sunken in the engraving: water ran in contained rivers, from a fountainhead in the shape of a god, through runs and terraces, past temples and faux-castles. There were pools with jets, statues with water cascading from mouths, battlements and elaborate walkways and streams. It looked barely real.

"Where did the water come from?" Bobby asked. "From a well?"

"Ah, well, what the lord did was rather clever," Olivia said. "He diverted the tributary of the Teviot away from a village. There was some very clever plumbing and engineering—it was ahead of its time."

"And the village?"

"The village is no more," Olivia said. She clapped her hands. "Now, I am sorry—I must go. I am so sorry your journey today has been fruitless. But we shall reconvene. I will get you down here as soon as is possible. Or we can meet in Edinburgh?"

"Edinburgh would be more useful for us," Bobby said.

They shook hands and began to leave.

In the dark hallway, Olivia gasped. She moved to a long wooden table and found two pieces of colourful paper. "You both must come," she said.

Tallis took one—it was an invitation to a party.

"A celebration of the agreement," Olivia said. "You will be pivotal in the handover of our masterpiece, of course.

Maybe a speech, and some entertainments. The great and good will be there, and so you must be too."

The party was in a few days time.

"The handover may not be wrapped up by then," Bobby said. "After all, we haven't actually seen *The Goldenacre* yet."

"Ah, but you will, you will," Olivia said. She was standing close to Tallis now. He could see tiny flecks of gold in her lipstick. She smelled of expensive perfume and vigorous health and cleanliness. She had indentations in the hair above her ears, left by glasses.

"We'd love to come, of course," he said, smiling, and held out a hand, and they shook.

Once Tallis had clicked on his belt, Bobby drove the car away, down the drive and out through the gates, which opened automatically. Soon they were on the road again, surrounded by the woods, and driving in silence. Birds broke and fled from the thick undergrowth. The sun throbbed behind a white sky.

They paused at a roundabout. Bobby slapped the steering wheel. "Un-be-fucking-lievable!" she said.

Tallis opened his mouth to say something, but didn't.

They drove in silence back to the capital.

As they neared the gallery, Tallis said, "I will make an arrangement to see the work as soon as possible."

The car pulled into the parking spaces behind the Public Gallery.

"You do that. This whole fucking thing stinks," Bobby said.

17

Shona's father had an allotment in the north of the city, near an old railway line. The allotments were hidden in trees, sunk between high tenements and large stone houses. They were shambling, chaotic: a ragged field of diggings and plantings, canes and hung strings, vegetables and flowers. A secret city planted inside the city.

Life was different here. And abundant. There was mulch and compost and weeds and birds, skittering mice and gleaming slugs and secret voles. They were dug on a wide and rich slope, looking out over the silhouette of old Edinburgh: the castle to the west, the spires and turrets of the Royal Mile, down to the palace of the Queen. Some allotments were abandoned, some were overgrown, some were neat and ordered. Hugh Sandison's was somewhere in-between: the result of a compromise between his haphazard enthusiasm for the soil and a more solid desire for ease.

Shona walked carefully down his duckboards. She had, as usual, slipped in mud and wet grass as she clambered her way to his lot. Her balance was precarious, her stick slipping.

His shed had been renovated in recent years. It stood close to the high fence that marked the border between the gardeners and the outside world. He was sitting in his wicker chair when Shona huffed into view. Her stick was clarty with mud, her shoes spattered.

"Hey, my darling," he said with a smile. He held up a battered enamel mug. "Fancy a brew?"

She nodded and smiled. He rose and they hugged. He unfolded a short camping stool and she sat, with a sigh.

"So, what's up with you?" he said. "And shouldn't you be at the office?"

He held the kettle under a metal stopcock. Water spurted in chokes.

"I'm really not convinced that water is drinkable, Dad." She had said that before. She had probably said it every time she visited him at the allotment.

"I'm no' dead yet," he said.

He made her tea without milk, and they sat together. The city purred away, through the trees. Shona looked at her father's patch. There was a row of vegetables and some bare canes, set at angles in the rich soil. He had planted roses, and they were healthy and towering. The long thorns were laminated and gleaming.

"How's the plants, whatever they are?"

"Well," he said, ignoring her deliberate show of ignorance, "the weather hasn't been great. The land feels soggy and soaked. So, you didn't answer my question. Shouldn't you be at work?"

She sighed. She tapped her stick, but the mud was still wet and clung. "Nasty story I am working on," she said.

He looked at her expectantly. Hugh had been a journalist for forty years. He had taken redundancy from *The Herald* and still read the papers, albeit usually with a shaking head. He was bald, with liver spots on his pate. He had a beard and a pink nose, and alert, watchful eyes. He wore brown cords and liked to iron his shirts. "They're all nasty, in some way or other," he said. "You know that, right?"

"I know, Dad," she said. Morag's tears were still in her

mind. They were still on her shoulder, sunk into the wool of her coat. "You've told me enough times."

He smiled and looked at his coffee. "Something wrong with these grains today," he said, and winced.

Shona sighed and stretched her legs. The sun appeared from behind a huge bank of clouds. It glittered on the wet soil, the tangle of fences and wires, sheds and hovels.

In as short a way as she could, she outlined what was happening at her paper—the new boss and the "digital transformation." She found herself getting angry and upset. So she stopped.

Hugh Sandison had listened. He tipped his coffee into the soil. A robin landed on the fence and skittered and fretted, its chest as red as blood. Then it disappeared. "It's the death knell, love. You know that. Papers are dying. Like the shipyards. Like car factories. But these fuckers—these so-called bosses of yours—are leeching it for all its worth, before it all goes down. The whole digital thing, it's a mirage." He waved his hand in the air, as if tracing a castle in some Saharan vision.

Shona nodded. She knew, somewhere unacknowledged fully to herself, that she had to leave the newspaper. If not journalism. She could not imagine doing anything else. She had the wounds bearing witness to her dedication. She stared into the mud and a tear formed. She brushed it away, surprised.

Her father put an arm around her and kissed her head. "You'll make the right decision, love, when it comes. Just like you did when you left the *Mercury*, when you left Glasgow for here. And when you made me a wee home. For which I am duly thankful."

She leaned into him. He smelled of sweat and coffee, and the strange minty scent he always had. "Dad, you need a bath," Shona said.

"Sure enough. But you spend so long in that bathroom, I never get a chance of a morning."

She smiled. He wasn't entirely wrong.

"So, tell me about this wee tale, then," he said, and sluiced out his mug from the tap.

Shona drank her tea—it tasted metallic and flat—and outlined the story of Love's death, and what his daughter had told her.

Her father made a new cup and moved his chair beside hers. "So, this fellow was in hock to someone? Owed money to some shady people?"

"No. Well, I don't know—who knows? He was probably in debt. His daughter said he was always working. And gambling. Maybe he was trying to pay people off. The man at the Arts Club basically said he was an addict."

"And this big painting he was working on, what was that? Who was it for?"

"Dunno. She didn't know. He was doing it for this Peters woman. I need to track her down."

"Maybe the Arts Club can help—they might have put her in touch with Love. His pals might have thrown her his way. If she is some loaded collector or someone like that. An investor in art. Maybe she is working for someone else."

"Don't know that she's loaded," Shona said, trying to remove a tiny, sour tealeaf from her mouth.

"Well, she had a big car and a driver. Doesn't sound like she was penniless," he said. "And she commissioned him: these personal commissions cost a bit."

She raised an eyebrow. A breeze blew her hair across her face. "Art expert, are we now, Dad?"

"I know a bit. Covered the Glasgow Boys in the eighties. Did a bit of auction reporting: there were always tales in those lots. Interesting people. And a spot of dodginess, too."

"How so?"

"Well," he said, and stretched out his legs, like his daughter. "Wherever there is money to be made—and there is in the auction trade, no doubt about it, even in the small city auction houses—there are people on the make. Small-time fraudsters. But also the big boys. The big gangsters were all drawn to it, you know."

Shona did not know. "Tell me more," she said, and threw her tea into the ground.

"Hey now. Those teabags aren't free now, Shona," Hugh said, irritated. He quickly found his temper again. "You should look up some of the big art heists. There have been some big thefts over the years. I remember one in New England, over there in the States, a way back—some woman, a serious collector, she had all these Master paintings stolen from her. Dutch stuff, you know all that Golden Age palaver. And they haven't ever found them again. You see, the thing is, they use it as collateral."

Shona raised her eyebrows, asking him to go on.

"Yep," he said, on a roll, "one of these paintings is worth so many million dollars or pounds or euros. So, stealing one—and these boys can steal anything if they want to—is worth it. All that value is in one place—in a frame, or rolled up. A single piece of stuff, a painting, is worth x-amount. Gangsters use them as trophies but also as stock, in a way. So if push comes to shove, they can resell them—maybe to another crim, maybe to some collector, via an intermediary. It's hard to sell again at public auction, but there's a whole load of ways that these people sell things between each other. Those paintings stolen in New England? They're probably on some villain's wall in Mexico or Colombia. Or in some mansion in China or Russia. See, if you're some bad man in Mexico and you owe some fella in Paraguay $20 million, why not nick a Master, easy done—comparatively—and give your man in Paraguay that, instead? If he's open to it and wants a Picasso on his castle wall, why no'? And that's just the underworld. There's still plenty of collectors who will buy things of dubious prove . . . produce. What's the word?"

"Provenance," she said.

"Hang on—isn't that some place in France?" He laughed.
"Dad," she said.

"Anyway. So, owning a painting is probably a canny investment for these types. You should look up what happened with that Leonardo down in the Borders—the *Madonna of the Yarnwinder*. I remember that tale. Some gang or other. Came up to Scotland and nicked it."

"I will, Dad, I will. But I am not sure this has anything to do with poor Robert Love getting his head staved in. He wasn't a Master. His painting wouldn't have been much collateral."

Her father looked into the wet mud. He reached down and pulled out a tentative weed and threw it away. "All I'm saying is, the arts world isn't all nice public galleries and museums and wine parties and all that. There are some dark corners. There's always been. It's a business like all others, after all. And where there's business, there's crooks, and where there's profit, there's bad people. We all know that."

"My old communist dad," she said.

"Oh yes," he said, nodding heartily. "And it'll all be proved right in the end."

Shona stared into her mug. She wanted to get back to the office—to somehow avoid any talk about the digital transformation, and do some research. She wanted to find this Catherine or Katherine Pieters. And more about this Tallis fellow.

"Thanks, Dad. Look, I'd better be off."

"Oh, come now, you've only just arrived."

She stood up and put a hand on his shoulder. "What's for supper, Dad?"

"Oh, some of my famous chilli con carne," he declared.

"Again," she said.

"Oh yes, once again," said her father, smiling.

18

Tallis was trying to speak to his son. And he needed to speak to Ms. Peters, so that he could see *The Goldenacre*. He could not get hold of either. But he really wanted to speak to his son.

Mungo was in the office, trying to make the internet work. It had stopped functioning, and Tallis could not send or receive emails. Mungo was staring at a small black modem.

Tallis imagined a backlog of angry messages from Melcombe. Asking him for updates, asking him to come back to London. Tallis realised, on the walk from the bus to the gallery, that the idea of returning to London did not fill him with any pleasure. Edinburgh was unknown to him, but it was full of quiet, and space, and its own living silence. You could feel it, the silence with its own tense gravity, flooding the streets, the private squares and gardens. You could feel it landing on your shoulders with a sudden tightness, as you walked its hills and streets.

He called Gretchen again and finally she answered. Was Ray there? Yes, he was, she said, and went to get him.

"Dada?" Ray said.

"Hey, dude," Tallis said. He found himself smiling.

"Mummy is away," the boy said. His voice seemed

ridiculously high. Tallis had spent too long in the company of adults.

"I know she is. But she is back soon. And I will see you soon!"

"I've been drawing this battle," Ray said excitedly, "it's like Narnia but different. Are you coming back tomorrow? Gretchen has made pizza. I had to do homework, which was so boring and not fair."

"No, I am not coming back tomorrow. I still have work to do."

"So who is going to look after me?"

"Gretchen, you know that."

"She's strict."

"Well, she loves you. Mummy is back in a couple of days."

"The men for Mummy came yesterday. They brought a new piano. It's white."

"Oh really, a new piano?"

"Yes, a big one in the piano room. Gretchen said I could play in the box. The black piano is gone. Are you doing the boring work?"

"Yes, the boring work. Especially as you are not here."

"I wish you had your old job, that was funner."

"This one can be fun, too," Tallis lied.

"I am going now. Bye," the boy said, and was gone.

The phone was put down, and Gretchen picked up the receiver. She said Ray was fine, eating okay, but he had kept coming into her bed at night. Holding his hair, a thumb in his mouth.

"Ah. Yes. He does that," Tallis said. Suddenly, unexpectedly, he began to cry. He wiped his eye. He passed a hand across his face. Wetness on his fingers.

"He's fine."

Tallis nodded.

"Thomas?"

Tallis shook his head. He wiped tears with the heel of his hand. "Yes. Kiss him. From me."

"I always do, Thomas."

Mungo loudly opened a small box with a rip and howl of packing tape. The call was ended.

"Ah, this must be the thingummy we have been looking for. How has your work been today?" Mungo said. He looked at Tallis, and a slight flinch ghosted across his white face.

Tallis nodded. A finger in his eye, pushing away a tear. "Fine, thank you, Mungo. Slow."

Mungo stood up, with a hand on the small of his back. "You shouldn't be working so soon after your shock," he said.

"What shock?"

"The . . . package."

"I'm absolutely fine, Mr. Munro. Are you nearly done here?"

Mungo nodded, and his voice took on another tone. "Oh, I think I've done myself a mischief. I can't work out this modem for the life of me. I'll call the IT man. And I forgot to say: that horrible Ms. Peters called for you."

Tallis sighed. "When?"

Mungo rubbed his hair. "Well, before I started doing this. You know, I came in here with that tea for you? I meant to say she had called, but then I saw the new modem box and I was distracted. She called earlier. I'll get the note. I'm pretty sure I made a note. A sticky one."

Tallis put a hand down on his desk with a slap.

"Mungo, what do you usually do when I am not here? What did you do before I arrived?"

Mungo rubbed an ear.

"I was the private secretary of George Newhouse, the curator whose room this was. But after he left, poor man, I have been working in Mr. Carver's office a bit, and helping out a bit in the press office. But I have no fixed role, really."

"Right. But now you do have a fixed role, don't you, in helping me?"

"Yes. Do you want me to get those messages?"

Tallis nodded and said he did.

Mungo left the room and shouted through from his small office. "So, Ms. Peters called, and also a man from the police."

"Can you please bring them in here?" Tallis yelled back.

Mungo came in with two yellow Post-it notes. "Sorry," he said.

"Mungo, has Carver mentioned Bobby and I visiting the Farquharsons?"

Mungo became suddenly pale. "No, he has not. But I haven't seen Sir Dennis," he said, whispering.

"Because I will have to go back there. They didn't have *The Goldenacre* on the site yesterday. So if you are nervous about that, I won't tell you when I go again."

Mungo shook his head. He bit a nail. "It's fine. It's fine. I was a little overwrought," he said. "You didn't see the painting?"

Tallis shook his head. "No. Bobby and I were left disappointed. She was quite annoyed. For good reason."

Mungo shook his head and disappeared back into his office.

Tallis called the police number. It was Reculver's number.

A rough voice answered. "Reculver," it said.

Tallis explained who he was, and why he was calling.

"Ah, Mr. Tallis," Detective Reculver said. "Thanks for calling. I need to ask you a question, but I propose that the substance of this remains something just between me and you right now. No need to come to Comely Bank."

"Comely Bank?"

"The wee house where the polis live," Reculver said.

"Okay," Tallis said uncertainly.

"Did you know the Scottish painter Robert Love? Was he an acquaintance of yours in the art world?"

"The artist who just died?" Tallis felt his stomach roll.

"Indeed, Mr. Love. 'Bob,' to his friends."

"No, not at all."

"Never met him? Or dealt with him, or his work?"

Tallis shook his head. "No, never. Of course, I was aware of his name, but in London I did not deal with his work or . . . He was a good painter. I was shocked to see the news."

"Never seen his work in the flesh?"

"No. Why do you ask?"

"Well, you arrive in town, man from the government, and suddenly a painter is deid," Reculver said baldly.

Tallis's heart leapt. "But . . ."

"Calm. Don't get in a fankle," Reculver said, and it sounded like he was smiling. "If you get any other strange post, let us know straightaway, won't you?"

"Of course, but why would I? Should I expect more?"

"Goodbye, Mr. Tallis. We shall be in touch."

The line went dead.

The room was silent. He stood and walked to the table and drank a glass of water quickly. He had sweat in the small of his back. He looked at a book that he had left on the table—a history of late Mackintosh works. Tallis opened it at a page with a plate of a painting. He sat and studied it intently. It was a grey and silver image of deep and gorgeous mystery. Two women floated in a dimension of magic. One seemed to be wearing a wedding veil, or perhaps the garments of mourning. Behind this beautiful woman was another: perhaps older, certainly darker. Around and about the women—who floated, who were without gravity, as if in a dream—were orbs of silver and white, globes that seemed to grow from the background. They could have been a strange fruit, or the stars of a galaxy. Or a pile of skulls in a catacomb.

He looked at the title: the painting wasn't by Charles Rennie Mackintosh. It was by his wife, Margaret Macdonald Mackintosh. It was called *The Silver Apples of the Moon*. It was created in 1912, years before *The Goldenacre*, but it had the same uncanny sense, a glimpse of the world beyond the veil. A vision from another place. Like *The Goldenacre*, it had also been created in pencil and watercolour, and highlighted with gold paint and gum arabic. It was painted on gesso-prepared paper and laid on cardboard. It was unclear whether it had ever been framed, or seen in public. The painting was included in the book, but the author seemed not to have mentioned why. Tallis flipped, annoyed, through its pages. Then he found the image again. It shimmered before him, glistening with uncanny loveliness.

"What a beautiful thing," Tallis said out loud.

"Well, thank you," Mungo said.

Tallis started. His assistant had appeared with another cup of tea. "The picture, here," Tallis said, pointing.

"Oh, that is lovely," Mungo said, craning his neck to see. "How pretty. Spooky too. Haunting. Is that in our store?"

"No. It really is beautiful—I really don't know much about Margaret Macdonald, which is my loss: I need to find out more. She was obviously spectacularly talented. Looking at this, it's clear she influenced Mackintosh. I wonder if that is a man or a woman behind this woman in the foreground. I think it might be a man now. Look."

"It's ambidextrous," Mungo said.

"Ambiguous," Tallis said. "It says here, this painting is untraced. This painting is missing."

"More mysteries," Mungo said.

The desk phone rang with a shrill bleat.

"I guess that is for you," Mungo said.

"I suspect so," Tallis said, "given this is my office." He

placed the book down and went to get the phone, and Mungo disappeared again.

"Thomas Tallis," the voice at the other end of the line said.

"Yes?"

"Catherine Peters." She spoke as if she was saying her name for the first time. A hard "C" and a propelled "P."

"Ah. Thanks for calling back."

"I am calling you again."

"Rightly so. Sorry. Yes, I . . . yesterday . . ."

"*The Goldenacre* is available for observation." Her voice was as inflexible as stone. Tallis couldn't place the accent.

"That is good news. Where and when?"

"At the Public Gallery Stores. I have already made the appointment with Sir Dennis. You can attend. Receive the details from his private office."

Tallis smiled and took the receiver in his other hand. He laid his other hand on the warm cup of tea. "Well, I shall attend—it is, after all, my duty to review the painting. I shall also invite Roberta Donnelly, the head of conserv—"

"There is no need for Ms. Donnelly to attend."

"With respect, Ms. Peters, it is also Ms. Donnelly's duty to inspect the painting before it can be officially transferred to the ownership of the Public Gallery."

"I shall discuss with Sir Dennis."

"No, I shall discuss it with Mr. Carver. Ms. Donnelly would also like to know where the painting has been conserved and who has done the work. It is very important we know all the details of its recent history as well as its life since 1927."

"Everything is in order. Goodbye, Mr. Tallis."

The line clunked. It was dead.

"Jesus fucking Christ," Tallis said. He sighed and made a diary note.

"Stop talking about me, Mr. Tallis," a deep voice said. A

large man entered the room—Theseus Campbell. "How goes it, Thomas?" His voice boomed around the room. He sat at the table and opened the Mackintosh book. "So, Friday: You will come to our house about seven?"

"That would be lovely—but I also said I would go to the Summoning event on Calton Hill."

"Ah yes, Vorn's event. Well, it should be interesting," Theseus said. "I may not go myself. But come for dinner. I have emailed you our address. I hear your visit to Denholm House yesterday was both surprising and unfortunate."

"Yes. Perhaps Bobby told you. *The Goldenacre* wasn't even there. All very curious. But my feeling is that the brother and sister aren't exactly communicating."

"I also heard that," Theseus said. He held a small book in his hands, an old tome on van Gogh and his brother. "I have heard that the son, the brother, is into all kinds of business. I guess inherited wealth isn't enough."

"The house itself is a mix of falling down and spectacular," Tallis said. "There are these ornamental gardens which, if rebuilt, could be a tourist attraction of some kind . . ."

"There is a reckoning to be had," Theseus said. He looked out of the window. "You know, my friend, it is going to rain. I hope the rain does not arrive for the Summoning. How many acres would you say the Lords Denholm own? Here in Scotland and down south?"

"I literally have no idea, Theseus. There seemed to be a lot of it yesterday. The place is surrounded by acres of woods. There is a lake."

Theseus nodded. "Coal mines in Wales and former plantations in the West Indies. That is the bulk of the source of their historic wealth. I looked it up. It's a hobby of mine, these kinds of unwelcome investigations," he rumbled. "That is how they build these edifices and collect this art. Historically, that is. I am not blaming Annunciata and Frederick, whatever their names are, personally."

"Perhaps unfair to," Tallis said, attempting to slow the monologue, but Theseus carried on.

"But let us not feel too good about removing their duty to pay twelve million in tax just so we can have another Mackintosh in our collection. Another pretty picture to be viewed by the white-haired, white middle classes who take public art for granted but would recoil at the deadly work it took to build the wealth to own it in the first place."

Tallis smiled. "You should speak to my aunt. She feels roughly the same as you."

"She sounds very wise, young Thomas," Theseus said, and, with a little bow, left the room.

Tallis looked out onto the parkland. No one seemed to be moving on the grass and amid the sculptures. The car park had a few staff cars, and a taxi with its light on. In the corner of the park was a large white four-by-four. He peered at it. It was at some distance, and partially hidden by trees. There was a driver. It looked like a large man, with grey hair cut close to his huge head.

Another man was walking towards the car. He was thin and in a grey suit. Tallis could not see his face. The men talked—the driver through the drawn-down window—before it began to rain hard, and the man in the grey suit ran back to the gallery.

Water on the windows sluiced down in a veil, another distorted pane of glass. Nothing Tallis could see was as it really was. The water bent light about its surface. The huge white car ground out of the car park and drove away, into the pitiless rain.

His mobile phone buzzed. It was a text from Astrella: *Gretchen said you called.*

He stared at it for a while, and did not know how to answer.

10:03 P.M.

I wonder if your voice message system is over-full, and this will be automatically deleted. If so, how apt.

Today wasn't a good day. I must say. I have had better, albeit not recently.

I had a dream; it was a memory. Some memories are dreams. This dream was real.

I was with some babysitter. One of the many. You were away, doing your thing. Being secret. Maybe you were in Moscow or Berlin. Washington DC. East Germany. It was a sunny day. The babysitter had a boyfriend, and he was driving this truck. The girl and I sat on the back, a flat-bed, and he drove fast along the road, and my hat flew off. There was no way for us to hold still as the truck moved—she was holding me, but we were sliding all over the flatbed, and giggling, and I was screaming with laughter, or just screaming.

The trees rushing by in a blur.

We picked strawberries that day. All day in the flat sun. It was so hot, I remember. And the strawberries so red. So sweet. My fingers were stained with the redness of them . . . Wooden punnets. It must have been the late 1970s.

I ate loads and slept in the front of the truck on the way back: just asleep on her warm legs, hearing pop music on the radio.

Where were you then? Fighting Communists? Some grimy coup in Africa? Assassinations in Iran? Turning some cancerous civil servant in Lübeck?

There wasn't a cloud in the sky, that day. I remember seeing the dome of the sky, properly, for the first time. How it deepens into dark blue, and is yellow-brown at the horizon. And the skiddy flat-bed, and my tiny body rolling over it. Anyway—I am only telling you this, so you can remember it too, when I am gone. But you won't be able to know if it is true, or not. Because you weren't there.

Bye.

19

Shona Sandison stared at her phone. Her father was making a racket in the bathroom, and she was wondering what to say to the Civic Gallery in London. Tallis had worked there. She did not really care about his life in London—nor would her paper's readers. But there was something shadowy about him.

She had to find out what it was.

And she had to make some calls before she spoke to the man himself. Sometimes, she knew, a reporter had to circle around a story—speaking to several sources, talking off the record, researching—before addressing it face on. She could do this with stories she was familiar with: crime, corruption, malfeasance. But Shona did not know about the arts world, how it really worked. And, given she could not bring herself to ask Ned Silver for help, she had decided to call the institution in London and see what happened. She was going to ask them outright why Tallis had left, and whether he had signed a Non-Disclosure Agreement. They may not answer. But it would rattle them, at the least.

Her father dropped something in the bathroom and swore loudly. "Nothing broken!" he yelled through the door.

"I'm on the phone," she shouted back. She was about to be. She called the number. It was still early, but someone in the press office of the Civic Gallery, South Bank, London, would answer. The phone was picked up by a young man with a tremulous voice. Shona introduced herself, and he did the same: his name was Nicolas.

"Hi, Nicolas, can I speak to your boss? The head of press?"

"External affairs?"

"Whatever you want to call it."

"I am afraid she is in a meeting right now. Can I help?"

"Can she call me if I leave a number?"

"She won't be able to today."

"That's some meeting she has," Shona said. "What's her name?"

"The head of external affairs, press and marketing?"

"Yes indeed, Nicolas."

"The head of press and marketing is currently unavailable," he said, suddenly robotic.

"What's her name?"

Someone was whispering on the line. It wasn't anyone in Shona's bedroom, and it wasn't her father. Someone in London was talking to this Nicolas.

"Erm. Can I ask you the nature of your query? Sorry—can you put the nature of your enquiry into an email and we will respond as soon as possible?" he said, quivering.

Shona shook her head. Out of the corner of her eye, her sodden dad slumped through the hall with a towel wrapped around him, bubbles still clinging to his hairy back. He was softly singing a Tony Bennett number to himself. Shona smiled.

"Is that possible?" the young man said.

"Are you reading from a cue card, Nicolas?"

"It's my second day here," he said, almost whispering. "I'm the intern."

"You sound like a hostage reading a prepared statement. Look, give me your email and I'll ping you some questions."

There was an audible sigh, breathed heavily down the line from London to Edinburgh. "Thank you very much, Sheena."

"One tip for nothing: get people's names right and you'll do all right. It's Shona. Shona Sandison."

"And how do I spell that?"

"I'll give you three guesses."

"Thank you."

"Nicolas—have a cup of coffee, read the papers, get some fresh air. Nothing's that important. I'll fire you my questions now. What's yer email?"

He spelled it out for her. "I will watch out for your message," Nicolas said, his voice less strained.

"Make sure you do," she said, and ended the call.

Her side ached, and she put a hand to it.

"Trouble at mill?" her father yelled from his room.

"Always. What's for breakfast?" she yelled back, opening her laptop.

An hour later, Shona slowly left the number twenty-one bus and walked through Edinburgh in the rain. She trudged down the stately wide boulevard of George Street, with its clothing stores and coffee shops. She turned into one, which was adjoined to a grand hotel. Her stick momentarily snagged on a carpet. Out of the rain, the coffee shop was dark and thick with coffee fumes and the slick scents of pastries. Men and women in suits huddled around small round tables. A shriek of steam burst from the coffee machine. There were shadows in the corners, and the light was pearly, diffuse. She stood in the queue, then noted with dismay that her colleague, Hector Stricken, was also in the queue. She was about to leave when he noticed her as he paid.

"Miss Sandison," he said. "Let me get you a coffee."

"Actually, I was just leaving."

"But you're only just here."

"Yeah, well, I saw you and thought, 'Fuck it.'"

"Nice. Latte with two sugars?"

Shona wondered if she had the energy to engage in conversation. She found herself nodding. "Go on, then. In a take-away cup."

"But I'm sitting in, Shona. Having some time to contemplate."

"Like a whelk."

"Exactly."

Shona smiled and stared at her phone and checked her emails, while Stricken, wearing the same anorak he always wore, with a ripped pocket, ordered. When the coffees came, she followed him to a table.

No emails, no replies.

"So," he said miserably.

"Aye, what," she said, sitting down.

"This 'digital transformation' at the paper—"

"A bucket of cold fucking spunk."

He laughed and looked at his coffee. "Not sure I want my cappuccino now."

Shona grinned.

"I am not sure what to make of it all," he said eventually.

Shona leaned forward, wiped brown foam from the edge of the plastic cup lid. "Look, Hec, they're fuckwits and they don't know what they're doing. We are the ones doing our jobs. They're the other guys."

"What I just don't get," Hector said, "is that the damn paper makes nine million a year for these stupid fuckers, and yet . . ."

"Sense doesn't come into it, Hector. They'll sack us, or make our lives so unbearable we will want to leave. We'll have to make our own choices. Not let these arseholes make them for us."

Stricken nodded. "What you working on?"

"This frickin' Love murder," she said, and shrugged.

"Of course. Nasty business. Poor fella," he said. "Was it a sex thing?"

Shona was incredulous. "No, Hector. It's some kind of robbery gone wrong. Something to do with money. That's when the murders get gruesome."

"Oh. I assumed it was a murder of passion."

"And what do you know about passion, Hector?"

He shrugged. "I've heard about it," he said, "as a concept. A rumour."

But Shona suddenly thought on it. It might explain why nothing was stolen. She had not asked Love's daughter about her father's ex-wives and current loves. She was annoyed with herself. "What you up to, anyway?" she said. She sipped her coffee. The café was filling up. Office workers escaping their computer screens. The windows were running with condensation.

"What, in between crushing bouts of existential angst?"

"Of course. That's a given."

"Yeah, well. I was looking at this film studio plan thing. Lots of digging in around Companies House, financial records and such. I'm not sure there's anything more to find out. Interesting story, though: it would have been Scotland's first major film studio. Good location, near enough to Edinburgh Airport, major roads. Land is owned by this development company, Oldmeg Reach. They were ready to go. They had recently bought more land, for an extension."

"Do we know any more about the Cullen murder?" she asked.

"Not a peep," he said, sipping. Froth was caught in bubble patches on his ginger stubble.

"Who's on it?"

"No one at the minute. Colm is sitting on it. It's an active case, no arrests, and that's about it. Someone's tried to rob the councillor in the bog and it's all gone sideways. That's my sense. He's fallen, slipped on piss or something, cracked

174 • PHILIP MILLER

his head, and the man's deid. The assailant has scarpered. It's a shame. Cullen was one of the good guys."

"Wasn't it his planning committee that nixed the studio?" she said.

He nodded. "It was. But anyone would have—the business case was paper-thin. And there was a sizeable patch of the land in the plan that didn't belong to them. They seem to have bought it now. There were all kinds of shenanigans going on. It really wasn't ready for planning permission. Not sure why they went for it. Impatience."

Shona pondered. Her hand moved over the pommel of her stick. Would a film studio knock off an awkward council official? Seems highly unlikely. Edinburgh wasn't overflowing with contract killers.

"Anyway so, there's no Hollywood on the Firth of Forth for the time being," Stricken said.

Shona looked at his face. It was long, with a straight nose, thin lips and receding hair. There were white flashes in the hair above his ears. He had large grey, watchful eyes and red stubble. There was something deer-like about him. "Tell me about this Oldmeg Beach," she said. She was down to the sugar in her coffee. It was sweet. The world suddenly seemed a sharper, brighter place.

"Reach," he said. He sat back in the chair and sighed. "Well, it's a development firm. A housing and commercial building firm. And it's part of this suite of companies that are essentially run for Lord Melrose. The list of directors is basically yer laird there, some other folks. It seems they have been trying to expand their investments. Diversify their portfolio. The family have a pile in the Borders, some existing property in Gloucestershire and a jam company. But they want to do more. So they've invested in this studio plan. Not that they intended to run it. They seem to have pots of money. They're behind half a dozen building developments in the Borders and the east of Scotland. Despite all of this, not sure there is anything in it. There's nothing I can hang a story on, that's for certain. One thing, though . . ."

"What thing?"

Stricken took out an opened, folded copy of the *Edinburgh Post* from his bag. He put it on the table.

"Yes, the paper we work for. So what?"

"No, this," he said, pointing at a large advert on page five.

The advert was for a housing development in East Lothian. Fifty new houses, blocky and bricked. It was a picture, an architect's painting: faceless people walked and played in the new streets. Faceless children played on swings. Gleaming cars sat in each driveway. OLDMEG REACH DEVELOPMENTS PRESENT NEWMEG BRAE the headline said.

"They've been buying a lot of advert and advertorial space in the paper for months now," Stricken said.

"So?"

"So, be canny. This new editor, he's a prick. Might explain why Colm is not that interested in Cullen."

"I don't give a fuck about that dick of an editor," Shona said. And she didn't.

"I don't, either—but just be careful. These arseholes, they'll ring the editor directly if you upset them, and he's so fucking spineless he'll come down on you, not them."

Shona shrugged. "Give us peace. What else you got?"

He reached into his satchel and brought out some dog-eared pieces of A4. "The list of directors," he said, "and I might get one of those pains au chocolat. Want one?"

"No, I'm allergic to chocolate."

"Who the hell is allergic to chocolate?" he asked, grinning, standing up.

"Special people," she said, looking through the papers.

"Special, right enough," he said, and walked to the till.

The papers had all been printed off the Companies House website and some other financial website she did not recognise.

Stricken was a good reporter, she conceded. He didn't file many stories—which, under the new regime would make him a target—but when he did, they were good, hard, exclusive.

According to the papers, Oldmeg Reach had two directors: Felix Farquharson and Olivia Farquharson. Oldmeg Reach was a subsidiary of another company, which appeared to have an office in Monaco, called Gododdin. That, according to one of the printouts, had four directors: the two Farquharsons, a David Ciseleur and a Katherine Pieters.

Stricken returned with a plain croissant and his pain au chocolat. He had already taken a bite of the latter, and a smear of brown was on his cheek.

"You eat like a fucking dog," Shona said.

"It's your constant charm and grace that I admire the most."

"I used to be a nihilist, but I realised there was no point."

"I don't understand," he said, sitting down.

"A joke, never mind," she said. She pointed to the piece of paper. "This Katherine Pieters: Do you know who she is?"

Stricken squinted and looked at the paper. "No idea," he said. "But the names are not uncommon."

"I know. Depends how you spell them. Can you see if there's any other companies with her as director? Can you see if she is on any boards? Ask any of your business pals if they have heard of her?"

"Slow down. Why?"

"As a favour."

He sat back and smiled.

"And can you get a number or email for her?" she added.

"I mean, why wouldn't I do all this work for you? You've always been such a lovely, supportive, sunny colleague, Shona. Ever since you appeared in that cloud of poison from Glasgow."

"Don't be a dick," she said. "It won't take you long. I'll tell Colm you've helped me out."

"Colm? He can get fucked," Stricken said abruptly.

Shona laughed. "Gododdin: What's that mean? Is that a person?" she said, pointing to it.

"I looked that up—it's some kind of old tribe, who lived hereabouts. I guess it appealed to Lord Melrose."

"This Ciseleur fellow?"

"I assume some French company secretary-type guy in Monaco. Not sure there's much on him."

"Look him up too, would you? As well as all the Pieters stuff?" she asked, standing up.

"Is it a name that means something?"

"Maybe. Maybe not," she said, "but you have to pull every loose thread, don't you? One loose thread unravels the whole jumper."

He smiled. "Such worldly wisdom in one so young."

"Ach. One of my dad's sayings," she said, and smiled. She took the croissant from the plate and bit into it. It was warm and buttery.

"Well, your old man would know, Shona. By the way, I bought that bun for myself."

"All property is theft," she said, and walked out of the café into the hissing rain.

20

Tallis had slept in, and then walked on Portobello beach. He could not face going to work. The thought of sitting in his office made his mind run cold. The day was dull, rolls of clouds stacked across the sky. The sea was lead, the sand damp brown. He sat on the smooth concrete lip of the esplanade. His mind flashed to the conservation room, to the flap of flesh and muscle in the box. The blood on his fingers.

Someone had talked with that. Someone had eaten, and kissed, and loved with that tongue, and now it had spoken again: some kind of warning to him, some kind of threat.

His phone rang. An anonymous number. It might be Astrella, he thought.

"Tallis," Melcombe said.

"Hi," Tallis said, as neutrally as he could.

"You on the train down?"

No, he thought. I am not. "Afraid not," he said, as blithely as he could. "I have still got a few meetings. Meet people. See a few documents. There's some in Glasgow. Some documents at Glasgow School of Art. I need to see them."

"Why? Just have them sent to you. Email exists," Melcombe said. "You're not on holiday. In the normal run of things you'd be done by now. You need to be here. I have other work for you. You're not helping me at all being up there."

The sea collapsed silently on the beach. Tallis wondered what to say or do. He did not want to engage with this man, or his job. Or anything.

"The line's dead. For God's sake. Tallis?"

"Still here, distracted by an email there, sorry."

"I need an answer from you, Tallis. When are you wrapping up?"

"I need to see the painting. I haven't. And I need to see the documents in Glasgow. None of those have happened yet. There's been delays. I'm staying with my aunt, as you know. None of this little extra time is costing the department."

There was a silence. He could dimly hear Melcombe clicking and unclicking a pen. "We need to have a chat," Melcombe said quietly, as if through his teeth.

"We just did. I'll be back in touch," Tallis said.

He ended the call. He slid off the concrete and walked on the sand. It was cold as his feet sunk into the damp beach. That morning, in bed, he had sent a text to Astrella. A neutral message, asking her how her tour was going. No response. It occurred to him that she might have texted the wrong person.

The night before, tired and with three glasses of Zed's red wine in his belly, he had looked her up on the internet. He had watched a video of Astrella Nemours playing at the Proms. She was playing Grieg's *Piano Concerto*, beautifully. The conductor applauded her afterwards, the BBC commentator purring. So accomplished, so good.

He looked around, after a time. The sea still churning, a large white car parked on the esplanade by the café.

Tallis picked the phone from his pocket and called Mungo to say he was working from home for the day. Mungo laughed. The white car had moved. Tallis walked back to Zed's house and, on the sofa, slept for most of the day.

He dreamt of *The Goldenacre*, held underwater by

clinging hands. After several hours of deep sleep, Tallis, fugged and slow, found a bottle of wine by the sink with a cork cockeyed in its mouth. It was half-full. He pulled out the cork and began to drink it.

He heard a buzzing noise, and a rattle. A burr in the air. He realised it was his phone. It was sliding with vibration along the kitchen table. He took a large swig and picked up the handset. He hoped it was Astrella. It was an international number of some kind.

He steadied his voice and answered. "Thomas Tallis."

"Thomas," a faraway, familiar voice said.

"Hello?"

"It's Celia," the voice said, becoming clearer, shedding digital fronds.

He only knew one Celia: Celia Newton. His former boss at the Civic Gallery. His heart was suddenly pounding. "Hello, Celia," he said.

"I know we are not meant to be talking." She sounded the same as she always had—a flat Midlands accent, with an edge. Red lips.

"No, I know," he said. "How are you?"

"Look, this is going to be a short call."

"Where are you?"

"Berlin, as you know. Didn't your father tell you?"

Strings pulled—strings bound into ligatures—strings wrapped around arms and legs, and jerked. "You don't know that for sure," he lied.

"Look, here it is: someone is digging around at the Civic. Some journalist. She's been asking questions. She somehow knows that we signed NDAs. So, there's that."

Tallis put his hand over his face. "Fucking. Great."

"Not sure if the Civic have given her anything. Luckily my director here knows it wasn't my fucking fault. I'm fine. But watch out for yourself. Someone knows something. Maybe they know how you got your present employment."

Tallis gulped. He wanted to drink ten bottles immediately. Or take something sharp and open his neck into the sink. "So, how is Berlin?" he said weakly.

"It's fine. Where are you?"

"Edinburgh. A job at the Public Gallery. For the government."

She laughed with a short, choking noise. "Nice—another job allocation by your father?"

"I have no idea."

"You should. I won't call again and don't call me. Be careful."

The phone call came to an end. He sat silently for a while, shame and disgrace washing over him. The sound of her voice had set his heart thumping and his mind awry. So he had to lose it. Tallis steadily drank the rest of the wine. He found a third-full bottle of whisky. He drank a couple of thick glasses. He found a tub of ice cream in Zed's freezer. He slowly ate it and finished the whisky.

He was now drunk, and had a shower. He banged his elbow on the wall. He stood in the hot torrent, pulling the pale shower curtain against his face. He imagined the other side, his featureless face screaming out from a blank sheet.

Tallis dressed and made himself an absurdly strong coffee. He left the house and, as the door shut, he realised he had left without his keys: Zed would be back later. It was fine. He walked as straight as he could in the direction of the bus stop. Children milled about the lane, holding balloons and small party bags. The balloons bobbed and thudded like decapitations.

Theseus Campbell lived with his family in an apartment in the New Town, the square mile or so of grand and elegant Georgian flats and houses at the centre of Edinburgh. The bus wheezed into town. Tallis glimpsed at the sea as the bus left the shore and headed inland, the water grey as stone, the sea deep and forgetful, clean and cold and forgiving.

The tone of Celia's voice still cut; it was hard and harsh. He nodded as the bus wound its way around Calton Hill—he deserved it. He deserved all of it. He could not endure it.

He could see, as the bus passed, the large tent that had been raised atop Calton Hill. The stone monument unfinished—the tent completed its width and length. Lights of mauve and purple, yellow and green, swirled inside. There were flashes and sudden booms of bass. In the trees, he could see people with the faces of beasts, swarming.

Tallis left the bus at Princes Street and walked north, in the direction of the New Town. Using the map on his phone, he found the street. It was in the crescent of a public square, with a gated garden at the centre: public and private delineated by iron. Trees stood stark against the sodium light.

He realised he had not brought any gift: no drink, no flowers. But he was already pressing the buzzer marked CAMP-BELL/ASH when he did so.

"Welcome!" Theseus's voice boomed from the speaker set in the sandstone wall of the building.

The door opened and Tallis pushed it. He was in a well-lit hallway, with a wide staircase rising. There were sweet-smelling flowers in large vases and a swirling carpet that was deep and rich.

"Come up," Theseus said, somewhere from above.

Tallis rubbed his face and walked to the bottom of the staircase.

Theseus's head appeared over the balustrade, a floor up. "Food is ready on *le premier étage*, Monsieur Tallis. Children are safely fed and watered and on their pads. Niamh cannot wait to meet you. Come up!" Theseus bellowed.

"I'll be honest," Tallis said, as honestly as he could. "I've had a drink already."

"Great! I'll have to catch up," Theseus yelled.

Tallis ascended the stairs to a large apartment. The living room had three sofas and many paintings. Next to a lit fire were two children, a girl and a boy, lying in pyjamas with electronic tablets lit and fizzing. They both had curling black hair. They looked up and smiled and then returned to their bleeping digital worlds.

A beautiful woman entered the room. "You must be Thomas," she said, holding out a hand.

Tallis stared at her face. It seemed, at that moment, it was the loveliest face he had ever witnessed. "That is me," he said.

"Ha-ha. Our friend Thomas has already begun his party," Theseus said.

"Excellent. Would you like more to drink?" Niamh said. It seemed she had an aura of snowy light about her.

"I would like more," Tallis said.

He sat down on a soft sofa. There was a large, icy, abstract painting over the fire. Above hung a chandelier in black and red glass. He tipped back his head to see it. His mouth hung open for a while. The glass glimmered and loomed. Fractals of tinselly rainbow frazzled.

"Isn't it beautiful?" Niamh said, handing him a glass of pink wine.

"Yes, yes," he said. "It's like a kind of heaven."

"It's so heavy. We had to reinforce the ceiling."

"Heavy," Tallis said. "It looks like an evil octopus. Leviathan. It looks like Cthulhu."

"We bought it in Murano," Theseus said. "Fifteen thousand. They shipped it over here in pieces and we had to put it together. Little hooks and chains. A massive project."

"I did most of it," Niamh said.

"True, true," Theseus said. "And so well, with your surgeon fingers."

Tallis looked into the large eye of his wine. Light swirled in globes and spheres. It was smeared around the thin walls of the glass; it refracted and spun across his face. His stomach decided to spasm. "Excuse me," he said, briskly. He staggered into the first corridor he could see.

"Second on the right, down the hall," Theseus yelled.

Tallis walked quickly to the second door and opened it. It was a large white bathroom. He closed the door with a kick and half-fell, half-ran to the toilet. After a short wracking retch, vomit shot from his mouth, through the sieve of his teeth, and in a greasy pink arc into the bowl. It seemed he was there for a while. He retched. And retched again. He knew he had made a terrible noise. He sat up on his knees. He found the toilet paper in the grim bright light and, shaking, wiped the vomit from the seat and the surrounds. He had vomited worse than this. This was just slippery remnants of whisky, ice cream and red wine. He looked down—his final lurch to the tiled floor had saved his clothes from the mess. His knees ached and he had bruised something in his side.

He sat for a while. The bathroom was immaculate. There were yellow and red plastic bath toys neatly stacked in a wicker basket. He was still drunk, but purged of any urgent illness.

Theseus came into the room, and sat on the edge of the bath. He was huge, and wearing brown slippers. "You ready for some food now?"

"I'm so sorry," Tallis said.

"You are forgiven already." Theseus gently tapped his knee with a large hand.

"I'm mortified," Tallis said, shaking his head.

"Niamh has seen far worse. She's a brain surgeon."

"Of course, she is."

"The kids are in their bedroom, if not in bed. They didn't hear a thing. Now come and replenish, young man."

They both stood up.

Tallis suddenly had the urge to call Celia back. He knew he wouldn't. And couldn't.

In a dark green dining room, with a large window looking out over Edinburgh Castle, Niamh was putting a salad bowl on a long brown table. There were candles in black glass, and prints on the wall. Tallis looked out over the city.

"It's a lovely view," Niamh said.

"A beautiful view," Tallis murmured.

"It's what made us fall in love with the flat."

"But my! Edinburgh is so expensive. It is a place where so few can reasonably live," Theseus said, shaking his head, opening another bottle of wine. It was gripped between his thighs, and he was yanking at the cork in a surprising amateur fashion. "God damn it all," he said. "This is why I drink beer."

Tallis looked out over the dark sea of shadow, the distant castle, all fuzzed and blurred with a shoal of yellow lights. The moon was full, and bright. "Views like this make you feel life isn't all bad," he said. "Not just a cycling carnival of pain."

"It's deceptive," Niamh said. "Fish?"

They sat and ate white fish and, heavy-headed as he was, Tallis felt almost sharp again. But he drank more wine. After the first course, he excused himself again.

"No loud noises now," Theseus said, chuckling. "Enough of your circus animals."

"Theseus," Niamh said.

Tallis laughed and held up a hand, as if asking for forgiveness. In the bathroom he locked the door and looked at himself in the mirror. His eyes were bloodshot, and his stubble was becoming a beard. Wild hairs were askew on his lower lip. His hair was too long and greasy. He was middle-aged and sad, and it wasn't attractive. "Fuck sake," he said. He pissed at length, then looked in the medicine cabinet. There was paracetamol, co-codamol, child's cough mixture and Calpol. There were iron tablets in a pink box, and a course of anti-depressants, with another box unopened. There was codeine and a painkiller, in what looked like US packaging, which he had not seen before. He drank some cough mixture, took some codeine and co-codamol, and picked up the American painkillers and put them in his pocket.

He exited the bathroom like a cat.

At the table there were three bowls of thick chocolate mousse. He rejoined Theseus and Niamh and they spoke of art and the art world, and he felt as if he was drifting above the conversation, adding funny puns and quips here and there, then drifting into another, more painless plane, all feeling and no thinking, and Theseus was laughing at or with him, and Niamh, so beautiful, like a dream of a perfect human being, looking at him in amusement or bemusement, and when they went to clear the table and make coffee he swallowed a few of the pills and washed them down with wine, and the lights outside flared and fizzed and whispered gorgeous things to his ears. He drank his coffee quickly and the furniture seemed to float, and Niamh said she was tired but delighted to meet him and he smiled back hoping she would say something else and Theseus theatrically yawned and said, "Do you mind, old man, if I don't come with you to the Summoning?" and Tallis said no, don't worry about it. Theseus said something about Tallis giving him a full review on Monday, and Tallis said yes, of course.

He said goodbye to them at the door, whispering loudly so as not to wake the children, and he gave Theseus a hug and he was a large grand beautiful man, and he kissed Niamh on the cheek and it was like kissing magical celestial flesh and her scent was all open roses and clean skin and open sky, and he wanted to drink it all in, and soon he was down the stairs and, for some reason, jogging along an empty street.

The cold air smacked his face and everything began to slow down. Everything was falling into divisions and circles, into divided worlds, into light and darkness, seen and unseen, real and unreal. He wondered how many pills he had taken, and a tiny faint rational voice asked how many units he had drunk, but then he couldn't count and soon he was running as fast as he could, pounding down the streets, past black railings and closed banks and open pubs, past the lit-up

Balmoral Hotel, gargoyle-ugly and soaked in fluorescence, full of wankers, and up ahead he could see Calton Hill, blazing with light. The monument was newly illuminated and its columns were decorated with strings of lights that flashed in rhythmic patterns, and its pediment had writing in ancient languages projected on its cold stones, and the faces of animals—fox and badger, deer and hound, eagle and owl and cat—circled around and about.

Tallis slowed, out of breath. He had run up the steep hill and a needling stitch cut into his side. There were people all about, moving in the darkness and the strobing light. People laughing and checking tickets, their faces flashing with mobile phone lights, with the sudden flare of matches, with the light from the monument changing their faces and eyes into red and blue, orange and green.

The large tent had a door in its side, and music was threading its way from inside to outside. Tallis bent over and caught his breath. He turned around and breathed deeply. He was at the top of Edinburgh, looking down over the city. The city was a sea of lights undulating amid darkness. The music from the Summoning was louder now, more intense, drums beginning to be struck, beginning to pound. It throbbed and pulsed and shook.

The pain in his side lessened to an ache and he moved unsteadily to the door. He could see that inside the tent there were many people, hundreds of people, silhouetted against lights, moving to the music. Tallis's mouth was all alcohol, and his mind was both numb and jagged. His back was wet. He put a hand to it, and in the changing lights the moisture on his fingers went from blood to water to plasma to slime and back to sweat. He was now in a messy, loud, busy queue for the door, and, at the entrance, two people with stag faces were giving out masks. Foxes and mice and deer and dogs and eagles entered the flashing door of the tent.

Tallis tried to find his phone in his pocket. He took it

out and dropped it. He knelt down in the flashing darkness: there was wet grass on his hands, and a forest of feet and legs about him. He found his phone and stood up relieved and elated, as if he'd saved a life. Suddenly there was a space before him, and he moved into it, closer to the door of light, where the couple in front of him were being given masks. The stag-faced people were asking the two women what their birthdays were, and they answered, and were given an insect and a wolf. The masks were expertly made and their eyes were not cut out, but somehow fashioned from glass or plastic and they bulged and looked and searched and stared, and the hairs on the masks looked real, the scales looked real, and the two stags approached him—they towered over him—two men or women in black, the antlers spread across the night, and they asked his birth date and he told them, 7 October, and they looked down into the night and drew from the strobing light a cat face and, as the stag handed it to him, he seemed to say, "Drowned kitten."

Forward, masked, he moved, into the light.

Tallis looked through the eye holes, glazed with red and blue, the elastic strap tight and sharp on the back of his head, and stood to the side straightaway and put his back to the warm tent wall. The tent was huge and filled with throbbing music and chanting voices. In the centre of the crowd was a circle marked by unmoving people in masks and, in the centre, Vorn, in pale clothes, head shaven, was chanting into a loud-hailer, and there was a golden light on the floor, some kind of screen, or some kind of fire. Vorn was chanting and dancing, hopping and leaping and singing.

Everyone in the tent seemed to have a glass in hand, small green glasses, and were shaking their shoulders and heads to the throb of the music and the rhythm of the chanting, and they were beginning to move as one. The people were all one, one ripple of felt music and insistent chanting. Moving up and down, like a wave, like the pulsing forces behind waves, in sequence and harmony and then out and up, up and down, all newly faced, all new fierce animal spirits moving about the central fire.

A small person with a mole face came to Tallis with a tray of glasses and handed one to him. A small plastic glass with green drink in it. He put it to his face and it smelled alcoholic and very strong and he wondered if it was absinthe, and in his other hand the mole had given him some kind of printed warning or advice, but in the shuddering darkness and light he could not read the writing, and he tipped the glass as he lifted his mask and most of the liquid dribbled into his hot, whisky-clogged mouth, and it burned and lingered and, Tallis dimly thought, yes, this is absinthe.

And he dropped the glass and felt for his pocket, as he nodded his head to the insistent beat, nodding to the throb of the pounding bass, and Vorn chanting over and over, some kind of incantation, some kind of spell or summoning, with the crowd rising as one and falling as one. He found the remaining pills and dropped one or two, skittling through his fingers, and put the rest in his mouth and crunched and they were sour and chalky but he licked crumbs around his gums and his teeth and they dissolved.

He was leaning now, hands free, against the tent as it filled with animals, and in the lights and darkness there were angry kingfishers and obsessive owls, eyes burning and turning, and the predator teeth of foxes and wolves, and dog eyes and cat eyes and the beaks of birds and lizards and the ears of cats and the striped masks of badgers and the many eyes of peacocks with their eyes and deadly beaks, and at the centre was the golden light, and Vorn chanting and moving about the circle like a planet orbiting the sun.

The music began to ripple and change and the audience and the animals began to clap and whoop and howl and a great melody rose from many pianos, many keyboards being struck and caressed, and four large screens suddenly illuminated on each wall, and on them Vorn was playing the gorgeous melody that rose and fell and drew into itself a countermelody that took a wrenching minor key, and the audience put their hands in the air as the beat hardened and quickened. Tallis had his hands in the air, too, as he bobbed up and down to the beat and the music, and he put his cat head forward, he stood on his cat toes as he tried to hear what she was chanting, but her words were fuzzed and distorted as she moved around and around the golden light.

The drink and the pills swum gasping around his thick and muddled head and Tallis felt a lurching and a pull, as if at sea, as if being dragged out to sea, and his body was light as driftwood, light as a twig in a flood, dragged to the current, as the music rose and fell. And on the big screens were fields and cliffs, streets and squares, towers and shopping malls, each flipping from one to the other, to and fro from place to place, from space to space, as the beat drove on and the chant chanted on, as Vorn sung and played and the audience cheered in waves.

And then the sound dropped and the audience dropped, and on the four screens there was Tallis—there he was, himself—walking into focus, walking into view from mist and fog, walking all in black, his face enormous, his face filling the screens as he walked in mist on an empty beach.

And the crowd whooped and cheered as the beat drove on, and Vorn's chanting drew on, and Vorn moved faster and faster around the golden light, the light flashing and sparking between the dark of her body and the dark of the bodies all about.

Tallis had stopped moving and he was holding on to the animals beside him, his fingers gripping and stressing, his eyes filled with himself, with the man on the screen, dead-eyed, drifting from the mist to full focus, and he backed up, and he began to move backward, and he turned and saw a field of eyes between him and the escape, because between where he stood in panic and the door to the open air was a field of animal souls, all staring at him. Foxes and wolves and dogs and hawks, each illuminated, each flashing and spinning, and their arms and claws and pads and nails in the air, eyes glinting and firing into the throbbing darkness.

And he ducked his head and tensed his shoulders and straightened his arms and pushed into them, but they would not move, they were solid and real and hard, and his furry cat face struck the fox before him, and the fox removed his mask and it was Carver, who bared his flashing spiky teeth and his red solid eyes, and hissed and bit and spat, and Tallis yelped and dove to the ground, and between every leg, which stood like trees at midnight in a midnight wood, were more faces, of animals he knew and beasts he did not know, and they hissed and shrieked and he moved back, running back into the woods, back past bark and branch, to the centre of the fire in the clearing in the dark and enclosing woods, and all around the million eyes of the wild stared into the clearing, but at the fire in the centre sat Vorn, and Vorn was dressed in rags and furs, and she held out hands and arms to Tallis. And fast through the trees came bounding the fox, the Carver-face, teeth bared, foam streaking from its killing face, and behind Carver-fox was a white wolf, with short white hair, with dark blood around its butcher's mouth, and dark blood on its ripping claws.

And out of the woods a dark purple tongue leaped and licked around the trees and the trunks and the branches, searching and finding, its slippery tip probing and slurping between wood and earth and rock, and Tallis leapt back, to the safety of the fire in the woods and the small tender frightened humans in the endless forest, and he fell back, through Vorn's arms, through the grip, over and over, tumbling and turning into the burning flames.

And into the flames, white and red and blazing, he fell, and down through a frame into a copper urban field, a cool metallic field between tall stone buildings, with moonlight on the slate roofs, and a straight road, and people around and about, sitting in the grass with trousers and caps and jackets, and long dresses and parasols, and gold all about.

And he was in cool grass, cold wet grass, glowing with light from the sun and the moon, and the lights of the dream city, and by his eye, just by the side glimmer of his eyes, as they closed, wet and cold in the golden acre, yellow with warmth and light and dew on his cheeks, there was a single robin, red-breasted, sitting perfect and tiny on a single budded twig, and it breathed and shook its feathers and sweetly piped a sweet, nameless melody.

21

Shona was with her father on the allotment when her phone buzzed in her pocket. She ignored it, and it shook in her pocket for a while and then stopped.

The allotment was cold and smelled of mulch and earth. It had rained the night before and the soil was wet and muddy in the hollows, and her father was digging a deep hole for some reason, his hairy hands muddy and glimmering with wet. He was kneeling, wearing filthy waterproof trousers and old wellies, his frown deepening, but happy.

Shona sat in his chair, in a bundled coat, drinking hot, sweet tea and watching the trees shake, and the clouds in vast ragged formations pass over the city.

The phone buzzed again—a voicemail. Who could be calling her on a Saturday morning? Work: potentially. A wrong number: quite likely. A crank call: possibly. A friend: unlikely. A spam call: most likely. She fished out her phone with a sigh.

"Don't answer it, love," her father said, digging.

"Too late."

"It's the weekend."

"Every day is a news day."

"And on the sixth day," he said, looking up from his work, a smear of mud across his hairy cheek, "they rested."

She checked the number, but it was withheld. Either spam or work. "Rightio," she said, and put the handset to her ear and listened to the message.

"Hi Shona. Sorry to bother you. Hector here," the voice said.

"Oh, Christ alive," Shona said. Her father shook his head and went back to attacking the earth.

"Sorry to call on a Saturday, and I guess your phone is either off or you are hungover or asleep or with your pa—"

She rolled her eyes. "Get fucking on with it."

"And anyway. I have to work, so there you go. Did a bit of a dig on your woman, that Ms. Pieters, as you asked. Turns out yes, she is a listed director, of a few other companies. All of them part of Gododdin, or in some kind of strange shell-relationship with Gododdin—I will explain shell companies to you one day when you have the patience—and seem to be connected to the Melrose family. She's a director of their jam and honey firm. Now, on one of the oldest companies, there's more detail. There's an address: there's no more details in the others. So it's an address in London, a place in Chelsea—nice. Believable. So I looked it up and . . . the address doesn't exist. It's a street called Gododdin Street. Total made-up place. Thought it sounds quite posh when you say it like that."

"So?" Shona said.

"And, of course, the Gododdin should be a giveaway. Anyway: false address and not a mistake either, or a misprint. Just made up. And, most interestingly, she is listed at that address with another person, a Catherine Peters. Same name, basically. What's the chances of a Katherine Pieters or a Catherine Peters in the same imaginary apartment? Zero. Anyway, winding back a bit. There is a company number for the jam firm. Quite a well-known brand, after all. So, I called it late yesterday, a man with a Geordie accent answered, and I said I want to speak to Ms. Peters, and he said leave a message and number and she'll get back to you. So I left my number and maybe we can meet. I'm still not sure why you want to speak to this woman. Maybe you can tell me, secret squirrel. There's more to this, I venture, but it might take a bit of digging. See you Monday. I've got the top prize this week: I am on a Sunday shift. Bye. Bye-bye."

Shona closed the call. The sun was now high and warm on her neck and arms.

"What was that all about?" her father said, not looking at her, but filling in the hole again. A single fat worm slowly writhed on the turned mud.

"A story I'm working on. I'm not sure where it's going. There's some kind of financial thing going on, and I don't quite understand it. Filthy lucre. Hector might work it out, though. Maybe we will work it out together."

"Hector might, he's a bright boy," her father said, nodding. "But I am sure you'll work it out. So is there something new? Some new information? Is this the Cullen murder?"

"No, that's all gone quiet for now," she said. "Funeral is probably next week, suspect we'll send someone along to get all the misery and heartbreak. Ask his wife and kids how sad they are. The usual."

"Aye, the 'how devastated are you?' quotes," Hugh said, flattening down the earth. "Poor wee John Cullen, he was one of the good ones. Head staved in, I heard. Nasty business."

Shona peered at her father. "How do you know he had his head staved in?"

"I still have my contacts and conversations." He grinned. "You're not the only ace reporter in the family." Kneeling in the wet soil, his face muddy, his thin hair under a heavy woollen cap and his beard bristling, he looked medieval.

"So, what did you hear?"

"I heard," he said, standing up slowly, levering himself with a dirty hand on a knee, "that it's all not quite as the polis quite said it was. It wasn't some mugging gone wrong. Cullen's head was panned in, I heard. Messy and violent."

"Head panned in?"

"Aye, like I just said. I need a coffee, and it sounds like you need one too. Would you be my darling and put the kettle on?" he said, pointing to the shed.

"Robert Love had his head 'panned in' too," she said, standing and moving to the shed.

"Two burst heids in a week," her dad said. "It's all a mucky business, my sweetness."

Shona clicked on the kettle, and something in her brain clicked. On the small black kettle, a red light came on. After a short while, the water began to boil angrily. "Fuck," she said.

"No need for that, Shona Rose Sandison," her father chirped from outside.

"I think I need to call Stricken back." The plastic shell of the kettle was shaking and shooting out steam. Shona bit her lip and looked for Stricken's number.

"It's your day off," her father said. He was washing his hands under the metal tap outside. "And I'm cooking tonight."

"I've had enough chilli con carne this week," she said.

"Impossible." He wiped his hands on his dirty trousers.

Shona phoned Stricken, but it rang and rang then went to voicemail. She rang the newsdesk at the *Post*. It rang for a while—the paper was being put together by a skeleton crew, and it was likely Stricken was the only reporter on duty.

"*Post*?" a voice said quickly.

"I'm looking for Stricken."

"Hi, Shona. How nice to hear your voice. He's away."

"Away? He's on duty."

"I know," the tired production editor, Taylor, said, "but he's out on a job. I'm guessing."

"Where to?"

"Your guess is as good as mine. Why don't you call him?

He's taken the pool car, so I guess it's farther than a walk. There's not much doing today so maybe he's just gone to the shops."

"Unlikely. He doesn't shop. Any idea at all where he is? I need to speak to him about a tale."

"Jesus," he said, "no, I don't. How would I know? Lemme look at his desk."

"Don't exert yourself too much," Shona said. She noticed her heart was beating faster.

"Jesus Christ, Shona, I've fourteen pages to fill, no ads and only one story. The only thing we got is the big fire in Glasgow—that's it. Why don't you come in and file some copy yerself. Wait a second."

The receiver was plonked down on a desk. Shona could hear Taylor stomping through the office. Other phones were ringing. A TV clearly had football on.

"Come on, come on," she said.

The handset was picked up again.

"What big fire in Glasgow?" she said.

"Art school burned down again," her father said, from the garden.

"Jesus, Shona, do you watch the news? Fire at the art school. Last night. I guess that's the splash. The Mackintosh Building is a ruin. Burned to the ground. No deaths, thankfully. But a disaster."

"Jeez," she said, "that's two fires there now."

"Yes—fancy writing a spread and an analysis piece by five P.M. on it?"

"No. It's in Glasgow, anyway, so no one east of Lenzie gives a fuck. Anything on Stricken's desk?"

"The usual jungle of shite. A Post-it note I left earlier. Some guy called for him. All a bit vague. So, nothing new."

"What was the message? We're working on the same story, Taylor. Was there a meeting planned or something?"

"He just left an address—there's not much detail: Oldmeg

Developments. I think that's one of those new housing developments out in East Lothian. Not sure that's enough of a story for our brave man Stricken to get his teeth into. As I said, he's probably off to the Gyle to buy some new waterproofs."

"Taylor—thanks," she said, and closed the call. While her dad whistled in the newly warm sun outside, she searched the internet on her phone for Oldmeg Developments.

"Aye, the art school, it's a rum do, I tell you that," her father said.

"Oldmeg. Here it is. Yep, it's a new housing development in East Lothian."

"They're throwing them up down there," Hugh said. "Edinburgh's population is expanding and will be bigger than Glasgow by—"

"Fascinating facts, Dad," she said sharply, staring at her phone. She called Stricken again, but again it went to voicemail. She looked at an online map: Oldmeg was off a new road, on a large plot of land—the nearest town was Haddington. She couldn't drive, and there was no train station.

She waited a moment.

"Dad?"

"Sorry, I'm sitting in the sun drinking coffee, being snapped at by my daughter. I'm busy."

"Like you never snapped at me. Can you do me a favour?"

"Well, I don't know."

She stood up, moved over to him and put a hand on his shoulder. "Sorry."

He supped his coffee.

"Can you drive me somewhere?"

He sighed and wiped a dirty hand on his face. He looked up at her, unhappy. "Really?"

"Really."

"What do I get?" he said, standing up, searching for his allotment shed key.

"I'll cook tonight."

He peered at her and leaned forward with his head tilted, as if she was talking in a different language. "Let's not make ridiculous promises," he said, and gently tapped her elbow.

They left the allotments and found her father's small car parked nearby. It was a blue Japanese model, with an automatic gearbox. Her dad used it to beetle to the shops and back, sometimes out to the beaches on the east coast, but his specific aversion to motorways and his general aversion to being anywhere but their flat or in his allotment meant it was little used, and thus was, for Hugh Sandison, fairly clean.

"Where to?" he said wearily.

She told her mobile where they were heading and the map started intoning orders with a flat voice.

"Oh, give us peace," her dad said to the disembodied voice, as they turned the car around and headed east.

The route took them through the elegant shore area of Leith, past the old docks, past Portobello and out onto the A-road, buzzing past car shops and storage yards. The radio news was all about the Mackintosh Building fire, and how it could have happened.

"Someone—somewhere—has well and truly fucked that up," her father said.

"True, true," Shona said, but she was distracted.

"I mean, it was a building site. Those are hazardous places. I doubt it was arson. But there's been a lot of fires in Glasgow recently. It's a rum do, as I say. Beautiful building. All gone. Ashes now. Lost forever."

Shona's mind was occupied. If Stricken was seeing Katherine Pieters, or Peters . . . She was the art collector. She was also something to do with the film studio plan. So, this woman knew both Robert Love and Councillor Cullen. Shona wanted to know what commission she had given Love. And how she felt about both Love and Cullen being killed.

Shona called Stricken on his phone again, but there was no answer.

Finally, the voice from the phone said they had reached their destination.

"Oh really?" Hugh said. They drove on, past a thick stand of trees. No sign of any houses. Farther down the straight road, a new road took off to the right. It led to an estate of blocky new houses, sitting alone in a plain of mud, with three large yellow earthmovers parked at the fringes. The landscape was open, stretching to a distant wood. The houses, more than a hundred, were standing in semicircles, roadless, as if they'd been dropped into the mud from above. They were unfinished, half-built, plastic hanging where their doors should be. They looked both new and grubby in their muddy paddock. There was no glass in the windows, which gaped. New saplings stood limp in metal cages. A forlorn playground was half-built, with a children's slide with no steps.

Shona texted Stricken—*Where are you?*—but the message would not send.

They turned off the main road and drove down the new road until the tarmac came to an end, and mud and stones and Caterpillar tracks began. Hugh switched off the car's engine; it was windy now, and Shona could hear plastic snapping in the air, but no other sounds. Other vehicles were parked.

"That must be your man's car," Hugh said, pointing at an old green Audi parked up on a verge. On the other side of the track was a large, gleaming white four-by-four.

They sat for a second. The field of mud lay dead.

"Wait here, Dad," Shona said, grabbing her stick.

"You be careful," he said, looking to her with large eyes.

"I'm fine."

"Sure thing, love." He looked away, nodding.

Shona got out of the car, and into the deep silence. The

houses stood cold and empty. They were blocky and bricked, with sloping roofs. There was a glossy sign by the entrance to the estate: *Old Meg's Copse, Deluxe Homes and Apartments*. Shona walked lopsided in the mud to Stricken's car, her wounded leg slipping. She put her hand on the engine. It was cool. There was no sound from the houses, just wind snapping through vacancy and plastic. She walked on, using her stick carefully in the uncertain mud. She was in amongst the new estate. The nearest building was a show house. It was closed and dark inside. She looked through the window—no one was there, just gleaming new furniture and a desk and phone. An ideal for living, with no one living.

She moved across the wasteland to the next house. Inside, the floor was blue boards, stapled down. She stepped into the dark building. Wires hung from unfinished ceilings. The wind whipped through loose fastenings. It caught the serrated edges of board and tarpaulin, whistling and moaning. A lamp hung from a thick black flex, unlit.

"Hector?" she shouted.

Her voice sounded empty, deadened by the wooden boards and new walls. She moved through the hall, to the back of the house. It looked out over the endless mud, the piles of bricks and large blue pipes coiling on the ground like guts sliding from a slit belly. Tarpaulins covered large supplies in bags and on wooden pallets. Bricks stood in neat piles. Three metal sinks lay side by side.

The houses stood quiet. She looked back, and her dad's head could be seen in his car. The wind blew her hair in front of her eyes. There was no one about.

She left the house and went to the central area of mud, a green yet to be seeded. Her feet were wet and clagged now, and her stick was clogged, slaked with wet earth and sand. She looked around at all the houses. There was nothing but emptiness, and the houses' four-square blockiness.

"Hector," she yelled as hard as she could. The wind took

her voice and slung it across the empty fields, the copse, the ripped plastic snapping. All the empty windows glaring. The wind whining.

A man quickly moved from one house to another. A huge man in black. He ran from a shadow, to another shadow, and then became one himself.

"Hey," she found herself shouting. She moved towards the house he had run into. But with a slap and thump, she lost her balance, slipped on the mud and fell flat on her behind with a clump. Her stick slid away from her hand.

"Fuck."

She heard a heavy crashing noise, as if a wall was being smashed. She reached for her stick, grabbed it and got up, her back and legs covered in slick mud and clumps of sand and grit. Her hair was all about her face. Limping, she made for the house. There was no door fixed, just a gap in bricks.

"Shona!" a voice yelped, from somewhere up above her. She looked up, and only saw the sky, shreds of cloud sliding by the unfinished roof. There was another crash. Shona's heart beat hard. Her mouth was dry. She gripped her stick hard and raised it, holding it over her shoulder, like a club.

Another crack and crashing noise came from inside the house.

"What's going on here, then!" a man shouted from behind her in a high, quavering voice. It was her father. He was standing in the mud, holding a shovel in his hands.

"Dad! What the fuck!" she yelled, her voice breaking.

"Shona!" a man shouted, as if from behind a wall, or trapped. There was a great clamour and the bashing of heavy boots. Calamity.

"What the hell is going on here, then!" her father yelled, in an unearthly voice. He had his eyes closed, was yelling into the mud and wind.

A large dark solid shape burst past Shona in a tumble of limbs and brutish force. She was suddenly bowled to the ground, back into the mud. Flat on her back, flailing, the sky wheeling. The man ran through the vacant estate, his boots heavy, splashing hard in the mud. Shona rolled onto her side. The large man, grey-haired, ran straight past her gesticulating dad, as if he wasn't there. The man held something small and hard in his hand. Her dad turned as he ran past, yelling at him.

"Dad," she shouted. She wanted him to stop. She desperately didn't want the man to come back and attack him. But he ran on, and out of sight behind the show house. Lying in the mud, she could see Stricken's face in the upstairs window of the house. Pale and frightened.

"What the fucking hell is going on here!" her dad yelled a third time, waving his shovel.

A guttural engine started somewhere.

Shona lay in the mud, her heart beating, muck around her neck and face. Stricken was leaning, sobbing, on a window pane, and her dad was yelling. The engine growled, and there was a loud percussion, a bang and rattle, and something large drove away at speed.

She put her head back in the mud and found herself laughing, until her side hurt with fire and iron. Then she began to cry with deep, wracking sobs.

22

There was a white wall. And then, appearing slowly from the unsteady turn of a revolving world, a grey wall. Circles and spirals moved, crawling across the grey wall and the surface of his eye, and then disappeared. The grey wall was now darker, and may have been a ceiling. Or the white wall was the ceiling. It was all too much. He wanted to sleep, or die.

He closed his eyes again and put his head under the soft, cool duvet. He felt terrible. Throughout his prone body, his muscles ached. His throat was raw from vomit and bile. Tallis put a hand to his head, and it felt like pulp. He smelled like grey meat. He was a patient now. But he had survived.

He was in a large clean, white bed, in a pale room, somewhere. Somebody was looking after him.

It was not Zed's spare bed. This was somewhere else.

He closed his eyes and felt for his groin. But he was dry. Under the duvet, with his eyes closed, and hearing nothing, he fell into sleep again, which came quickly, a wave of warm, black silence and painless peace.

Tallis was later woken by a large hand on his head.

"Wakey, wakey, rise and shine," a deep voice said quietly, with humour.

The cover was pulled back, and the face of Theseus

Campbell looked down at him. The room was darker, the white walls now ochre and mauve. "You've slept all day, my man. Here, sit up, there is tea."

With the effort of an older man, Tallis pulled himself up. He heard children's voices down a corridor. For an instant he hoped it was Ray.

Foxes and wolves and trees. Darkness and fire. Tallis closed his eyes. A hot mug of tea was placed in his hand.

"Drink up. It is nearly the evening," Theseus said softly.

Tallis drank the tea. It was hot and sweet and stung his mouth and throat.

Theseus moved to sit in a soft chair in the corner of the room. There was an empty fireplace and a pale carpet. Wooden shutters were latched shut over a window. "Niamh checked you out." Theseus was wearing a dark blue cord suit. His eyes were kind. Tallis wondered if he looked like God. "And she said you were catastrophically drunk and high, and you were a lucky boy not to swallow your own copious vomit while you lay down there on the hillside. You're dehydrated and hungover and maybe a little poisoned. But you'll survive."

"Pity," Tallis said, staring into the swirling tendrils of tea steam.

"And, apart from crawling out of the tent on your hands and knees, running off into the darkness and then throwing yourself down the hill, landing betwixt and between a ditch and an iron railing—you managed not to embarrass yourself too much." Theseus sipped his own drink and raised a theatrical eyebrow.

"Oh man," Tallis said. His head throbbed in a cruel, insistent way. He wanted the swift, harsh release of a whisky.

"We washed your clothes. I found your mobile phone, but not your wallet, I am afraid," Theseus said. "Your trousers are absolutely ruined."

"Can I wear them home?"

"I shall drive you home. Portobello, isn't it?"

Tallis nodded. "Home for now," he croaked. "How did you . . . How come I am here?"

Theseus took a long draught of his coffee. He put his head back to the wall. The children in the kitchen were laughing at something. A cartoon was playing. "After you left, and I cannot say it was my idea—it was Niamh, to be perfectly frank—we were worried about you. You were too drunk. You had also dropped some of your medicine, or whatever it was, in the bathroom."

"Fuck," Tallis said, holding the tea to his cheek.

"Fuck, indeed," Theseus nodded. "So after a little bit of a tense and contentious conversation with my beautiful and intelligent wife, I decided to attend Vorn's event. It was fairly fun. I arrived and received my mask—I was given a panda; I would have preferred a lion, but there we are—and, after being initially entranced and then a little bored by the video work and the music and so on—my clubbing days are long behind me—I was nearly knocked off my feet by a lunatic crawling through the crowd to get to the door."

"Ah, fuck," Tallis said, pushing the hot cup farther into his cheek. How frail the human body is, but how resistant to death.

"I didn't think too much of it," Theseus said, his head resting in his hand, "but Mungo was there. Other members of staff, as well. Of course."

"Was he?" Tallis said, groaning.

"Yes, indeed. He was wearing the face of a ferret. Suitably. He mentioned to me that the crawling man may have been you. He recognised your shoes."

"I was trying to get out," Tallis said. His empty stomach turned over loudly.

"You succeeded," Theseus said. "Admirably. You left the tent and lost your footing somehow—probably because you were absolutely paralytic—and then rolled and fell all the way down the grassy side of Calton Hill. Like a drunk skunk, you came to rest at the railings at the bottom."

"You found me."

"Well, there still was a queue of people trying to get into the tent. They could not fail to notice a man, with a cat mask on, crawling to the lip of the hill and then tumbling down. So I followed the trail of wreckage down to where you were. I stood you up, you vomited. I sat you on a step and called a taxi, you keeled over and were sick again, and then we were here. Oh, you vomited in the taxi, also. The man had to be paid extra. It added to the drama of the evening. We dragged you upstairs. Niamh helped. But fear not: I undressed you and put you to bed. I have two children. So dealing with throw-up and poo is not new to me. You are, however, surprisingly heavy."

Tallis nodded. "I am grateful," he said. "I am glad I am not in hospital."

"I am, too. I live with a surgeon, so I sought her advice. And who needs the embarrassment? A drunk and sodden man in A&E receives little sympathy."

Tallis looked at Theseus, who smiled back at him. He clapped his hands. The clap was as painful as his ears being boxed.

"I suggest you get dressed. Your mobile is charging."

Tallis nodded. "I did a terrible thing at the Civic Gallery. I did a terrible thing. An unforgivable thing," he said.

Theseus closed his eyes for a time and then opened them. He stood up. "I think hangover confessions are the worst kind. And few things are unforgivable. We all make mistakes and have aberrations. Myself included. Let us talk on this another time."

Tallis put his hand to his face. He had a great desire to see his son, and kiss his head, and hold him. To hear him say "Dada" again.

"Did you harm anyone at the Civic?" Theseus asked.

"Not really. Mainly myself."

"Did you harm any*thing*?"

"A thing, yes," Tallis said quietly.

"A thing is not a human. We all suffer when humans are treated as things, and things are valued more than humans. So, that is fine. Be at peace."

The sugar from the tea worked around Tallis's body. "Did Mungo ever tell you his story?" he said.

"Mungo has recited many a tale," Theseus rumbled.

Tallis shook his head. "There was one. One about being in a cave under the ground. Subterranean. Seeing shrimps in the underground lakes, under the stalactites?"

"He has not."

"I wish it was my memory. Not his."

"What memory would you change it for?" Theseus said softly.

"The night I met my wife. Knowing I was in love with her. On the steps of the university, our first kiss. Her face under the morning light the first time we woke up together. I don't want that memory anymore. I do not want to anymore compare the past with the present."

"You would prefer it to be an underground cave, tiny animals swimming blindly in the dark. Knowing nothing."

"Yes. In the earth. Knowing less."

"I am not sure how you could substitute one precious memory of yours for another, a memory which holds no meaning," Theseus said.

"There is only one way," Tallis said, and turned his face to the pillow.

Theseus left the room. He bellowed something hearty to his children and strode down the hall.

Tallis's clothes were in a cleaned and ironed pile at the foot of the bed. He slowly dressed. He had grazes on both arms, and on his knees, one of which was wet with drying blood. One of his feet was developing bruises. His back was pummelled and felt like ham. He could feel large bruises rising across his skin between his shoulder blades. His fall to the bottom of the hill had been through obstacles, and over rocks and hillocks, and his body had a sensitive report of every strike and percussion. The trousers were ripped at the knees, and a back pocket was torn away. After a time sitting on the bed, Tallis flapped his way down the hall, to the kitchen. Theseus was lifting up one of his children and put her down again, over and over. Father and daughter were finding it hilarious. Laughter boomed and skittered around the room.

"Theseus, you'll make them sick," Niamh said.

She was leaning against the wall, in a suit. Tallis looked at her and felt sudden and overwhelming shame. Instant death seemed a good option. He saw the rack of knives and pondered it.

"So, the kraken wakes," she said.

"Thank you for—"

Niamh held up a hand. She shook her head. "Get better," she said.

Tallis and Theseus walked in silence to the car, parked outside on cobbles. It was early evening and the sun still illuminated the stone buildings all around.

"You have not seen it, but the Mackintosh Building at the Glasgow School of Art, it is no more," Theseus said, as he drove.

"What?" Tallis said. The shock snapped him back into the now.

"Yes. Indeed. A terrible thing. It burned down last night. When I first saw the news, I thought it was a report marking the anniversary of the first fire in 2014. It took me a while to realise that this was a new fire. A thorough conflagration. It is gone."

"I was due to see it, on Monday—and also see Edie Bradley," Tallis said. He felt sick again, the car's movement swirling his stomach and mind.

"Ah yes, the Bradley mission. Of course. My secret agent. But yes, I am afraid Mackintosh's building has suffered a biblical conflagration. It looks like the building will have to be pulled down. The fire took hold fast, and it has been destroyed. The walls still stand, remarkably."

"Disaster," Tallis said. "I thought they were renovating."

"They were, and were nearly done," Theseus said, pulling the car onto the road to Portobello.

"Does anyone know what started it?" Tallis asked.

"Not yet."

"Poor Mackintosh."

"What was your business there?" Theseus asked.

"I was going to look at some documentation—a sketch by Mackintosh of *The Goldenacre*. Some attendant notes, I had hoped."

Theseus nodded. "They may be ashes now," he said. "Although there are Mackintosh archives at Glasgow University. Bobby will know. Speak to her."

"Thank you, Theseus, I shall."

"Send Edie my warmest regards. Good luck with your mission," Theseus said, smiling. "Oh, and some more bad news before you go."

"I'm ready for bad news. If I didn't have bad news, I would have no news."

"Vorn told me she was videoing the event on Friday night for another work. So your escape is probably caught on camera. Not your violent topple, though."

"Fucking great." Tallis screwed up his eyes. He saw circles and shapes. The hot mad eyes of a fox, the bloody claws of a monstrous bear, hurtling through a forest.

Tallis left the car with a crooked wave. He walked slowly down the side streets to the seafront and his aunt's house. Every footstep on the cobbles juddered his battered body. Lights were on at the house. Through the window he could see Aunt Zed talking to Jack, who was standing with a glass of wine. There was a glow from the television, and from the kitchen. Steam rose from a pot on the stove.

He stood outside, listening to the waves break on the grey beach.

On the television screen, there were flames. Great fires rising from a black ruin, rising above a city. Firefighters on high ladders, pumping jets of water into the flames, which nevertheless drew on, and rose higher and higher above Glasgow. Red and yellow flashing off stone and concrete and glass, and the destruction of the past. If the sketch of *The Goldenacre* was in the Mackintosh Building, it would be part of that smoke now, part of those flames. Gone forever. Drifting up into the clouds. Somewhere caught on the wind. Moving in a cloud of ash over the Atlantic.

He took a deep breath and walked into his aunt's house, where he said hello and climbed the narrow stairs to bed, where he slumped.

Tallis looked at his mobile phone with dread. He had several missed calls, and five new voicemails. He couldn't bear to listen. He would in the morning. Before he climbed under the covers, he texted Mungo, asking him for Vorn's phone number. He wanted to ask something.

23

"So, how did it go?" Shona asked.

It was late morning and she and Stricken were sitting in a pub. They had both reported the incident at the building site to the police. They had given statements, as had Shona's father. He seemed to be back to himself again, after his manic behaviour in the mud.

"Och, fine. I just told them what happened. You got there just in time," Stricken said, holding a pint of lager in two hands. "Just in fucking time. What a mad thing. Mad."

He had a large plaster on his forehead where he had cracked it against some beam or other in the half-built house. He had a black eye, deepest black near the bottom of his left eye, yellow and purple above it. Shona's gin and tonic arrived.

Stricken was off work. Shona had received a call from Colm, asking her to come to the office. A chat with the editor. She pushed it to the back of her mind.

"It was lucky the place was still a building site," she said. "Plenty of places to hide."

"And that he couldn't face killing all three of us."

"Run me through what happened again," she said, taking a sip.

Stricken supped his beer and slowly spoke. He had arrived

at the site and parked. He had arranged to meet the man, and Catherine Peters, at the showroom. Then the man had turned up, holding something in his hand, and came for him, and Stricken had run. There had been a muddy chase. A clarty game of cat and mouse. Stricken, after running into, hiding, and then being chased out of two houses, had run into another and leapt up the stairs. He had pulled a piece of dry wall across the gap in the wall and leant against it. The grey-haired man had kicked at the temporary wall and battered it with his fists, but Hector had held firm. He wasn't sure how long he could have held out, if Shona and her father had not arrived.

They sat quietly for a while.

"It was quite absurd. Bizarre, really," he said, not smiling, "running from house to house, this maniac after me. Never been so scared in my life. And I've been to a fair few Aberdeen vs Rangers matches."

"It's all those bloody Munros you climb, Hector—finally, that pointless activity has brought you some benefit. You're fighting fit."

"I feel terrible and quite shaky today."

Shona nodded. He looked shaky. "Get drunk and forget," she said.

"Easier said than done, Shona."

She traced a circle on the tabletop with a finger. "So, what did the cops say to you? I gave my statement at the freaking station and then she shooed me away. My old man was with them for even less time."

"A man chasing a bewildered hack around a half-built housing estate in the middle of nowhere isn't a routine number for them, I'd imagine," he said. "But there's not much for them to go on, is there? I guess they are tracking down Ms. Peters and asking her for her side of events."

"Did you tell them about what he was carrying?"

"Yes, of course. But I could barely see it. You know if

he had crept up on me, he could have killed me. He would have had a clear shot. I wasn't paying attention when I got there—I was trying to get some bloody phone reception, holding my mobile around up in the air like it was a kite or something—and he drove up, engine blazing, did this dramatic stop, mud and water everywhere, and jumped out of that massive truck and kind of flew at me. If he'd been more—"

"Like a ninja."

"Yes, like that, he could have got me. Thanks to the Wee Man, he didn't. It was fight or flight, and I sure as fuck wasn't going to fight." He blew out his cheeks. He was pale. "I think I need to go home, actually."

"I've got this flaming meeting with the boss," Shona said. The bubbles of tonic popped in her nose.

Stricken paused. "The cops said they would have a good look at the housing estate, try and trace the four-by-four by its tracks. At the station, I got your friend, Reculver. Strange fellow, isn't he? He seemed to be wearing makeup."

"Aye, he does that. Always has. It's just who he is. What did he say they would do about Ms. Peters?"

Stricken shook his head. "He said something vague. I did think, this morning on the bus here, that the madman may have had nothing to do with Ms. Peters. Some other reason he could be there. I guess? Stealing things from the building site?"

"No chance. Are you mental? You arranged to meet her there. She doesn't show up, but the huge psycho-killer does. It's obvious there's a link."

"A killer, Shona?" Stricken said, leaning forward. "You don't know that."

"What was he trying to do? Play tig?"

Stricken thought in silence for a while. He looked to Shona. "You going to get time off?"

"Not a chance. I don't do time off."

Shona hadn't voluntarily had time off for years. She had lost half a year of her life, recovering from the injuries she had sustained in Glasgow. Endless nights in the pale, white wards. The healing of wounds. Spotting stars through the only window in the ward. The moon and lonely Venus. All the galaxies, beyond. She loathed the feelings of futility and emptiness that accompanied inaction and lack of work. So, she would keep working.

"I'm off," Stricken said. He slid off his stool. Shona noticed more scratches and bruises on his neck. "Be careful, Shona, and mebbe don't poke around this Peters thing. Let the police do their thing."

"I won't. I'm not going to do a thing now," she lied.

"If that fella is linked at all to the murders, we need to keep our absolute distance."

Stricken moved forward, and it looked as if he was about to attempt a hug, but Shona's instant flinch led him to hold out his hand, for a shake. She shook it. His hand was cold and sweaty.

"Thanks for coming out on Saturday," he said. "I'm still not clear why you did it, but I'm damn sure you and your mad dad scared him off."

"Just doing my job," she said, grinning. "Now away home with you."

Stricken sloped off, his red anorak gleaming through the press of people queuing to order a drink.

Shona sat for a while, staring into her glass. The gin slowly warmed her mind, smoothing off the edges. She thought about texting Reculver, but it was too early for the investigation, if there was one, to have found much out. Maybe Peters was in custody now, or being interviewed. She wondered if the Geordie who had answered the phone was the big man with the grey hair. His white four-by-four sounded like the same one Morag had seen outside her father's house. She started tapping in notes to her phone: *Love's funeral, Cullen's funeral.* Then there was Mr. Tallis. She decided to visit the Public Gallery. Maybe she could meet him, accidentally.

Shona finished her drink. She needed to be at the office and was about to leave when her phone buzzed. She slumped down again. It was Reculver.

"You all right, hen?" he said.

"Good morning to you, too."

"So, you're alive. Well, we need to chat. Can you meet me at the Botanics in, say, an hour?"

"Yes, but I have a shan meeting at work now. After that— in an hour and a half?"

"By the East Gate."

"Fine."

She left the pub, and it was a short walk to the office. The news editor, Colm, was waiting when she arrived. He was outside in Rose Street, smoking a short brown hand-rolled cigarette. Smoke dragoned around his face.

"Boss wants to see you," he said, wincing, blowing a sharp gust from the side of his mouth.

"I know. That's why I am here." The gin was doing its work. She felt louder and less wary.

"You all right?" he said, dropping the stub, grinding it with his shoe.

"Thanks for asking," Shona said. "Yeah, fine. Stricken is shaken up, though. You should have a word with him."

"I'll let him get over it. He's signed off sick. He'll shake it off. Come on, let's do this with as little pain as possible."

"Do you know what this is about?" Shona said, as they walked into the office. She had a fair idea.

"I'll let the Big Man explain," Colm muttered, in the lift.

Shona gently stubbed her stick, spattered with pale dried mud, on the lift floor. The lift doors opened slowly on the second floor. They had to walk together across the newsroom to get to Ronald Ingleton's glass-walled office in the corner of the building. Some eyes moved across Shona's face as she walked. She kept her vision on the door to the office. Fingers clacked on pale grey keyboards. A silent TV scrolled news: some kind of political demonstration in the centre of the city.

Colm said something quiet to Ingleton's secretary and pulled down his rolled-up sleeves, then he opened the door for Shona and they both walked in.

Ingleton was standing by the window, peering at his mobile phone, checking some kind of sports website. He was small and shaven-headed, with a gym-pumped torso and thick black glasses. Fifty years old, with grey around his ears.

"Shona Sandison," he said. "Please sit down." His voice was nasal and thin.

Shona nodded and sat, leaning her stick against the metal table leg. Colm sat beside her. As Ingleton turned to close his mobile phone, Colm winked at her.

"Colm, I'd prefer you look after the desk," Ingleton said, nodding at him.

"It can wait ten minutes."

"I'd rather you look after the newsdesk."

"Well," Colm said, and stood up. He put a brief hand on Shona's shoulder as he left. He closed the door firmly.

Ingleton sat down. His large watch clunked on the table. Shona looked at his face, all smooth lines and flat, pale flesh. He had a thin, pink, stippled mouth, like the lips of a healed wound. "I hope you are okay," he said. "After your adventure." He laughed a little and then stopped.

"I'm fine."

He sat motionless.

"I've had worse," she added.

"You have." He nodded, looking at her stick.

"So, do you want a run-down of what happened?"

"No, I've heard enough," he said, crossing his arms.

"Okay, then," she said, and made an effort to stand up.

"Hold your horses. No, I want to talk to you about this," he said, and pointed to her chair. He took off his glasses and rubbed his eyes with two fingers. "Before you went to this housing development, did you bother to do any background checking on it?"

"I went to support Hector. I was worried about him. Turned out I was right to worry."

"You are right to worry," he said. "But not about that. Thing is, Shona—you don't have to concern yourself with the things . . . that I have to concern myself with."

Shona winced. He seemed to be gathering things together in his taut frame.

"You write your wee stories and whatever. And that's all fine. You supply content for the paper and, I hope, going forward in the direction of travel on the road that we are travelling—our, what I call, our digital transformation—you will play a part. All you content suppliers out there will have a role to play." He gestured to the office through the glass walls. "But there won't be any, if we carry on the ways we are going. Look, we need unique, compelling content for our platforms going forward on the path what we are taking. That is understood."

"Excellent," Shona said. "I am interested in unique compelling content. And discontent."

He blinked and continued. "But I also need to mind the books. The actual income of this business. One of our main incomes is from advertising, that's not changing. But also as we go forward I am looking at the commercial opportunities out there, and more and more I am looking at commercial partnerships with businesses. They also offer us unique and compelling content, and we benefit in kind."

"You are talking about adverts for companies, which we will write."

"No, Shona. Commercial partnerships." His glasses were back on, and he was looking into the corner of the room, where there was only a crease line of shadow. "Commercial relationships."

"Right," she said. "'Advertorials' is, I think, the word you are looking for. Not journalism. Puff pieces."

He shook his head briefly. "And," he said, still staring away from Shona and into the corner, "we already have interesting possibilities with several commercial entities, and one of them is Oldmeg Reach."

Shona looked at the table. Stricken had been right to warn her. She felt suddenly annoyed. And also relieved: she knew entirely what this meeting was about. "Who is Oldmeg Reach?" she said. "Should I know him? Strange name."

Ingleton's hand was on his smooth forehead now. He seemed to be in mild pain. "Oldmeg Reach is a growing—it's big already, but it's growing—housing company. Developments. Lots of exciting developments. And we are entering into a commercial—"

"Writing puff pieces for them in exchange for money. As I said."

Ingleton turned to her. "Writing content in return for valuable income, which then helps us move away from making necessary adjustments to our ongoing cost base of staff," he said, his flat voice returning. "To cut to the chase, to boil it down. From you, I need a memo explaining why you and Stricken were trespassing—as I understand it—on one of their developments." He started to tap the tabletop with a finger. He briefly looked at his watch.

"I am sure Hector can explain himself," she said.

"I don't think Stricken has the wherewithal to be causing these kinds of issues all by himself," Ingleton said.

Shona raised her eyebrows.

"How many years has he been at this company? How many stories has he really broken?" Ingleton said.

"More than you have."

Ingleton sat back in his chair. The light filled his glasses.

It looked like his eyes were two pools of empty sky. "Thanks for your time," he said.

She stood up and grabbed her stick.

"And mind, your note will be forwarded on to Oldmeg Reach," he said, "so that we can all come to some kind of resolution. And you will drop whatever story you have going on, until I say otherwise. Colm knows already. He has other things for you to be working on."

Shona thought of something to say, but did not say it. She left Ingleton's office, pushing shut the door as hard as she could behind her. She walked through the office as quickly as possible and was out into the world before her fury subsided. Shona stopped in the street and collected her mind. She did not want to walk anymore. Her side hurt and her back ached.

She found the right bus and arrived at the East Gate early. She tramped up the path to the Royal Botanic Gardens from the main road, past hand-holding couples and a man pushing a double pushchair with two sleeping children. Their heads lolled to each side, locks falling over their smooth faces. At the entrance, there was a small café. She sat on a metal chair outside. The botanical gardens were both parkland and glasshouses. The grass was well trimmed and the trees resplendent. Neat beds of vegetation stood around bridges and water. There was a river and a pond. Here, the city was reduced to a hushed whirr of noise. People slowly perambulated its paths. It did not seem real.

Waiting for Reculver, she searched on the internet for Katherine Pieters and Catherine Peters, Catherine Pieters and Katherine Peters. But she got an overloaded jumble of websites, some Facebook pages that looked all wrong, some random Twitter accounts. But nothing on a woman of that name as a company director, or as an art collector.

She slapped her phone down on the metal table.

"Don't break it now," Reculver said. He sat down heavily.

He was in a three-piece suit, with red socks and well-polished brown shoes. He had a long coat on and a trilby. He looked like he had stepped through a portal from the 1940s, with added mascara. He had a large pale plaster over one ear.

"Another domestic?" she said, pointing to his ear.

"Plook," he said. "Not every wound has to be an injury, Shona."

"Good place to be bitten," she said.

"Shona—are you drunk? How are you? What a curious business down there in Haddington. I assume you're not too traumatised."

"Nah, I'm fine. Very curious," she said. "What do you know about it?"

He sucked his teeth and peered into the café. "I fancy a cuppa," he said. "Well, the answer is no, we don't know much about it. But we have found the car."

"The four-by-four?"

"Yes," he said. "It wasn't hard to find: it was full ablaze in a lay-by off the A1. Completely incinerated. The Fire Service ladies and gentlemen had a job containing it—the hedge beside it had caught fire. So had an overhanging tree. The boys in the lab think they might have something with the tyre marks, but it's an old model and hard to track, and the mud on that site was liquid. It was like paint. We will have the engine number, of course, but it was all very professionally disposed of. Fast burn, high temperature. Nothing much there. Thoroughly immolated. A lot of fires around at the minute."

"Was there anyone in it?"

He grinned and pulled at his injured ear. "Shona Sandison—no. There was not. I may have mentioned that first. Anyway, so there we are."

"That it? Well, at least it shows they were trying to hide something."

Reculver rolled his eyes. He picked at lint on his collar.

"Yes, someone was. This whole Peters business," he said, "what do you know of it? Tell me everything."

"Why?"

"Because some of my tetchy colleagues in financial crimes are interested."

"Oh, really," she said, reaching for a notebook in her bag.

"None of this is on the record," he said, looking around. "Or anywhere near the record."

There was no one near. An old couple stopped to stoop and point at flowers.

"This name, Peters, has come across their radar," he said. "That's all I am saying. I can't say any more. This name, I mentioned it to a colleague. It set off some alarms. Some recognition. For starters, there is little to no digital imprint for this woman. No social media at all. You have probably already checked that. I am not telling you anything new, on that score."

She nodded.

"So, tell me everything you know about this woman." He put his hands together on the table. They were broad and hairless.

"For what reason?" She put her hands on the table too.

"Because you can have the eventual story, if it leads to anything."

"So, you are investigating—or someone is?"

He smiled. "Tell me everything."

"Get me an espresso and I might do."

He sighed, stood up and stomped over to the café door. "This is bribery," he said.

When he returned with two hot cups, Shona told him what Robert Love's daughter had said. She told him about a Ms. Pieters who had ordered a commission from the artist, and that her driver sat in a white four-by-four. It had been a commission that seemed to bother Love.

Reculver nodded and made notes in a small red notebook.

His handwriting was as square and linear as ancient cunei-form.

Then she told him about what Stricken had found, and how a Ms. Peters was listed as a director on the companies run from, or by, the Melrose family.

He made more notes. His face was impassive. The brim of his hat laid hard shadows on his face, lines down from his nose to his jowls, and across one painted cheek.

She finished, and he fell into silence and toyed with the edge of his hat.

"Is that some kind of fancy dress hat?" she said.

He looked at her fiercely. "This was handmade in Italy. To order." He tapped the table with his pen. "Curiouser and curiouser," he said eventually.

"Reculver," she said. "I have been curious. Where is that name from? It's unusual."

"You're unusual. It is quite simple. My dear father was a man of Kent. Or a Kentish man, I cannot remember the exact phrase, it all depends on your relation to the Medway. The name is very old, from down that way."

"I always assumed it was made up," she said.

"Every name is, at some point, made up, Shona," he said.

She rapped her phone on the tabletop again.

"It's weird, isn't it, that a Pieters and a Peters seem to be connected to both Love's death and Cullen's, too?"

"I admire your imagination. But there's fuck-all to con-nect her to the Cullen murder," he said slowly. "In fact, the Oldmeg Reach people were going to reapply for planning permission, and I think Cullen knew about that, and had some contact with them over a revised offer. So, it's a big jump to somehow connect that little affair to his death. I still suspect some low-life jumped him in the pub. The Love case, though: we don't have much. We have the boot stamp. It's from a standard man's boot. We have a savage murder, quite nasty, quite unusual."

"Savage?" Shona said. "In what way?"

"I'm not telling you that, and I certainly don't want his daughter to know," he said. "Tongues will wag."

"Go on, tell me."

He shook his head and sighed. She was not going to find out. "All I can say, Shona, is that the arts world seems to be a small place. So, Morag did not meet Ms. Pieters?"

"Not fully. Just in passing."

"Description?"

Shona closed her eyes, trying to remember. "She didn't like her. At all. I think she said she was tough-spoken, maybe a bit posh? And with the huge man in the car. Who I think we now seem to have met."

"That's not much. She's a shadow," he said. "A wraith."

"Wraith?"

"A ghost, Shona. There's no address, there's no tax data, there's nothing. Just a name. But she has actually met people. She exists in the material plane. She has this intermediary on the phone. The Geordie. He might indeed be the man who chased you around the building site. He might be the man who introduced some new ventilation to Mr. Love's head."

Shona winced. "Did you try to call the number Stricken had?"

"Yes. Nothing, it's gone dead. Disconnected. We have a colleague from the Borders visiting the company now; it's at some industrial unit near Hawick."

"There's definitely something up, then," she said.

He smiled. "Yes, there is absolutely something, as you say, up. But why would anyone murder a painter, a quiet, troubled but innocuous painter in a quiet part of Edinburgh? Even if this Ms. Pieters was a pushy so-and-so, wanted her big commission perfect and delivered yesterday. That's no prelude to murder."

"Maybe she got the painting and then didn't want to pay.

She sent her driver, this Geordie, and there was some kind of row?"

"A row over a fee that ends in a savage murder?"

"Well, I dunno," Shona said. "If it was the same guy, he wasn't exactly normal. He was trying to kill Hector, for starters."

"Or maybe he was just trying to scare him," Reculver said, shrugging.

"There's money involved."

"With these horrible, gruesome, cruel crimes, it's usually about money. You can't beat greed. It's the original human sin from which all others flow. It will destroy us all in the end."

"You getting religion, Reculver?"

"I pray every week. Go to the Mass at the Metropolitan. I figure it's a safe two-way bet," he said, with a smile.

They both sat for a time, holding their warm drinks and staring off into the gardens. The sun gleamed on the green, on the nodding flowers, the towering trees. A child's voice cried somewhere amid the parkland.

"So how has Pieters's name come up at financial crimes?" Shona asked.

Reculver peered at her. "I'm no' telling you. But there's more companies involved in this than just the ones your colleague found."

"Really?"

"Yes. And we are always interested when large sums of money appear from nowhere to buy buildings or businesses, or, in this case, land. One thousand acres near the Queensferry Crossing, all paid directly in one lump sum, almost as if it was paid in cash? Curious."

"I thought you said the film studio business had nothing to do with this," she said.

"You're clever, Shona." He stood up. "Let's just say, Ms. Peters or Pieters is now a person of interest to us. We just need to find her."

"Is there a clock ticking?"

"There's always a clock ticking, Shona. Time runs down-hill. Mr. Love's death is an open case. We have little to go on. We don't even have any CCTV that is useable. This commission, this Ms. Pieters, is someone we are now very interested in. I will need to speak to Morag, too."

Shona shook her head. "I can't give you her number."

"Come on now," Reculver said, his arms outstretched.

"If you have to speak to her, surely you already have a number for her?"

Reculver smiled. "Just testing." He started moving away. "All of this is off the record," he said. "And if you find anything else, tell me first." He stomped off, out of sight behind trees and leaves.

"Will I fuck," Shona said. She looked at the internet on her phone again. She typed in: "money laundering."

3:32 A.M.

Surely your mailbox is full now. Do they auto-matically delete? I'm going to stop asking if you listen.

It seems that someone knows about what happened at the Civic. Celia called. You will remember her. You sorted her out, didn't you? So it may all come out into the open, and my career—my so-called career—will be over. And then what? Maybe I'll finally follow in your footsteps. I'm in the fucking government already. I've become quite good at lying and cheating and deceiving and skulking about. Anyway, I thought you'd better know. If this is a way of telling you.

Goodbye.

24

The train was closing in on Glasgow, and Tallis woke up. Everyone in the carriage was asleep. Two men snoring on each other's shoulders. A woman opposite with her laptop open and her eyes closed. It was as if they had all died. High rises emerged on either side, like giants rising from the earth. It was raining, the drops crying their way along the windows. The train entered a tunnel, darkness flung like a cloak over the carriage, and his fellow passengers woke. Queen Street Station emerged, all curving glass, noise and clamour.

Tallis was to visit Edie Bradley, who lived in the Glasgow suburbs, a place called Milngavie. He had been taught by Mungo how to pronounce the word—Mill-Gye. He was on the mission from Theseus.

He descended from the train in a haze, found a taxi and managed to correctly pronounce Milngavie. The taxi moved off, and he watched the city slide by. There was noise and shouting, people shopping and moving, cars everywhere, and rain, drenching its gleam on metal and glass. Water ran in new becks down the littery sludge at the edges of streets, past soaked homeless pleading for money, past neon betting shops and burger joints, past burned ruins and ruinous Victorian buildings, past ugly concrete and some shivers of fugitive grace and beauty. Past the smoke drifting from the Mackintosh Building, past the embers and the destruction.

After a time, leaving the tenements and the noise behind, they entered wider streets and fields of silent geriatric bungalows. In the distance rose high rises and stark, bare, precipitous hills. The taxi pulled into what could have been a country road and drove to the end, where a low, single-storey house sat behind a stand of trees.

"There you go, boss," the driver said, and Tallis paid and alighted, and the taxi drove away. The air was fresh and wet. The city hummed and groaned behind him. Ahead, the view was hills and trees and the long path to the Highlands. Cars flashed by on the main road. A bell, somewhere, dinged as he moved through a small white gate. The garden was looked after but slightly overgrown. There were flowerbeds glistening with the new rain, some heavy trees, and toys for toddlers on the long grass of the lawn.

A woman stood at the door, white-haired, with a pan in her hand. "Good morning, Mr. Tallis," she said. Her voice was clear and sharp.

Tallis greeted her, and she ushered him inside.

"Now, my son was here yesterday with his children—my grandsons—and they made a terrible mess, so I am afraid I am just doing some tidying up. And they used this pan, an old and much beloved pan of mine that has survived many burned scrambled eggs, the cooking of my husband, and many a house move, to melt something awful in. I have no idea what it was, but I think it's ruined—don't you?" She showed Tallis the pot. It had something black inside it, something charred and evil.

"It may need a soak," he said.

"I think it may need to be taken to the dump. And I do love going to the dump. Shall we have tea before work?"

They were in a large kitchen that had a broad cast-iron stove and a large, white ceramic sink. The watery light gleamed on everything, on plates and cutlery, on glass-framed pictures on the wall, on a cat's water dish, on Edie's thick white hair. She heaved a water-filled old kettle onto the stove, which pulsed with heat. The radio was playing classical music.

"Now tell me, Mr. Tallis, are you related to Thomas Tallis, the composer?" she said, leaning back against the warm stove. She had sinewy arms and strong fingers. Her eyes glittered.

"No," he said, his hands on the kitchen table. "No, sadly not. At least, not as far as I know."

"You will have heard Vaughan Williams's 'Fantasia on a Theme by Thomas Tallis,' of course. Divine music. Now my late husband and I disagreed on this; I think the Romanza in his Fifth Symphony is his most beautiful music. That Romanza is some of the most beautiful music written in the last hundred years. Now Reggie disagreed, but we disagreed on many things. He always said, 'Oh, you're not listening to me,' and I would say, 'I am very much listening, my darling Reggie, but I am disagreeing with you, and that is a different matter altogether.' And so marriage goes, of course. I was blessed. I am alone now. So, how do you like your tea?"

Tallis said hot, brown and sweet.

"Oh, me too," she beamed. "This is going to be a terrific day. Now, Mr. Tallis, you are not here to turn me from the path of righteousness, are you?"

"I might be," he said.

Edie smiled, then served tea and said she was going to get documents. She thumped up the stairs to a room above. There was some kerfuffle and a large hairy white cat bounded down the stairs and sloped into the kitchen. The cat came over to Tallis and rubbed itself on his leg, then jumped up onto the surface next to the stove. It licked its paws. Five long white hairs stuck tremulously to Tallis's calf.

"Now, Rosa there was just lying all over these, I am

afraid," Edie said, hauling in a large pile of papers. "She, like me, mourns her own late husband, Karl, and Karl was a beautiful cat, but also rather fat and he got terribly . . . well, terribly motionless, and he quietly died a few years ago. He is now sleeping under that cherry tree in the garden. But, unlike me, Rosa has no children, so she rather thinks I am her child, which is funny, as in real years I am sixty years older than her, but I suppose in cat lives she is—sixteen times seven, whatever that is—much older than me, so maybe she is right."

"Cats often are right about these things," Tallis said.

She smiled. "Indeed so. Oh, Theseus did say I would like you. And Theseus, that gorgeous man, has sent you."

Tallis nodded. "With an offer."

"I am afraid, dear sir, I do not want to hear your offer. My mind is made up. I cannot abide these works of art being in your gallery, hung up like pelts or stuffed lions' heads, anymore. I cannot live with it. I cannot bear the weight of those works on my conscience. Can I tell you something strange?"

"Of course," he said. He felt like his journey was now pointless.

"That, somehow, objects contain not only their history, but the history of their owners. That they somehow absorb and thereafter contain the pains and joys of the humans they have connected with. Been owned by. Been bought and sold by. Is that odd of me?"

"That they have memories," he said.

"Yes, exactly. And in this case, are not these paintings drenched in pain? In sorrow and loss? Bought by the proceeds of slavery? Yes, they were. My family became rich on the backs of slaves. The wealth cascaded to me. And it is my decision to rid the Bradleys of this inherited guilt."

Tallis smiled and shrugged. "Is not everything we own therefore drenched in other people's pain? If I buy a new computer, does it contain the terror of the miner of precious metals in Africa, the exhaustion of a child in an electronics factory? The sweat of the sailor on the cargo ship, the boredom of the warehouse worker, the anxiety of the shop assistant?"

Edie smiled. "Maybe they do, Mr. Tallis, which is why our world is slowly sinking. Our everyday life is freighted with inherited and transferred pain." She gently clapped her hands. "I will be removing the Bradley Collection from public view, and I have already made a deal! With Sotheby's in London. So, that is set. They will sell, and the collection will be no more. No more proceeds of crime. They have told me that the collection will reach a significant sum. However, all my inherited books and documents and ledgers and so on, they will go to the National Library of Scotland. For study. For sober reading. But not everything in my family was bought with the profits of crimes against humanity. We have assessed and figured. So the Public Gallery will be given, from me to you . . . Now, let me see."

She licked a finger and found an index. A neat document sat before her on the table. There were pages of images, each with its own typed history.

"Four drawings bought in the 1970s, with my husband's money, twelve of my own watercolours, seven 'mixed media' works from the 1990s—now they were my accountant's words, not mine—and . . . Well, here it is, for you to read. I shall drink tea and you can ask me questions. We have about an hour because I want to start work in the studio at midday. But as for the greater Bradley Collection: it will be sold. The money will be going to a host of good causes! The plans are exciting."

Edie sat back in her chair and smiled. Tallis took the document and read it. Rosa the cat curled into a ball by the stove and purred loudly. Time passed slowly as Tallis ran his eyes over words and pictures. There was some good news for Theseus here. But mainly bad. Just like history.

He marvelled at her watercolour paintings. So beautiful and strong.

"It's provenance," Edie said softly, after a time, "isn't it? Your job?"

"Yes, that's right." The document had every detail he needed. There was nothing more to add. Edie had typed it herself.

"Provenance. Histories and memories and family trees. Lovely," she said.

He put the papers on the table. "I don't think we have much to discuss."

"No. I hope I am setting an example for others to follow, in some way. Maybe the marbles will go back to Greece. Maybe the bronzes back to Benin. Maybe all those ghastly bodies, back to Africa and Canada and Egypt."

"Maybe."

Her eyes glittered. "It is time for the west to divest. And it also rhymes. Which is nice."

"Theseus will be very disappointed. He had thought his offer, of some kind of institutional recognition, would—"

"Theseus knows his history," she interrupted. "He is part of history. He should know this is all long overdue. It is a bill that has long needed paying. I am doing that now. I do not want my grandchildren to be ashamed of me. They will one day find out how my family made their money. Then they will understand."

Tallis nodded. He did not want to leave, but Edie needed to paint. Her cat stood up and yawned, and a tender pink maw studded with white sharp teeth opened.

"I will give you all the papers," she said. "Before you go, do you want to see my studio?"

"I would love to."

"Isn't it awful, so awful about the art school?" she said, as they walked. "I grew up in Glasgow, so I did not go to art school there—I wanted to travel, to get away, so I went to

London instead. But such a beautiful building, those studios that Mackintosh designed, the light . . . it was so beautiful. And now, all gone. It has been cremated, hasn't it? Not even given a decent burial."

He followed her through a door in the back of the kitchen to a broad and open white space with two walls of windows that looked out over the hills and fields, facing east and north. There was a canvas on an easel, half-painted, a shifting dimensional spray of colour and shadow. Beside it on a table was an island of oil paint, dried and coagulated, squeezed from tubes onto board, piled into a melted model city of colour and hue. Paintings were stacked against the red brick walls. A large frame, with no painting, stood against one of the windows. There were pots of brushes and a radio, playing orchestral music. The cat sauntered into the studio and hopped onto a small, soft-topped stool.

"How wonderful this place is," Tallis said. He looked over the landscape. He briefly saw the face of a fox, its teeth bared. His dream returned, the one of death, a dream of drowning and falling, a fall from light to cold darkness. He felt weak.

"You look pale," she said.

"I am fine, thank you. I was sick at the weekend."

"Do you like my frame?" she said, pointing to the empty wooden oblong.

Tallis moved closer to it. In the pale wood, there had been carved a geometric pattern, and each corner a kind of symbol.

"It was made for a new commission, by a very talented framer based in Edinburgh. He is awfully good. It had to have these symbols on it—they are based on the rings found on old stones and stone circles in the Highlands. The ancient ways. Not the Beaker People. They are rather beautiful. He did a terrific job. My old friend Bob recommended him." She gasped and put her hand to her mouth. She was now holding

238 • PHILIP MILLER

a short brush, and its white hairs splayed on her flesh. "Did you hear about poor Bob? Robert Love? I was so shocked. How can that happen? Absolutely devastating. I heard it was a robbery but, of course, Bobby never had any money. Everyone knew that. Stupid robber! Didn't do his research. And then he's killed him. I mean, so terrible."

"Yes, a terrible business," Tallis said, a finger on the wooden frame.

"Awful, quite awful."

"Senseless."

"Senseless," she echoed.

They stood a while in silence. Edie's eyes were closed.

"Who made this frame?" he asked.

"Jack Miles. He is a rather irascible old man, but he is terribly good. I have some more works to frame—he will be doing them for me. Prints and paintings, both. I have this ambitious idea for a series of paintings based on my recent travels in Latin America, and I want something rather different—he said he would do them for me, he is terribly good at decorations and other unusual and out-of-the-ordinary frames. I'm afraid my framer in Glasgow has retired, and has, would you believe, rheumatism. Of all things. I said to him, 'Ivor, wear a copper band, like everyone else does.' He wouldn't hear of it. But yes, about two months ago, I saw Bob at the Glasgow Arts Club. He was buying everyone drinks, what with I do not know, maybe a horse came in for him at last—at long last—and he said, 'Go to Jack, Edie, he's the best in the biz,' so I did. He couldn't recommend him highly enough."

"Jack worked with Mr. Love?"

"Oh yes," Edie said, pulling a smock over her head. "He just made a very delicate and unusual, specific, bespoke frame for him, another commission. This one was very delicate, very fine, Bobby said to me. It was some big number he was doing for a private client, and you know how they are. Picky bunch. Jack pulled it off, anyway. Bob said the collector was very specific and exacting, and Jack did it just right."

Edie smiled and said: "Goodbye, Mr. Tallis, you know the way out. If there are any issues, ask Theseus to call me. Every call from him is a tonic."

She turned to her work.

Tallis walked back to the kitchen. It was silent now, apart from the groaning stove and the dripping of the rainwater. He picked up the files and put them in his case. He moved to the front door and, standing outside, texted Gretchen and Astrella together and asked how Ray was. And if they could speak that night, or if a video of the boy could be sent to him. The text whipped off into the wet Glasgow sky.

He called a taxi and began the long journey back to Edinburgh, city of secrets. At the station, he deleted all the messages and voicemails from Melcombe. He blocked his number.

He waited for the train, with his mind as heavy and unreal as a fever.

25

Rain fell on the trees and the grass of the graveyard, pattered and spat on the people dressed in black and the umbrellas that they held. The mourners stood around the fresh grave, which had been cut with clean lines into the damp soil. The priest spoke. A folded cloth of fake grass stood to one side, livid green, and on it Robert Love's coffin sat, its wood and brass gleaming.

Shona stood back. She was under an elm tree, dressed in black, leaning on her stick. She had arrived as the coffin was carried, as if on water, smoothly from the church to the graveyard.

Rain was falling in gouts and flurries. The sky was grey. Morag, who had not noticed Shona, was also in black, her bump even bigger, it seemed, and holding the hand of a bearded, tall man. Crawford Dudley, the Trinity Arts Club president, was close to her, his eyes red. Morag leaned into the bearded man as four men lowered the coffin into the grave. Her face crumpled and an arm was placed around her shoulders.

Shona moved closer to the tree. Her mother's funeral had not been in a graveyard such as this. It was at a crematorium in Glasgow's Southside. Her father had not cried at the funeral. He had been all cried out. After, there had been a wake in the old Press Bar, with her father's old journalist friends in sombre voice. Her mother's friends had been silent in the corner, drinking brandy and gin and tonic. Her mother reduced to the contents of a pot, her ash filling its shape like water.

The mourners walked past Shona, their feet silent on the wet grass.

Morag came close, wiping her face, leaning on the man beside her. She looked up and saw Shona. She whispered something to her partner and he nodded.

"Well done," Shona said to Morag, as she came closer.

Morag smiled and her eyes filled with tears again. She wiped them away. She blew her nose. Rain fell again, and they moved closer under the canopy of leaves.

"Martyn said God is crying," Morag said.

"God must do a lot of crying," Shona replied.

Morag smiled and nodded.

"I spoke to the police," Shona said.

"They've been all over the house." Morag's voice hardened. "But I don't think they've found anything. They want to look at his bank accounts. Good luck with that." She smiled and shook her head. Her hands were on her stomach. "I looked in his diaries, and there was just the usual: horse races, dog tracks, lottery numbers, football scores. But there was no name for that man who was with that Pieters woman. I'm sorry."

"Have you heard from her?"

"No, nothing. But I've not been in the house much, and Daddy didn't have a mobile phone. There's nothing in his emails, either."

Shona nodded as they stood in the silence.

"The only thing I have found, in the mess, was a strange thing I had not seen before. A sweet thing. But it wasn't anything to do with his work, I don't think."

Shona looked at her, expecting more.

"A little Christmas decoration," Morag said, smiling and crying, "which he had clipped to the easel. The easel was all knocked over and smashed up, but the little robin was attached still. A wee robin, with wings and its breast made from fake feathers. Bright red. I wonder if he was painting something for me, for us—because we told Dad we thought Robin was a nice name, a good name for the bump, because Robin could be a boy's or a girl's name, and he said . . ." She suddenly began to weep and Shona put an arm around her. Morag wept with great lurches and sobs. The rain still fell.

Morag's partner, Martyn, appeared, with sad brown eyes and a bristling beard. "Thank you," he said to Shona, and put his arm around Morag. Through the tears, Morag said something to Shona she could not understand or hear, and the couple walked slowly away. Mourners waited by the gate, and black glossy cars glimmered in the rain.

Shona waited by the tree, and they all slowly left, fallen leaves drifting in the purposeless eddies of a stilling pool.

2 6

Thomas Tallis was to see *The Goldenacre*, at last. He was in a taxi to the Public Gallery's stores in the north of the city. A text buzzed on his phone: *I will come to Edin. with Ray*, it said. *I will be in hotel. Can we talk soon s.v.p? A.*

Tallis stared at the text from Astrella. He closed his phone, then he opened it again to check that the message was still there. It was. He texted back: *That would be lovely. I am nearly done here, but can stay a few more days.*

The Goldenacre had been deposited at the stores earlier that day. Neither Olivia nor Felix Farquharson would be present at the viewing. Olivia was abroad, apparently. Felix was unwell.

Sir Dennis Carver was making his way there. Bobby Donnelly was in the taxi with Tallis. She had zipped her coat up to her chin and was cycling through emails on her phone. The taxi lurched and growled its way through the city. It passed stone avenues and crescents, and a wide green park with dogs scampering under a cold white sky. After a time, the taxi entered different housing: stippled old council housing in grids and rows, and high flats. There were sharp railings around abandoned lots and low pubs, with flat roofs. The taxi drove past a concrete harbour, slimy with weed, where two sad boats huddled together, leaking. They came to a fence, which surrounded a large, metal-walled building beyond. There was an intercom and the taxi driver spoke grumpily into it—the gate slid open and they passed through. They left the taxi and walked to the security entrance.

Bobby swung out a lanyard from under her coat.

"How are you, Bobby?" Tallis asked.

She looked at him blankly. "Fine, thank you. I just want to spend as little time as possible in a windowless room with Sir Dennis Carver."

"Terrible news about the Glasgow Art School," he said, as they waited to be let into the metal hanger.

"I hope they had insurance," Bobby said.

"Have you heard any news on what happened?"

"I doubt we will ever know," she said.

A man through thick glass nodded at Bobby's pass and a door slid open. They both signed in. At the other side of another door stood Carver, waiting for them in a black suit, white shirt, black tie. His hair was shaved shorter, his metallic face as hard and angular as an anvil. Eyes like incisions.

"Hello! Shall we go to work?" he said brightly.

"Well, of course, Sir Dennis," Bobby said gaily.

"Marvellous," Sir Dennis purred.

"Looking forward to finally seeing it in the flesh," Tallis said, as eagerly as he could muster.

"You sound like a giddy child, Thomas," Carver said. "But after this you can, of course, return to London. So, I understand your excitement."

The walls were white and windowless, and the floor was grey and hard. Double doors led to the main storeroom. It was cavernous. Sculptures stood in neat rows. Christ and David, old gods and anonymous Roman busts. Neo-classical sculptures and a large Victorian statue of a naked woman in a stream. There were many rows of high shelves and racks holding paintings, framed and unframed. Some were leant against the walls.

"This way," Carver said, his feet clicking on the floor.

"You look happy, Sir Dennis," Bobby said.

He frowned. "Actually, I am feeling rather impatient, Roberta. Impatient."

"Where is Ms. Peters?" she asked.

"I am afraid that she is abroad. She's terribly busy."

They passed through the store to another corridor, and off it, a door was open. In the centre of a bare room under dim light, a store technician was standing, wearing white gloves. Before him, a painting was laid on a table.

The Goldenacre.

"Thank you," Carver said to the technician, who left.

They stood around the table. The light was yellow and diffuse.

"Well, there it is," Bobby said quietly. "The grand prize."

"The apex of Mackintosh's art and work. Beautiful, is it not?" Carver said. "A masterpiece. We should be very grateful. And now in public hands, forever."

Tallis stepped forward and looked at the painting. The colours were faded. The dark hills were grey. The stone of the buildings pale. The frame was new: although it was scratched and chipped, and it had been glazed. Light rebounded from the glass and distorted the painting beneath. The robin in the foreground stood prim on its twig. The gold and silver glittered. Tallis stood on his tiptoes to look down on it. He bent over it. He put a finger to its glass. The robin looked lifelike, real. It looked as if it had been painted yesterday. He leaned over it more. The robin was askew. As if it had just landed on that twig. Clipped to it like a decoration.

"Thomas, let us not manhandle the painting before we can even show it to the public," Carver said, putting a firm hand to his shoulder. All bone fingers, no flesh.

"New frame," Bobby said. "The painting looks in worse

shape than the last photograph. Those blues and greens are very washed out. The paper may be damaged. I wonder if it is coming away from the board?"

"I don't believe it is a new frame," Carver said. "I understand it is the old one, but renovated. The board is fine."

"Frame looks new to me," Tallis said. "That wood is not aged at all. Look at the varnish."

"Yes, new," Bobby said.

"Ms. Peters said it had been thoroughly restored, and thus it all makes thorough sense," Carver said.

They stood, looking at the painting. It was as if the surface was the glinting skin of a pool, and something precious could be seen through unclear water at its bed. They stood as still and silently as the painting itself.

"A wonderful thing, is it not? All in all," Carver said. "Shall we now depart?"

Tallis did not want to leave.

"Are we scanning it?" Bobby asked. "X-ray? UV?"

"You shall in time, Roberta," Carver said, smiling.

"I need to see more of it, in better light," Tallis said.

"I'd like to do some of my own observations in the lab," Bobby said.

"Mr. Tallis, I think your journey ends here. It is now completely in our hands," Carver said, smiling just at the corners of his mouth. "Mackintosh's final painting, this work of genius, now safely transported to our stores. It will be unveiled to the public next week. There will be a grand press conference for the launch of our historic 'Mackintosh and the Spook School' exhibition next year. Now, let us depart." He moved his hands in a pushing motion.

The technician appeared again in a swish of nylon.

"Thank you, Gavin, you can lock up now," Carver said, leaving the room. He strode down the corridor, his shining black shoes resounding on the hard floors, like clippers snapping on wood.

Tallis and Bobby walked after him. Past the statues staring with blank eyes, past the racks and shelves of paintings, they moved in silence. They both signed out and Bobby called for a taxi. Carver was gone. They stood by the thick plate glass door, looking out over concrete ground and metal railings, and beyond the scrubland to distant brown square houses while the wind whipped and hissed.

Tallis wrapped his arms around his sore body. Bobby came closer and looked at him.

"What do you think?" Bobby said.

Tallis clutched his chest harder with his arms. His mind as black as the bottom of a midnight lake. "I don't think it's real," he said.

Bobby made a whooshing noise. "What do you mean?" she said very quietly.

"It's a copy. A fabulous copy. But a copy."

"Thomas, how can you know?" Bobby stamped her feet and briefly leant against the concrete wall. "How can you say that?"

"Does it look right to you? Could it have been conserved so badly that now it looks fake?"

She sucked her teeth and shook her head.

Tallis asked her again.

"Can I just say it looked like the right painting to me?" she said. "Sure, some of the illumination is heavy-handed, but was it not always? The blues and greens are washed out. But it's the picture. It's *The Goldenacre*."

Tallis put his hands to his eyes, which he closed. He knew he was right. "It's not real. I don't know what to say. I can't quite say why, either. It doesn't look like *The Goldenacre*. It is a version of it. But not the original. As soon as I saw it, I knew. Like a model of a thing, not the actual thing."

Bobby peered at him. "Are you absolutely sure?"

Tallis looked at her. "Yes. Either the family have been fooled, or we've been fooled, or everyone is fooling each other.

I will have to do more investigating. I don't want to. I will probably have to speak to my boss, God help me. It's made everything more difficult."

"You're right." She walked away for a few paces, and then came back. "Fuck." She squinted at him. "Didn't you have some kind of freak-out at the weekend? Is this part of the hangover? Are you messed up?"

He shook his head. His skin crawled. "No. Did you see the frame, Bobby? It's brand-new."

She nodded. "But the frame isn't the painting. The actual image: it's what I have seen in documents, and so on. The ones we saw at Denholm House. And no one gives a fuck about frames."

"Did you see the robin, Bobby? The robin is all wrong. It is too vivid. I don't know what more I can say. This is unknown territory."

The great gate to the high security store opened and a black taxi beetled into the drive, rubber grinding on concrete.

"King Dennis," Bobby said, "this painting is his great prize, and he seems to think it is real. The family—what's going on there, I don't know. Why aren't they here today? But they clearly believe it's the real deal, and they've done a £12 million deal with your fucking government for it."

"Yes," Tallis said. "But—"

"Why should this be a copy?" Bobby interrupted. "The line of ownership is intact, isn't it? It's solid. It's a direct line from the original purchase: from the artist to now. It's not left Denholm House. It's been photographed several times. It's had damage, but that is well documented. It's nigh-on a hundred years old, it's been hanging in that godforsaken pile all this time. It might be a bit worse for wear. It's been touched up, perhaps. The frame might indeed be some half-cocked new one. We can look into that. But why should the actual painting be a copy, Thomas? It doesn't make any kind of sense, at all."

"Carver wants us to go along with the lie," Tallis said. "To submit to the illusion. But I cannot. It's not right. The robin . . ."

Bobby shook her head.

They both stopped talking as they climbed into and sat in the taxi, which was to take them back to the Public Gallery.

"This is actually incredibly serious, if you start telling people this," Bobby said, at last. "If you are going to do something to stop this happening." She pushed her hand through her hair. "*Are* you going to stop this happening?"

"I cannot say right now." The car pulled into the grounds of the Public Gallery. "I don't know what else to say."

As the taxi pulled up, Bobby looked fiercely at Tallis. "It's unprofessional of you to even say that. Just after looking at it for three minutes. I would say nothing, if I were you. Absolutely nothing to anyone."

They both got out of the taxi.

She came close to him. "Seriously," she said softly and slowly, "I think you need to sleep on this notion. And for fuck's sake don't tell anyone else."

"I will sleep on it," he said, nodding. "Maybe we can see it again. In some proper light, not in that jail cell."

"Look, I'll ask. I need to see it again, too," she said, rubbing her eyes. She started to move into the great mass of the building, which hung above them like a stone cloud. "You coming in?"

"I need a walk," he said.

She shook her head and walked through the doors.

Slowly, Tallis walked to the back of the gallery. There was a footpath that led down, via a terrace of steps, to the river below. He walked down to the Water of Leith, which was high and burling white over boulders and rocks. There was a low bridge, and he walked halfway across it. He leaned on the railing and watched the water pound its way to the sea.

He closed his eyes and thought of the painting again. Under the dim light, in a dark room. Lying flat, like a corpse. Like the plan of an idea. Lying on a slab like the broken bodies of Robert Love and Councillor Cullen. No longer human, with just the appearance of being a person.

Maybe he was wrong? But he wasn't: the robin was so alive. As if it had been painted last week. It was not Mackintosh's graphical, cold, eerie depiction. This version was alive with life. Fizzing with it. Not a pattern or a decoration, but instressed with movement, with imparted energy, with potential.

He pulled at his hair and face. What could he do with his shame? It was drowning him. Had soaked into his body and inundated his mind. He had to be rid of it.

He looked at his phone. He called his father. Somewhere overseas. The mobile phone number rang and rang, as usual. No answerphone message, as usual, and then a brief, piercing beep. Tallis spoke quietly, as if whispering to a priest behind a grill. "I need to know some things. About this man, this man who might be against me, Dennis Carver. He said he knows you, or knew you. I'm in Edinburgh. I know you don't call, but here I am. I need help."

He closed the call and carried on walking, over the bridge to the other side of the Water of Leith, until he found a bench. He sat on it and listened to the water battering over the rocks. A man with a dog walked past, and the bristling little dog briefly came to see Tallis. Gleaming eyes and tight, spiky hair. Its whole miniature body seemingly wagged by its delighted tail. It bounded off.

His phone buzzed and rang.

His heart leapt.

He looked at the screen: no number supplied.

"Hello?" he said.

"Hello, Mr. Tallis," a woman's voice, a Scottish voice said.

"Yes?"

"Your secretary there gave me your number. I hope you don't mind."

"Did he, now?"

"I'd like to meet you for a quick chat."

"Who are you? Sorry, I must have missed it. I can't quite hear you, I'm beside a river."

"Are you fishing? My name's Shona Sandison, I'm a reporter for the *Post*."

He stood up and walked around in a tight circle, with his phone tightly pressed to his ear. "Yes," he said.

"I'd like to meet and have a chat."

"About what? Maybe you are the one fishing."

"About how you left your job at the Civic Gallery, landed at the government, and why you are in Scotland."

He closed the call. He put his phone in his pocket and strode down the track. He did not know where it was leading. Branches whipped off his shoulders and mud spattered. He pounded on. The river valley was tight and dark.

His phone rang again. Another withheld number.

"Fucking Christ," he said. He took the call.

"Sorry, we were cut off," Shona said.

"No, I closed the call, Ms. Sanson. I am not sure I need to speak to you. I left galleries and now work for the government. It happens all the time. It's boring but it's not a crime. Or news. Any more inquiries I would put to our press office in London. That's the usual way of doing things."

"Sandison. I do know you signed a Non-Disclosure Agreement," she said. "I know other things. But I need to meet you to chat about it all. Let's not have a row. Shall we have a coffee? If there's a story here, I may have to write it, of course. Maybe there isn't. I am not an expert on the arts world, or art. Maybe, Thomas, you can help me. Let's put it that way."

He pulled the phone away from his face.

The path forward was narrow and dark, and led only to

the sea. An old stone bridge hung overhead. It cast a shadow over the water, stones and trees. The surging water was angry and white, crashing and separating over rocks. There was no way to return. He was at the bend in the river.

"Maybe I can," he said.

They made arrangements to meet.

27

Tallis was back in his temporary office. He called for Mungo. The door opened and Mungo put his head around the edge.

"You called, master?"

"Mungo, I need to speak to the visual artist known as Vorn. Could we find a number?"

"To apologise?" Mungo's face was impassive. His hair was a distressed red rag.

"No, Mungo," Tallis said. "Not to apologise."

"How did the viewing of the painting go? Is it beautiful?"

"It's not my kind of thing. Beauty is in the eye of the beholder. *The Goldenacre* itself is beautiful, yes. Mungo?"

"Yes?"

"Could you also call Denholm House for me—that is Lord Melrose's house in the Borders—and find out for me when their celebration party is. Roberta and I were invited to some kind of reception, but I have lost the invitation, and I didn't note it down. And can you inform whoever answers the phone that we have viewed *The Goldenacre* today. Thank you."

"I shall do," Mungo said. "And there is some good news and bad news."

"What is the good news?"

"No parcels for you today."

"Well, that's good. And the bad?"

"A very rude man called for you. He said you had to call him directly."

"Was he called Mr. Melcombe?"

"Yes, that is right. Mr. Melcombe. He was rude."

"Well, can you kindly call him back and ask politely if he can go fuck himself," Tallis said.

"I am not sure, as your temporary secretariat, that I would recommend that course of action."

"That's fine, Mungo. I will inform him myself."

Mungo left the room and the door gently closed.

Tallis sat back in his chair. He looked at his phone, the lock screen image of Ray: a small face, smiling. He thought of the small candle he had lit in the cathedral. The wax becoming liquid, and the small flame, nubbed and a-quiver, dripping its light on stone walls and columns. The columns towering and luminous, as if he were in a great ship lit in the dark of the sea, or in a forest as the sun rises.

His lived life lay behind him, with all its failures and compromises. Paths to other lives were now shut, and other choices could have been made, but were not. There was no changing them now. The landscape behind him was cast, and cooled. Most of his life was done. Now he had to be rid of the consequences of his failures. He had wallowed enough. He had to make something good, and something right, to engineer a hard truth. And hope that the truth, once struck, could kindle the shame into a flame and burn away his guilt.

He left his chair and moved over to the window, leant on it. The glass was cool on his face. *The Goldenacre* opened before him: the ghosts in the grass, the shadows of giants in the mountains. A bird on a tree, singing a silent song. Angels in the green, angels in the blue. Where was *The Goldenacre*? It was not in that store. It was not in that frame. Maybe it had been destroyed in that fire, all those years ago, and the lord had covered it up, replaced it. Maybe *The Goldenacre* had never existed. Did Mackintosh really have the energy to leave his deathbed in London, dying of that dreadful cancer, to come to Scotland and create that work?

Maybe the Lords Melrose had maintained, out of vanity or insolence or arrogance, it was a true Mackintosh original. It would not be the first fraud to live in a country house. Not the first fraud to hang, celebrated, on a rich man's wall, and privileged lies often remain unquestioned. Who would gainsay it?

Mungo returned with a note, with both a number and an email. Tallis thanked him and returned to his desk. He called the number. It rang for a while.

"Hello," Vorn said.

"Hello, it's me, Thomas Tallis. You filmed me."

Vorn was speaking from somewhere outside, somewhere where leaves and branches were thrumming with swirling air.

"I'd like to meet," Tallis said.

"We can," she said. "I am working this afternoon, until about five. You can come after that, if you like."

Vorn told Tallis her address, and he made a note and hung up. He stood and opened the office door. Mungo was sitting at his computer, playing an online card game.

"Mungo," Tallis said.

"Indeed," Mungo said.

"Cast your mind back to the day that horrible package came," Tallis said. He sat on the edge of the table.

"I am casting," Mungo said, closing his eyes. Freckles around his eyes, his red hair glinting in the harsh office light.

"How did the package come to be in my office? Did you put it there?"

"Yes," Mungo said. "Which is why my fingerprints were all over it, probably. My DNA all over it. I'm amazed I've not been arrested, to be honest with you. That big police fellow with the makeup."

"But how did the package come to you?" Tallis asked, lowering his voice.

Mungo opened his eyes. He closed them again. "Now, I picked it up from the front desk. They had it, because it had been delivered. They rang me and said there was a parcel for you. I just wandered down there and picked it up."

"Did you tell the police that?"

"Yes, Thomas, I told them it had been delivered."

"Was there a delivery sticker or note?"

"I guess there must have been."

"Because, Mungo, what I remember is a clean box, with my name on it, but no stamp or sticker. No delivery note."

"Maybe it was inside one of those plastic delivery envelopes, and I took it out."

"Well, was it?"

Mungo put his head in his hands. "You know, it wasn't. I can't be a hundred per cent sure, but I remember seeing the box on the front desk. Maggie on security was there, she had called me up, said it had been left there."

"Maggie?"

"Yes, she is in today—do you want me to speak to her?" Mungo said excitedly.

"No, that's okay, Mungo, don't worry."

"It's really a good question though."

"Thank you, yes it is—now go back to your card game."

Mungo blushed. Patches of pink mottled around his cheeks.

"Don't worry, save all your hard work for whoever uses this office next."

Mungo grinned, and then frowned. "You're not going?"

"Not yet," Tallis said, and held out a placatory hand.

"Well, good," Mungo said, with emphasis. He added, "That party at Denholm House? You remain cordially invited, as is Bobby. I am sure Sir Dennis will be there too."

"I am sure. Thank you, Mungo." Tallis walked past

Mungo, out into the main gallery office corridor and down the spiral stairs to the lobby. At the front desk, a young couple were coming through the main doors, chattering and laughing. Clear light filled the entrance hall and signs gleamed. Maggie was sitting in a tartan uniform behind the long, low slab of a desk.

"Hi, is it Maggie?" Tallis said.

"Mr. Tallis." She smiled, looking up at him through fine black-rimmed glasses.

He sat on the desk. "Remember that day the police were here, about that package that was sent to me?"

"I do," she said. "The police interviewed me. You can ask Brian, if you like, he's my manager and—"

"No, it's fine, I don't need to speak to Brian. I was wondering: Who delivered the package? Was it a courier company? What did you say to the police on that?"

She sat back in her chair. "I didn't say anything to the police on that," she said, looking to Tallis with a steady stare. "Because, you know, they never asked that. And, till this minute, I never thought on it."

"Me neither," Tallis said, smiling.

"Nope, it was just there on the desk when my shift started at six A.M. that day. It was there with some letters and periodicals, I seem to remember. Is that helpful?"

"Thank you, Maggie," he said, and walked slowly back to his office. On his desktop was Detective Reculver's card, with a mobile phone number printed on it. He rang it.

"Reculver," a gruff voice said. It sounded like he was driving, the mobile on speakerphone.

Tallis introduced himself.

"How can I help you? Or can you help me?" Reculver said. "Whichever it is, can this be quick, I'm steaming down the A1."

"I'll be brief. The parcel that the tongue was in . . ."

"What about it? It's still in the lab."

"Is it being tested, swabbed, or whatever it is?"

"Well, I can't tell you any more about that."

"Any other prints on the package?"

"I can't rightly say," Reculver said. There was a pause. "Hello?"

"Sorry, just navigating a stupid tiny roundabout. No one builds junctions anymore. No, basically. I think that's all we had; whoever did the foul deed was wearing gloves or somesuch. I shouldn't be telling you this. Is that it? Just a check-up by you, is it?"

"Did you find out where the parcel came from?"

"It was delivered, wasn't it? It's not in the forefront of my mind right now."

"Can you check?"

"Excuse me, Mr. Tallis, with greatest respect, I don't take requests. I'm not a cabaret singer, luckily for the world. I am sure one of the officers checked all that out. When I am back in the office I shall check, how's that for you? As I am sure you know, we have two murders in Edinburgh to be investigated and it's taking up a lot of my time. I will have to go now. I will check for you. And here's another fucking roundabout. I'll have to go. Thanks for the call."

The line went dead.

Tallis rubbed his neck and back and then sent a text to Gretchen, asking how Ray was doing. He also looked up where Vorn lived and decided to walk there, through streets wide and silent. He walked slowly, his body still aching from the weekend, new thin scabs tender on his knees and elbows. Vorn lived in a flat near The Meadows, a green expanse in the south of the city. A wide and long field, it was ringed by old trees and crossed with paths. By the time Tallis was at the park, it was warm, and the sun was unhindered in a dark blue sky. He reached the flat, which was high up in a block of old Victorian tenements. He pressed the buzzer marked "Vorn."

"Enter," a voice said, and the heavy door clicked open.

Up the stone stairs, plants sat in red pots, and flowers hung down from railings and landings. A bicycle was attached to the top railing. The final landing had one door. Vorn was standing in it, tall and shaven, wearing all white. "I have cookies," she said.

Tallis entered the flat, which smelled sweetly of baking. The hall was white, and the floorboards had been painted green. Vorn led him into the main room, which was spare and overlooked The Meadows through a large bay window. Tallis could see the parkland, the shaking trees, the spires and towers of the university. Beyond, the city murmured. In the fireplace a cluster of Christmas lights blinked. Against one wall, in a recess, sat an upright piano. Tallis sat on a hard white sofa. On the wall by the fireplace hung three animal masks: badger, snake and mouse.

Vorn reappeared with a plate of cookies and a glass teapot filled with steaming amber liquid. "Provisions," she said, and sat on a stool by the window.

Tallis took a biscuit and bit into it. It filled his mouth with sugar. He noticed there were no mugs or cups. Perhaps he was to drink directly from the teapot's spout.

"What do you want to talk about?" Vorn said.

"Your event the other night."

"I heard it was a little bit too much for you. Someone told me."

Tallis nodded. "I must admit, I had a little bit much to drink beforehand." He realised he should have been embarrassed but did not feel so. "But it was a spectacular event," he added.

Vorn nodded and crossed her legs. "It seems to have had an effect. Whether the world changes or not, I don't know. I am planning more."

"I heard you videoed the event, or recorded it in some way," Tallis said, crumbs on his knees.

"I was recording. I will use it for the next Summoning. There will be more masks as well: seagulls, whales, seals, fire foxes, anacondas, pandas and spiders, frogs and tigers."

"I was wondering if I could see the film, your recording?"

Vorn frowned. "It lasts for hours and hours, Thomas. I haven't reviewed it all yet. You missed the animal masquerade at the climax."

Tallis smiled. "I would like to see the moment where I made for the exit."

"I am not going to delete it or censor the final version."

Tallis waved a hand. There was a row of scattered black scabs on his knuckles, and a neat blue puncture-bruise in the meat of his hand. "No, I don't want you to do that—I just need to check something."

Vorn was briefly still, showing no emotion, expressionless, and then stood up and walked across the room. "Is this an official request from the government?"

"Consider it so," Tallis said.

A silver laptop was on the piano stool. Vorn came back with it and sat beside Tallis. She had the scent of soap and silk. The laptop was flipped open, and Vorn opened the digital film file. There had been more than one camera. There was an array of different angles, each with its own box on the screen. Vorn's cursor moved over them.

"I think this will be the best one," she said. "From the apex of the tent."

Vorn clicked on a window, and the film appeared. The Summoning began once again, but this time Tallis could see it from above: the view from an escaped soul. People danced in masks in semi-darkness and in silence. The dark was cut and slashed by lights and flashes. The central golden light—a kind of artificial fire—glowed and strobed. Only partially in the shot, Vorn danced and chanted. There were many eyes in the rippling darkness, and many teeth bared in the hostile shadows.

Vorn turned up the volume, and the music juddered and pulsed. Shards of electronic noise rippling over a pounding beat.

"Jesus," Tallis found himself saying.

"Don't worry," Vorn said.

The film played for a while. Creatures moved in the fiery dark. There was bristle and hair and teeth and gums under glittering, icy lights.

"I'll fast-forward," Vorn said softly.

The film moved at triple pace—beasts hopping up and down, eyes flashing like strobes, blurs and buzzes of movement. Arms shivering like grass in the wind.

"Here we are. There you are, look," Vorn said quietly, and pointed.

Tallis saw himself. A man in a cat mask, his hands in the air. Shimmering in the fast-forward. Shaking as if with electrocution. Vorn pressed pause. There was Tallis masked, his clothes a shambles, amid the press and the mass of the dance.

"Shall we carry on?"

Tallis nodded. The film proceeded at normal speed. In the black and silver and red and green lights, Tallis danced, then suddenly looked behind. His head turned first. Then he turned his entire body around. The back of his head was on camera. He seemed to stop still. Frozen stiff as the tumult roiled about him.

"Does this zoom?" Tallis asked.

"A wee bit." Vorn pressed a key and the picture jerkily expanded. There was the back of Tallis's head, fuller in the frame. The film continued. Tallis was frozen and the rest of the crowd was dancing and moving, eyes of animals glittering. Now, larger in the background, he saw the face of a fox, and above the fox, a bear.

"Pause there," Tallis said.

Vorn pressed pause. The fox and the bear stood still. The fox, a mask on a slim, black-clothed body, was halted.

The bear's face, partially obscured by a dancing hand, hovered above a large man's shoulders.

"Carry on," Tallis said.

"Please?"

"Sorry," Tallis said, nodding. "Please press play."

The film rolled on. Suddenly Tallis dropped out of sight. Vorn expanded the frame again. Tallis was no longer there. Dancers were looking down, and some were moving out of the way of something. One, with an owl mask, seemed to fall, jerkily collapsing out of shot.

"Sorry," Tallis said.

"No one was injured," Vorn said quietly.

In the background, there seemed to be a scuffle at the triangular shadow of the door. A glimmer of a distressed body, flitting into the dark.

Tallis sat back and breathed out heavily.

Vorn paused the film. "I shall get some cups," she said, and left the room.

Tallis stared into the screen. In the darkness, behind the dancers and the light, out of view, his body was tumbling, rolling, bouncing down grass and into and over rocks and bricks and, at the end, meeting a sudden end in a grid of metal. He had wanted to die.

Light glimmered in silvery petals on the warm glass teapot. Vorn came back into the room and poured two cups. Tallis sat back and drank the tea, warming as it was.

Vorn carried on watching the video, playing with the angles, the views from the different cameras. There were angles from each corner of the tent, and from the centre of the golden light. There had been a camera directly over the entrance to the Summoning. There was a huddle of people there, some entering, some leaving, others with their masks off, talking. Some were smoking, some drinking, with tiny glasses of green liquid in their hands.

"A lot of people," Vorn said.

"It felt like death," Tallis responded.

"A lot of people want to touch the line of death," Vorn said. "I did once, too. But what did the writer say? Humanity's innate aversion to suicide prolongs our needless grief."

Vorn had clear skin, as smooth as alabaster. Pale lips, and pale eyelashes. A shaved head, unblemished.

Tallis looked back at the laptop. There, by the yawning door of the tent, stood a man he recognised, holding a mask in his hand. Tallis leaned in, to look harder. The man was standing with two others. One was clearly Carver, holding the fox mask. Sleek and poised.

"Friends?" Vorn said.

"Not as such. Is there a better angle of this moment, so I can see this man's face?" Tallis pointed at the screen. The man next to Carver was wearing what looked like red trousers and a gilet. The bear stood nearby, looming.

"This is all very interesting, Mr. Tallis," Vorn said. "Will you be able to tell me what we are doing here? I have an appointment in about fifteen minutes."

"Is there a better angle?" Tallis said.

Vorn raised her eyebrows and cycled through the angles and views. "I'm not sure there is."

"Could you zoom in on the one we had before?"

"I am sure I can."

The previous angle was restored. The man was indeed wearing red trousers.

"Let me go back a bit—I think he turns his face to the camera a little bit more," Vorn said.

The frames reversed. The face turned, the shoulders rotated. Grainy and flickering with colour. Vorn zoomed in on the face. It was Felix Farquharson. His long face, his shaggy hair. Talking, animatedly, even angrily, to Carver and a grey-haired man in his bear mask. Something was bothering Felix. One of his hands was up, pointing.

Tallis nodded. "That's all," he said. He sat back and put a hand to his face.

"Are you okay?" Vorn said, putting a light hand on his shoulder. "You are pale."

Tallis turned to Vorn. "Thank you. And sorry for my rudeness, and my insistence."

"Can I ask you what you are doing?"

Tallis stood up and looked over The Meadows. Shadows were lengthening over the grass. Car lights flickered and students were walking back from the university. The moon had appeared, glimmering over Arthur's Seat, like a circular passage cut to another place, a realm of light. "I'd better go," Tallis said.

"You had," Vorn said.

Tallis thanked Vorn again. At the door, they shook hands.

"I shall see you again," Vorn said.

"I doubt it," Tallis said, and left.

By the time he was on the path he was running.

28

"Shona," Stricken said. He tried to catch her attention by waving.

The two of them were in the coffee shop. Colm had called them both that morning, saying there would be a big meeting about redundancies at the newspaper, and they would both be expected to attend.

"What, Hector?" Shona said to Stricken. "Don't interrupt my misery when I'm enjoying it so much." She was curled in a large armchair. She was half-heartedly looking online for journalism jobs. They all seemed to be in London, and poorly paid.

"Shouldn't you be at work?" he said from the chair opposite.

"I am working."

"At least we will get payoffs."

"I don't want a payoff or a bung, Hector—I want to be a news reporter. In Scotland," she said, putting her phone down on the table. She was due to meet Thomas Tallis soon. In the old cathedral, St. Mary's, with its three spires.

"Me too, me too," Stricken said.

"Well, it won't happen with this editor. This is what happened at the *Mercury*. Some arsehole comes in, talks about digital a lot, talks about necessary cuts to preserve the future of 'the brand.' No one talks about the newspaper but instead some hazy apparition of a website. Then reporters leave or are laid off, and, within a year, the shoddy online product doesn't make any money, and the paper closes. Another newspaper dies. Ends."

"But our paper makes money." Stricken was dressed, as usual, in waterproof clothes and walking boots. He rustled. He had not shaved for a few days and a ginger beard was sprouting, spotted with hard, white hairs.

"Doesn't make a sod of difference. You have to remember, Hector, the people who run newspapers don't actually like journalists. They fear and look down on reporters. They fucking hate old-timers, like my old man. Or me. Or you. And, at heart, they're worried that one day we will report on them."

"Oh, come off it, Shona. Not everything is a conspiracy."

"A conspiracy is just a plan you are not part of, Hector."

They sat in silence for a while. Music tinkled and the world whirred outside.

"Anyway, the reason for our meeting . . ." Stricken said.

"For you to buy me a coffee and quit talking? Thanks," Shona said.

"Nope, I've had a lot of time on my hands, and—"

"Don't tell me you've taken up cooking, or fucking folk music."

"No." He turned his head to one side and grinned. "And what's wrong with folk music?"

"Don't get me started. Ned Silver loved all that 'Oh me canny man's gone off to sea' shite."

Stricken shook his head and reached into his haversack and took out some paper.

"If it's your poems again, Hector, I'd rather slit my throat."

"Nope, it's murders."

"More interesting, then," she said.

Stricken leaned forward, pointing at the printed paper. It was a sheaf of cuttings. "That mad man that chased me around the houses?" he said.

"Yes, it's still quite fresh in my memory, Hector."

"He was holding something in his hand. Now, I didn't see what it was. But it might—might—have been a tent peg, or some kind of metal spike anyway. Robert Love had his head staved in, did he not?"

"He did."

"And our late Councillor Cullen had, apparently, his head bashed in, too."

"Go on."

"I called a contact at the cops. And don't look at me like that—I have contacts too."

"I'll allow it," she said, making a winding motion with her hand.

"He said—well, he said not much—but he did confirm that Cullen died from catastrophic head injuries. So, I searched for murders with head injuries. Not assaults and manslaughters, not familial madness and all that, but proper murders: gangland hits, hard men offing each other, all that. Serious organised crime."

"Right." Shona noticed an over-enthusiasm in Hector's voice, which grated. "Have they got anywhere with Cullen?"

"Nope, nowhere. But look, there have been six murders with very similar descriptions in the last five years." He shook his cuttings. One sharp corner of paper dipped into his coffee cup, catching a dab of brown and cream. "Two in Manchester—one with a piece of sharpened central heating piping that was left in the fella's head."

"That would be pretty sore."

"Indeed. Another in London. Three in Newcastle."

"What are those warring gangs down there? The Hurlocks and the—"

"Hurlocks, that's right," Stricken said, "and some

Russian-backed team. It all got crazy for a while, a couple of years back. The police upped their game and slapped down on it all. National force got involved. I think, going by all reports, the Hurlocks emerged as 'winners,' whatever that means. Certainly they're loaded. The family live in big mansions in Northumberland, apparently. It's all quite well covered in the *Chronicle* and the *Echo*."

"Yup," Shona nodded. "So you're saying that Cullen and Love were killed by some mad Geordie gangsters. A wee Edinburgh councillor and an obscure Scottish artist. Killed by a Newcastle team."

"I'm not, no. I can't see a connection at all." Stricken slapped down the paper. "But it's interesting. It's not all guns and knives. Someone is killing folks, quite efficiently, with a spike in the head."

"Our madman?"

"Maybe." He sipped his coffee. "I certainly felt like he wanted to kill me with a spike to the head."

"Did you hear about the four-by-four?"

"Burnt out."

"Like us." Shona looked at the time—it was time to go. "See you later, I'm off."

"Off where?"

"The big one, Hector. Off to write the big one."

Stricken smiled, scratched his beard. "You should. Show them we're still value for money."

"I know I am," she said. "You know the editor has asked me to send him a report of what happened at the building site? And why we were there?"

Stricken went pale.

"I'm not writing a word for that prick," she said, and gave Hector a brief goodbye wave.

Shona left the coffee shop and began walking to the cathedral. It was raining and she pulled up her hood. Water darkened the pavements and gave a polish to slates and stone.

She passed through Charlotte Square, silent and empty in the rain, and through a crooked medieval lane, and reached a long, wide street of Georgian buildings. At its western end stood St. Mary's Cathedral, a dark mass with spires, three fingers pointing into the sky. She reached the grassy land that lay around the cathedral. The building loomed above her. She had never been inside before. It looked sullen, dark and redundant, an empty mass of hollowed stone. Shona walked around the black, towering exterior of the cathedral. The rain ceased and the sun emerged from behind fast-moving silver clouds. She walked to its entrance and through a tall stone aperture, and then plain glass interior doors, to the cavern of solemn stone inside.

Shona was suddenly in a place of silence and captured space. The crucifix on the altar seemed to burn in the revealed sun. But the cathedral was empty: no one sat in the pews, no choir in the stalls, and the seat in front of the organ was vacant. Shona walked slowly down the aisle, her feet and stick rapping on the stone.

Lights burned in a space from the corner of her eye. She turned her head and candles were flickering on a small metal table beside one of the towering pillars. Tall, pale, thin candles and, in small tin cups, smaller flames. An icon hung above them, glittering in rich red and gold. She walked over to the candles. There was a blush of heat. Light shifted in the air. A cloud of shadow passed through the silent forest of stone.

"Are you going to light a candle?" a male voice said.

Shona turned around. A middle-aged man in a long overcoat stood before her. He had ruffled hair and a two-day beard. His hands were in his pockets. His eyes were large and watery. He looked like he had not slept in days.

"No, I'm not. Why would I?" she said.

"Just to add to the light." He held out a hand. "I am Tallis."

She took his hand. It was weak and pale. They shook. "Shona Sandison," she said.

"You wanted to talk to me."

"You agreed to talk to me. Shall we go somewhere with coffee?" she said.

He looked around the cathedral. He seemed worried. There was no one around. The sunlight was beginning to warm the space. "Did you come here alone?" He looked to the doors.

"Yes, only me," she said.

"No one else?"

"I wasn't followed, if that is what you mean. Shall we move somewhere else?"

He nodded and then shook his head. "Here is fine," he said, and sat down on the end of a pew. He picked up one of the decorated knee cushions and put it on his lap. It had been roughly woven, in bright primary colours—a design in red and blue and white, depicting a saint. "Ah, Saint Jude," he said, with a small smile. "How apt. Do you know your saints, Shona?"

She looked at Tallis. He was pale. Where his neck emerged from his white linen shirt, there appeared to be the edges of a large bruise, mottled in pink and red. There were crumbs of black dried blood in his hair. "No, I have no idea about saints. My father is an old communist, so we never went to church. My mother did, though, every week. Not sure it helped her much."

"Did you ask her?"

Shona ignored the question and sat down in the next pew and turned around to face him. "So . . ." she said. She took her notebook and a pen from her bag.

"This won't be on the record, I'm afraid," he said.

"I think we can discuss that."

"I will leave now, actually," he said quietly, "if you don't agree."

Shona nodded. She had been in conversations of this type many times before. "That's fine—this is all off the record. But I will need to make notes for my own benefit. I wouldn't want to get any facts wrong."

"Unattributable," he said.

"Okay."

Tallis nodded. He swallowed hard. "You say you know something about how I came to work for the government?" His voice quivered.

"I heard you left the Civic Gallery in London under a cloud and had to sign a secrecy agreement. There's ways I can find out what happened. But I'd love it if you'd tell me."

"No. This won't go like that," he said clearly, if shakily. He shook his head. "This is how I propose this conversation goes, if you don't mind. I will give you a bigger story and, in exchange, you will not write about why I had to leave the London Civic. In particular, you will not bother my former boss about it all. I have to tell you something else, something more important. You can quote me—off the record, if you like—for that story."

Shona nodded. "How do I know if it will be a better story than your mysterious exit from your job at the gallery?"

"I will tell you both," he said. "And you will hear for yourself." He rubbed his face with his hands.

The sun was now unhindered in the sky outside. Light had filled the vessel of the cathedral. The distance between the world as it was, and the world as it should be, had never felt wider.

"Are you ready?" he said.

"Yes," she said, raising her notebook.

"Well. Where to start?" He gestured a hand, its knuckles scabbed and red with swelling, towards the altar. "This could be a confessional. I haven't told anyone this before. Not my wife. Not my family."

"I don't do forgiveness," Shona said.

"Neither do I. That's the problem."

"Have you been in a fight?" Shona pointed at his hands.

He looked at his knuckles, as if surprised. "Only with myself," he said, in a quiet, patient voice. He breathed out and closed his eyes.

Shona leaned forward and grinned. "Are you always so downbeat, Thomas Tallis?"

He smiled too. "Do you know music?"

"I know what I like."

"Well, in music, without the downbeat, you cannot truly measure time."

"There's an upbeat, too, Thomas."

"There's always an end, as well," he said. "And then, the silence."

Shona nodded and waited for him to speak.

"I worked at the Civic Gallery in London, SE1, for ten years. I was an assistant curator there. I helped stage exhibitions. I curated a few myself. I became interested over the years in artworks with muddled or mistaken histories, or of disputed provenance. Strange, twisted alleyways of history. I helped with a quite well-known reattribution at the National Gallery. And that became an ongoing concern. I was settled there, at the Civic. I met my wife, former wife, while working there. It was all fine, for a while."

"For a while. What does your wife do?"

"She is a musician. But she is irrelevant to this. My marriage to her began to fall apart. No one to blame. Just one of those things." He wiped an eye with the sleeve of his coat, and Shona noticed the left-hand pocket of his coat was ripped. "Certainly not her fault, anyway," Tallis said. "Not her fault. Perhaps we should never have married in the first place. Who knows?"

"Children?"

He wiped his other eye. "Yes, we have a son. Anyway, as that all began to collapse around me, my boss and I began a stupid little thing. A messy little affair. Squalid. She is married; I was married. We spent a lot of time together, and we liked each other. It was all pathetic. Predictable."

"One thing led to another," Shona said.

"One thing always leads to another, unless time decides to stop," Tallis said. "Yes, one thing led to another. Christmas drinks, clinches in alleyways, stupid texts, unfortunate emotional outbursts. Turning up at her house at two in the morning. Guilt. Sweating like an animal. All that." He sighed. "But Celia—I mean, my boss; her name isn't important—she brought it all to an abrupt end. She wanted to repair her marriage. She felt guilty. And so on."

"This all seems very personal and painful but doesn't seem—"

"Unfortunately, this is where my behaviour became inadvisable. Destructive," Tallis said. He turned to one side, so Shona could only see his dishevelled profile. The deep bruise on his neck was vivid. He put his face into his hands.

"If you want some time to yourself . . ." Shona said.

"No, I am fine." He turned back to her. "We would always meet for our squalid clinches in the stores. The stores of the Civic are underneath the main building. Two floors of basements. Darkened spaces down there. Places to be hidden, and to hide. Underneath London's surface. So we would meet down there. Plenty of times. And the last time, we had an argument. It was mainly my fault. I didn't want her to leave me alone. I knew she did not love me. And I did not love her. But we were still entangled. It was a mess. But anyway, at this last meeting, this . . . terrible meeting, I was clumsy. I lost my balance." He was speaking in a quiet monotone.

"Anyone can lose their balance," Shona said.

"Someone else once said that to me," Tallis said, smiling slightly, looking at her. He swallowed hard and continued. "I lost my balance. I was behaving erratically. There was a painting down there, a beautiful painting. It happened to be in the way of my clumsiness. A rare study: *Madame Camus at the Piano*, by Edgar Degas. It was a preparatory painting, half-finished and not as fine as the completed version, but still wonderful. And so interesting—on the canvas there were still signs of Degas working it out, all there on the painting. It was a work in progress. It was not often on show, for that very reason. It was being brought out of store. We were going to show it again to the public, give it new life, show it beside its better-known fellow painting. Anyway. I destroyed it. It was broken." He stopped talking and looked up into the far ceiling of the cathedral.

"You destroyed it?" she said.

"Yes. It was wrecked. Irretrievably lost."

"How?"

"I don't need to relive it."

"How much was it worth?"

Tallis shifted in his seat. "Who knows? It had never been bought or sold. And its monetary worth is beside the point. Its value was something else. It was priceless."

"How did you lose your balance?"

Tallis shook his head and tightened his arms around the prayer cushion. He was not going to tell her.

"I take it accidentally destroying a painting isn't an ideal situation for a curator?"

He smiled briefly. "No, Shona. It tends to be looked down upon. It's not ideal."

"And your boss, what did she do?"

"Well, she knew it was a catastrophe, of course. She was horrified. She was upset. I think she felt, rightly or wrongly, part of the whole disaster. We discussed what to do, and we—for a change—felt honesty was the best policy. We both told the director of the Civic. A mortifying scene. There was a terrible period after that. I was signed off, sick. Essentially we were sacked, but we both signed NDAs and the gallery would not acknowledge what had happened. They had some help, covering it up. The painting does not exist anymore, officially. It never existed."

"What if someone wants to see it?"

"They would have to know it was once there," Tallis said. "And it is no longer on the Civic's records. And you'd be surprised how few people really dig around for these things."

"But what if they did?"

"I don't know. A Degas scholar, perhaps? An Impressionist curator looking for unusual discoveries? There are few arts journalists around anymore, to look into these things. Again, you'd have to know it had been there in the first place. As Augustine said, 'How can I find you, if I do not know you?'"

"Saints again. I don't know what you are talking about, but I am sure you are right."

"So, there it is," he said. "Pitiful, really. I was given—I found—a job in government. And now I am here, in Edinburgh, working, for the time being, at the Public Gallery."

"The government do not know about your incident?"

"No, of course not," he lied.

Shona nodded. The doors to the cathedral opened and two elderly women walked in. They wore hats and thick brown coats. They walked up the aisle and nodded and smiled at Shona and Tallis. They headed for the choir.

"Well, I have not heard a story like that before," she said.

Tallis covered his face with his hands. He seemed to be mumbling something to himself. Shona waited for him to reach composure again. He smelled of sweat, tears and old wine.

"You won't hear a story like this again," he said. "We can go for that coffee now, if you like."

"Yes, I know a place nearby. But you need to tell me the other story."

Tallis stood up and put the prayer cushion carefully back on the floor of the pew. There was fresh colour to his cheeks. He seemed relieved. "Oh, I think you'll find it much more interesting."

"What if I want to write both?"

"Then I would deny everything. The Civic won't help you. No one will help you. You'd probably get somewhere. But not close to the true version. Not the actual, correct course of events."

"But you just told me the story," she said, as she followed him down the nave to the door.

"Perhaps. Or did I?"

"Are you always this grim and mysterious, Mr. Tallis?"

"No. I am not. But I have lately lost all my mirth."

"I know what you mean."

The cathedral filled with a sudden burst of music. The organ played huge chords. The vast sounds rang from rock and glass. Its abrupt attack made Shona flinch, and she leaned into Tallis.

"So, this second story—the one you want me to write—is this about something in London too?" she asked loudly.

"Oh no, it is about a matter right here, in Edinburgh, in Scotland. Right now." Tallis held the door open for Shona. "And I would like for you to run it in your newspaper. Is that possible?"

"Potentially. If you give me enough detail."

"I will give you all the detail."

"Thank you. Wait, you haven't destroyed another painting, have you?"

"No, but I hope to," he said, as they walked out into the daylight.

The sun shone on puddles and wet stone. The rain had been, fallen and gone.

<u>6:34 P.M.</u>

I've told a reporter everything.

This painting, it's a fraud. There is one part of it . . . the bird. There is a robin. I don't know whether there are robins in limbo or purgatory, or wherever you are. But this one was painted so much brighter and better than the Mackintosh.

I don't know if Dennis Carver believes it's real, or not. I don't know why a fake would be made. Or where the real version of The Goldenacre *is.*

I will see Astrella and Ray soon. I won't ever see you. All I have of you is this phone number.

What could you have possibly done? Did you tell too many lies, or cover up too many? What are you doing with all your memories? Can you even think straight? Can you listen to your fucking voice messages?

I want to forget. I want this all to be over.

Bye.

2 9

Tallis and Aunt Zed were walking down the esplanade as the tide came in over the grey sands of Portobello.

A newspaper article would be published, and he would probably lose his job.

Shona had called him back, to check some details. But she could not call him anymore, as his phone was out of battery. He had left it in Zed's kitchen. He was done with it all, now. Melcombe could call, he could email—he would receive no reply.

The sun was setting. Shadows grew on the beach, and the air was cooling. The lights of the seafront cafés and pubs glowed on the concrete path. Zed's arm was through his. They walked slowly and quietly, heading for the fish and chip shop.

"I suspect I will probably go soon," he said at last. "You can have your spare room back, and I will be out of your hair."

She looked up at him. "Back to London." She leaned her head on his shoulder.

"I don't think this new job is going to work out at the government," he said. "I am not sure, shall we say, I will get through my probation period."

"Are you sure? But what will you do?"

"Something close to Ray. If I can."

"Maybe you could move here?"

"No, not here. I need somewhere that is extrovert, to counter my introversion. Edinburgh needs coaxing. I prefer to be coaxed."

"That's one way of putting it, I suppose," Zed said. "But it is such a beautiful city. You could give it more time, Tommy."

"Beautiful, yes, but then so is a necropolis."

Zed laughed.

"Also, in London, no one sends me body parts in the post," Tallis said.

They reached the chip shop and bought three fish suppers. Jack would be home soon. The sunset bled a deep blood orange across the sky and they walked home in silence.

At the house, Jack was slumped on the sofa, watching TV. "Thomas, there's been calls for you," he said, not looking up. "A fella called Mungo. He says to call him on his mobile phone."

"Mungo called me here?"

"Yes, several times. He said he tried your mobile, but no dice."

Tallis walked upstairs in the gloom and plugged in his phone, which came to life, lighting the room with its sub-sea glow. He had several missed calls. He ignored the voicemails and called Mungo.

"Oh my God," Mungo said loudly. He seemed to be out of breath.

"What's the matter?"

"I've been calling you, over and over."

"I know, I'm sorry, it was dead."

"Have you seen the website of the *Post*?"

"No, should I?"

"You should read it—right now," Mungo shouted.

"Should I?"

"Sir Dennis is silent and mad. The press office are beside themselves, and—"

"I will look, and call you back, Mungo," Tallis said, his insides sliding.

He looked on the internet, and found the *Post*'s website. They had run Shona Sandison's story early. By design, or mistake.

QUESTION MARK OVER £12M MACKINTOSH MASTERPIECE

Exclusive
By Shona Sandison, Senior Reporter

A £12 million masterpiece painting given to the Public Gallery in a blockbuster deal could be a fake, sources have told the Post.

The Goldenacre, *a painting by the world-renowned Scottish architect and artist Charles Rennie Mackintosh, is due to be unveiled by the Edinburgh gallery next week. The painting, owned by the late Lord Melrose, who died aged 81 last year, has been given to the Public Gallery as part of the Acceptance Instead of Tax scheme run by the UK government.*

But senior sources have sensationally told an investigative team at the Post *that the painting given to the galleries could be a FORGERY.*

It is understood that the senior staff at the gallery are in uproar over the "fraudulent" artwork, which is being held at the gallery's top-security stores.

The Public Gallery did not return inquiries by this newspaper last night. And the office of the late Lord Melrose, at the ancient family seat of Denholm House in the Borders, could not be reached for comment.

A senior curatorial source said: "There is great consternation here, as the painting in our stores is clearly not The Goldenacre *by Charles Rennie Mackintosh, a beautiful painting which he made in the last year of his life.*

"What we have been given looks like a very fine copy. We are trying to urgently find out whether this fake has been hanging on the walls of Denholm House all these years, or whether something more sinister is afoot.

"But several senior members of staff have now seen this painting, and it is not The Goldenacre.

"It begs the question: Which painting did the UK government see when it agreed to offset £12 million in inheritance tax by transferring this shoddy fake to a public collection?"

A source said that it looked like the painting had been copied by a talented artist, but that some details were wrong, or painted substantially differently from archived images of the work.

It is possible that the copy was created recently, the source said.

The frame of the painting, which dates from the 1920s and has hung in Denholm House since it was purchased by the Farquharson family, is also believed to be new.

The Post *understands that the painting was due to be unveiled at a glitzy launch at the gallery next week, and that director Sir Dennis Carver had told colleagues that acquiring the painting was the highlight of his long and illustrious career.*

The Public Gallery has been working with a senior UK government official, Thomas Tallice, on the deal. Mr. Tallice, who worked for the Civic Gallery in London for a decade before joining the government, was unavailable for comment last night.

Tallis read the article twice. Shona had done a good job, although his name was spelled incorrectly. He considered calling her, to ask why it had been put online, and not saved for the paper for the morning. But it didn't matter. The story was out in the world and would take on a life of its own.

He had missed calls from the Public Gallery press office and from a private number. He had also missed a call from a civil service number in London. He would not call them back.

He sat in his bedroom until Zed called from downstairs. His fish was getting cold.

Zed was on the sofa, watching TV, picking chips and shards of fish from the papers on a plate on her lap. "Delicious," she said, as Tallis went into the kitchen. Jack was at the kitchen table, eating in silence, scooping food into his beardy mouth. Tallis sat there, too, and began to eat. The room was full of vinegar and salt, a tang of sauce and fish.

"Jack," Tallis said, "you fancy getting a pint after this?"

"Oh, that's a wonderful idea," Zed called from the sofa. "You two boys go out for a drink. There's a lovely pub just down on the beach, Thomas. You go there."

Jack raised his head and looked at Tallis. "It's a school night, Thomas," he said.

"I know. Just a pint and a chat."

"Let's wait till another time," Jack said, and filled his mouth with chips. He had large, hairy fingers.

"You have a lovely time," Zed said. "I can't believe how delicious this fish is. Must be fresh. Straight from the sea. Jack, you should see this by-election debate. They're all lunatics."

"I need to talk to you about something," Tallis said quietly. He put a finger on Jack's plate.

Jack looked up. "About what?"

"About *The Goldenacre*, about your frame." Tallis put a chip in his mouth.

"I mean," Zed exclaimed from the sofa, "they're just such liars."

Jack looked at Tallis with steady eyes. "Thomas here and I are going to pop to the pub, Zed," he said.

"Great," she said, "I'll record this for you."

Tallis and Jack ate their food in silence. They put the plates to one side and got their coats from the hooks in the tiny hall. They walked in the dark to the pub that looked out over the now inundated beach to the black sea.

Inside, it was quiet. They found a table and sat.

"I'll buy," Jack said and walked slowly to the bar.

Tallis waited. His phone was on his bed, ringing and buzzing in a dark room on a woollen blanket.

Two pints of dark beer were set down on the mats on the tabletop.

"So . . ." Jack said. He pushed his tangled hair back from his ears.

"Robert Love painted a copy of *The Goldenacre*," Tallis said.

Jack sipped from his pint.

"You provided the frame," Tallis added. "Am I right in thinking that?"

"I've worked with Bob Love," Jack said. He took another sip, and foam hung from his moustache.

"On this *Goldenacre* copy," Tallis said.

"What are you now, Tommy, the polis?"

"I'd rather they weren't involved."

Jack turned his pint glass around. Then did it again. He sat back on his seat. "Is there a problem?"

"Have you got your phone?"

"Aye."

"Look up the *Post*'s website. Top story."

Jack fished into his pocket and took out his old phone. As he fiddled with it, Tallis drank the beer. It was heavy and sour. He looked out of the window, to the sea, where an oil tanker slid across the horizon.

"Well," Jack said. He put his phone on the table.

"Well, indeed," Tallis said.

"Is that you quoted?"

"No," Tallis lied.

"What a fuck-up," Jack said.

Tallis drank more from his glass, and he felt the alcohol swirl in his blood.

Jack sighed, wiped his mouth and began to speak. "Bob asked me to make a big frame. He gave me the dimensions, and these patterns he wanted, at the corners. He said he'd had a big commission. Told me it was all private, not to mention it. Why would I? I don't go around telling people what I'm doing."

"Did he say who had commissioned him?"

"Aye, he said it was some posh woman," Jack said. "Kathy Peters. Working for Lord Melrose."

"Why did he tell you that?"

Jack flashed Tallis a look. His eyes glittered in the golden pub light. "Bob and me go way back."

"And now he's dead."

"And now he's fucking dead." Jack took a swig from his beer. "I think it had something to do with his debts," Jack said quietly.

"His murder?"

"Aye. I think he owed money to bad people."

"How do you know?"

"He was thinking of selling up, selling the house, moving away. Moving to an island. Up north. He was talking about that. But his daughter, she's about to have a baby. That would be his first grandchild. So, I think he was having second thoughts. But I thought he was scared."

"Scared?"

Jack nodded. He drank from his pint.

"Did you see what he was working on?"

"I saw what he was working on. This is a couple of months ago. A large watercolour. I caught a swatch of it when I was coming around with his wood samples. For the frame. He wanted light wood, pale wood. I could see into his studio from that long hall of his. He was being weird about it. He saw I'd seen. He shut the studio door. He'd never done that before—he liked having people in and around him when he worked. He wasn't precious about it. He was like that, was Bob."

"Was it *The Goldenacre*?"

"I saw a corner. Maybe a quarter of it. Big thing on his easel. Then we had a few words."

"What do you mean?"

"A rammy, an argument."

Tallis waited for Jack to continue.

"He didn't want me to put the picture in the frame. He said he had someone else to do that. But I'm the bloody framer, I said to him, that's what I do. We had words about it. But he paid me, in cash. I took the frame around to his. This is about three or four weeks ago. That was that."

"You never saw it framed?"

"Nah. It pissed me off. Not for the first time with Bob." He took another drink. He pointed to his phone. "This is bad news."

"It is."

"They can't trace that frame to me," Jack said firmly.

Tallis sipped his beer and tilted his head.

"Fucking stupid," Jack said. "Why would they want a copy of it? I figured, I was thinking—"

"Go on," Tallis said.

"That they wanted the copy to replace the original, once the original is at the Public Gallery. A replacement. Something to remember the painting by, on the wall in their house. An honest replica. That's an understandable thing to do, right?"

"Right," Tallis said, nodding. "An honest replica."

"But, so, why all the secrecy?"

"How secret was it?"

"Well, Bob was being all MI5 about it: 'No one can know. This is one where we both just do the job and forget about it.' Think about the money, he was saying. Don't tell anyone. But I daresay he was paid a bit. I got paid above and beyond for the work I did."

"How much?"

Jack squinted at his pint. "More than enough."

"This woman, the one working for Lord Melrose—did you meet her?"

"No."

"How did you know about her?"

"Bob told me. I've already said that."

They sat back and drank in silence. The sea covered the beach outside.

"What's going to happen with this?" Jack said at last, pointing to his phone again.

"I think I'm out of a job."

Jack nodded. "Shame, that."

"I'm not sure it is," Tallis said.

They finished their drinks and walked back to Zed's house in silence. It was dark, the only light from electricity. The sea was soundless. Distant cars hummed on the main road in and out of Edinburgh. The moon was hidden.

They got to the door.

"I'd be obliged if you wouldn't mention this to—" Jack began to say, gruffly.

"I won't, Jack," Tallis said. "I want Zed to be happy."

Jack nodded.

"Someone deserves to be," Tallis added, and they walked through the door into the warmth and light.

30

"Why the fuck was it online last night?"

"A fuck-up with the website," Colm said. "Something to do with the metadata. I dunno. This is what happens when you email copy from home and don't put it in the system yourself: shit fucks up. There's no one here to check things. It's the splash this morning, so quit the moaning. Good story. Nice tale. We need a follow-up."

"But it was online last night, so who is going to bother buying the paper this morning?" Shona said.

"Because of the rest of the newspaper's unique, compelling content," Colm said tiredly. "Anyway—we need a follow-up. Let me know ASAP. Bye."

Shona threw her phone across her living room. It landed on the sofa.

Her father was loudly putting his shoes on in the hall. "Your language is terrible, oh daughter of mine."

"I learned it from you," she said.

Hugh shambled into the living room. He was wearing waterproof trousers and a thick coat, ready for the allotment.

"What a shambles," Shona said. "If it's an exclusive, don't put it on the internet the day before it is due to be printed. For fuck's sake."

"I've no idea what you're on about. You going to work or not?"

"I guess so. I'll come with you on the bus for a bit. Might help my brain."

They left the flat and walked out to the estate. There were pebble-dashed blocks of flats and low-rise houses. High bushes were trimmed and untrimmed. There was a single row of shops: a fried chicken takeaway, a betting shop, a hairdresser, a Co-Op. The sky was clear, but it was cold. Two boys circled the path on bicycles, chatting.

"Got any idea for a follow-up?" her father said. He had a woollen hat balanced precariously on his head.

"No. It's a one-source story. And that source isn't answering my calls."

"One source—tricky one. They speak to you once and that's probably that. Unless they fall in love with the chicanery of it all. The spy craft."

"I will badger the Public Gallery until they are forced to say something," she said. "Now that it's in the public domain. They have to respond in some way."

A double-decker bus arrived, wheezing and grinding over the hill. They boarded and sat downstairs: neither of them were fond of stairs.

"Why does your allotment have to be so bloody far away?" Shona said. She looked out the window as the estate passed by and the bus skirted a large football stadium.

"Because the planners could not imagine that the workers wanted gardens. Or to plant vegetables."

"Is that so? Planners like Cullen."

"Good men like Cullen," he said. "Good men can make bad decisions."

The phone rang loudly in her pocket.

"Could be the big one!" her father exclaimed.

She smiled and answered the phone. There was a screeching noise. A warp of feedback, which pierced and jangled. She held the device away from her ear. "Jesus," she said, and closed the call.

The phone buzzed again. She answered.

"Reculver," a harsh voice said.

"Hello."

"So, who is your source?" he said. The feedback whined again.

"I can't tell you that. Sort out your bloody phone."

"You walking down a tunnel?"

"Are you? I'm on a bus."

"That's an interesting story you have today."

"Ta. Is there anything else I can help you with?"

"You going to the party tonight?"

"I don't go to parties. What party—you having one?"

"You wouldn't like my parties. No. There's one out at Denholm House, down there in the Borders. The Farquharsons planned it to celebrate the handover of *The Goldenacre*, I hear."

"I doubt I am invited to that," she said. "How could I get in?"

"With some difficulty. Your article has set some hares running today, especially with our financial people. Good job. Is this Mr. Tallis your source? The sketchy civil servant from London?"

Shona smiled. "I'm not going to tell you, Reculver."

"I'll take that as a yes."

"Take it any way you want. Why are the financial cops involved?"

"Do you know this Tallis fellow?"

"I've already answered that."

"Know much about him, who his friends are?"

"Why are the financial cops involved?" she asked again.

"Naughty. Good luck. Any more details spring into your head, let me know. Bye."

The call ended.

"This is my stop, love," Hugh said, as the bus came to a halt on Ferry Road.

She helped her dad descend from the bus to the path, and they walked slowly to the allotments. She was silent and distracted. She should have been in the office, but she didn't care. There were no stories in the office. There was a germ of a story for a follow-up, but not enough. But she had an idea. A seed.

"You're pondering," her father said.

"Yes. Give me a minute, Dad, I'll be along in a while."

She stopped on the path. He walked on. They were on a cycle path, and it was quiet and damp: rain had left the green gleaming, the stone wet and glossy.

She took a deep breath. She called Ned Silver in London.

"Ned Silver?" he answered.

"Nedward, it's Shona."

"Wait a second," he said breathlessly.

She could hear the sound of quickly walking feet, and a door opening and closing. Then the sounds changed. There were indistinct voices, and the grind of traffic. The distant rumble of aircraft.

"Okay, I can speak now," he said. "How are you?"

"Fine. Did you see my story today?"

"I did. Great story. I'm not sure I could have done it better."

Shona shook her head. "I know. Look, who from the gallery would be going to this party at Denholm House tonight? The Farquharsons are holding some shindig to celebrate the handing over of the painting."

"If it's still happening . . . I guess Sir Dennis, the director? Maybe Roberta Donnelly, the head of conservation. Some of the board of the gallery, I suppose. Mr. Tallis, perhaps—but I don't know whether he would go."

"Roberta?"

"Donnelly—she is head of conservation. Relatively new. Her colleagues call her Bobby. Irish. She never speaks to the press, though, so good luck with that. And the press office will stop you speaking to her."

"Thanks. Is the conservation department in the main gallery?"

"Yes, it's . . . Why?"

"Thanks, Ned."

She closed the call before he could speak anymore. She gripped her stick hard and walked down the path to the entrance to the allotments. She could see the small figure of her father bent over amidst the soil and plants and the tumbledown sheds, wire, wicker and wood. He was leaning on his spade.

"I know that look," he said, turning around. "Don't worry about me. Be safe."

She stumbled across the final duckboards to her father and hugged him. He smelled of sweat, freshly turned soil and coffee. "Dad, you need a shower," she said.

"You're the only one who hugs me." He smiled.

On her way back to the road, she called for a taxi to the Public Gallery.

31

Tallis was trying to tie a tie. He folded and pressed, coaxed and yanked the slithering, silken tongue. He could not get it right. He passed the slip over and under itself. The liquid fastening fell apart. His fingers shook. "For God's sake," he said. A loop of tie bunched up near his throat.

The morning had been taken up by a meeting with the gallery's press office. He said he knew nothing about the *Post*'s *Goldenacre* story. Nothing at all. The press officers were vexed. But they were saying nothing to the press, to the BBC, or other broadcasters—no statements, no quotes.

He had expected Carver to call him in, to send him back to London on the spot. But he had not. Indeed, there had been no messages from him. Not an email or a note. And no post. No letters—or parcels. Nothing from Melcombe, either.

Mungo's head appeared at the office door. "What are you doing?" he said. "I heard strange noises."

"Trying to put my tie on. I must have done it thousands of times. Now I cannot seem to do it at all."

"Maybe you're nervous."

He yanked the tie again, and it finally slipped into place.

"So, you are going to the big party with Bobby?" Mungo said.

"Yes, I am."

"Even after—"

"Yes, even after that rather silly and speculative piece in the paper today. Some shoddy reporting, Mungo." Tallis was wearing his black dress shoes, which he had polished, and he had shaved that morning. His skin was smooth and smarting, tender.

"It could all be a bit of scandal," Mungo said. He had sat down at the long table.

"It could," Tallis said.

"Strange that the article mentioned you like that."

"It spelled my name incorrectly. I guess because the article is questioning the painting's provenance, it would seem relevant to mention the government's involvement." Tallis stood up.

"Are you leaving, Thomas?" Mungo asked quietly.

Tallis looked to the floor. "Quite possibly." He smiled. "I think my work here is done."

Mungo put his head in one hand. "I meant, are you going to the party soon?"

Tallis laughed. His first laughter in a while. "Yes, as soon as Bobby is ready."

Mungo left the room, and Tallis walked to the window. He looked out over the parkland that surrounded the gallery. The trees still shook in the breeze, the leaves moving like the sea. He would never know this place, or what it could mean to him. He meant nothing to the place. He had made no impression on it, and his time here would be lost, like the water breaking on the rocks under the bridge at the bend in the river.

Mungo returned and said Bobby would be leaving in half an hour. "I am so sorry—I forgot—you received a call from that detective."

"Reculver?"

"Yes, he called earlier, wanted to speak to you again. He was quite abrupt."

"I'll call him tomorrow." Tallis thanked Mungo, who left. He took out his phone and called Gretchen.

"Hello?"

"Hi, Gretchen, it's me, Thomas."

"Ray is right here," she said.

Ray came to the phone. He breathed heavily into the receiver. "Hello, Dada," he said, in his fragile, tender voice.

"Hello—how was school today?"

"Dada! Fine. Finlay and me made a big dragon for the learning bubble and we did gym."

"That's great. I am proud of you."

"Mummy is back tomorrow," Ray said. "She said she had a present for me. Gonna go now. Love you."

"Love you, too." Tallis heard the phone being handed over, but then feet running back.

The little voice again. "Dada?"

"Yes?"

"When you back?"

"Soon."

"Come back soon?"

"I will. Soon."

"Bye!"

Tallis could hear his son's feet scampering off to the TV.

"He's happy," Gretchen said.

"Thank you," Tallis said. "Kiss him goodnight, from me."

Tallis walked down to the car park. It was getting dark, and the moon was high. A car had its lights on, its engine turning over. Bobby, in a suit, was waiting by the motor.

"Good evening," Tallis said.

"Evening," she said. Her hair was up in a bun. She was wearing makeup. "Nice suit, Mr. Government," she said.

"Thanks. It doesn't fit me anymore."

"I can tell. Get in. Let's get this whole charade over with."

Tallis stepped into the car. There was someone sitting in the back. It was Shona Sandison.

"My niece is coming with us," Bobby said.

"Your niece," Tallis said, looking at Shona.

Shona grinned back at him. She was wearing a dark suit.

"Yes. This is Natasha," Bobby said.

"Hello, Natasha."

"Nice to meet you, Mr. Chalice," Shona said.

Tallis winced and smiled.

"I thought she might enjoy tonight's ceremonies," Bobby said.

"I'm sure it will be eye-opening," Tallis said.

"Welcome to the pantomime," Bobby added.

They drove through the centre of Edinburgh, lit up in the night like a theatrical set, its stage empty. They did not speak for some time, as the car left the city and headed into the countryside. Bobby was wearing perfume.

"There will be fireworks," she said, at last.

"I suspect so," Tallis said. "Especially if Carver is there."

"No, I mean there will be fireworks. Colourful explosions. Entertainments."

"How lovely," he said.

"Twelve million can buy you a lot of Roman candles," Bobby said.

Shona snorted in the back seat.

"You know that's not how things work," he said.

"Who knows how things work?" Bobby said.

Tallis nodded. He looked to Shona. "I didn't know you had a niece."

"I didn't, either," Bobby said. "But she could come in useful. I figured, what the hell. No one there will know . . . my niece."

"No one knows me," Shona said. "Not in these circles."

Tallis turned to Bobby. "So are you coming round to my way of thinking?"

"No. But I know I don't like Sir Dennis Carver's way of thinking. Let's see what happens."

They came to a dark junction, the headlamps flickering off fence and thorn bush and tree. A pair of eyes glinted in the gloaming. A pale cat ran across the country road and skittered back into the darkness.

"Watch out kitty cat," Bobby muttered.

They came to the long straight road that led to Denholm House. There were lights in the trees, a glowing in the forest. The high brick wall ran beside them. The gates to the house were lit by burning braziers, and the gates were open. They drove slowly to the gates, where a woman dressed for a party checked their invitations.

She peered into the back seat.

"That's my niece, Natasha," Bobby said, smiling.

"There are no plus-ones on the invitations, I am afraid, madam," the woman said.

"Oh, now that's a shame," Bobby said. "We've driven all this way—and, as the Public Gallery, perhaps we are allowed a wee extra pass?"

The woman stood back and seemed to talk into a microphone in her collar.

"Jeezo," Shona said.

The woman reappeared and smiled. She waved them in.

They drove through the woods, the road lit by lanterns. Other car lights blazed behind them. The forest closed around them. Denholm House was lit by spotlights, its towers and crenulations sharp-edged in the false light. The house seemed to blaze in white and black in the plunging night. The island at the centre of the lake was lit. Beyond, the ruins of the sunken garden vanished into a deep-sea darkness.

Party guests were steadily moving into the house from minibuses, taxis and cars. Men were in black tie, some in kilts, women in suits and dresses. They walked slowly, as if drugged.

A shimmering projection hovered on the door to the house: *The Goldenacre*, huge in quivering light. The robin on its twig, glowing on the stone and wood. At the door, Olivia Farquharson stood in gold and silver, grinning at the visitors, shaking hands, her long pale arms hung with jewels.

"Blimey," Shona said.

"Keep quiet, and keep your eyes open, Natasha," Bobby said.

"Of course," Shona said. "God. So, this is how the oligarchy live."

"Yes: these are the people my father served," Tallis said.

A field in the trees had been roped off for cars, and they parked. They moved silently to the door.

"Ah, Mr. Tallis," Olivia said, "How nice of you to come." She looked at him and smiled.

"Delighted to be here," he said.

"And Roberta," Olivia said, keeping her smile wide.

Bobby introduced Shona as Natasha—Olivia barely acknowledged her—and they entered the house, Shona limping. The entrance hall was illuminated by projections of *The Goldenacre*. All the furniture had been removed, and the room was wide and high, and full of people. Sweat and hair, alcohol and perfume.

People with trays of drinks and food moved among them. A string quartet played in the corner. Their music cut into the air, which was thick with shouting voices and laughter. There were echoes and shouts and reverberations. Tallis took a drink from a tray that seemed to float past. He lost track of Bobby in the press of bodies. He found himself standing alone, by the quartet. The musicians were serious and focused, and their bows moved up and down in savage movements. He saw himself in a long mirror. His tie was askew, his face pale, his eyes looked back at his eyes and did not see them.

"Is this normal?" a voice said.

Tallis turned around. Shona was standing beside him, leaning on her stick. She had a drink in her hand. "The party or the drink?" he said.

"Everything."

"No, it's not normal. It's all too much."

"It's kind of obnoxious."

"Every single person here—and everything they believe in—is awful," he said.

"Fair enough," she said, with a grin. "You'd know." She touched his elbow with her stick. "Did you know the painting is here?" she said.

"Where?"

"Come with me," she said.

Shona moved uneasily through the party, leaning on her stick, pushing past arms and shoulders.

Tallis followed her. He felt he was floating. He was in the dream again, caught in the current.

Shona stopped suddenly at a door to another hall. "Fuck," she said.

"What is it?"

She turned to him. "That's my editor over there with those men," she said. She nodded towards a group of men in suits, laughing. Ronald Ingleton grinning, with his slick hands thick around a drink.

"Would he recognise you?" Tallis said.

"Of course, he fucking would."

"Well, let's move then."

"Fucking hell," she whispered. "I should have known he would be here."

"Why?" he whispered back.

"Because he's a dick."

They moved through an arched doorway, into a large panelled room. In the centre was a painting on an easel, in front of an empty stone fireplace. Shields and parts of armour hung on the wall, and the wooden floor gleamed.

Tallis found himself walking quickly to the easel.

"Is that it?" Shona said. Her eyes flicked nervously between the painting and the door.

Tallis stood before it.

There was the jewel-like detail and the luscious sweeps of watercolour. The waves of grass and the silken tenements. The spirits in the field amid the flowers and, in the background, the looming shadows of the hills. In the foreground, the tiny robin, pale and delicate on its single porcelain twig. The frame was battered, and used. This was the painting, *The Goldenacre*.

Tallis stared at it for a while. He was in the dream, but a real dream—the painting as real as a mirage.

Shona was beside him. Music drifted from the other room. Feet boomed on the wooden floor. Tallis moved closer to the painting. He put a finger on its frame. It was cold wood. Real.

"An absolute masterpiece, is it not?" Carver's voice said.

Tallis turned, and Sir Dennis Carver was standing in dark suit and tie, still as a standing stone. "The real deal," Tallis said, nodding.

Shona took some steps back. She stood close to another group of people, melting into them, and slipped away.

"Worth every penny," Carver said.

"Indeed," Tallis said.

Carver came close, and they stood in front of the painting together. It looked back at them with old eyes.

"My old friend Henry Melcombe will need your resignation rather soon, I suspect. But we need not speak about that unpleasant matter tonight," Carver said.

Tallis shook his head. His heart began to thump. "No," he said.

"But it was interesting to make your acquaintance," Carver said, and put a cold hand to his shoulder. "How unlike the father, the son can be."

Tallis pulled away. "And that thing we saw the other day? What of that?" he said, turning to Carver.

"What of it?"

"A poor copy, is it not?"

"And you know so much about being a poor copy, Thomas."

Tallis bit his lip. "That fraud you attempted to pull," he said, as loudly as he could.

No one seemed to notice, and Shona was gone.

Carver smiled. "Thomas, calm down. I think you must have seen a ghost. An apparition. We did not see anything unusual the other day. Perhaps you were still recovering from your unfortunate breakdown on Calton Hill."

"Bobby was there with me. She saw it, too," Tallis said.

"Bobby can see *The Goldenacre* here, and she surely knows you were mistaken. And she won't cry to the press, as others do. Like a weeping child."

Tallis looked Carver in the eye. His face was a grey mask. "You went to a lot of trouble to make that fake," Tallis said. "There must have been a lot of money spent to try and fool the world."

"I think, Raymond Thomas Tallis, there is only one fool here." Carver turned sharply on his heels and walked away.

Tallis put his face in his hands. He opened his eyes and the painting was still there. Shona reappeared beside him. She took a picture of the painting with her phone.

"This, I am afraid, is real," he said. "This is *The Goldenacre*." He felt sick.

She seemed unruffled. "So, they've switched them," she said.

"So, you believe me?" he asked, looking at her face. The crowds were thickening about them. Eyes peering at the painting.

Shona shrugged. "Yeah. Why the fuck would you make a story like that up?"

"Good question," he said. "I wouldn't."

"You're a fuck-up, not a liar," she said gently.

"You're a good person, Shona," Tallis said, looking into her dark eyes. "Despite it all. And a good journalist."

She smiled. "Let's not exaggerate, Thomas."

He looked around the large, busy room. "Have you been spotted?" he asked.

"Not yet. I'm hiding."

Bobby walked over to them.

"This is it," Shona said.

Bobby peered at it. She looked to Tallis, and he nodded.

"I'm just going to the cloakroom," Shona said, and limped quickly away.

Bobby walked around the easel. She stopped at the rear of the painting. Her eye had been caught by something. She was about to speak, when Olivia moved into the room. She announced that she was about to say a few words to the assembled party in the main hall. Everyone slowly moved from the rooms, down a wide corridor, and into a large chamber. There were many footsteps on wooden floors, on stone floors. Above them a frieze of knights and animals bounded the walls and extended to the ceiling. Swords and pikes were attached to the walls. A fire flashed in the large stone fireplace. More drinks and food rested on low round tables. Heat from the fire bloomed and rose.

Tallis, Shona and Bobby stood near the back of the hall. Before them were a hundred people clinking glasses and murmuring.

Shona had found a hat from somewhere. A red beret and a green silk scarf. It made her look mad.

Olivia stood at a raised wooden lectern. "And so, here it is," she said, and pointed to the wall above the fireplace. A projection of *The Goldenacre* appeared. The audience clapped and someone cheered. "Tonight marks both a welcome, and a farewell," she said. Light glittered on her jewellery. Stars about her neck and ears. Her eyes shone. "For tonight, the favourite painting of our late father—*The Goldenacre* by that Glaswegian genius Charles Rennie Mackintosh—officially leaves the tender embrace of our family and passes into public ownership, into the arms of the Public Gallery of Edinburgh."

The audience applauded. Bobby and Tallis stood silently. Shona had turned on the Dictaphone on her mobile phone and was holding the device to one side of her body.

"This is a moment long in preparation. It is sad that my brother, Felix, cannot be here tonight. I know he wanted to be here. And he would have loved to see so many friends and supporters here at our ramshackle old house tonight, marking this historic occasion. Sadly, yesterday, he fell rather ill while on business in Newcastle upon Tyne, of all places."

People murmured. Someone said "shame."

"Typical Felix," a man shouted, and the crowd laughed too loudly.

Olivia nodded and carried on. "And he is now in hospital there, in the tender care of the Geordies . . ."

Shona looked to Tallis. He blinked back.

". . . but he assures me he will be released soon. He has a sore head: but, worst of all, he has been forced off the booze. He assures me he will be back in fine fettle soon. I am sure he sends his best wishes."

The audience clapped. There was some more cheering. Tallis could see Carver, his arms crossed, looking down at the floor, standing close to the stage.

Olivia spoke on. She outlined how the painting had entered the family collection, and how her parents and grandparents had loved it, and desired that it never leave the house. "But then, in his inconsiderate way, my father sadly died," she said, with a smile, "and left us his great gift of land and home and possessions, but also a rather large inheritance tax bill. And this is where Sir Dennis Carver, who as many of you know was a close and old friend of the family, stepped in. I shall hand over to him . . ."

There was sustained applause.

"I won't watch this," Tallis said. "I can't stay here."

Bobby nodded. She whispered to him, "Thomas, have you seen the reverse of the painting?"

He shook his head.

"Let me show you," she said. "It's very interesting. Where are you going?"

"Out," he said. "Bye." He touched Shona on the elbow and gestured that he was leaving the room.

She nodded. "This is all kinds of fucking dreadful, isn't it?" she whispered.

"Don't worry, Shona. Everything that happens, happens for the last time."

Shona peered at him.

Tallis turned to the scene: the celebration of the painting, the deal that had been done. He could not grasp it. Tallis realised he could not see what was happening, or why. There was just talk, and people clapping, and a fire, and walls decorated with money and paint and weapons. There was some kind of spectacle and, behind it, money being exchanged. That was all. The rest was noise.

He left the room through the open double doors and walked back to the anteroom where *The Goldenacre* stood. He was moving across the floor when a hand grasped his shoulder. Tallis turned around, but the grip remained. A large, grey-haired man was holding him. The man was in a suit. His face was like a slab; his eyes dead and grey, as if painted on plaster. He dropped his grip.

"Ms. Peters would like to see you," the man said in a hard accent.

"Catherine Peters?" Tallis said, rubbing his shoulder.

"Outside," the man said, gesturing for Tallis to follow.

Tallis looked about him: there was no one in the room. The grey-haired man walked away, his heavy feet creaking on the wooden floor. Tallis did not have to follow, but he did so, glancing at *The Goldenacre* as he passed. The robin glimmered in twilight. He briefly thought of turning back and rejoining the people in the hall. But he wanted to know more.

A door led to a short, cold, stone corridor, and then to another door, with a circular iron handle. This led outside, and the man held the door for Tallis. They were on a gravel path between the house and the lake. The air was cold but clear. He followed the man into the night.

The man produced something hard and glinting from a pocket. He flicked something, and a beam of light appeared—it was a torch. The two men walked in silence along the gravel path. The path skirted the lake, which lapped gently. There was the smell of weeds and algae and dank water. The path turned and headed towards the Sunken Garden. They walked into the net of ruins. The air was colder. The woods, all about, were silent and dark. They walked on a grassy path, and the torchlight flickered on broken walls and splintered columns. Pediments lay half-sunken in tangled grass. They skirted the edge of a large abandoned pool, its border stones slimy, its voids choked with grass and moss and weed. The garden's centre was a pyramid, tens of feet high. It, too, was collapsed and broken, like a lost sacrificial altar in the jungle. They came to its door—a rectangle of stone into nothingness that briefly lurched in the beam of light and then was lost—and waited.

The large man said nothing. He trained the beam of light on the ground before them.

On the far shore, Tallis could see people leaving the house and standing, amid newly lit braziers, on the edge of the lake. There were three cheers and scattered clapping. Suddenly there was a shriek, and a firework leapt into the air. It exploded in a fizzing flower of light, which faded back in a blink of colour to the night. It was followed by red and blue explosions, whirring skirls of light and applause. There was a pop and crackle and fireworks detonated from a small island. There was more cheering, and the shimmering reflections of sudden light on the sullen water.

New uncertain light flitted in the darkness. A torch held by a woman. She came close, wearing a long coat. It was Olivia Farquharson. She held the beam now steady in her hands.

"Thomas fucking Tallis," she said harshly.

"I thought I was meeting Catherine Peters," he said. He suddenly shivered.

"You are," she said. "You met her on your first day of work. I was wearing a hat and glasses—enough to make me forgettable, it seems. And when you came here last week you didn't seem to see me at all: Dennis told me your father was always far more observant."

The big man put a hand on Tallis's shoulder. He gripped.

"So," Tallis said.

"So, indeed," she said. Her face was pale and hard. "You should know that you have fucked everything up, royally," she said.

The fireworks continued to burst in the air. The blue light suddenly lit half her face, and then it fell into darkness. There were explosions and ricochets. Sparkling light fell slowly.

"Where is your brother?" Tallis asked.

"Trying to find millions from somewhere." She moved closer to Tallis. "You see," she said, stabbing the soft ground with her shoes, "my twin is many things, and indeed, many things to many people, but he is also really fucking stupid. Expensively educated but thick. And arrogant. So when my father's discreet and time-tested operation was taken over by Felix, things fell apart. He tried to diversify. The fucking property deals. Housing estates with sloppy developers. And the cherry on top, some idiotic film studio scheme."

She shook her head. The grey man stood silent.

"My father had dementia, towards the end. Very sad. I should have stayed far away and kept my hand invisible, but something drew me back, and I have to be reacquainted with all this . . ."

She gestured to the ruins. Tallis's phone buzzed in his pocket. Someone was calling him.

". . . this disaster area. And my brother, millions in hock to these gentle, forgiving souls from Tyneside. And then I discovered his last little wheeze: giving a valuable piece of collateral to these gentlemen, to cover his huge fucking losses. As if a painting was some kind of fucking cheque. As if it could ever be cashed. And all this just as I was negotiating the completely legal deal with your blessed government. And God knows, we need that deal: the house needs a new roof, the tax bill is very large and our income is best not scrutinised too heavily. Felix declined to tell me that we did not even have the painting anymore."

"So, you had it copied," Tallis said.

"No, I did not," she said, looking back to the house. Music was playing somewhere. "That was the idea of Sir Dennis. Daddy's old pal. Not his best idea. Not anywhere near his best idea. It seems I am surrounded by idiots. But I trusted him. After all, if the director of the Public Gallery says some kind of light art forgery is doable, who is to argue against that? He chose the artist. He was in charge of that. Luckily, for my family—for me—I have great experience in cleaning up messes, mainly my brother's."

Tallis realised he was shaking. "Why did Love have to die?"

She shrugged. "He was a third-rater. He was asking for too much. And his work wasn't good enough, not nearly good enough. Other people along the way have annoyed us. You are the last loose end. You have yourself to blame. We tried to warn you off."

Tallis felt colder. "The tongue?"

"Yes, the fucking tongue. Jesus Christ," she said, spitting out the words, flicking her eyes to the large man. "This savage monolith here, he borrowed it from Mr. Love, and Sir Dennis thought it would make for some kind of rather literal warning. He thought it would scare you."

"It did," Tallis said.

"Not enough, clearly."

"The police will be on to you. They know about the tongue."

"They will not prove a thing—how could they?" she said lightly. "They're slow and stupid."

"What about the councillor?"

"Fat Cullen?" she said tiredly. "He let us down. We were tired of him. Now, sadly, we have journalists asking all sorts of questions. Luckily, they get bored quickly. We can wait them out."

She looked to the edges of the lake, where people could be heard laughing and talking—the fireworks seemed to have paused. She came closer to Tallis, her eyes glittering. "Thomas. Your annoying interference has convinced that old idiot Carver that he must take the real fucking painting. Our friends in the north have been generous. We, and they, didn't want a public fraud scandal on our hands. Too many questions. So, there it is, in the house again. Shortly, it will leave. We get our very useful tax break, but our impatient friends lose an asset. So now we owe a lot of bad people a lot of good money. Well done, Thomas Tallis."

The grip on his shoulder became tighter, the fingers as hard as bone without flesh.

"What is happening?" Tallis said.

She passed a hand over her face, and pulled a hair back behind her ear. "There is no way for you to win, Thomas," she said quietly. "But, you should be proud of your efforts. They were nearly enough." She turned around, the beam of light from the torch with her. It flashed on tree trunks, old stones and ruins, and then she was gone, a slim pale light against the night.

The Geordie turned Tallis around. Tallis tried to remove his grip, but he could not. He was suddenly wrestling with something that wasn't a man. The man's head, like a boulder, his eyes as dead and bright as moonlight. The man's hand was tight around his throat. Choking him. Tallis tried to prise the fingers from his neck. He could not. Pain bloomed in his neck and mouth.

Suddenly there was a percussion in the air, and splinters of light, exploding and falling. Fireworks shattered nearby. There was laughter and cheers. Another crack echoed and threw jagged light on the ruins and the trees.

The man's grip suddenly loosened amid the shrapnel of light and noise, and Tallis squirmed free, nails dragging across his skin.

A swooping violent hand flew through the dark, inches from his face, but he dropped to the ground and then staggered up, running furiously in the darkness.

More fireworks burst and, in the strobing light and dark, the Sunken Garden wheeled around him. Tallis ran half-blinded through the slippery darkness, into the ruins, the maze of stones and shadows. Behind him the night moved with intent.

He suddenly dropped, falling down into a stone gully half-filled with water, and slid under, suddenly pitched into an icy black depth. There was a brief moment of freezing water and utter dark, a writhing against slippery stone, and then, gasping, he rose. Amid the stones, he saw the man, huge and silent, move away, walking slowly deeper into the ruins. Light flashed again, a field of sparklers cracking high in the air.

He crawled from the trench, drenched and heavy and suddenly solid with cold. He crawled across the mud and stones, and there was a door and he rolled himself to it. Tallis was surrounded by stone now, in an alcove cut into a broken monument in the dark. He breathed deeply. He pulled out his phone—it was still working, a rectangle of light.

There were more flashes and percussions over the water. He took his breath, his chest straining for breath, water pouring in streams from his hair and clothes. He looked at the ruins before him, most sunk in darkness, lit in flashes by the fireworks. Somewhere amid the obelisks, the pyramids and crumbled steps and terraces, the murderer searched for him. As the explosions cracked, and the crowd cheered on the banks of the lake, he quickly and wetly flicked through the names on his phone—he did not have Shona's number saved, he did not have Bobby's. But he had his father's.

A sudden peacock flame of blue and silver and red spread in fire and light over the house, the lake and the ruins, and the crowd purred and clapped.

Tallis, shivering now, called his father. It had always gone to voicemail. Maybe it would not now. He turned in a heap to the stone wall—in the flashing dark it looked like a mausoleum. The phone rang and rang. It went to voicemail.

"Help me," he said, as clearly as he could. "Help me, Dad."

He closed the call. He looked to the house and lake again. The fireworks seemed to be over—the crowd as one was moving away, and smoke moved over the face of the water. Tallis crouched now, and then ran unsteadily to the next ruined outcrop. He looked around: nothing. Just the ruins, and the silence, and the trees. He moved again, to a shattered pillar, and could see a clear lane of grass and gravel and flagstone running from where he stood to the safety of the house. He moved along this path, running, slipping and soaking. His phone was in his hand. It lit up—someone was calling him. It buzzed and flashed. His eyes widened, and his heart leapt.

A heavy hand, hard as stone, smashed into the back of his head.

Tallis fell heavily to the wet ground, his soft face hitting a low, jagged, ruined wall, his skin suddenly hot from blood, his tongue bitten hard and ripped in his mouth.

He lay unmoving on the grass. His phone, buzzing and lit blue, turning with a light vibration on a wet flagstone, out of reach. Tallis tried to speak, and could not, his mouth a mess of blood and torn flesh, his cheeks swollen, an eye mushed. He saw dimly the light of the huge house, rippling on the lake. He saw the darkness of the trees, beyond. He heard a song, rising above the sound of human laughter. Thomas Tallis thought of his son, and he kissed him.

The shadow of the tall man knelt over him. With a punch, he drove a hard spike of metal into Tallis's skull.

Tallis saw light and heard music.

Then starless night and endless silence.

After a time of quiet, the Geordie steadily pulled what was once Thomas Tallis to the edge of the cold lake.

3 2

The press conference was being held in the main exhibition space of the Public Gallery. It was a bright and warm day.

Shona Sandison had been offered a redundancy package from the newspaper. An offer of money and a swift exit. As she expected.

She walked slowly up the drive to the gallery, her stick clicking on the tarmac. She had a copy of that day's *Post* under her arm.

The headline was in large type on the front page:

MOCKINTOSH!

And below, a subdeck: "New Art Shock: £12M 'Mackintosh' Is Not a Mackintosh. Exclusive by Shona Sandison."

Her last story for the paper: the headline was not completely accurate, but the story was. Bobby had given her all the details, on condition of anonymity. Tallis had simply disappeared. He had run off, into the night. He would emerge again, she thought. He was probably drunk as a skunk somewhere, she thought.

As she walked slowly through the warm air to the gallery she could see other journalists arriving. That fellow from the

Times was there, the Scotland reporter from the *Guardian* was making her way in. A BBC satellite truck had parked. Hacks were getting out of black taxis.

Shona was not the only one leaving the newspaper. The *Post* was asking all its senior staff to leave. Stricken had refused—he said he would rather be sacked.

Shona was thinking it all over. Her father had his pension, his allotment, and his chilli con carne. She did not have many options, and a mortgage to pay. The idea of a cheque was enticing. But the idea of leaving journalism was not, in any way. What else could she do? She had a vocation, not an occupation. She would put the decision off as long as possible. Journalism—the game of it, the chase—filled a void. She did not just want to be left with the void.

The lobby was full of journalists chuntering and chatting, cameras being swung about, and TV crew trying to barge past them all to set up in the gallery.

"Oh, here she is, Mrs. Exclusive," someone said, as she walked in.

"You snooze, you lose," she said.

Someone groaned and someone laughed.

"Hey, Shona. I heard they wanted you suspended," the old BBC man said quietly out of the side of his mouth, as he unfolded his camera.

"Only from a tree, Bill," she said. "But here I am."

The gaggle of hacks all shuffled through to the main gallery, where *The Goldenacre* was resting on a stand at the front. Beside it, there was a security guard wearing white gloves. A table with two chairs sat beside the painting. One would be for Theseus Campbell, she figured. He was the new, interim, director of the gallery. Sir Dennis Carver had been signed off, sick, for a month.

The journalists all sat down. Some took off their coats, others took out pens and pads and Dictaphones. Light shone into the room through high windows. *The Goldenacre* gleamed on its stand. On a screen behind the table, there was an image of the painting's reverse. A portion had been magnified to a far greater size. There was writing—tiny writing, in pencil, more than ninety years old.

A press officer from the gallery walked in, suited and smart, and so did Dr. Roberta Donnelly, who glanced briefly at Shona as she made her way to the table. Heavy steps brought Theseus into the room. He was wearing a loud tartan suit and brogues with red socks.

The murmuring of the journalists quietened down. Pens were clicked and notepapers ruffled. The press officer thanked everyone for turning up, and said that Dr. Donnelly would speak first. There would be a press release issued afterwards, and Drs. Donnelly and Campbell would be available for brief on-camera interviews.

Bobby stood up. "What a turnout. I welcome you all here to the Public Gallery on an auspicious day," she said. "And I would like to start by acknowledging the support and help of my colleagues today as we reveal a very exciting discovery for the Public Gallery. As some of you may have read in the papers today, after intensive research, we are today announcing a new and historic attribution for this beautiful work of art, *The Goldenacre*."

Cameras clicked. Shona could see Bobby in tiny form on the monitors on the back of the TV cameras.

"As you all know, this painting has been transferred to the public collection, passing from the ownership of the estate of Lord Melrose. The painting's remarkable ownership history was verified by a UK government official."

She stopped, and the press officer handed her a glass of water, which she sipped and returned.

"In our scrutiny of this painting—this beautiful dream-like image, so emblematic of the Glasgow School—we started to question its established attribution. There were some interesting facts about the painting. It is unlike any other painting created by Charles Rennie Mackintosh in the final years of his life. It is, indeed, unlike anything he had painted for many years before his death. Before his fatal illness, he had been producing some lovely watercolours in the south of France. They are clear and free from adornment or elaboration. They document landscapes, vistas and villages. They are not fantastical, as this is. He fell ill in France, with the oral cancer that eventually killed him. Before he died, he and his wife, Margaret Macdonald Mackintosh, returned to London. After an operation that deprived the great man of his speech, he died in December 1928."

Shona looked at the projection, which shone brightly over the heads of Bobby and Theseus. The writing on the back of the board was a name, drawn in a stylised pattern: *Macdonald Mackintosh*.

Bobby described how Charles Rennie Mackintosh had not been ever recorded as having travelled any farther than London, on his return to Britain. She said how he often sat in his garden, in Willow Road, Hampstead, after his operation. There were no mentions in any documents, diaries or letters of Mackintosh leaving London.

"So how was *The Goldenacre* created?" Bobby said, standing closer to the work. "For years—indeed, ever since it was bought by a previous Lord Melrose in 1927, one year after Charles died—it has been at Denholm House in the Borders. It was not loaned or shown elsewhere. And apart from one accident, when it was nearly destroyed in a fire, it had not been closely observed. Once we could properly study this gorgeous creation, however, we could also study the reverse of the painting. Which for decades had been hidden, overlooked or ignored. The evidence can be seen, most clearly above, on the screen: *The Goldenacre* was not created by Charles Rennie Mackintosh, but by his widow, the artist Margaret Macdonald Mackintosh. She signed, in very small pencil, as you can see, its reverse. This reattribution has been confirmed by a preparatory sketch, which we have found in the archives of the Glasgow School of Art. Luckily, it was off-campus when the terrible fire struck the Mackintosh Building. The sketch clearly shows workings in Margaret's hand, and features various studies on the strange perspective, which is probably from a top-floor flat somewhere in the Goldenacre area of north Edinburgh. We have an image of the sketch, and the autograph, should you need it."

Shona smiled. The gathered journalists all started murmuring, and some hands went up to ask questions. Bobby carried on.

"I am happy to answer questions. But the reattribution answers a lot of questions that *we* had: How did Charles come to Edinburgh to sketch and work on this painting? Why is it so different to his other work of the preceding years? The fact is that Margaret, in the midst of her terrible mourning, created this work in the months after he died. And in its ghostly figures, in its beauty and dreaminess, it not only looks backwards in time, to their youth in the so-called 'Spook School' of Glasgow, but also laments her husband's passing. Look at these ghostly figures in the high grass: they could be ghosts, or spirits in purgatory. The shadows over the Pentlands allude to the shadow of death. The perspective, which is so high and so unusual: this also could have a spiritual meaning. And this small robin, so beautifully painted, which you can see here perched on this twig in the foreground, is, I think, a depiction of the spirit of her dearly departed husband. An animal spirit. This is, and remains, a significant work. *The Goldenacre* by Margaret Macdonald Mackintosh will have pride of place in our newly updated collections of Scottish women's art. Now: Questions?"

Shona sidled to the door. A journalist asked whether this meant the painting was worth less than the £12 million previously announced. As Bobby prepared to answer, Shona left the room. The lobby was quiet. A redheaded youth in a smart suit was talking animatedly to the security guard behind the desk. She walked past him and out into the light. Shona fished out her phone and called Hector Stricken.

"Could be the big one," he answered cheerily.

"Give over," she said, smiling.

"So, scoop! How was the press conference?"

"Just as I thought it would be."

"So, we looking into this sudden Carver disappearance?"

"I am. I don't need your help."

"What about this Tallis fellow—you spoken to him?"

"Och, I'm sure he is just lying low somewhere. Licking his wounds."

"I hear they dragged the lake."

"So I hear. He wasn't there. I tell you—he's in a bothy somewhere, drinking."

"Did they interview you?"

"They did. I didn't have much to say."

"His family are thinking of doing a Missing Person event with the polis, you know?"

"No, I didn't. Well, I do now. Why are you calling me?"

"You called me, Shona."

She smiled. "Just checking you're paying attention, Hector. I was going to remind you that you owe me a drink."

"I don't. But it's funny you should call, because I've been looking at some interesting financial documents I've dug up here . . . And this morning, while you were peacocking around the arts world, I had a wee chat with your pal and mine, Detective Reculver."

"Tell me more," she said.

33

Ray was playing in the sand on Portobello beach. The sun was shining, and he had plastic toys, as bright as flags, about him. Jack was using his hands to help him dig a large hole. Ray smiled as Jack dug like a dog, the sand rising and falling in swift arcs behind him.

On the esplanade wall, Astrella and Aunt Zed sat and sipped takeaway coffees as they looked out to sea. Zed held Astrella's hand. Astrella's dark hair was cut short.

"Have you met Mr. Tallis before?" Zed said quietly.

"No, never, Zelda," Astrella said. "Raymond was always very absent."

The sea's tide was slowly turning. The beach was shortening. Jack picked up Ray and plonked him in the hole in the sand. The boy burst out laughing.

"But he has a family to meet now," Astrella said.

"He has always had a family," Zed said, and leaned her head against Astrella. She put her arm around her, as they watched the boy play.

"I am looking forward to meeting him," Astrella added.

"It's thirty days now," Zed said softly. "Thirty long days."

Astrella nodded. "They will find him," she said. "They will."

"I wish I could see him again," Zed said.

• • •

Inland and upstream, Sir Dennis Carver walked quickly beside the Water of Leith. The police were at the gates—two unmarked cars and a white van. He needed to walk. He had slipped out of the back entrance of the Public Gallery, down the steep path to the river, and was on his way into the city. There would be a train south, a switch, and a plane.

The river trail came to a wide and long bend in the river. A stone bridge loped overhead, casting shadows onto the water. A man wearing a hat was leaning on the railings, looking into the river. As Carver passed, an arm came out and grabbed him. There was force and sudden energy.

"Excuse me," Carver said loudly. "Do you mind, I—"

"I do mind," the man said.

The man was of medium height, with a heavily lined face, and wearing neat country clothes. An overcoat and large, watery eyes. The man held on to Carver and directed him to the fence. In a gloved hand, the old man was holding a short, black, silenced gun.

"Raymond," Carver said.

"Dennis," Raymond Tallis said.

They stood awhile this way in silence. The water bit and crashed over the rocks at the bend in the river. Cars passed by overhead. They could have been old friends, reminiscing. Or comforting each other. A woman walked quickly by, a small dog rustling the grass beside her.

"How nice to see you again," Carver said.

"It's either me, or the rough boys up the road," Raymond said.

"I don't know what you mean."

"You can turn around now. I'd wager you could strike a deal."

"No, I'd rather not," Carver said thinly.

Raymond gently nodded the gun and moved forward. "Why did you do it, Dennis?" he said.

"I didn't," Carver said. The gun was now pressing into his lean belly.

"Try again. The painting. My son."

"I was merely a conduit," he said, closing his eyes. "I was to pass the painting to other people and create another one. That was it."

"To your friends in Newcastle."

"And their friends."

"Felix Farquharson: Where is he?"

"Doing his penance, somewhere."

"They will need their money."

"They do, indeed," Carver said, eyes closed, nodding.

"Did you get a cut of all that laundered money over the years, Dennis?"

Carver opened his eyes. "The money was invested sensibly in legitimate business, Raymond."

"And you got a cut."

"Their father was very close to me. We were old friends. It is a shame his son is a fool. His daughter is rather wiser."

"Where is my son?"

"I don't know. That is the truth."

"Think again." Raymond raised the gun to Carver's mouth.

"I do not know. I would ask our friends in the north."

Raymond took a step back. "I am going to kill you now, Dennis."

Carver was pale. He raised his hands. His fingers tremulous. "Please don't, Raymond."

"Don't whinge, Dennis."

Carver looked around. He saw the path, the busy bridge above. The water rushing from the silent hills to the silent sea. "There will be witnesses. The police are just there."

Raymond seemed to shrug. "It doesn't matter."

"All I did was commission a painting. That is not a crime. I tried to warn Thomas. I tried to help him."

Raymond winced at the name. The gun did not move. "You killed my son," he said.

"I did not," Carver said, his voice rising, his voice louder.

"Someone did. You are close enough."

"Maybe you did," Carver said.

"Goodbye, Dennis."

Raymond stood back swiftly and pulled the trigger. His practised arm trembled with the force. The pistol's report was lost in the roar of the white water.

Carver slumped to the ground. Raymond leaned over the crumpled body and fired three more times into the destroyed head. Blood and brain and bone drenched grass, gravel and stone.

Raymond looked around, but there was nobody on the path. He put a hand to his face. Morning after morning, he had known that his boy was gone. Everything seemed too large now—the city, the river, the sky. With a short flick, he threw the gun into the Water of Leith. It disappeared in the foam and wave. He walked slowly along the path, until it came to a steep set of stairs. With aching knees, he slowly climbed to the top. Step after step towards the light. After a final step, he was at the bridge. A police motorcyclist sped past, its lights silently flashing.

He saw a bus stop, which he walked to, and waited for transport. Eventually, a large maroon bus pulled up. He stepped on.

"Can you take me to the beach?" he asked. "And how much will it cost me?"

ACKNOWLEDGEMENTS

This book was written with the aid of a Robert Louis Stevenson Fellowship, organised by Scottish Book Trust, to whom I owe great thanks. Thanks to patient friends and early readers: Jackie Copleton, Allan Donald, Simon Stuart, Cristina Dello Sterpaio, Rosie Ellison, and Alison Rae at Polygon, who encouraged and supported. Thanks also to Robbie Guillory, for picking me up. And with love to Hope, for everything.